"Immersive, atmospheric, and brimming with magic, *Wraithwood* presents a skillful take on Arthurian legends, harnessing a gothic manor and ensemble of enchanting characters to create an unforgettable read. A treasure for any booklover. Alyssa Roat is a wizard at her craft."

~Caroline George, author of Dearest Josephine (HarperCollins)

"In *Wraithwood*, Alyssa Roat strikes a balance between intrigue and whimsy just right for young teen readers. It's a perfect summer read!"

~Lindsay A. Franklin, award-winning author of The Story Peddler

"An instant classic. You can't help but fall in love with all the characters, especially Brinnie. I'm incredibly picky with books I like, and I fell in love with this one. Arthurian legend like you've never seen it before, and all incredibly complex characters. You can tell the author threw her heart and soul into this book, and I cannot wait to find out what happens next in Brinnie's adventure."

~Hope Bolinger, author of the Blaze trilogy

"The irresistible first book in a planned trio, *Wraithwood*'s world is both magical and familiar. Supernatural revelations enter the story in an unobtrusive way: chairs float in the air; a bedroom emerges from a blanket in a wizard's hovel; an impenetrable maze proves to be the best estate security. But it's Brinnie's empathetic search for answers, and for her own identity among the wizards, that will carry affectionate interest in her story forward into the trilogy's next volumes."

~Foreword Reviews

WRAITHWOOD

THE WRAITHWOOD TRILOGY

BOOK ONE: WRAITHWOOD

WRAITHWOOD

THE WRAITHWOOD TRILOGY

BY
ALYSSA ROAT

MOUNTAIN**BROOK**FIRE

Wraithwood
Published by Mountain Brook Ink under the Mountain Brook Fire line
White Salmon, WA U.S.A.

The website addresses shown in this book are not intended in any way to be or imply an endorsement on the part of Mountain Brook Ink, nor do we vouch for their content.

This story is a work of fiction. All characters and events are the product of the author's imagination. Any resemblance to any person, living or dead, is coincidental.

Scripture quotations are taken from the King James Version of the Bible. Public domain.

ISBN 978-1943959-95-2
Published in association with Cyle Young of Cyle Young Literary Elite.
© 2021 Alyssa Roat

The Team: Miralee Ferrell, Kristen Johnson, Cindy Jackson
Cover Design: Indie Cover Design, Lynnette Bonner

Mountain Brook Fire is an inspirational publisher offering worlds you can believe in.
Printed in the United States of America

DEDICATION

To Mama, Daddy, and Steph, my biggest supporters.

Chapter One

BRINNIE'S HEAD SMACKED AGAINST THE WINDOW as the car hit a bump. The driver clung to the steering wheel, his knuckles whitening.

"Just a rough patch here," he assured her.

Brinnie clutched the armrest as the shuttle jolted and bounced back and forth. She forced a smile. "Okay."

The trees outside the window looked like they were dancing as the station wagon swayed. Their roots pushed up through the dirt road, seeming to grasp with gnarled hands to reach out and trip the shuttle. *Even the forest doesn't want me to be here.*

Brinnie ducked as a sign hanging from the back of the passenger's seat declaring "Thank you for choosing to ride with us. My name is Bert" swung and almost hit her in the nose. The driver—presumably the said Bert—tapped on his GPS with one hand while gripping the wheel with the other. The device seemed frozen.

Figures.

Within a few moments, the car ground to a stop on the side of the road.

"Sorry, miss." Bert ran a hand through his dark hair and pulled on a weathered cap. "This old thing isn't going any farther."

Brinnie bit back a sigh and climbed out of the vehicle. She was hit by a wave of humidity that felt like someone had thrown a bucket of water in an oven. She snapped a hair tie off her wrist and pulled long strands of dark hair already sticking to her face into a ponytail. How was air wet? Arizona wasn't like this.

I bet wherever Mom and Dad are isn't, either. They could have taken me with them.

Bert pulled her bags from the trunk. She put on her backpack and picked up her small suitcase. She felt like she should be bringing more for an entire summer, but she didn't need much—only basic summer clothes, a handful of toiletries and miscellaneous items, and of course, a stack of books. She didn't expect there to be much to do besides read in the middle of upstate New York.

"It's only about a mile away, I think," Bert said. "We won't be walking for long."

"You're coming with me?"

"Of course." He tipped his cap. "I have to see you get there safely. And"—he held up his frozen GPS ruefully—"I can't leave you out here with no signal."

She cracked a real smile for the first time that day. "I appreciate it."

Bert locked the cab, and they started down the road. Brinnie stepped carefully to avoid the ruts and potholes.

"I've never been out this way before," Bert said. "I didn't know anyone lived out here, to be honest. Who is it you're staying with?"

"My uncle."

"I'm sure you'll have all sorts of fun, then. All this nature and country living."

"Yeah." Nature was fine. But unknown uncles?

Mom and Dad had informed Brinnie two weeks ago they were going to visit her sister helping refugees for the summer at the medical station. She had been thrilled until a week later, when they told her she wasn't coming.

"What do you mean I'm not going?" Brinnie had demanded.

Mom didn't even look up from the eggs sizzling on the stovetop. "Fourteen is too young to be allowed in the hospital, and it would be too dangerous to leave you alone all day. We're just going to help out with all of the work until Anna has her baby and the new doctors arrive, then we'll come home."

Brinnie's spoon sank into her cereal bowl. She glanced from Mom, still stirring the scrambled eggs, to her father, who nonchalantly reached for the newspaper while sipping his coffee. "And it won't be dangerous for you? Am I a danger magnet or something?"

"Don't be dramatic, Brynna." Mom pursed her lips.

Dad shook out the newspaper and opened it, fixing his eyes on the page in intense concentration. Brinnie looked closer. Last week's newspaper. And he was on the ad section. *Come on, Dad. Not sneaky.*

Sometimes she wondered how he ever got his doctorate.

"It's not the safest area of the world," Dad said calmly. "We should be fine, but who knows? We'd prefer you not take a risk like that quite yet."

"So you're leaving me alone all summer?"

"No. You'll be staying with your, um, uncle Merlin." Dad glanced at Mom.

Why were they acting weird? "Do you mean Uncle Marty?"

"No." Mom chopped at the eggs with a spatula. "My brother, Merlin."

"You have a brother?" Brinnie exclaimed. "Since when?"

"It never came up." Mom changed the subject quickly. "He's agreed to let you stay with him for two months." She tossed her apron over a hook and headed out of the kitchen. "I'm running late. You two can have all the eggs."

And then she had practically fled from the kitchen.

A pothole the size of a bathtub brought Brinnie's mind back to the present. *Merlin,* she thought, stepping around it. *Who names their kid Merlin?*

They began ascending a steep incline, and all Brinnie's attention diverted to keeping her footing. *So instead of doing something worthwhile, I'm climbing hills in the middle of nowhere.*

Finally, the incline leveled out, but the overcast sky decided to drizzle.

Really? "Has it been a mile yet?"

Bert held his phone in the air for a few moments, searching for a signal, then shrugged and put it back in his pocket. "It was a mile a while ago. Guess I misjudged. But we should be there soon."

The suitcase wasn't feeling so small anymore.

The drizzle became a steady rain, and Brinnie's jeans clung to her skin while her toes squished in sodden shoes as the dirt road turned to mire. *This backpack better be as waterproof as the advertisements said.*

Even Bert was losing his chipper mood. "Got to be soon," he muttered.

Brinnie's feet were numb and both of her arms felt ready to fall off from carrying her suitcase in one hand and then the other, but still the road stretched on ahead with no sign of their destination. She finally allowed Bert to carry the suitcase. "Do you think maybe we're on the wrong road?"

Bert shook his head. "This is the only road around here, according to the GPS." He held out his phone, still stuck on the same screen. "Here's the road we turned off from in the car, and we left it about here."

"I don't see Wraithwood on here."

"No, it isn't there." He pulled a paper out of his pocket, the one that Brinnie's mother had told her to give the driver. "Says here to turn onto this road and the place is about fifteen miles out. We came close to fourteen before we started walking. Your mother been here recently?"

She shook her head. "Not in thirty years."

He whistled. "A lot can change in thirty years. Hope it hasn't, though."

They kept walking as the gray sky melted into dark blue. *Please don't let us be lost in the dark.*

She spotted something ahead. "What's that?"

A wrought-iron gate loomed about ten feet high, blocking the road. The iron twisted in strange and beautiful designs, and the two halves opened in the middle. Or at least, they would have if the gate wasn't closed. On either side of the gate, a dense hedge fenced them out. This must be the place. Wraithwood Estate. *What a name.* It sounded straight out of nineteenth-century British literature.

Brinnie tried to pull the gate open, but it didn't budge.

"It's locked." Bert pointed to a heavy bolt and padlock on the other side. He rattled the gate and called, "Hello!"

His voice echoed through the dark woods, but no one could be seen on the other side of the gate. Brinnie joined him in calling, "Hello! Hello! Anyone there?"

No one came.

"I'm sorry, miss. We can go back to the car and I'll help you find a hotel. We can try again tomorrow."

4

The thought of trekking all the way back to the car made Brinnie shudder. "I appreciate it, but we can't turn back now. Maybe I can climb over the gate."

He looked at it with doubt. "I suppose you could try."

She took off her backpack, set her foot in the metalwork, and hoisted herself up. She hesitated for a moment. What was she doing, trespassing over a creepy old gate? What if it wasn't even the *right* creepy old gate? *Well, they can't blame me. We need help.* She clambered to the top, squeezed between the spires, and descended on the other side.

"I don't think I can shimmy over like you can," Bert said.

"If you stay there, I'll get someone to come open the gate. I'll be right back."

"I'm not going anywhere."

Brinnie took off at a jog up the gravel road, which led through a well-kept garden and lawns. Shrubs grew in neat rows bordering perfectly green grass. Hopefully this was the right place, or she could be in a lot of trouble. Within seconds, Brinnie could see the house. She stopped and stared.

The house was a mansion sprawling outward and upward. She counted four stories, and it stood twice as wide as it was tall, with red brick walls and a slate roof—except on the right side of the house, where a large dome capped the wing instead. The dome seemed to be mostly made of glass and was almost ridiculously incongruous with the rest of the mansion, looking as if it should be part of a capitol building.

If this is Wraithwood, I can't believe Mom grew up here.

Brinnie skirted the circular drive and ascended the steps to the door. She lifted the brass knocker, took a deep breath, and let it fall.

No one answered. She knocked again, but still saw no sign that anyone was home. She didn't know whether to be more relieved no one was there to chase her off the property or discouraged at the prospect of hiking back to the car. At least maybe in this case, Mom and Dad would be forced to take her with them. Time to trudge back to the gate to tell Bert the bad news.

"Hello!" a voice called.

Brinnie jumped and turned around to see a small woman with gray hair bustling down a path that came from the left of the home. Brinnie stepped off the porch to meet her.

"I'm sorry, dear," the woman said, puffing along. "We never use the front door, only the back. I had to come around, you see, since the front door is all locked up tight, and oh!" She came to a stop right in front of Brinnie, and her eyes widened. "You look just like..." She shook her head. "Never mind. Silly of me."

Okay... "Sorry to bother you, but is this Wraithwood Estate?"

"Why, yes, it is. Why do you ask, dear?"

"I'm supposed to stay with my uncle for the summer. Merlin Ludovic. Does he live here?"

The woman stared. "Your...your uncle?"

"Um, yes."

"I thought you looked...but that's not..." The woman titled her head, brow furrowed.

Brinnie squirmed. "Does he live here? I left the shuttle driver standing outside the gate, and I'm supposed to go back for him."

The woman straightened, breaking off her stare. "Oh, yes. Yes, of course." She bustled down the road. "So sorry, we must let him in at once."

Brinnie followed her to the gate, where she pulled a key out of her apron pocket and unlocked it.

Bert smiled in relief. "Thought you might have forgotten old Bert."

"I would never." Brinnie shouldered her backpack and picked up her suitcase again.

The woman gazed at the suitcase for a moment before clapping her hands together. "We must get you inside. You two must be half frozen."

As they followed her up the drive, she said, "I'm Mrs. Winslow, by the way. The housekeeper, you know."

"I'm Brynna. Brynna Lane. But everyone calls me Brinnie. This is Bert...um, I don't know your last name."

"That's all right. It's a tongue twister. Thomtonson. I just like Bert."

"A pleasure to meet you." Mrs. Winslow led them around the

corner of the house to a much smaller door. "If you ever come this way again, Mr. Thomtonson, I recommend you use the other road. It leads very nicely past the town of Lyle to here. I imagine you had to leave your vehicle behind."

"Past Lyle?" Bert shook his head. "I should've known."

The door led into a warm, dim kitchen with a fire dancing in the hearth. Mrs. Winslow had them hang their light summer jackets, now soaking, over the fireplace. Then she set a kettle on the squat black stove and pulled three chairs in front of the hearth.

"Thank you," Bert said, "but I really should be going now that I know Brinnie's all right."

"Nonsense! You'll stay the night, of course," said Mrs. Winslow.

"Thank you, ma'am, but I'd best be heading home or my wife will be worried sick."

Brinnie's heart beat faster. She hardly knew Bert, but his presence was the most familiar to her at the moment. She didn't want to be left at this giant house alone. Not yet.

"Well, at least stay long enough to drink some hot tea," Mrs. Winslow said. "Your wife wouldn't want you to catch cold, either."

He raised his hands in surrender. "I can't argue with that. Thank you, ma'am."

Brinnie breathed a silent sigh of relief.

"It's my pleasure." Mrs. Winslow turned to Brinnie. "Now, you, dear. What's your mother's name?"

"Eira."

Mrs. Winslow's eyes crinkled as a smile bloomed. "I knew Eira was still out there. How is she? Is she well? Married?"

"She's fine. Yeah, married, to my dad."

"Ha ha! I knew it. And you, dear, you look just like her. I'm going to have a talk with that Merlin. He's busy now, but once he's available, I'll introduce you all."

"Okay..." *Was he not expecting me?*

Mrs. Winslow poured them both tea into teacups that looked at least a hundred years old. Brinnie took her cup with delicate fingers, afraid to break it, but it felt solid. The smooth flavor settled comfortingly on Brinnie's tongue, the warmth seeping into her bones. She examined the design of tangling vines and roses on the cup as Mrs. Winslow heated tomato soup on the stove. She served the soup with homemade bread, soft on the inside and crunchy and flaky on the outside.

While they ate at a small table in the kitchen, Mrs. Winslow stepped through a doorway off the kitchen. "Marcie, dear!" She called out the name with more gusto than was evident in her small frame. In less than a minute, footsteps sounded on stairs and a short, plump young redhead appeared in the doorway. "Marcie, I need you to prepare one of the guest bedrooms for me. Probably the blue room."

"Yes, ma'am." Marcie hesitated, looking at the guests as if a couple of exotic birds had chosen the kitchen for a roost, before ducking out of the room.

After they finished eating, Bert sat back. "That was the best soup I've ever had."

Mrs. Winslow's cheeks glowed. "Why, thank you."

He stood. "I'll be on my way. Thank you very much for your kindness."

"It was a pleasure. Here." Mrs. Winslow pulled a flashlight from a drawer. "Take this with you."

He took the flashlight and winked at Brinnie. "Keep out of trouble, little lady."

She held herself back from jumping up and begging him to take her with him so she could make a desperate bid to convince her parents they'd made a mistake. She took a deep breath. "Thanks, Bert. Be safe."

"Sure will."

Mrs. Winslow and Brinnie escorted him to the gate under the shelter of a big umbrella, then he was gone.

As Bert faded from view, Brinnie couldn't stifle an enormous yawn. Mrs. Winslow's blue eyes softened. "Time for bed, I think. Follow me, dear."

Brinnie followed her back to the house and into the kitchen, where Mrs. Winslow lit a lantern before leading Brinnie into a general sort of room with a staircase in the corner. Mrs. Winslow carried the lantern to light the way. *Is there no electricity?*

They went up one flight to a long hall with multiple doors on either side. The one closest to the staircase on the left stood open. "This one is the blue room, for you, dear. There isn't running water in the house, but the washroom building is right outside the kitchen door. It should have everything you'll need."

No running water either? A little more rural than she had anticipated. More than a little. Mom could have given her some warning.

The washroom, at least, had electricity and running water. After making use of those small touches of modernity, Brinnie brought her things upstairs, carrying a suitcase in one hand and a lantern in the other. Mrs. Winslow was tidying the kitchen, but she said she would be downstairs in a room off the kitchen if Brinnie needed anything.

Brinnie set the lantern on the nightstand and put on her pajamas, taking in the room with its light blue walls and white furniture. Gauzy curtains hung over the window, and the same material draped a canopy bed. *Not creepy, thank goodness.* But when she looked down, her hands were still shaking. How many others were in the house? Only Mrs. Winslow and the young woman? More? Who?

She climbed into the queen-sized bed between the cool, clean sheets. It felt luxurious, especially after being wet and cold. She took a deep breath. *You're fine. Mom and Dad wouldn't have sent you here if it wasn't safe. Rustic, maybe, but safe. Just go to sleep.* She turned out the lantern and snuggled under the covers. Within seconds, her long day of plane flights, a car ride, and a grueling trek put her fast asleep.

Sometime in the middle of the night, Brinnie woke with a start. It took her a moment to remember where she was. Pitch darkness surrounded her except for the lightning that flashed occasionally outside, but that didn't bother Brinnie. She had always had excellent night vision. She sat up and looked around. What had woken her?

Maybe it was the thunder. But the rainstorm had already begun picking up when she had gone to bed. She must have slept through a good deal of thunder already.

Wraithwood. British literature or gothic horror? She shuddered and listened for what could have woken her.

There it was—a creaking, thumping sound in the hall.

She tried to convince herself it was only the noises of an old house. Goosebumps broke out on her arms as the noise grew louder. There was no way she could sleep until she was sure. Cautiously, Brinnie climbed out of bed and eased open the door, peeking out.

A flash of lightning illuminated the hall. It was gone in a second, but it seared a picture into her mind. She closed the door quickly and leaned against it. A tall, dark figure had been coming down the hall toward her, a black cloak flapping behind him, his boots thumping on the creaking floorboards.

Chapter Two

BRINNIE COULDN'T BRING HERSELF TO MOVE as the footsteps thumped closer. Her heart pounded. She pressed her back against the door, as if that could keep the figure out.

Then, the footsteps grew fainter. It seemed the cloaked specter had passed her by.

Even after Brinnie worked up the nerve to tiptoe back to bed, she lay shivering and wondering. Was the house haunted? *Just my luck.* She didn't dare sleep. Her arms clenched to her sides, ready to spring, she kept her eyes glued to the door.

But eventually, she must have fallen asleep. When she woke again, light poured through the wide window on the wall opposite the door. She attempted to calm her racing heart by slipping out of bed and gazing out the window.

It overlooked the back of the house, where a merry lane meandered far into the distance. Brinnie could barely make out a small gate in a short, white picket fence. Low, shady trees scattered the green lawn, with benches placed under a few of them. A flower garden grew next to the washroom, and a small vegetable patch lay outside the kitchen door. Beyond the washroom sat a small shed, perhaps a chicken coop, and even farther away Brinnie could make out a larger shed by the gate, painted the same white as the fence. The backyard, unlike the front, seemed a pleasant and inviting place, especially with the sparkling newness that came after the rain.

Her shoulders began to relax. Whatever she saw last night, she doubted it would show its face in the sunlight.

She dug through her suitcase and put on a T-shirt and jeans, along with a pair of clean socks. Only a few things in her suitcase had gotten damp thanks to its hard, plastic exterior. A small blessing.

She put her long, black hair into a ponytail while looking in the full-length mirror in the corner. *Did Jane Austen design this room?* Then she made her bed, stuck her suitcase back in the other corner, and ventured downstairs to see what was for breakfast.

In the kitchen, Mrs. Winslow bustled about the stove. "Good morning, dear! Have a seat. The eggs are about ready."

"Can I help at all?"

"If you would like, you can get the plates out of that cupboard there."

"How many?" Brinnie opened the cupboard.

"Five today, I believe. Your uncle got called out late last night, so he shouldn't be down until later."

Last night. Was it her uncle she had seen in the hall? Now she felt like an idiot for freaking out. But why would he be dressed like that?

When breakfast was ready, Brinnie sat with Mrs. Winslow, Marcie, and another man and woman she didn't know. "This is Mr. Winslow, my husband." Mrs. Winslow patted the man's arm. "He's our fine groundskeeper."

He nodded to Brinnie. "Howdy do." His bright blue eyes sparkled, the laugh lines around them crinkling. Brinnie liked him immediately, though she sensed a slight hesitance in his smile.

"You already met Marcie briefly. She's our new maid." Mrs. Winslow nodded toward Marcie, who bobbed her head, her cheeks turning almost as red as her hair. "And this is Miss Edna Burtle, secretary and bookkeeper."

Miss Burtle looked down her thin nose at Brinnie as if she were a beetle in a glass case to be evaluated. Her dark hair was streaked with gray and pulled severely into a bun, and she wore a dark gray dress to match. *Why do I feel like she's going to peck me?*

Brinnie felt Miss Burtle's eyes on her throughout the meal, which made it difficult to eat. No one said anything, making it even more awkward. A few times, Brinnie caught one of them staring at her out of the corner of her eye, but when she turned, they immediately looked away, intent on their plates. Mrs. Winslow opened and closed her mouth several times before Miss Burtle asked abruptly, "So your parents said that you were to stay the summer?"

Brinnie set her fork down. "Yes, two months. They're visiting my sister Anna overseas. She's a doctor and she's having a baby, so my mom will help around the house and my dad will help her husband, David, in the hospital, since my dad's a doctor too. There were supposed to be replacement doctors coming, but, paperwork delays." She shrugged, then hesitated. "I didn't know my mom had a brother until they told me I was coming to stay here."

Mrs. Winslow fiddled with a napkin. "I'm sorry you haven't been able to meet your uncle. He's been very busy."

"That's okay." *What is he so busy with out here in the middle of nowhere?*

"Best be going. Work to do." Mr. Winslow stood.

The others followed suit, placing their dishes in a crate in the corner before disappearing, leaving only Brinnie and Mrs. Winslow. Mrs. Winslow picked up the crate that held the dishes. "I need to wash these up. You can join me if you like."

Brinnie followed as Mrs. Winslow took the crate to the washroom and set it on a counter beside an industrial-looking sink.

The washroom intrigued Brinnie. On the left sat a washing machine and dryer, and on the right were the big sink and a modern refrigerator. At the back, two doors led to two complete bathrooms, each with a shower, toilet, sink, and mirror. A telephone hung next to the washroom door, and lightbulbs dangled from the ceiling.

"How come the house doesn't have running water and electricity?" Brinnie asked.

Mrs. Winslow dunked a plate and began scrubbing. "Oh, it's an old house. It wouldn't work too well, you see."

Brinnie tried to imagine wiring the huge house. Point taken. She dried after Mrs. Winslow washed. Then they returned to the house and Mrs. Winslow put the dishes back where they belonged.

"I suppose I should give you a tour of the place, since you'll be here a while," Mrs. Winslow said, shutting the cupboard. "You already saw the yards. You're welcome to roam around as you wish, but I don't recommend leaving the property. It would be easy to get lost in the woods around here."

No kidding. She didn't need another escapade like yesterday.

"Now, you saw the washroom, and this is the kitchen. Mr. Winslow and I have a room through this door over here." She bobbed her head to the door across from the stairs while setting cups in the cupboard. "The room that the stairs are in is a storage room. That used to be the servants' staircase back in the old days."

"What about that door?" Brinnie indicated a door occupying the wall opposite the entrance to the kitchen.

"The dining room. We don't use it. It's best that you don't go in the front of the house—everything is all shut up, and it may not be entirely safe."

That must have been why she didn't answer Brinnie's knock at the front door. "Are you renovating?"

"No. It's just old." She clapped her hands together and turned. "I'll show you the rest of the second floor."

Brinnie followed her up the stairs. "Two doors down from your room is Edna's, and across from hers is Marcie's. We keep the other rooms closed, but you can explore if you would like."

Four doors lined either side of the hall, and huge double doors stood at the end of it. "Where do those lead?" Brinnie pointed to the double doors.

"There's a sort of sitting room or parlor in an area at the top of the grand staircase. We don't use it, and the doors are locked."

The grand staircase. Fancy. It seemed a waste that so much of the house wasn't being used.

Mrs. Winslow pointed back to the stairs they had come from. "Those stairs keep going up to the third floor. That's where your uncle keeps his work, and you must not go up there, or you might disturb it."

"Is he a scientist, then?"

She hesitated. "Something like that. He sleeps up there too, which is why you won't often see him, I imagine. You won't want to go up to the fourth floor or the attic, either. They haven't been used in decades. Not safe at all."

Brinnie plotted out the house in her mind and came to a roadblock. "Wait, so there's only the kitchen, dining room, and the grand staircase on the first floor? It must be a really big staircase."

Mrs. Winslow laughed. "No, no. There's also the ballroom, the parlor, the study, and the library."

"Library?" Brinnie could already sense the books calling her.

"Yes, I suppose it would be all right if you saw it. It's on the other side of the house from the kitchen, but it opens onto its own portico, so we'll head around the back. You can go in there whenever you like, but you must be careful. Some of the books are very old. And you mustn't pass through the library to the front of the house."

They went back down and out the side door by the kitchen and followed a winding path to the other side of the house.

When Brinnie saw the portico, her breath caught. A slanted roof covered a small porch enclosed with white lattice, and three dainty white steps led to the path. Inside, a porch swing swayed across from white wicker chairs. Two French doors with huge glass panes opened onto it from the house. It was so different from the rest of the red brick exterior.

Brinnie drifted closer. "It's absolutely beautiful!"

Mrs. Winslow nodded and looked at it tenderly. "It was built for Elaine."

"Elaine?"

"Your grandmother." Mrs. Winslow gazed at the portico. "I can see her sitting in the porch swing now, curled up with a book. This was her favorite place."

Brinnie tried to picture it, but she had no idea what her grandmother had looked like. Blonde, like Mom? Or had her hair grayed like Mrs. Winslow's? Did she have Mom's blue eyes? "I didn't know that was her name. Mom doesn't ever talk about them."

"Some memories are too painful, dear." She bit her lip for a moment, then shook her head. "Let's go in, shall we?"

Brinnie followed her up the steps. Mrs. Winslow inserted a key into the French doors and swung them open. Brinnie stepped in after her, eyes wide.

Stained glass dappled the lower level with rainbow light. The library soared upward, encompassing all four stories. The ceiling curved in a giant dome, the dome she had seen the day before during her first view of the house, letting in soft golden rays of sunlight. Rich mahogany shelves full of books lined every wall of the library's three tiers, broken only by the swath of stained glass.

On the ground floor, an old-fashioned rolling ladder allowed easy access to books ten feet up. An ornate conference table dominated the center of the room, surrounded by twelve carved chairs. A leather chair or two sat in the corners, and a few especially old books sat in cases on stands. Across the room, more double doors, these heavy and imposing, closed off the library from the rest of the house.

Mrs. Winslow led Brinnie up the twisting staircase next to the outside door, not speaking, as if she knew that any words would break the spell. The second tier ringed three quarters of the room, excluding the stained-glass wall, like a large balcony that looked down on the ground floor. Rotund armchairs and a long sofa were arranged in a sitting area at one end, but the rest was devoted to books. Short shelves lined the balcony railing. Brinnie found even the railing beautiful, with twisting posts carved out of wood.

The third tier looked much like the second in that it was a balcony, but it ringed the entire room.

"Up there," Mrs. Winslow said, pointing to it, "is where the most delicate books are kept. We won't go up there. But you're free to use this library whenever you like. Just be careful. You can take the books on the short shelves out of the library, but you should leave the rest in here. Some are very, very old."

Brinnie nodded, feeling as if she was being entrusted with a special secret or inducted into a prestigious society. Her opinion of Wraithwood was rapidly improving. "This house is amazing."

"Yes, it is. I have some work to do, so I'll leave you here for now. Don't forget to come out in a few hours for lunch."

"I'll try." But with so many books, she wasn't making any promises.

After Mrs. Winslow left, Brinnie browsed the books on the short shelves of the second level. To her delight, they were all classics, mostly children's books—*Treasure Island, The Adventures of Tom Sawyer, Ivanhoe, Anne of Green Gables.* The worn covers and cracked spines suggested they had been well-loved. Brinnie spotted a book she hadn't read before, *The Story of King Arthur and His Knights,* and pulled it out. She brought it downstairs with her and out onto the portico, where she took up residence on the porch swing.

It took her longer than she expected to get into the book. Her mind wouldn't stop spinning. Her situation didn't seem real. *And I haven't even met Uncle Merlin yet, but apparently he roams the corridors at night in a cloak.* She didn't know what to think, so she lost herself in the book instead, distracting herself for the next two hours.

A male voice jolted her out of her reading. "Stars above!"

Brinnie startled at the exclamation. She looked up to see a tall man standing across the portico. She had been so engrossed in the book she must not have heard the doors open.

As soon as she saw him, Brinnie knew this man was her uncle. He had the same bright blue eyes that she and her mother had. After his eyes, she noticed his old-fashioned moustache and reddish dark-blond hair. He wasn't wearing a cloak and boots, but his clothes were just as strange. He wore an outfit Brinnie had seen in old movies, a Victorian costume like the men used to wear in the late eighteen hundreds, with a vest and beige pants. However, Brinnie mused, in some strange way it looked natural on him.

"Sorry to startle you," he said, his diction formal, articulate. "I wasn't expecting to find anyone here. You must be Brynna. Forgive me for not greeting you when you arrived. I didn't know until late last night. I had assumed your mother would send you a bit later than this, perhaps at the end of the month."

How was that miscommunicated? "That's okay. Mrs. Winslow took care of me."

"Ah, you've met everyone, then?"

"Yes, this morning."

"Very good." He hooked a thumb in his vest pocket. "I suppose Mrs. Winslow will be unhappy with me since I didn't warn her in advance that you were coming. I only received the letter a day or two ago and hadn't gotten around to it."

The letter? Mom didn't even talk to him? "You didn't know when I would be coming?"

"Not precisely." He extended his hand. "Pardon me. I haven't introduced myself. I'm your uncle, Merlin."

"And I'm Brinnie."

They shook. She eyed him curiously, taking in his polite smile and calm manner, but she couldn't read anything else. Was he excited to see her? Annoyed? Did he care one way or another?

Where have you been all my life?

"I suppose Mrs. Winslow has given you the tour. Yes? Well then, it's twelve o'clock, and Mrs. Winslow always serves lunch at noon. Come, she'll have something wonderful, I'm sure."

Brinnie tucked the book back in the library to continue reading later. Normally, she would think any grown man who wore dress-up clothes was crazy, but her uncle seemed quite sane.

Hopefully.

Chapter Three

SURE ENOUGH, MRS. WINSLOW WAS LADLING SOUP into bowls when they came into the kitchen.

"Something smells good." Uncle Merlin inhaled deeply.

Mrs. Winslow whirled around. "Merlin Ludovic, I don't want to hear anything from you until you tell me what on earth you were thinking, arranging for your niece to stay here without telling anyone!" She shook a spoon at him.

"I intended to tell you, but she arrived earlier than I expected." He moved toward the sandwiches. "Shall I set these out?"

Red blossomed across Mrs. Winslow's cheeks. "You aren't getting off that easily. You knew? You knew what happened to Eira and didn't tell us? Eira's alive. She's married. She has children. Two! Did you know that? You have two nieces."

Alive? Brinnie's mouth opened slightly.

"Yes, I was aware of that." Uncle Merlin's expression remained impassive. "We can talk about this later." He reached for the sandwiches again.

"Stop that!" She pulled the tray away. "You didn't think that perhaps we might like to know these things?"

"Hmm." He looked over at Brinnie. She had her mouth open to ask a question, but it froze on her tongue under his cool gaze. "There are reasons, you know. I think lunch now and talk later, if you don't mind."

Mrs. Winslow hesitated for a moment, then sighed. "Fine. But there *will* be talk later."

The household gathered for a lunch of soup and sandwiches at the kitchen table. For Brinnie, it was even more awkward than breakfast. Marcie kept looking at Uncle Merlin like he might burst into flame or turn into a pumpkin at any moment, after which her gaze would turn to Brinnie, whom she regarded with wariness. Miss Burtle continued to watch Brinnie like a fascinating insect. Mrs. Winslow fussed and offered Brinnie salt at least five times, while Mr. Winslow kept his eyes fixed on his plate, as if that would keep him from noticing the uncomfortable situation.

Only Uncle Merlin didn't seem to be on edge. He complimented Mrs. Winslow on the soup and asked Mr. Winslow how repairs on a fence were coming along. Then he asked Brinnie normal questions like what grade she was in and what subjects she liked best. She'd finished her freshman year of high school, she replied, and she liked English and history best.

"Excellent subjects," he said. "My favorites as well."

Brinnie noticed him fiddling with a button. Was he nervous too?

The silence returned and everyone finished their lunch. Uncle Merlin broke the spell. "Has anyone seen Bruno lately?"

"I can't say I have," Mrs. Winslow replied.

Uncle Merlin frowned. "Oh, bother. I believe I know where he is." He hesitated. "Brynna, would you like to join me?"

"Um, sure."

They put their dishes in the crate, then Uncle Merlin led Brinnie out the door. They followed the path through the yard to a chicken coop enclosed by a whitewashed fence. As Uncle Merlin lifted the latch on the gate, a large brown dog came flying around the corner, barking and wagging his tail. "Ah, there you are, Bruno! Poor old boy, I must have shut you in last night." He opened the gate. "There you are."

Bruno escaped the yard and capered about his master. Brinnie watched Uncle Merlin's stiff expression melt into a warm chuckle that lit up his bright eyes.

So he is human.

Suddenly, the dog paused and seemed to realize Brinnie was there. "Hello, there." She reached out a hand for him to sniff. He pushed her hand aside and bounded into her, licking and wagging his tail, nudging her to pet him. She obliged, laughing, until he jumped all over her and tried to lick her face.

Uncle Merlin looked on with a smile. "Would you like to see the chickens? You can check for eggs if you would like."

Salmonella! Mom's voice screeched in her head. But Mom wasn't here. "Sure."

The chickens scratched in the yard and ignored Brinnie when she entered the coop. Uncle Merlin showed her how to gather the eggs as she engaged in a scavenger hunt.

"You know," Uncle Merlin said, "you can come collect eggs whenever you like. Just bring them back to——"

His voice abruptly sounded farther away. Brinnie turned to see that he no longer stood beside her. Instead, he was standing outside the chicken yard with a look of surprise. But his expression smoothed in an instant, and he didn't stop talking. "To Mrs. Winslow. Unfortunately, I have things to attend to, but feel free to explore. I'll see you at suppertime."

He nodded and strolled away, leaving her blinking with her mouth open. *What the...?* He must have moved while she wasn't paying attention. He must have. *Pull yourself together, Brinnie.*

Still, she stared for a few moments before turning back to the chickens.

During the next four days, Brinnie only saw her uncle at meals. After that, he would always disappear, as if he wasn't keen to be around his newfound niece. It seemed he and her mom had that in common.

No one seemed to know quite what to do with her, so she did her best to entertain herself, whether that meant cooking with Mrs. Winslow, wandering the expansive grounds, or taking care of the chickens. Within a day, she had named all the spastic birds after prominent politicians, and within two, she knew the best places to sit and read—in the rose garden, by the stream, and in her favorite tree.

It's not the worst place to spend the summer. Her parents still should've taken her, though.

At least she was making headway with the members of the household, or so she hoped. On the second day, Miss Burtle rolled her eyes when she saw Brinnie sitting in the library with a book. "Of course, you would be getting them dirty instead of clean."

Brinnie closed her book, responding to the cutting words with a forced smile. "What would you like help with?"

Miss Burtle seemed a bit taken aback at her pleasant offer. Brinnie suppressed a genuine smile. She had years of practice with Mom's disapproving comments. Miss Burtle was no match.

"Well," Miss Burtle replied, "if it wouldn't trouble you and your busy schedule too terribly, you could make yourself useful by dusting. This room doesn't keep itself clean, you know."

So Brinnie learned how to dust and polish the shelves and how to clean the books without damaging them. Miss Burtle sniffed. "You've left plenty of dust behind."

But Brinnie noticed Miss Burtle never redid them.

Brinnie had begun to wonder if she would spend the entire summer in such a manner when Mrs. Winslow asked on Saturday evening, "Did you bring something nice to wear, Brinnie? We'll be going to church tomorrow."

"Church?"

"Yes. You attend back home, don't you?" Mrs. Winslow sounded anxious over the condition of Brinnie's family's souls.

"Yes, usually." Unfortunately. With her mother's anxious eyes fixed on her the entire service, as if Brinnie were a child who might start screaming or misbehaving without that gaze shooting daggers, it wasn't exactly pleasant. "I just didn't think there would be any churches around here."

Mrs. Winslow relaxed. "Oh, good. We'll be leaving around six-thirty, so be sure to be up bright and early."

The next morning, Brinnie woke with the sun and put on a nice button-up shirt and a good pair of jeans. She'd heard people back East were a bit fancier about things, but she figured the outfit was churchy enough.

Evidently it was not. When she came down to breakfast, she was surprised to see the women in dresses and the men wearing ties. Uncle Merlin looked almost normal—men's fashion must not have changed much in that regard over the last couple hundred years.

"Did you forget about church today, dear?" Mrs. Winslow asked.

Brinnie blushed. "I didn't bring any skirts."

Miss Burtle looked scandalized, but Mrs. Winslow paused to think. "You all go ahead and eat. I'll be right back."

Mrs. Winslow returned as everyone finished eating. She carried a dress over her arm and a pair of shoes in her hand. "Here, dearie. Go try these on."

"Thank you." Brinnie took them and hurried up the stairs into her room, where she changed into the dress, coughing at the mothball smell that indicated it had sat in a drawer for years. Then she slipped on the shoes and turned to the mirror to take a look.

The dress itself was pretty, though dated, pale blue with three-quarter length sleeves and a hemline halfway between the knees and ankles. It fit perfectly, with a few ruffles on the bodice that matched the little white flats. But it looked horrible on Brinnie.

It was meant for a blonde girl, like her mother. Or even for a girl with golden, honey-colored hair, like her sister. But it definitely wasn't meant for the jet-black hair Brinnie had inherited from her father. The dress also drew attention to the stark whiteness of Brinnie's skin. She didn't look sickly—her skin tone was even. But she was the palest girl she had ever seen. She could never tan, no matter how hard she tried. She had inherited that from her mother, whose skin was pale like her hair. Brinnie's striking, icy blue eyes, also from her mother, peered back at her in the mirror, brought out by the dress and contrasted cruelly against her dark hair.

Hello, Vampire Girl. She cringed at the reminder of her grade school nickname. This outfit pointed out every oddity in as cruel and stark a fashion as possible. Mom would send her back to her room to change immediately if she came out in something like this.

She trudged down the stairs. *She won't really make me wear this, right?*

No such luck. Mrs. Winslow clapped her hands together. "You look lovely, dear! Just like Eira. That was her dress, you know."

Uncle Merlin looked up from his tea at Brinnie. His expression softened, almost sadly, then returned to its unreadable nature. "All right. Let's go."

They trooped down the lane in their Sunday best to the white building next to the gate that Brinnie had passed many times but never explored. From inside the big open doors came a loud mechanical sound like a motorcycle starting up. The vehicle pulled out of the garage and Brinnie stared.

Mr. Winslow was driving an old topless Ford Model T. It puttered and popped as he drove it out of the garage and stopped for everyone to get in.

The heck? Brinnie climbed in front. Uncle Merlin opened the gate for the car to go through, then closed it again once it had passed. He climbed in next to Brinnie. "Apologies for squeezing you in the middle, but you're the smallest," he explained. Mrs. Winslow, Miss Burtle, and Marcie all sat in the back seat. "And we're off."

Mr. Winslow raised his voice over the noise while they puttered and bumped along the dirt road. "We call her Black Beauty," he told Brinnie. "And a fine vehicle she is, too."

How do you compliment a car? Call it shiny? Instead she went with, "It could be in a museum."

"Ah, old Beauty wouldn't like that much. She's adventurous, and she's got a lot of life in her yet. Just takes a little care."

"Keeping the car in working order is Tom's pet project," Uncle Merlin said. "He's quite the mechanic."

It took quite a while to get to church, bumping over hills and through trees that lined the road, at a meandering pace in the old vehicle. Eventually, the dirt road widened into asphalt, which in turn led into a little town with a sign proclaiming, "Welcome to Lyle, An Old-Fashioned Small Town." They first passed a small gas station and convenience store. Next to it squatted a diner called Bob's Fine Hamburgers, with Lyle's Best Grocery on the other side of the street. A clothing store came next, then a few other small shops. *I didn't know these cutesy towns actually existed.*

They passed a few houses after that, charming places with porches and front lawns. Front lawns. A luxury no one in her Southern Arizona neighborhood could afford to keep alive. They made do with cacti and decorative rocks.

A gradually sloping hill rose on the far side of the houses, at the bottom of which sat Lyle Elementary and Middle School, and at the top, an old whitewashed church with a steeple and cross. Vehicles ranging from minivans to cars to tractors filled the parking lot, and the hill teemed with people.

Mr. Winslow parked in the dirt lot and everyone got out of the car.

A smiling old lady in a flower-print dress greeted Mrs. Winslow with a wave of her cane.

"Good morning, Barbara!" Mrs. Winslow said.

"Good morning, Elsa. Who's this?"

"A relative of Mr. Ludovic's, Brynna."

Brinnie reflexively stiffened, pasting on the polite but unremarkable smile her mother had taught her to perfect. She offered a small wave. "Hello."

"Oh!" The woman peered at her. "A pleasure to meet you, young Brynna. I'm Mrs. Miller. How long will you be staying?"

"For the summer, ma'am."

Mrs. Miller raised her eyebrows at Mrs. Winslow. "Strange doings there, Elsa. No place for a young girl. But I suppose you know that."

"Yes," Mrs. Winslow replied tightly.

"Take care, then. I must speak with Maryanne." Mrs. Miller hobbled off.

Strange doings? Brinnie followed Mrs. Winslow to the church building. *Makes me feel so much better about the creepy old mansion.*

The others were already inside, and many people greeted Mrs. Winslow as they walked over. Old-fashioned pews lined either side of the aisle, facing the pulpit. The choir stood ready on the risers, and most of the churchgoers were streaming inside to take their seats.

Brinnie and Mrs. Winslow joined the rest from Wraithwood in a pew near the middle. By now, half the church seemed to know about Brinnie and was straining for a look. She fought the urge to squirm, instead sitting straight and gazing ahead, hands in her lap.

The organ struck an opening chord, and everyone stood. The preacher, a balding man with glasses, welcomed the congregation formally. Then the choir opened the service with hymns, which were sung in their entirety, every verse. *Thank God for hymnals.* After several hymns and the collection of an offering, the pastor prayed and everyone sat.

"Today," the pastor began, "I would like to address an issue that we all have to face in some way or another–the spiritual forces of darkness. Satan prowls the land, lying in wait for the unwary. Most often, he tempts us with sin, but at other times, he tempts us to serve him.

"The Bible speaks harshly against witchcraft and dark magic. In Leviticus 20:6, the Lord says, 'As for the person who turns to mediums and spiritists...I will also set My face against that person and will cut him off from among his people.' In Exodus 22:18, He declares, 'You shall not allow a sorceress to live.'"

Brinnie had the uncanny feeling that the preacher looked directly at her as he spoke. *Why witchcraft? Shouldn't we be talking about sin or godly living or something?* Maybe he knew about her fantasy novel obsession. She suppressed a smile at that. They were probably having issues with unruly, superstitious teens in the community. She glanced around at the young people in the pews, but turned away quickly when she saw them looking right back.

Then, it happened again. Uncle Merlin was sitting on her right, closest to the aisle. Suddenly, he wasn't sitting next to her anymore. She turned around and saw him sitting in the pew behind them with wide eyes. The woman next to him scooted away in horror. *When did he...? How did I miss that?* For a brief second, he looked as surprised as she felt. Then he sat listening to the sermon as if nothing had happened.

"Witchcraft—the giving over of oneself to the devil—" the preacher continued booming.

Brinnie's mind raced. It was like the other day at the chicken coop. Had Uncle Merlin moved without her noticing? He must have. It was the only explanation.

"Beware those who engage with darkness. Repent! Turn from your evil ways. Do not bring iniquity into the house of the Lord. On the Day of Judgment, He will see your evil deeds written on the scroll and will cast all who did not serve Him into the fiery pits of hell. Repent, for the day is near, and no one knows the time of its coming!" The preacher bowed his head. "Let us pray."

Everyone stood for the benediction. Brinnie blinked several times, suffering from sermon whiplash. With the final "amen," people began streaming out the doors. Uncle Merlin rejoined the Wraithwood group. Brinnie wanted to ask him what had happened, but he was halfway down the aisle, smiling and nodding to members of the congregation like nothing had occurred.

A potluck lunch was served outside the church. Children played in the grass, adults sat at fold-out tables or stood around chatting, and the youth did a mixture of both. Brinnie hoped one of the teens might introduce themselves and invite her over, but none did.

Well, this is awkward. She excused herself to use the ladies' room.

She pushed open the door to reveal a small, two-stall bathroom. Empty. She closed the stall door in relief. Someplace to hide.

Two seconds later, she heard the main door swing open and what sounded like two women come shuffling in. *You've got to be kidding me.*

"Did you see that girl?" an old-sounding voice asked hesitantly.

"The new Ludovic?" A deeper, middle-aged voice scoffed. "How could I not?"

Brinnie cringed. *Awkward. Again.*

"I heard she's staying with them the whole summer," said the older voice.

The middle-aged one barked a laugh. "If she makes it that long with Merlin. Considering what he tends to do to family, I don't find it likely."

"That's just gossip. The police said—"

"We all know that investigation was a sham."

Water ran for a moment as the older woman sighed. "Do you really think he'd hurt the girl?"

Brinnie gripped the toilet paper dispenser. Then let go. *Gross, don't touch that.*

"I don't know what to think. All I know is that the old Ludovics didn't die naturally and *he*"—she sneered the pronoun like it was dirty—"had something to hide."

Goosebumps rose on Brinnie's arms.

"But," the woman continued, musing, "the girl doesn't look quite right either. Witchy, if you know what I mean. Like she might be into the same sort of things." Her voice sobered. "Might not be her that needs to watch out. Might be us."

The older woman made a shuddering noise. "Enough of that. Doesn't seem right to say that kind of thing in a church."

The two ladies finished their business and left. Brinnie stared at the stall door. Her haven of solitude didn't feel like such a safe place anymore. She pushed the door open and walked woodenly to the sink. As she washed her hands, she looked in the mirror. *Witchy.*

She yanked off a paper towel to dry her hands. The witchcraft sermon was ridiculous, just backwoods superstition. But murder was another story. *Mom said they died in an accident when she was a teenager.*

But was that true?

Chapter Four

BRINNIE WANTED TO ASK ABOUT HER grandparents. She opened her mouth a few times, but never brought herself to do it. *Don't be ridiculous. Obviously, they weren't murdered.* She didn't want to admit to herself that half the reason she didn't ask wasn't because she thought it was silly, but because she was afraid what would happen if it was somehow true. If Uncle Merlin did have something to hide.

Instead, she amused herself. She read for hours, wandered the grounds with Bruno, learned how to cook with Mrs. Winslow, kept the gardens with Mr. Winslow, organized the library with Miss Burtle, and cleaned with Marcie. The only person she never saw was her uncle.

On Thursday, Brinnie was slicing bread Mrs. Winslow had baked. "Wouldn't it be a lot easier and quicker to set out store-bought bread?"

Mrs. Winslow shook her head. "Many things would make cooking easier and faster, dear. In fact, it would be easy with all these modern inventions never to cook at all."

"Then why not use them? Wouldn't that save a lot of time?"

She laughed. "What do I need more time for?"

"Well...for doing other things."

"I love to cook. So I cook. Tom loves to garden. So he does. It would be much easier for him to plant a few trees and cut the grass every once in a while, I suppose, but he does much more than that. Imagine the grounds without the rose gardens and the hedges and the orchards." She pointed a wooden spoon at Brinnie. "Easier and faster are not always better. What better things do you have to do?"

"Nothing, I guess." Brinnie dropped her gaze to the bread.

That seemed to be the philosophy of Wraithwood. No one ever complained or seemed to be working. Brinnie almost felt on edge at the slow pace. She loved not being in a hurry or having something that needed to be done by a certain time, loved spending hours reading or playing in the rose garden with Bruno, but guilt tended to nag at her conscience. Her mother's voice echoed in her head. "Can't you be useful, Brynna? Where have you been? *When Anna was your age..."*

Brinnie shook that thought away.

The only not-quite-tranquil times were at meals, when she would sometimes see Uncle Merlin. Marcie's fear of him was obvious, and ever since Sunday, Brinnie couldn't help regarding him with suspicion.

She gripped the knife tighter and moved on to cutting tomatoes.

He disappeared often, sometimes for days at a time. Brinnie was never sure if he was in the house or not. She never saw him leave, but it seemed she would know if he were upstairs.

"What does Uncle Merlin do for a living?" Brinnie had asked Mrs. Winslow one day while washing dishes.

"How am I to know, dear? That would be a question for Edna."

Why wouldn't *you know what your employer does for a living?* But she had asked Miss Burtle anyway when they were dusting in the library.

"What business is that of yours? Cheeky girl," Miss Burtle had replied.

A tomato squirted, breaking Brinnie out of her reverie. She set down the knife. "I think I'm going to go help Marcie."

Mrs. Winslow nodded. "Lunch should be ready in half an hour."

Brinnie climbed the stairs with determination. If Marcie had any idea, Brinnie was certain she would tell.

She found Marcie in what she called the Lavender Room. Brinnie peeked around the door and smiled. *Of course.* The walls were light violet and the bedspread and curtains were a dark purple, with a chair and dresser to match. Marcie said it was meant for a purple queen.

Brinnie had learned two things about Marcie once she had grown comfortable enough to talk. One, she loved theater, especially Shakespeare. And two, she liked nothing better than a chance to practice her acting skills.

"Ah! The queen is pleased." Brinnie turned up her nose and strode across the room with pomp.

Marcie turned around and curtsied. "It is my honor, Your Royal Highness."

Brinnie sat upon the chair with as much dignity as she could muster in her jeans and T-shirt. "I shall promote thee to Head Designer of the castle and thou shalt dine every evening at my royal table."

"Oh, Your Highness, I do not deserve such an honor."

"Rise, fair lady. It pleases the queen to do so."

"But Your Highness, how can I rise? I have not knelt."

Brinnie's posh act cracked and she snorted, which sent them both into giggles.

Marcie put a hand on her hip. "So what are you doing here, purple queen? Come to help clean?"

"I would be happy to. But I actually had a question."

"Fire away."

"Do you have any idea what my uncle does for a living?"

A sudden change came over Marcie's smiling face. She turned and began meticulously scrubbing the doorknob. "No. No, I don't."

That was perhaps the third thing Brinnie had learned about Marcie. Despite her love of theater, Marcie was terrible at concealing her own emotions. Like now. "You don't have a general idea?"

"No."

Brinnie turned in the chair to face her better. If anyone was safe to question, it was Marcie. She hadn't been at Wraithwood as long as the others. *Can't possibly be complicit in the potential and highly unlikely murders.*

She decided to take the humorous route. "People at church seemed to think he was a witch or something—or whatever a man witch is called."

"All I know is that everyone here has been very nice to take me in, and I don't ask questions." Marcie's voice trembled, and she refused to make eye contact. "That's more than anyone else would do for me."

Brinnie sat up straighter and decided to back off with the questions. It hadn't been that long since Marcie had stopped looking at her with the same suspicious anxiety the maid held toward Uncle Merlin. The last thing she wanted was to lose their tentative new friendship. Instead she asked, "Take you in?"

Marcie sighed. "Yes. My husband—Jerry, down in Lyle—he drinks a lot, you know. I didn't know that when I married him. I was barely eighteen. He didn't treat me right, and I had to get away for a while. I couldn't go back to my family. Not after they told me to stay away from him. I had to prove to myself that I could live on my own. I guess the Wraithwood folks heard the gossip, and they offered me a job for as long as I needed it." She glanced at Brinnie. "I don't know if the rumors are true or not, but I do love these folks."

"How old are you now?"

"Nineteen. Jerry's six years older than me. That probably should've told me enough, but I was stupid."

"You're not stupid." It came out with more force than Brinnie intended it to, but she softened it with a smile. "And in the end, this isn't a bad gig at nineteen, you know? Full-time job. I'd think more fun than fast food."

Marcie chuckled. "Don't remind me of my high school job." Then she sighed. "I love him, Brinnie. I really do. But I can't live with him." She picked up her cleaning supplies. "Anyway. On to the next room?"

It took until after lunch for Brinnie to get her next shot at asking questions, while helping Mr. Winslow in the rose garden. "Mr. Winslow, what does Uncle Merlin do for a living?"

He scratched his head. "For a living? Not sure, really. I think he has some money in stocks. Far as I know, they do pretty well."

"Oh." A speculator? How would that work way out here? She looked at Mr. Winslow sideways as he snipped off dead roses. *What are you all hiding?*

⁂

"Chill out, Donald." Brinnie shooed the chicken into the coop and shut the door. They were all skittish from the strong wind that had come up. Dark, ominous clouds built in the overcast sky as she checked the security of the latch.

After her failure to get answers yesterday, her prospects looked even grimmer today. The Winslows, Miss Burtle, and Marcie had gone into town for the day. Something about visiting an ailing friend, going to a book club meeting, seeing family.

And of course, her uncle was nowhere to be seen. He had bid everyone who was leaving for town goodbye at breakfast, and then, as usual, had disappeared.

Bruno followed Brinnie to the house and into the kitchen. He was supposed to stay outside, but storms were an exception, and he knew it. Seconds after Brinnie closed the door, thunder cracked and the heavens let loose with sheets of rain.

Brinnie looked around for something to do. There was no one to cook for and nothing to clean, since she and Marcie had cleaned everything yesterday. *Library it is.*

She turned toward the door and stopped. She didn't know where the umbrellas were kept. Even more tragically, she didn't have any books in her room at the moment, even ones she had already read.

That rain did not look pleasant. "Bruno, I'm thinking about being a bad girl."

He looked up at her from where he lay next to the hearth and yawned.

I don't see why that side of the house is any more dangerous than this side. It's all one house. She wavered, hearing her mother's voice in her head. *For crying out loud, Brynna, can't you stay out of trouble for two minutes?*

She winced at the memory. She didn't even remember what she had done. Maybe she broke something. She couldn't have been more than five. After that, she had never gone to play at a friend's house again—and she didn't think that was a coincidence.

It'll be fine. No one will know. I won't stay there. I'll just walk through and go to the library. By the time she wanted to come back, the rain would have stopped and she could return the right way.

For a long time, she looked at the doors that led to the dining room. Then she nodded and strode over to them. She reached out to push open the door when a hand came down over her wrist.

She screamed and leaped back. Heart thundering, she found herself under Uncle Merlin's cool gaze.

"I—I was just..."

"Hmm. Mrs. Winslow might have forgotten to tell you. That side of the house is rather dangerous."

"Oh." Brinnie wished she could disappear. She should have known if she tried to do something she shouldn't that she would get caught.

She looked up and saw Uncle Merlin blinking at her, but it seemed as if he was looking right through her, a puzzled expression on his face. Then, with a strange, sudden shift, the world seemed to tilt. Uncle Merlin was standing slightly to her left, but she could have sworn he had been standing in front of her. She stepped back in surprise.

With that step back, he looked directly at her again and smiled as if nothing had happened. "I came downstairs to ask if you would like to play a game. Not much else to do on a day like today."

What was that? "Um...sure."

"Splendid. Come." He turned around and headed for the stairs. She followed, her mind racing. It was the third time her uncle had seemed to appear and reappear...literally.

She trailed him up the steps, but when they reached the landing, he kept on going. Brinnie hesitated. Uncle Merlin waved her on. "It's all right. You have permission to come up here."

The stairs led to a small room with a chaise lounge, a few stuffed chairs, and a game table. Double doors to one side led to the rest of the floor, or so she assumed. Outside the window, lightning flashed, illuminating the old-fashioned furniture eerily. Too eerily for Brinnie's taste. *I'm alone on the third floor with a man I hardly know, who is rumored to be a murderer or occultist at worst, an eccentric at best.*

He strode over to the game table and pulled out a sturdy wooden chair. "Please, have a seat." She sat down and he sat across from her. "Do you know how to play chess?"

No, she groaned inwardly. Death would be better than chess. "Yes."

"But...?"

"But last time I played I tried to lose as quickly as possible so the game would be over."

He laughed. His smile almost looked like Mom's, but warmer. "I feel the same. Can't abide the game. Incredibly dull, lasts entirely too long, and I always did wonder, what were the two kingdoms fighting about anyway?"

He can't be a complete psychopath, then. "Exactly! Besides, the king is always such a coward, making the queen do all the work, that I

34

almost want him to lose."

Uncle Merlin nodded. "Quite. Well, let's just fix it."

"Fix it?"

"Yes." He pulled out a drawer in the table. It was full of chess pieces. "Why not make it interesting?" He set the white king on his right, and Brinnie noticed an elaborate geographical map underneath the glass tabletop, with hills, valleys, rivers, forests, and mountains, but no names. "This is King Arlon of Adiron." Uncle Merlin wrote the word "Adiron" across the table with a dry-erase marker.

Brinnie stared. "You play Dungeons and Dragons?"

He blinked. "Dungeons and...? I was simply suggesting a modified game of chess."

Brinnie stifled a snort. *Okay, so apparently we're so far removed from society that he doesn't know about D&D, but I'm willing to play "modified chess."*

Brinnie took out the black king and set him in the far corner from King Arlon. "And this is King Mirdon of Mordrin." She scrawled "Mordrin" across the corner.

"King Arlon's castle is on the Plains of Silisia." Uncle Merlin placed the castle-looking piece on a wide plain on the map near his right hand. "He rules his people justly, and the peasants and noblemen alike have plenty. Most of his subjects are simple farmers who till the fertile soil of Silisia Valley."

Brinnie couldn't help grinning. She'd read Narnia in kindergarten and cuddled *The Fellowship of the Ring* instead of a teddy bear. At least, until Mom told her *Lord of the Rings* was too scary for a second grader. "King Mirdon's castle is high in the craggy Mountains of Armon. He is sly and clever. His people live in fear of him and his terrible army. They eke out their existence from the hard rocks of the mountains, if they are lucky, and if they are not, they spend their lives in the dark mines of Dromir, mining gold, silver, and jewels to grace the decadent halls of King Mirdon's black palace."

Uncle Merlin nodded appreciatively. "King Arlon has no desire for war, only for peace and prosperity for his country."

"But King Mirdon delights in war." Brinnie reined in her grin to match the tone of what she was saying. "His dark mind joys in conquest and destruction. He watches his neighbor jealously, thinking what great wealth he could accumulate from the produce of Silisia. He no longer wants to pay for the goods of Adiron—he wants to take them for himself."

Uncle Merlin nodded. "A pause for a few rules so the game will run smoothly. First, everything that happens must be reasonably possible. For example, if King Mirdon's army invented helicopters and flew to Silisia, that would be unreasonable, in which case I would say 'Veto.' However, if King Mirdon's invading army rode in on horses with manes dyed purple, that would be unreasonable, but reasonably possible, so I would say 'Fair.'"

No dice then. She pictured her uncle hunched over a pile of dice with half a dozen other nerds and suppressed a giggle. "Fair. So what do you call this game?"

The corner of his mouth turned up. "Wizard's Chess—at least, a simplified version."

"Never heard of it. Cool."

Over the next three hours, the game raged as the vicious Mordrin invaded Adiron, taking down city after city in dramatically narrated confrontations. Brinnie had never had so much fun with a game. Never had anyone to swap vivid imaginings with, especially since Mom had told her she was too old for pretend for as long as she could remember. *Maybe those eighties nerds were onto something.*

The Mordrinians surrounded the castle of King Arlon in the dead of night. The remnant of Adiron's men had retreated there in a last desperate hope of resisting the onslaught. King Mirdon came to watch the final death throes of Adiron.

"The captain of the forces came to King Arlon. 'My lord. Our supplies of food and water are all gone. We stand not a chance.'" Uncle Merlin switched voices. "'Perhaps not, but we shall die as men, not as cowards,' King Arlon replied. 'If we must go down to the grave, we will go down fighting for the freedom of our people from the darkness and tyranny of Mordrin. At dawn, we shall meet them once and for all on the field of battle.'"

"The Mordrinians await the Adironis on the field below the castle," Brinnie replied, arranging her pawns. "They know they do not have long to wait before victory will be theirs."

"In the darkness before dawn, the gates of the castle open. In silence, the forces of Adiron creep out onto the field, hoping for a surprise counterattack." Uncle Merlin nudged his pawns toward hers.

"But the sentinels of Mordrin see the move and sound the horns."

"With a shout, the Adironis rush toward the camp."

"They are met almost immediately by a solid wall of Mordrinian shields. Mordrinian arrows decimate their numbers, and they are cut down by swords and spears from every side."

"Every side?" Uncle Merlin asked.

"Three sides, anyway. The Mordrinians want to cut off their retreat."

"Fair." Pawns and other chess pieces clustered the Plains of Silisia, moving as rapidly as the two could speak. "King Arlon makes a charge and breaks through the line."

"Only to be surrounded once again by a horde of Mordrinian warriors." Brinnie turned to her king. She rested her fingertip on the chess piece's pointy head. "Meanwhile, King Mirdon watches from a nearby hilltop, drinking in the sight of destruction. He is well pleased with his conquest.

"But beside him, his son, Askil, sits brooding." She slid the knight she was using to represent the prince closer to the king. "Askil had participated in the conquest of the city of Annaim, and what he saw sickened him. The people there had been living so happily before the surprise attack. He had looked in a window and seen the smiling faces of a simple farming family. He had never seen any of the Mordrinian peasants smile. They only grimaced as they bore pain and heavy burdens in the cold of the mountains. He felt it was wrong when the Mordrinian warriors slaughtered the peaceful peasants. And all for what? For more wealth for the Mordrinian royal family and more misery for everyone else.

"Askil knows that his father is the reason for the fighting, and that he will never put a stop to it. But if his father was not there..."

Something about the story felt oddly familiar as Brinnie continued, the game board fading from her vision, replaced by her imagination.

"'Father?'

"'What do you want?' Mirdon asked impatiently.

"'I want to apologize for what I am about to do.'" Brinnie could see Askil's face, his horror at what he was going to do and his certainty that it was the only way. She could see the anguish it caused him. "And with that, Askil drew his sword and plunged it into his father's heart."

Brinnie saw it before her, as if shadows were playacting what she had said. A yell of agony ripped from the throat of the shadow Mirdon.

She heard a crash—and came to herself to find that Uncle Merlin had knocked his chair over. He grabbed her arm and pulled her from her chair, pushing her behind him, her back to the wall. He pulled a knife seemingly out of nowhere and pointed it at the table. He looked around the room warily, knife at ready.

"What are you doing?"

"Quiet," he commanded. He took a cautious step forward. Slowly, he investigated the entire room. Lightning flashed, illuminating his serious face. After he had checked every place a person might be hiding, he slipped the knife back into his vest and turned to Brinnie. His brow furrowed.

"What...what was that all about?" Brinnie's legs trembled, and she leaned against the wall for support.

"Hmm." He looked at the game table, then at her again. "I heard a noise. It startled me."

"A noise?" How did hearing a noise warrant a drawn knife? "What sort of noise?"

"A sound like someone yelled." He fiddled with a button on his pocket. "Did you hear it?"

"I was too into the game to notice anything," Brinnie admitted. *But pulling a knife is still a pretty extreme reaction.* "It was probably the wind."

"Yes. Yes, the wind." He passed his hand over the table, as if feeling for something. It seemed he might ask something else, but instead he pulled out a pocket watch. "Stars above! It's already three o'clock. Everyone should be back in an hour. Come, let's go downstairs."

Brinnie couldn't believe they had spent almost five hours playing the game. So long that Uncle Merlin was losing his grip on what was real? That he was hearing things? "That was the best game of chess I've ever played."

Uncle Merlin stopped at the top of the stairs. "I'd entirely forgotten. No one won yet."

"No."

"We can't have that."

They returned to the game table. Askil halted the army right as the Adironis were about to be utterly defeated. A truce was declared between the two countries. The Mordrinians rejoiced to have a new king, one who was kind and fair and relieved much of the heavy burden placed upon them by his father. King Askil and King Arlon became not only allies and trade partners, but friends. Both countries thrived once more.

"And so," Brinnnie said, "Mordrin became a country of peace and prosperity, and the dark mountains didn't seem so dark anymore."

Uncle Merlin waited a moment, then asked, "That's the end?"

"Yes. Unless you want to add anything."

Uncle Merlin shook his head. "You seem to delight in losing."

"What do you mean?"

"You elaborately engineered the story so your side was sure to win, then you sabotaged it yourself."

"I never wanted to win. I wanted Adiron to win all along."

"But the point of chess is to win."

"But I don't like chess."

They looked at each other for a long moment, then both broke into grins. "Come," said Uncle Merlin. "We should go downstairs. I need to telephone town. I doubt the Winslows and the rest will be coming home in this storm."

As Uncle Merlin braved the weather to make a call from the washroom, Brinnie's smile faded. *I know nothing about him, but he's a darn good storyteller.*

The door whipped open as the wind took it from Uncle Merlin. He slammed it shut. "They won't be coming home until morning. They're all at Jack's in town. He owns the mechanic shop. It seems the car broke down, and there's too much rain and mud for anyone to drive down these old roads."

The two of them ate a dinner of sandwiches in the light of the lanterns. Brinnie wanted to ask questions about what had happened upstairs earlier, but Uncle Merlin sat staring past her, lost in thought. She looked down at her plate. *We're the only two people in the house...all night.*

Brinnie lay in bed that night clutching a pillow against her chest, as if that could protect her. The thunder and lightning, the creaks and groans of the old house, and the whistling wind made for an eerie night. Uncle Merlin had escorted her to her room before heading to bed himself, but now that she was alone...

She pulled the covers over her like a hood, trying to shake a chill that stemmed more from fear than cold. She knew her fear was irrational, but she hated being the only one on the floor. A strange part of her wished Uncle Merlin was in one of the rooms in the hall.

One day and you go from "He's a potential murderer" to "He's a nice guy, I wish he was around" just because it's dark? Pull yourself together.

She took a fortifying breath, turned off the lantern, and shut her eyes.

Chapter Five

BRINNIE SAT ON THE LIVING ROOM carpet, holding a bright pink plastic horse. Its name was Whinny—Brinnie's Whinny.

A knock on the front door startled her.

Mommy came out of the kitchen and opened it. When she saw the figure standing on the other side, she shrieked.

The mustached man raised an eyebrow. "Not the reaction I imagined for our first meeting in twenty years."

"Merlin!" Her mouth snapped shut and she grabbed his arm. "Get in here before someone sees you."

The strange man stepped into the living room, not fighting the pull on his arm. His gaze swept the room and landed on Brinnie for a moment. She froze as he seemed to study her.

Mommy shut the door and let go of the man's arm. "What are you doing here?"

"What am I doing here?" His eyes left Brinnie and returned to Mommy. "I'm your brother."

"Hush. What if someone followed you?"

"I'm quite certain no one has." He straightened his sleeves. "It would be rather difficult to get from Wraithwood to a few blocks from here in less than a second."

Mommy's eyes narrowed. "You can't be here just for a nice visit. Why did you come?"

"Because two and a half years ago you disappeared entirely. I kept an eye on you in Washington—"

"Merlin!"

"Without your knowledge, of course. But then you left Washington, and no one knew where you had gone. I did hear some interesting stories from the hospital, though—snow in the delivery room—"

"You didn't go snooping around."

"Of course I did. It took me two years to find you here—clever name changes, homeschooling your oldest, and all that—but I found you eventually." His tone hardened. "Now, what do you think you're doing?"

"What..." She balled her fists. "I'm trying to live in peace, if you would quit stalking me."

"I'm trying to keep you safe. How can I do that if I don't know where you are? Do you know how hard it was to fake another death without having the police come knocking? I told the authorities you moved out, led the townspeople to believe you were dead, and staged the circumstances of your death for the—ahem—others. If it weren't for me, you would be dead."

"Well, I do thank you for that. But did you have to come all this way to tell me?"

"No, I came 'all this way' for the safety of your daughter."

Brinnie awoke with a start. Her window showed the early grayness before dawn. The dream lingered in her mind, clear and fresh as a memory, unlike the haze that usually surrounded dreams. So real and yet so bizarre. Yes, that had been their old house. She held vague memories of Whinny the plastic horse—she thought it was still in her closet somewhere. Uncle Merlin had looked like Uncle Merlin, but a bit younger. She recognized a younger Mom from pictures. Brinnie knew she was born in Washington. *Twenty years...* She did the math. She was two in the dream. Anna was sixteen at that time. It made sense that Mom wouldn't have seen Uncle Merlin in twenty years, if she hadn't seen him since they were born.

Brinnie shook her head. It fit too perfectly. That couldn't have all been a dream. There must have been at least some memory mixed in.

She got dressed, brushed her hair, and tiptoed down the stairs in her socks. She was about to slip on her shoes to go to the washroom when the door opened, revealing a thick fog enveloping the house. Uncle Merlin shut the door behind him and took off his muddy shoes.

"Good morning. I called town. It seems the road is a bog from all the rain. The car's fixed, but they won't be back until this evening, when everything dries out enough to drive."

Another day of only the two of them. "At least it's fixed, and it isn't raining anymore."

"Indeed. Shall we see about breakfast? I was thinking about hot cereal myself. Rather chilly out there."

As they prepared breakfast, it took Brinnie a few tries to work up the nerve before she asked, "Did you ever come visit us when I was younger?"

He glanced at her with an expression she couldn't read. "Yes, when you were very young. Why do you ask?"

"No reason." Something prevented her from mentioning her dream. "I just thought I remembered something about it."

"Hmm." He removed a boiling kettle from the stovetop.

"Did you come often?"

He took a minute to reply. "No, only once." He jerked his head toward the cupboard. "Some apples up there."

Brinnie took down an apple and began slicing it to put on the cereal. So Uncle Merlin *had* come to their house when she was young. But how much was memory, and how much was a dream?

They ate breakfast in relative silence. Brinnie hoped he would say something else about his visit, but she couldn't bring herself to ask. "Tomorrow's Sunday," she said finally.

"Yes."

"Are we going to church?"

"Of course." He seemed to notice her disappointment at the news. "Do you not like it?"

"It's not that." She pushed her food around. "It's just, I don't know, a little...different, I guess."

"The people of Lyle are good people. They're simply mistaken about some things." He sipped his tea. "Pastor Denison cares about the congregation, even if his sermons might sound a bit harsh."

Brinnie thought anyone who called people witches wasn't exactly a good person, but she kept that to herself.

A strange sound interrupted her thoughts—a clacking, thumping sound like...like a knocker. Uncle Merlin stiffened and set down his spoon. "Someone at the door. I'll be back in a moment."

He stood and exited through the dining room. Brinnie didn't react at first, caught up in wondering who would be knocking. Then she blinked and stared at the dining room doors. Didn't he say the front of the house was dangerous? Did he forget?

She had finished her breakfast by the time Uncle Merlin came back. He brought with him a short, round man wearing a pork pie hat who waved his arms as he spoke. "I tell you it will be tonight—it's the perfect time. We should strike now before—"

"I agree, Oswald," Uncle Merlin said. "But we have time enough to talk in a moment. It wouldn't do to take cold from wet clothing."

"Yes, yes, of course." The little man trundled over to the coat rack by the door and hung up his sopping wet coat and narrow-brimmed hat. He pulled a handkerchief from his pants pocket and mopped his wet face and balding head. Brinnie raised an eyebrow at the man's old-fashioned hat and handkerchief. Apparently, he was stuck in another century as well. "Quite a downpour out there," the man commented.

Brinnie's eyebrow rose even higher. She glanced out the window at the overcast sky. She didn't see any rain.

She had been standing near the cupboard tidying up when the two came in, so the stranger hadn't seemed to notice her, but as he turned around his eyes widened. "Ach! Merlin, who is this?"

"Forgive me. This is my niece, Brynna. Brynna, this is Oswald Goddensfeld, a colleague of mine."

"Your niece?" Goddensfeld asked.

"Yes."

"Ah, a pleasure to meet you, young lady."

He stepped forward to shake her hand, and the world seemed to shift. Brinnie had been sure Goddensfeld was an older man, probably in his late forties or early fifties. But as she reached out to shake his hand, he seemed to be in his early forties—no, his thirties. Yes, he appeared to be in his early thirties now. And he had been almost entirely bald a moment ago. Now she saw no more than a palm-sized balding patch on his crown. She blinked as if to clear her vision. "Nice to meet you, too."

Goddensfeld hesitated for a moment, then turned back to Uncle

Merlin. "You know, I'm going to save my questions about this for later. For now, we need to talk. I received word from Mary—"

"Excuse me, Oswald, but I don't think Brynna is particularly interested in our business affairs."

Goddensfeld's mouth pinched into a small circle. "Oh. *Oh.*"

"Let's go up to my office. I'm sorry, Brynna, but I must attend to matters of business. Would you mind taking care of things?"

"Nope, go ahead."

As the two men left the room, Brinnie stared after them. *I'm losing my mind.*

After cleaning up the breakfast dishes, Brinnie stepped outside to feed the chickens, hopping from foot to foot to avoid the biggest puddles. Bruno came with her, quite pleased with himself, since he had received the remains of Uncle Merlin's breakfast. As Brinnie scattered grain to the clucking, fluttering hens, her thoughts drifted back to Mr. Goddensfeld. What sort of business was Uncle Merlin in?

"Brynna!"

Uncle Merlin strode up the path toward her, his coat flapping and his expression troubled. "I have to leave right away for an urgent matter. I called town and they're going to try to make it home as early as possible, but I'm afraid I'll have to leave you here on your own for a few hours."

Brinnie's heart thudded. Sunny Wraithwood with Mr. Winslow in the rose garden and Marcie taking an afternoon stroll? Wonderful. Foggy Wraithwood all alone? Not so much. "That's all right. I'll be fine."

"Good. I'm very sorry about this. I would recommend you stay in the house. It wouldn't do to wander around alone."

"Okay."

He nodded, but hesitated. "All right," he said at last. "I don't know when I'll be back, so don't be concerned if you don't see me tomorrow. Until then."

Brinnie watched him disappear around the corner, then she scattered the rest of the grain before returning to the house. Bruno's tongue lolled out of his mouth as he followed her. *At least he isn't concerned.* She knew she wasn't supposed to, but she let him into the library with her. It was the brightest and least scary room in the house. *How old are you, Brinnie? Get a hold of yourself.* She sat in an armchair with a book, and Bruno draped himself across her feet.

She read for about an hour before she heard it—the sound of the knocker. Her heart thumped once. They'd never had visitors before today. She wondered if she should answer the door. *But what if it's a kidnapper or something?* No one would know what happened to her. She knew she was probably being ridiculous and rude, but whoever it was would be fine if she didn't answer.

She went on reading, but the knocking persisted. Finally, she put the book down. The best thing to do would be to look out the window and see who it was, but she couldn't do that, since she would have to go into the front of the house. But she couldn't go outside, either. That would be the worst thing to do if it was someone dangerous.

Eventually, the knocking stopped. Relieved, Brinnie returned to her book and her heart slowed to a normal pace.

She heard a rattling sound. Her eyes darted to the knob of the door leading to the back yard. It was turning. Her heart leapt. She hadn't locked it. In fact, she didn't know if it had a lock. She dropped the book and ran up the stairs, diving behind the short bookshelves.

Bruno skittered and scrambled up the stairs after her, thinking it a fun game indeed. It was impossible to hear anything over his racket, so Brinnie cautiously poked her head above the bookshelf, where she could see below without being seen.

A little woman in a purple skirt suit stood on the main floor. A matching hat perched on her bobbed red hair, and even her stockings and heels were purple. She scanned the room with one hand on her hip. "Merlin! Merlin Ludovic! Where on earth are you? I've been knocking for hours. This is serious. We need you at once." She stomped around the library's first floor, looking behind each chair and row of shelves, as if he were a naughty child playing hide-and-seek. Finally, she looked up and spotted Bruno standing next to Brinnie's hiding place, panting and nudging her. Brinnie tried to push him away.

"I know someone's up there," the woman called out, "so you might as well come down, or I'll have to come up there after you."

Brinnie froze. Should she stay hidden or give herself up? The persistent woman would surely climb the stairs and find her anyway. She rose, gripping the top lip of the bookshelf with her fingertips. "Who are you?"

"Who am I? I should be asking you the same question. What are you doing in here?"

"Um." Brinnie wasn't sure how to answer such a question. "Reading."

"Oh, please. I mean *why* are you in here?" She shook her head. "No, don't answer that. Just tell me who you are."

"I'm Brinnie."

"That doesn't really tell me anything." The purple-clad woman waved a hand impatiently.

"I'm Merlin Ludovic's niece?"

"Ha!" She crossed her arms. "You can come up with something better than that. Merlin doesn't have any family."

"Well, who are you?" Brinnie demanded.

"Me? I'm Lydia Tynsdale, for all that's worth." She took a step toward the staircase and rested her hand on the railing. "Now, does Merlin know you're in here?"

"Not exactly, but—"

"No buts! Where is he? I have important things to tell him, but be sure I'll tell him about you, too."

Brinnie took a deep breath. "I'm allowed to be in here. I come in here almost every day, and Uncle Merlin knows it. He went away on business."

"Of course he did." Lydia Tynsdale tapped an impatient finger on the stair railing. "Where to?"

"I have no idea."

"Of course you don't. You're from Lyle, aren't you?"

"No."

"Fine, then. Where's Elsa Winslow?"

"She's in town."

Ms. Tynsdale threw her hands in the air. "Is there no one here?"

Great. The strange lady didn't seem sinister, but she couldn't be sure.

"That's a question."

"No, it's just me. But they'll be back soon."

"Wonderful!" She shook her head and strode back and forth, her heels clicking on the wood floor. *Odd*...for a brief moment, Ms. Tynsdale's red hair looked long and blonde, trailing halfway down her back. In the time it took Brinnie to blink, the lady's reddish bob reappeared above her shoulders as she turned on her heel toward Brinnie. "Wonderful. And who are you *really*? A relation of the Winslows?"

"No, I told you the truth. Uncle Merlin is my uncle."

"Stop wasting my time. I don't really care if you've been lying. I just want to know if you're someone who can help me."

"What do you need help with?"

"Hmph!" The woman's snort echoed in the cavernous library. "I can't tell you until I know who you are."

Brinnie sighed. "I'm Brynna Lane. My mother Eira is Uncle Merlin's sister."

"Eira isn't your mother. She passed away years ago."

"No—as far as I know, she's still alive."

Ms. Tynsdale narrowed her eyes. "That's impossible."

"It's true."

"If I find out you're lying to me..."

"I'm not!" Would this woman never stop? "Why does everyone around here think she died? She hasn't lived here in a really long time, but that doesn't mean she's dead."

"Why didn't you tell me that right away?" Ms. Tynsdale stabbed a finger toward the ground. "Come down here. Oh, I could strangle Merlin! Why didn't he tell us? He knew, didn't he?"

"I think so?" The woman seemed to know Uncle Merlin, and even Mom. Brinnie decided there was no harm in talking face to face. She took a few steps down the stairs.

"I can't believe it. After all these years...But we don't have time for this now. We have to go. Write a note and get in the car. We have to hurry."

Brinnie jerked to a stop. "No. I don't get into cars with strangers."

"Don't be silly, I'm not a stranger. We need everyone we can get."

"For what?"

"For riding pink unicorns." If eye-rolling were an art form, the purple lady would be Picasso. "What do you *think* what for? Now come on." She headed for the door. "Oh, and what do you do, by the way?" she called over her shoulder.

"I call the police when suspicious people try to persuade me to go with them," Brinnie said, retreating up the stairs. Bruno, perplexed by her indecision, stuck to her heels.

Ms. Tynsdale spun around and put her hands on her hips. "Oh, please." Her eyes widened. "You don't know, do you? That makes it more difficult. Well, you see—"

"That will be enough, Lydia." Uncle Merlin stood in the doorway. His voice drowned out whatever Ms. Tynsdale was about to say. "Aren't you supposed to be at the office?"

"The office?"

"Yes. We had a huge workload come in. We need you there." He glanced at Brinnie. "I doubt Brynna could be of much help at the moment. Perhaps later she can learn to make copies and such if she would like, but we're too busy right now to teach her."

"Merlin!" Ms. Tynsdale exclaimed. "How could—"

"We should go." His tone left no room for discussion. "Brynna, I came back because I forgot something. Glad I did. I suggest you go to the kitchen and lock the door." Then he turned to Ms. Tynsdale and gestured to the door. "Ladies first."

"Wha—! Merlin Ludovic!" Ms. Tynsdale's stance, feet apart and hands on her hips, told Brinnie she had no intention of moving.

"Good*bye*, Brynna." Uncle Merlin herded Ms. Tynsdale out the door, seeming to move her by the sheer force of his will.

As the door closed behind them, Brinnie stood staring at it for several moments. Then she shook her head and made her way down the stairs.

"Yes, your uncle's coworkers are a bit eccentric." Mrs. Winslow poured Brinnie more tea that night after Brinnie had related the day's happenings. Mr. Winslow, Miss Burtle, and Marcie had all gone to bed, and Mrs. Winslow and Brinnie sat at the kitchen table sipping chamomile before doing likewise. "Nice people, though."

Brinnie accepted the cup. "Why does everyone think my mom is dead?"

"Oh, she's been gone a long time, you know. People assume things."

"But you asked me about her, too." Brinnie leaned forward. "Did she run away?"

Mrs. Winslow fiddled with her spoon. "No, no, she was eighteen. An adult. Perfectly normal a girl her age would leave the nest."

"How come we never visited? I didn't even know Mom had a sibling until this summer."

"That's the way of families nowadays, I hear."

Why is everyone so evasive? But she didn't ask any further questions. What was the use? She finished her tea and then said goodnight.

Chapter Six

IT WAS THE SAME DREAM. AGAIN, she sat on the floor playing with the horse. Again, Uncle Merlin came to the door and the conversation played out exactly as it had the first time. But this time, the dream kept going.

"No, I came 'all this way' for the safety of your daughter," Uncle Merlin said.

Mommy crossed her arms. "Anna is perfectly safe."

"I don't mean Anna. I mean Brynna Gwynneth. Why on earth did you give her such a name?"

Mommy hesitated.

"It's because she's one of us, isn't she?"

"No, that doesn't mean anything—"

"This is Brynna, isn't it?" Merlin strode over to Brinnie.

"No! No, Merlin, please—"

"Eira. You can't do this. Let me look."

Mommy wavered a moment, then stepped aside. Merlin knelt next to Brinnie. "Hello, there. Are you Brynna?"

"Yes. I Bwynna."

"I'm your Uncle Merlin. Can I look at your eyes?"

He put his hand under her chin and tilted her head up. "Look to this side. Good. Now look over here. Good job. That's all."

Brinnie could see his sad but resigned face in the foreground and her mother's teary eyes in the background as the dream faded away.

Brinnie bolted up in bed, heart thumping. All the strangeness of the day must have gotten to her. Here she was having that weird dream again. *But how much of that really happened?*

She tried to return to sleep, but after fifteen futile minutes, she rose and gazed out the window. Gentle moonlight fell on the yard. She picked up a book from the nightstand and climbed under the covers, opening it to where she had left off. She read for a while until her brain had settled down. As she returned the book to the nightstand, she realized she had never turned the lantern on. How had she read for half an hour in the dead of night without a light? *The moon must have been bright enough.* She rolled over and soon fell asleep.

Sunlight filtering through the window woke her. With a sigh, she rolled out of bed, pulled on the horrible blue dress, and brushed her hair. She had never dreaded church this much before. She tromped to the door and reached out to open it when someone knocked.

She opened it to see Marcie standing there, lavender fabric draped over the young woman's arm.

"I found one of my old dresses and took it in a bit. I think it should fit you now."

Brinnie's scowl melted away as Marcie held out a silky dress. "How sweet of you! You didn't have to do that."

"Oh, it hasn't fit me in years, and it isn't doing any good collecting dust. Try it on! I want to see how good my seamstress-ing was."

Brinnie invited Marcie in and tossed off the horrible blue dress with gusto, pulling on the purple one instead. She turned in front of the mirror, pleased to see that the cut looked like it was actually made in the twenty-first century, unlike the blue dress.

Marcie gave herself a high five. "Seamstress Marcie for the win. Fits like a glove."

The two were still giggling when they joined everyone else at the breakfast table. Uncle Merlin still hadn't returned. Brinnie's giggles died as she noticed the Winslows and Miss Burtle casting glances at each other. "Is everything okay?"

"Why shouldn't it be?" Miss Burtle snapped.

Stung, Brinnie began peeling a hard-boiled egg in silence. Marcie shrugged and offered a sympathetic grimace.

After an uncomfortable breakfast, everyone went out to the garage and piled in Black Beauty. The vehicle bumped and puttered noisily, but it felt silent to Brinnie without any conversation. Mr. Winslow scanned the road as he drove, Mrs. Winslow's eyes kept darting over her shoulder, and Miss Burtle watched the trees like a hawk. The anxiety level was such that even Marcie looked puzzled, but she kept her mouth shut, as usual.

They reached the church where the typical greetings and small talk ensued. Many asked after Uncle Merlin—was he well? Yes, they replied, he was simply away on business. Meaningful looks often passed between townspeople at this reply. Brinnie wondered what they were thinking.

Brinnie followed her group as they meandered into the building. Last week, everyone from Wraithwood had split up to socialize, but today they stayed in a tight knot. They all sat in the same pew as the week before while the churchgoers trickled in to take their seats, filling the sanctuary. The Winslows and Miss Burtle separated Brinnie from Marcie, cutting off any potential diversion from another fire-and-brimstone sermon.

Brinnie groused to herself until she heard Mr. Winslow whisper to Mrs. Winslow, "One in the back, by the door, I reckon."

Mrs. Winslow nodded slightly. She turned around to greet a woman in the pew behind them. Brinnie glanced over her shoulder. There wasn't anything or anyone by the door except a man in a simple black suit. Nothing about his appearance set him apart from any other man in the church, but something intangible made Brinnie shudder. Their pew sat halfway from the door to the pulpit, but even from there Brinnie could see a hard glint in the man's eyes and the thin, set line of his mouth.

Mrs. Winslow turned back around to Mr. Winslow. "Should we leave?"

"He'd be sure to notice us and follow us all the way back."

"What should we do, then?"

"Sit tight, I guess. Pray extra hard."

The doors closed and the service began. Brinnie stood with the congregation for the hymns. "Praise the one who breaks the darkness with his liberating light," she sang as she stole a glance over her shoulder. The man still stood there, his body stiff, shoulders rigid. He wasn't singing.

After the hymns, prayer, and offering, Pastor Denison began the sermon. Brinnie imagined he might be making excellent points—or offering dire warnings of hellfire—but she was too distracted by those next to her to listen. She knew the Winslows and Miss Burtle were watching the man in the back. Marcie alone seemed oblivious. She sat stiffly, biting her lip, looking equally perplexed and amused by the old woman beside her who had fallen asleep on her arm.

When the service ended, Miss Burtle and the Winslows stood quickly. "Lose him in the crowd," Brinnie heard Mr. Winslow say. "Drive home before he knows it."

Marcie disengaged herself from the old woman who had been using her as a pillow. While the elderly woman yawned and tottered off with her husband, Marcie scooted past Miss Burtle and took Brinnie by the arm. "I thought she'd never wake up. You haven't met my folks yet. They all caught colds last Sunday, so they weren't here. I'd like to introduce you."

Marcie made to lead Brinnie away, but Mrs. Winslow stopped them. "We're heading out now."

"I was going to introduce Brinnie to my sisters," Marcie replied.

Mrs. Winslow glanced at the door. "I'm sorry, dear, maybe another time." She took a deep breath. "I think I left the oven going."

The way she blurted out the words as if they pained her made Brinnie think the fib would be obvious—that and the fact Mrs. Winslow hadn't used the oven that morning. But Marcie exclaimed, "Oh, no! We'd better hurry back."

They made their way through the crowd and out the door. Mr. Winslow and Miss Burtle had made a quicker escape and already waited in the car. As soon as Mrs. Winslow, Brinnie, and Marcie got in, Mr. Winslow started the engine and pulled out of the parking lot. Mrs. Winslow watched behind them. Curious, Brinnie turned around to look. A sleek black car followed them from about fifty yards back.

"You may want to drive a bit faster, Tom," Mrs. Winslow warned.

Mr. Winslow nodded but didn't change his speed. He waited until they approached a bend in the road, then stepped on the gas. Around the corner, the road forked. Mr. Winslow yanked on the steering wheel and sent the Model T crashing through the underbrush into the trees on the side of the road, bouncing Brinnie three inches off the seat before grinding to a halt. As Marcie yelped, Brinnie turned around to look at the road. The black car sped around the corner, but it slowed at the fork. It almost came to a stop but sped up again and zipped down the wider road that led into Lyle.

"Sorry about that," Mr. Winslow said. "Clumsy driving. Think we'll have to push."

Everyone got out to help push the buggy back onto the road. Brinnie's dress stuck to her back and legs in the muggy afternoon heat.

She braced her hands on the fender next to Marcie. "Sorry I've gotten this dress sweaty already."

Marcie waved her off. "That's what laundry is for." Her footing slipped a bit on the roadside grass and she had to grab the bumper to stay upright. She only laughed. "Ovens, snoring old ladies, out-of-control vehicles—it's a day of surprises."

Brinnie didn't offer any commentary on the fact that one was a lie and one, she was almost certain, was intentional. Finally, they heaved the car back onto the road, and they all piled in again to go turn off the imaginary oven.

Brinnie wasn't sure what happened with the man and the black car. She didn't see either one again on their way home.

She spent most of the day reading and keeping an ear out for Uncle Merlin's return, but by evening, she'd seen no sign of him. She was about to climb in bed for the night when she realized she'd forgotten to brush her teeth. She grabbed her toothbrush and headed down the stairs in her pajamas. She reached the bottom of the stairs when she heard the outside door open and close.

"Merlin!" she heard Mrs. Winslow exclaim.

Brinnie padded in her bare feet to the doorway that led from the storage room into the kitchen. Uncle Merlin stood in the light of a lamp on the table, his shoulders stooped. He bled from a cut over one eye, and smaller scratches and bruises covered his arms and the rest of his face. The dark circles under his eyes made him look ten years older.

"Hello," he rasped.

"Merlin, you're a mess!" Mrs. Winslow herded him toward the table. "You sit. Let me get you some bandages."

Neither seemed to notice Brinnie where she stood in the dark, so she didn't move. Mrs. Winslow poured Uncle Merlin a cup of tea from the kettle and began digging around in a drawer. He sipped it and sighed. "Thank you."

She pulled out antiseptic from the drawer. "What happened?"

"We lost." He winced as she dabbed at the cut over his eye. "We didn't stand a chance. We retreated while we could."

Retreated?

Mrs. Winslow shook her head, pressing her lips together.

"It's our numbers. How can we expect to win when they have so many more people?"

"Have they gotten a lot of new recruits?"

"Their numbers have been increasing with the population. That's to be expected. The problem is that our numbers aren't increasing at all—in fact, they're dropping."

There was a brief moment of silence. *The population? What sort of office is this?*

"I hate to be the bearer of bad news," Mrs. Winslow said, "but there was one at church today."

Uncle Merlin stiffened. "No."

"We lost him on the road. Merlin, how did he know?"

He reached up to feel the cut she was bandaging, but she swatted his hand away. Instead, he drummed his fingers on the table. "Their intelligence is twice as good as ours. I suppose I knew they would find Lyle eventually. What did Brynna think?"

"I don't know, but she's smart. She's going to start figuring things out."

Or you could just tell me.

"I don't know what to do with her." He looked at the ceiling while Mrs. Winslow dabbed another scrape under his eye. "Is she in more danger if she knows or doesn't know?"

56

She placed a hand on his shoulder. "You promised Eira. I've always tried to stay out of things between the two of you, but maybe you should talk to your sister."

"Because that went so well last time." He sighed and passed a hand over his face. "I hope I can find out quickly and send Brynna home. If only Eira wasn't so stubborn..."

"Merlin." Mrs. Winslow leveled a stern look at him. "*Can* you send her home?"

Brinnie's breath caught.

He looked down, his brow furrowed. "I don't know. For her sake, I hope so."

Brinnie tiptoed back up the stairs, teeth brushing forgotten. *Mom, what have you gotten me into?*

Chapter Seven

AGAIN, IT WAS THE SAME DREAM. AGAIN, it repeated itself—Brinnie playing on the floor, Uncle Merlin coming to the door, and then him looking at her eyes. Again, the dream continued from where it had previously ended, with her mother's tears and Uncle Merlin's troubled expression.

He stood up and turned to Mommy. "Eira—"

"No!" Mommy was crying. "It's fine. No one will ever know."

"All they have to do is look at her."

"It will go away."

"After more than a decade. Even after that, how is she going to hide what she is?"

She crossed her arms. "We've done it for years."

"We can control ourselves. She can't. If she does something strange, they'll find out. You can't keep her locked in a closet." He paused. "Do you know what it is yet?"

"No."

"The snow?"

"That was me. Everything starts frosting over as soon as I touch her. That's why I helped my husband find a job here in the desert. It warms me up some." She brightened, uncrossing her arms. "I think she's just a Helper, Merlin. She won't cause any trouble at all."

"It's possible. But it's more likely you react to her because she's one of us. Besides, if she's a Helper, they'll want her more than ever. She'll be so easy to control." His eyes narrowed. "They didn't quite believe the death scenario—they're still keeping an eye out for you. And if they find you...we'll lose her. She has to come to Wraithwood."

"No!" Mommy clenched her fists and took a deep breath. Her volume returned to a normal level. "I left for a reason, Merlin. I didn't want any part of all that anymore. I'm a normal person now, and my daughters are normal people. Thank you for your concern, but I'd appreciate it if you'd just leave us alone." Though harsh, her voice trembled.

"It's none of my business if you try to run away from who you are. But you can't put Brynna's life in danger because of it. I understand you don't want to go back. But at least give Brynna to me. She won't last a year away from Wraithwood."

Mommy stepped in front of Brinnie, partially obscuring Brinnie's view of Merlin. "No! Absolutely not. Are you crazy? She's my daughter."

"It's simple. I can erase all her birth records right now and be back in half an hour. You're new here. No one will know she's missing. Or we can do it legally."

"Even if I would ever agree to that, what would I tell Andrew? You tell me that."

"What do you mean?" Understanding came over his face. "Your own husband doesn't know? Any of it?"

"I told you, I didn't want any part of it. How could I tell him something crazy like that? How could I put him in that sort of danger?"

"Of all the..." He shook his head and turned around to look at a picture on the wall.

"Merlin, listen to me. Having Brynna was an accident. It was a mistake. I'm not going to let it ruin everything, so just—"

Merlin turned slowly. His expression remained neutral, but his eyes flashed. "Eira." His low voice was slow, even. "Never, ever call anyone a mistake. And never blame Brynna for your problems." His glance flicked over her shoulder and settled on Brinnie. "Does she know what we're saying?"

Little Brinnie stared back at him.

"No, she couldn't. She's only two. Play with your horsey, Brinnie."

Brinnie half-heartedly galloped the plastic horse across the carpet.

Merlin strode forward and gripped Mommy's shoulders. "Her life *is in more danger every second she spends away from Wraithwood. Sooner or later, they will find her. Then it will be too late."*

She shook him off. "They won't. It's been twenty years since I left Wraithwood, and they haven't found me."

"Are you sure of that?" His tone was ice. "I've kept track of you, and I'm only one man. They're many. Has it ever crossed your mind that perhaps they're waiting for the right moment? They know they can't make you do anything, and you're already doing what they want— staying out of their way and not fighting against them." Their eyes locked, the two of them glaring at one another. "Perhaps what they care about is your children. It's quite possible that they know where you are, and they're just waiting for the right moment to take her."

Mommy went pale, paler than usual. Then her face turned red. "How dare you! How dare you come into my house and terrorize me! You can go back to where you came from, you—" She broke off into sobs.

Merlin's expression softened. He reached out to her, but she pulled away. He sighed. "I didn't intend to make you feel this way, Eira. I only wanted you to see reason. At least tell your husband about this, please? How is he going to protect Brynna if he doesn't know she needs protection?"

"I can't do that. How dense are you? At least Andrew and Anna should be able to be safe. If they knew about all this—"

"I see. Well, then." He paced slowly. "At least promise me this— if anything happens that exposes Brynna or threatens her safety, you'll send her to me immediately."

She crossed her arms again. "Of course. I'm not stupid."

"And if you don't find out what she is by then, you must send her to me when she's fourteen." Before she could protest, Merlin held up a hand. "No, listen. She can spend the summer at Wraithwood. I'll evaluate her, run some tests. She'll never know what I'm doing. When I find out, I'll let you know."

"For what purpose?"

"You know how it is. Sometimes the most powerful ones don't show it until then. It would be best if she's at Wraithwood when it happens— if anything too...explosive happens."

"And then what? What do we do after that?" Hopelessness caught in Mommy's voice.

He hesitated. *"We'll have to wait and see."*

"In other words, you'll keep her at Wraithwood." Somehow, she managed to glare down her nose at him, even though her head only reached his chest. *"Fine. As long as my family doesn't suffer for it."*

"Is Brynna not your family, Eira?" Merlin asked softly. *"Am I not?"*

Her fists uncurled. Her mouth opened, closed, as her gaze dropped to the carpet. Her angry pose, arms crossed, now looked more like she was hugging herself, bracing against a gale. *"Just go,"* she whispered.

Merlin nodded once. *"You've promised, Eira. I will see her in twelve years, if not sooner."* Then he vanished, leaving only empty space.

Brinnie's eyes flew open. Moonlight danced on the guazy curtains as they floated on the breeze from the open window. Still night. *Did that really happen?*

She rose and went to the window, gripping the windowsill. *Who were they hiding from?* Her spine prickled. And who did they think wanted to kidnap her? Her mind raced, trying to break through her body's sleepiness. *This summer couldn't have been planned out that long ago.* And what sort of tests? It seemed ridiculous, except that what she had heard in the kitchen earlier was every bit as bizarre. She sighed and leaned her head against the window frame. She wished she could call her parents and listen to their familiar voices. Especially Dad's.

She thought of how she would tell him about her dream if he were there, and how he would interpret it until she was laughing, no longer concerned. "You see," he would say, assuming the worldly air of a psychologist, "this dream was really a result of your last meal. Merlin represents an onion, and your mother is cabbage. If you cook them together with a pinch of butter, they're quite tasty."

"Dad," she would giggle, "you can't have a pinch of butter."

"Why not?"

"Because...you just can't."

"You see, I've found the problem! You have a narrow view of butter. That's why you're having strange dreams. I call it the Butter Complex."

She smiled to herself over the imaginary conversation. The dream clearly wasn't the result of a butter complex, but her sleep-fogged mind wasn't going to figure it out tonight. She went back to bed. As she waited for sleep to come, she heard Uncle Merlin's voice in her head. *"Summer at Wraithwood...fourteen...she'll never know."*

The next morning found Brinnie sitting on a bench under one of the trees in the yard. A warm breeze ruffled the pages of the book she was trying to read, but her mind kept returning to her dreams and the kitchen conversation.

Footsteps crunched on gravel. She looked up from her book to see Uncle Merlin coming toward her. He hadn't been at breakfast, perhaps because he was exhausted from being gone for so long. As he came closer and his scratches became more apparent, she was tempted to ask him if the paper shredder at the office had attacked him. "Good morning," she said instead.

"Good morning." He looked at the sky. "Lovely day, isn't it?"

Ten points to Uncle Merlin for most original conversation starter. "Yes."

An awkward silence fell. "Mind if I join you?" he asked finally.

"Sure."

He sat at the other end of the long, curved bench. He seemed to be evaluating her, and she tried not to squirm. "You met some of my, um, coworkers."

"Yes." The silence ran on. Finally, she couldn't stand it anymore. "What do you do? This is the weirdest place, and there are people saying all sorts of weird things, and then you disappear for days. And someone was after us in an actual car chase! I don't get it."

She blushed and started to apologize, Mom's voice ringing in her mind, scolding her for rudeness, but he shook his head. "No, you're quite right to wonder."

It seemed he wouldn't say anything at all as he looked off into the distance. Then he turned back to her, a strange sadness in his eyes that she didn't understand, as if he saw her future and it was a tragic one.

Wow, a little dark there, Brinnie.

"I can't tell you exactly what I do or what this all means. My job is a secret one."

That's not much of an answer. "Is it dangerous, what you do?"

"Yes, somewhat."

What did *that* mean? "Are we—I mean the Winslows and Miss Burtle and Marcie and I—in danger? Like, will anyone want to bomb the house or something?"

She expected him to laugh. Hoped he would. "You are not in danger, per se," he said, his tone anything but mirthful. "No one who would want to harm me or any of you knows where Wraithwood is. As long as you are here, no harm will come to you. If there is ever even the slightest threat to your or anyone else's safety, trust me when I say I will take all precautions. I may ask you to do strange things at times, but I ask that you simply do as I say, even if it doesn't make sense."

Blindly follow the secretive man I hardly know. She remembered her appropriate-for-adults manners this time. "Okay."

His shoulders relaxed at her simple answer. "I didn't want to worry you, but I thought it would be best if you had some explanations."

You call these explanations? "Of course."

"I'm sorry I didn't let you know sooner."

"That's all right." *Kind of.* "Thank you for telling me."

After a few more moments of light conversation, he excused himself, leaving Brinnie to her book and her thoughts. He had explained nothing—but she didn't think he had lied either. As long as everyone was safe, she wouldn't push the subject.

At least not yet. And not to his face.

⚜ ❦ ❦ ⚜

That evening, Brinnie helped Mrs. Winslow make mashed potatoes to go with ham and fresh peas and carrots from the garden. As they all sat down to eat, a knock sounded on the back door.

"I've got it." Marcie set down a plate of rolls and brushed off her hands as she headed for the door.

"Were you expecting anyone?" Mrs. Winslow asked Uncle Merlin.

He shook his head and began to rise.

The door opened, and Brinnie turned to look when she heard Marcie gasp. "Jerry!"

A mess of a man stood outside the door. His rumpled clothes hung loosely on a too-lean form, and his eyes were bloodshot, his brown hair tousled. He rubbed a hand over a few days' worth of stubble on his cheeks. "Marcie," he slurred. "Been missing you."

She stepped back. "What are you doing here?"

"Lookin' for my wife, that's what." He leaned against the door frame. "Why you gone and run off on me? I'm not good enough for ya? That it?"

Marcie seemed to shrink, shoulders turning inward. "I just needed some time to myself, that's all."

"Been long enough. You can come back now."

Uncle Merlin started to step forward, but Mrs. Winslow laid a hand on his arm. "Hold on," she whispered. "Give her a moment to tell him herself before you chase him off."

"To where?" Marcie asked, straightening her shoulders. "That dirty little trailer with the beer cans everywhere?"

"Look who's all fine and mighty!" He waved his arm, swaying. "Guess you think you're something else now, huh? Livin' with the warlock? He's turned you against me, hasn't he?"

"Of course not." Her voice trembled. "You're drunk. Maybe you should come back when you're sober."

Jerry snatched for her arm, but she jerked away. He tottered like a leaf in a windstorm. "Not drunk, and not goin' away without you, you little—"

"Excuse me." Uncle Merlin strode up behind Marcie. Or did he? Brinnie hadn't even seen him move from the table. One moment Marcie was alone, and the next, Uncle Merlin loomed behind her, his gaze hard. "Are you harassing my employee?"

Jerry glared. "If it ain't Mr. Fancypants himself. You know what we think of you in town, you—"

"Eh-hem," Uncle Merlin cleared his throat over whatever the man said. "I would thank you not to curse in front of the ladies. Now, what seems to be the trouble?"

"The wife here up and left me for no good reason, and I came to bring her back."

Uncle Merlin's eyebrows rose at the claim of "no good reason." He deferred to Marcie. "Do you want to go with this man?"

"No, sir."

Uncle Merlin nodded. "I'm sorry, sir, but I'm afraid you'll have to leave."

Jerry uttered such a string of profanities that Uncle Merlin couldn't drown them out with a polite "excuse me" or a cough. He took a step forward, forcing Jerry to retreat, and stepped out with him, shutting the door firmly but quietly behind them.

Marcie hovered near the door, wringing her hands.

Mrs. Winslow went to her and drew her back to the table. "Come sit down, dear."

"I just..." Marcie hesitated. "Jerry can get violent when he's like this. I don't want Mr. Ludovic to get hurt."

Miss Burtle coughed and quickly took a sip of water.

Mrs. Winslow seemed to hide a smile. "I'm sure he'll be fine, dear."

Uncle Merlin returned a few minutes later. He took a seat and plopped potatoes onto his plate as if nothing out of the usual had occurred. "I've seen him down the path."

Marcie's cheeks were bright red. "Thank you," she whispered, looking down at her plate.

Mrs. Winslow patted her hand, and no more was said on the subject.

Brinnie eyed Uncle Merlin. *Who is he?*

The next morning, Brinnie was curled up in a comfortable chair in the library engrossed in a book about the Persian Wars when she heard a door open.

She peered over the railing, and her eyebrows rose. Miss Burtle entered the library through one of the heavy doors that led from the library to the "forbidden" rest of the house—holding an old flip phone to her ear.

Mom had claimed there would be no cell service out here.

"I don't know why he didn't tell you." Miss Burtle ran a finger along the books on a shelf, squinting at the titles. "I don't know. You know how he is...He's not available right now, he's in Madrid...Something to do with Alverez...I'm sure I don't know, but it's Ludovic's orders."

Evidently Miss Burtle didn't notice Brinnie, so she tried to be invisible behind her book while she listened.

"He said he's expecting some trouble there in Chicago, but not bad. He has Goddensfeld and Tynsdale on it, I believe. Breckinridge and Austin are already there. I'm looking for those maps..."

Brinnie watched Miss Burtle rifle through a shelf full of maps and atlases before pulling out the right one. "Ah, here they are. Yes, at the museum, that's about five blocks from you...North...Yes, exactly...No, I don't think he's coming. But if you have trouble, be sure to call, and he'll come... He went to Barcelona late last night, Madrid this morning, and that was only twenty-four hours after the last disaster. I think that's a good enough reason for him not to come even if he does get back in time...Castelon! Why on earth...Certainly we don't want them involved. I'm sorry, but Ludovic's made it very clear that we can handle this on our own. Is that all the information you need? All right. You, too. Goodbye." With that, she left the library.

How did Uncle Merlin get to Madrid just last night? Brinnie shook her head. No, that must have been someone else they were talking about. Madrid, Barcelona, Chicago...She'd never heard of Castelon. Or was it code? Was he actually a spy or something? Was Miss Burtle his assistant?

Sooner or later, I'm going to find out.

The rest of the day passed uneventfully. Miss Burtle seemed to be a bit harried and more than usually snappy, but otherwise life continued as usual.

Uncle Merlin returned that night. Brinnie heard his voice in the hall, talking to Miss Burtle at a very late hour, apparently filling her in before he went upstairs.

Brinne didn't see him the next day until late morning in the rose garden. She held the stem of a pink rose, shears in her other hand as she snipped at a length perfect for a vase to place in the middle of the kitchen table. She carefully added the rose to her basket, avoiding the thorns.

She heard footsteps on gravel and looked up to see Uncle Merlin sauntering along the path. He had dark circles under his eyes, but he greeted her with a bright smile.

"Good morning." He stopped and examined one of the bushes. "Eira and I had a competition when we were young. We would see who could grow the best rose bush—the highest, the greenest, and the healthiest—and whoever lost did the other's chores for a week."

Did you also have spy competitions? She counted the roses in her basket. Six should be enough. "My dad and I did something like that, but with sunflowers. Both of ours only grew a few inches and then died, though."

He chuckled. "Don't have much of a green thumb?"

"Not at all."

"I'm the same way. Eira always won." He cupped a yellow blossom and inhaled. "Granted, she won most of the games we played back then."

A rare glimpse into her mother's childhood. "What kinds of games?"

"Oh, dozens of them. We played Sardines, where we competed to see who could fit in the smallest space, and Heat, where we each had a thermometer and tried to make a room the hottest—set my hair on fire once with that one—and Cold, which was the opposite, and of course the normal hide-and-seek and racing and competitions to see who could hold their breath the longest or swim the fastest or throw the farthest. Once I jumped off the railing in the library and sprained my ankle trying to fly when we were pretending to be birds."

Brinnie couldn't help feeling wistful. "You must've had so much fun." Anna was too old to ever play with.

That strange sadness Brinnie had seen before flitted across his countenance. "Yes, we did." He was quiet for a moment. "I've been working on a bit of a project—a research project. Would you mind helping me?"

"What is it?"

"If I told you, it would ruin the results. But would you mind being a test subject?"

Test subject? That's not ominous at all. "As long as there aren't any electrical shocks or blowing people up."

"Not that I know of."

She shrugged. She had nothing better to do. "Okay."

She followed him back to the house, stopping in the kitchen to stick the roses in a vase.

Uncle Merlin waited at the foot of the stairs. "Some of the experiments might seem a bit strange, but it's nothing dangerous," he said.

"Will you tell me what it's all about at the end?"

"Hmm. Yes, somewhat."

Descriptive as always.

She followed Uncle Merlin up the stairs to the third floor. This time, he passed through the lounge to the double doors. He opened them to reveal a long hallway, off of which at least a dozen doors opened. Brinnie wasn't sure what she had been expecting of the secret third floor, but it wasn't something so normal. She was relieved and disappointed at the same time.

He opened the first door to the left. "Welcome to Room Number One."

Inside, a large grid was painted on the floor. Lights were affixed to the ceiling, and though Brinnie knew they must be operated by battery, they also had cords running to something that looked like a sound booth in the corner. Each light hung directly above a square. Brinnie did a quick count—six squares by seven squares, forty-two in all, each about a foot and a half in width.

"You'll stand somewhere near the middle," Uncle Merlin instructed. "Then, I'll start flashing the lights one at a time onto the squares. You must jump to each lighted square without stepping in another square or out of the grid."

"That's it?" What exactly was he testing? Then her eyes widened. *Testing. Like in the dream.*

"Yes. Fairly simple."

"Okay." She stood in the middle of the grid. "Ready."

Uncle Merlin disappeared behind the sound booth. A light flashed on the square next to her, and she stepped into it. As soon as she did, another lighted two squares away. She hopped. Then another square lit on the other side of the grid. There was no way she could jump that far, but she gave it a shot. She landed one and a half squares short, and the lights all flashed and gave off a buzzing noise. Then they shut off and a new square lighted three away. She jumped to that one successfully, but then another lit across the grid. She missed, and the lights flashed and buzzed.

The game grew increasingly frustrating. The lights flashed faster and faster, and many of the jumps were impossible. *What on earth is he testing?* Brinnie panted, sweat beading on her forehead. She hoped Uncle Merlin would come out and declare the test over, but he didn't. The lights kept flashing until finally she stopped in the middle of the grid after yet another buzz with her hands on her hips, chest heaving. "This is impossible!"

"No, I've seen it done," Uncle Merlin said. "Keep at it."

She did, for another fifteen minutes. Then Uncle Merlin seemed to take pity on her and stepped out of the booth. "All right, the test is over."

Brinnie gasped for air. "Did you get good results?"

"Hmm. Some interesting ones."

"How does anyone do it? They must have really long legs."

He smiled but didn't answer the question. "Would you like to try something else?"

Not really. "If you would like."

Uncle Merlin brought out a stack of paper. He counted out fifteen sheets. "The goal is to keep all fifteen sheets of paper in the air for fifteen seconds without them touching anything or being attached to anything."

Are these some sort of problem-solving IQ games? Brinnie's mind whirred. If it was only one paper, she would blow under it and keep it in the air, but she couldn't do fifteen at once, and they were too heavy to do them in a stack. She next considered a giant fan, maybe six, to keep the papers in the center of the room. "Do you have any fans?"

"No. An excellent idea, though."

Brinnie bit her lip and squinted at the paper. "What about magnets?"

He seemed to think for a minute, then laughed. "It seems you've got me. Large magnets on all sides, yes? With small magnets attached to the paper, and like charges facing one another?"

"Exactly."

"Yes, I do believe you could do it with the proper equipment. But I don't have it. You'll have to try something else."

She wiped sweat from her brow. There were no nuances in his instructions that she could exploit. If he had simply said "in the air" she would have pointed out that they were already technically in the air, but they couldn't be touching anything or attached to anything. "What do you mean by touching or attached to something?"

"I mean touching a wall or attached to the ceiling by a string or something of the sort."

"Then if I built a small plane with a motor and put the paper in it..."

"Yes, I suppose. But I'd rather you tried another way. I'd rather you just did it."

"Did what?"

"Try to keep the papers in the air."

"How?"

"You would have to try."

Peeved, she picked up the paper and began throwing it one sheet at a time into the air, blowing and waving at it madly. She was sure she looked ridiculous, and she began to become lightheaded from all the blowing, but she couldn't keep more than two papers up for more than a second. "It's impossible!" she gasped.

"Hmm. I've seen it done."

Brinnie glared at the papers on the floor. *This is stupid.* She picked them up again and tried folding them into parachute-like shapes, but it still didn't work. "Someone might be able to do it, but not me."

"All right. Thank you. That's all the results I need."

"You got data from that?"

"Yes, very good data."

What is this, a test of how frustrated he can make me with an impossible task? She began picking up the papers, and Uncle Merlin helped.

He seemed to realize she was still put out. "I'm sorry it was so maddening. Eira and I enjoyed it as children."

"You did this when you were kids?"

"Yes. It's an ongoing experiment."

Brinnie opened her mouth to ask more questions, but Miss Burtle appeared at the door, jaw tight and one hand clenching a handful of her skirt.

"Yes?" Uncle Merlin asked.

"I need to speak with you."

"Of course. Thank you very much for your help, Brinnie. You can go downstairs now."

Translation—leave so we can talk about secret stuff. "Okay."

As Brinnie reached the top of the stairs, she heard Miss Burtle say, "It's bad. They're attacking Riverdell."

"Riverdell? How on earth—"

"I hoped you would know."

"No. Our intelligence suggested they would be after Chicago next. They're attacking Riverdell itself?"

71

"Yes!"

"But that's impossible."

Brinnie pressed herself against the wall, listening.

"That's what they told me on the phone," Miss Burtle said. "They're at a loss as to how it happened, but the fighting is intense."

"I have to gather reinforcements. Have someone keep Brinnie distracted and watch her. Don't let her go outside. If they got past Riverdell..."

"I'll take care of it."

"Thank you." Footsteps headed her way.

Brinnie jolted and scurried down the stairs. She heard Uncle Merlin on the stairs above her, feet thumping a quick staccato. She ran all the way down and then tried to casually walk toward the kitchen while keeping her breathing even.

She turned around, expecting to see Uncle Merlin there—but he wasn't. Confused, she stepped into the kitchen just in time to see him disappear through the door that led to the dining room. She froze and stared.

Chapter Eight

"Hello!"

Brinnie whirled around. Marcie came down the stairs smiling, broom and dustpan in hand. "I gave your room a sweep-up, since I was doing the hall anyway."

"Oh, thank you." Brinnie stepped out of her way, eyes drifting back to where Uncle Merlin had disappeared into the dining room.

"No problem." She manuevered around Brinnie and headed for the back door. "What have you been up to this afternoon?"

"Being a test subject for Uncle Merlin's experiments." *I could swear he was right behind me. I heard him behind me.*

"That sounds a little scary." Marcie descended the steps outside, dumping the slight bit of dust from the dustpan into the yard.

"Not really." Brinnie slumped into a chair at the table. *"Have someone keep Brinnie distracted and watch her."* What was she, of all people, going to get into?

Miss Burtle swept into the kitchen. "Where are the Winslows?" she demanded.

"I think Mr. Winslow is in the orchard," Marcie offered, "and Mrs. Winslow said she was going out to the rose garden."

Miss Burtle brushed past her and out the door without a reply.

Marcie watched her go, her mouth quirked to one side. "She seems upset about something—more than usual, anyway." She shrugged and gave Brinnie a sweet smile. "You thirsty?"

The two were pouring themselves some of Mrs. Winslow's lemonade when Mrs. Winslow herself entered, face pale.

"Is something wrong?" Marcie asked.

"No, nothing for you to be concerned about." She glanced at Brinnie and bit her lip. "Would you like to help me make an apple pie, dear?"

"That sounds great." *Though it would be even better if you told me what Riverdell is and who's attacking it.*

Brinnie and Marcie helped Mrs. Winslow get out the ingredients for the pie and were beginning to measure them out when the door opened and Mr. Winslow stepped in. He came in quietly, as he always did, but Brinnie's eyes widened at the object in his hands—a rifle. He set it next to the door and exchanged a look with Mrs. Winslow, who pressed her lips together and looked back down at the table.

"What's cooking?" he asked.

"Apple pie," Marcie said.

"Mmm." He nodded and pulled up a chair nearby.

"Where's Edna?" Mrs. Winslow asked.

"Library."

"By herself?"

He seemed hesitant to answer. "No," he said finally.

"Who's there?"

Again, he appeared reluctant. "Tynsdale."

Brinnie cocked her head. Ms. Tynsdale?

Mrs. Winslow nodded. "Good." She continued to bang around the kitchen, stirring so the spoon clanged against the side of the bowl and clacking measuring cups on the table. Brinnie flinched at the ferocity of her apple chopping. *What on earth?* Mrs. Winslow was usually quiet and efficient in the kitchen.

By the time the pie was in the oven, it was time to make dinner. Mrs. Winslow set pasta to boiling and Marcie and Brinnie helped her make a meat and vegetable sauce. Mr. Winslow sat in the corner, cleaning his gun. "Are you planning on going hunting?" Marcie asked him.

"No." His words came slowly. "Good to have a gun in working order. Been a while since I cleaned it."

"What do you shoot?" Marcie asked.

"Heard about some foxes. Want to keep the hens safe."

Brinnie saw Mrs. Winslow try to hide a smile and wondered why.

"I don't shoot anything else. Just warning shots."

"Oh." Marcie seemed to realize Mr. Winslow wasn't going to swap hunting stories and turned her attention to the cheese she was grating.

The dining room door opened with a squeak. The Winslows both startled and Mr. Winslow gripped his gun, but they relaxed when Ms. Tynsdale stepped through.

Ms. Tynsdale looked around at everyone. "Good. All in one place. Hello, Winslows. Hello, Brynna. You must be Marcie. Pleased to meet you. Lydia Tynsdale."

"The same to you." Marcie watched Ms. Tynsdale like a wide-eyed hare afraid of being eaten.

"Good to see you, Lydia," said Mrs. Winslow. "Where's Edna?"

"Coming. Merlin gave her a few more people to call, and Ribsnor is coming through by door. She thought she should help with him."

In the split second of silence that followed, a man's voice shouted, "Ludovic, how dare you take me this way! I refuse to travel in such a manner!" Then a door slammed.

Mrs. Winslow banged the spoon around in the pot of pasta, but Brinnie had already heard.

"There he goes," Ms. Tynsdale commented.

Mrs. Winslow continued clanging. "*So.* Have you eaten yet, Lydia?"

"No, not since breakfast. Been a little busy."

"Good, because dinner is ready." Mrs. Winslow set out a serving spoon. "Pasta with meat sauce and zucchini."

Ms. Tynsdale inhaled. "It sounds—and smells—delicious."

Miss Burtle entered with a scowl a few seconds later, a few gray hairs out of place. She, too, came through the dining room door.

A whole lot of people keep going in and out of the "super dangerous" front of the house.

They ate dinner and then pie for dessert, but the tense expressions didn't fade from the faces of the Winslows and Miss Burtle. Brinnie couldn't tell how Ms. Tynsdale felt, but Marcie's eyes darted nervously from one to the other.

After dinner, Marcie and Brinnie helped Mrs. Winslow clean up while Miss Burtle and Ms. Tynsdale returned to the library—again through the dining room door—to make more calls, Ms. Tynsdale said.

Once they finished tidying up, Mrs. Winslow suggested, "Why don't you two get some rest? It's getting late."

Marcie and Brinnie went to the washroom together to get ready for bed. When Brinnie looked back, Mr. Winslow stood silhouetted against the light in the doorway, holding his rifle. "Marcie, something weird is going on."

Marcie bit her lip. "I'm sure it's all right."

"Don't you wonder what's happening?"

She stepped into the bathroom. "I try not to wonder. Around here, it's best to be blind."

She shut the door, leaving Brinnie alone with her frustration.

In her room, Brinnie sat on the ledge near the window and looked out at the shadowy leaves blowing softly in the nighttime breeze, the moonlight dappling the lawn. Bruno loped toward the house, where Mrs. Winslow would let him into the kitchen for the night. Brinnie inhaled, trying to breathe in that peacefulness. Her mind went back to the man's voice she had heard. It seemed strange how quickly people appeared and disappeared at the house, like Ms. Tynsdale and Mr. Goddensfeld. She wondered why they came to the front when the tall, heavy gate was locked, as it always was. She knew, because she often passed it when she wandered the grounds. Who let them in? Who knew they were coming? Maybe they had their own keys.

Brinnie climbed into bed and lay staring at the ceiling, trying to make sense of things. She persuaded herself to stop trying to figure out Uncle Merlin's top-secret activities, only to find herself trying to decipher them again. Finally, she sat up and decided to go downstairs and get a glass of water. Maybe that would help her fall asleep.

She padded downstairs in her socks. Everyone should have gone to bed already, but a light still shone in the kitchen. Blinking, she paused in the storage room to allow her eyes to adjust to the brightness. Voices drifted from beyond the doorway.

"So, let me get this straight." That was Ms. Tynsdale's voice. "Brynna and Marcie still have no idea?"

"None," Miss Burtle confirmed.

"How on earth does that work? Can't they see what's right in front of their noses?"

Brinnie leaned against the wall beside the doorway, out of sight.

"There's a bit more to it," Mrs. Winslow's voice broke in. "The people of Lyle think Merlin has some sort of occult powers. Or at best, the less superstitious think he's insane and perhaps a murderer. That's what Marcie has grown up hearing. The poor girl. I can see she feels guilty about accepting kindness from us. She tries to keep her eyes shut to it all. If she didn't, she thinks she would have to admit to herself she's living in a house of evil."

"I can see that. But what about Brynna? She doesn't seem too dense."

"It's been difficult," Miss Burtle said tersely, "and some of us haven't been doing too well."

"Right. And remind me why we aren't telling her? Merlin told me not to, but he didn't say why."

"He made a promise to Eira, oh, about twelve years ago. He tracked her down and persuaded her to send Brinnie to him when she was fourteen—Brinnie was very young at the time—since Eira wouldn't come back and wouldn't give Brinnie up. But Eira made him promise he wouldn't tell Brinnie anything, just run the tests, find out what she was, and send her home."

Brinnie pressed a fist to her clenching stomach. *Dream confirmed.*

"And how does he think that's going to work?" Ms. Tynsdale snorted. "The girl may be blind to what's going on around her, but she can hardly fail to notice that. Besides, we can't afford to send her home. The enemy will snap her up as soon as she goes back anyway. It's the foolhardiest plan I've ever heard."

"She has survived almost fifteen years without attracting attention." Mrs. Winslow sounded less than certain.

"Come on, she's a Ludovic. Once she finds herself, she'll be causing all sorts of trouble. We need to make sure she stays here."

"It's not our decision." Miss Burtle's words were clipped. "You'll have to talk to Merlin about it if you want to disagree."

"I will. He'll see for himself soon enough that what he's proposing is impossible."

Mr. Winslow cleared his throat. "It's late. I'll take first watch."

Brinnie ran back upstairs before anyone could come out and see her. *So everyone is lying to me and Ms. Tynsdale wants to kidnap me.* Her mind raced. She couldn't contact her parents—their access to cell service was spotty at best, and her only means of communication was by letter, which would take far too long. No one here could be trusted. She was on her own.

She had no convincing evidence that anything sinister was going on, but if all of this was true about enemies, and if certain people wanted to trap her at Wraithwood, she needed to know. Not to mention that she was apparently a test subject.

The longer Brinnie thought, the more she realized she needed more information before she could make her next move. And whenever her uncle and the others were up to something, they seemed to disappear through doors she wasn't allowed to access.

She needed to investigate the front of the house.

Chapter Nine

BRINNIE FORCED HERSELF TO WAIT ANOTHER thirty minutes, until she was sure everyone had gone to bed, if not to sleep. Those thirty minutes felt like an eternity. She tried to read to occupy herself while she waited, but after reading the same sentence ten times, she gave up.

Her heart thumped and her hands trembled. *Is this what it's like to be a normal teenager, sneaking out and breaking rules?* If so, she was glad she had never intentionally disobeyed her mother. But not tonight. Tonight, too much was at stake.

She opened the door and crept out into the dark, silent hall. Again, she was struck by the fact that she could see perfectly well, even without lights or windows. *Is my night vision improving?* She had never gone sneaking around at night before, so she didn't know.

Downstairs, a feeble light emanated from the kitchen, as if from a single candle. Mr. Winslow said he would take first watch. He was probably sitting in there with his rifle across his lap. She wasn't sure how she would get past him, but she would figure that out as she went along.

She peeked into the kitchen from the storage room. As expected, Mr. Winslow sat in the corner, his rifle across his knees, the chair tilted back and his head resting on his chest. Brinnie let out a breath. He looked asleep. Bruno was lying on a blanket in the other corner, but he merely peered at her out of one eye, yawned, then laid his head down again.

She tiptoed across the kitchen to the door. Halfway there, she heard a snort and whirled around to see Mr. Winslow shake his head and look up, blinking. She froze, wishing she could melt into her surroundings. She had a plan—if he caught her, she would tell him she came down for a drink. But that plan flew from her head the moment he looked at her. She remained motionless, staring back at him.

But his gaze passed over her. He grunted, put all four chair legs back on the ground, and stretched. Then he stood and turned toward the outside door.

It was all Brinnie needed. She darted past him, and two seconds later she was on the other side of the dining room door.

She stood there for several seconds, sure Mr. Winslow would push open the door at any moment and ask what she thought she was doing, but he didn't. Somehow, he had looked straight at her and hadn't seen her. Now she was home free.

She took in her dark surroundings. She stood in a large, long room with high ceilings and wood paneling. A huge brass chandelier hung overhead, but the most interesting feature in the room was the enormous wooden table surrounded by high-backed chairs of the same rich wood. It would seat thirty people, at least. The legs and sides of both the table and chairs were carved with amazing delicacy for such heavy pieces. *It's like the dining hall of a castle.*

She came closer to investigate, her stocking feet padding over the hardwood floor. She looked down. Her socks collected no dirt. Intrigued, she wiped a finger across the table's surface. It had a slight film of dust, but not the layer she had been expecting. It seemed as if it had gone without dusting for a week or two, not months or years.

Grand double doors stood at the other end of the dining room, and she walked to them. She set her hand on one of the handles, took a deep breath, and pushed it open. She winced and froze as it creaked. *Count to ten in case someone comes to investigate.* No one did. She stepped through and closed the door behind her.

What she saw took her breath away. The ceiling soared high, and an enormous crystal chandelier hung from the center, twinkling softly in the bits of moonlight filtering through the windows. To the right was the front door, and to the left a grand staircase swept upward, a red carpet leading up the sleek wood of the steps, which started at the bottom about twelve feet wide and tapered at the top to about five. The handrails swooped down the length and ended with intricate curliques, all carved of smooth, dark wood.

Brinnie spun in the middle of the room, gazing in awe. She stepped to the front door and imagined herself as a fine lady in a flowing dress, entering Wraithwood to the sound of refined chamber music and the polite laughter of elegant aristocrats dressed in ball gowns of every hue. She looked to the small closet to her right and pictured a butler taking her coat.

The floor beneath her imagined heels was once again clean. Only a slight film of dust covered the few portraits and paintings that hung on the walls. She drew closer to the portrait nearest to her, of a beautiful woman with bright blue eyes and golden hair. The woman offered a kind smile to the painter, and she held a book in her hand. Brinnie looked at the background. Yes, it was the porch off the library.

She would have liked to gaze at all the paintings, but she knew time was limited. Past the stairs was a different room with furniture draped in white sheets—*the parlor?*

To the right of the stairs, toward the library, were white doors. Were they the doors that led to the library? She pushed them open and stepped inside.

Her footsteps slowed as she entered a spacious room that was definitely not the library. At one end stood a raised platform, presumably for musicians. Around the edges sat a few chairs, but the rest of the fine white floor remained bare, perfect for dancing. White Grecian columns lined the oval room, and crown molding added to the effect. Looking up, Brinnie saw a beautiful painting of a mixed sky of both clouds and stars, midnight blue and azure, covering the entire ceiling.

She retreated from the ballroom and through the parlor to a door of average size and made of polished dark wood. This time, what she saw when she opened it was surprisingly ordinary—a large desk piled with papers, filing cabinets along the walls, a computer, and various other office accessories. Double doors opened off one side—they had to lead to the library. This office must be where Miss Burtle spent much of her time.

Curious, Brinnie looked at the computer. It was turned off, but under the desk, she saw foot pedals like a bicycle. She grinned. So that was how it worked. She imagined Miss Burtle pedaling away to generate electricity for the computer and stifled a giggle.

Now she had seen the front. It wasn't dangerous or run down. It was beautiful, and it looked like it had been cleaned and used recently.

She wasn't sure what that meant, though. Why had they lied to her about it? Why didn't they want her there? Her gaze trailed to the papers on the desk. Maybe the answers were there.

Somewhere, a door creaked open. Her heart skipped a beat. The door closed again, and she heard voices. Without stopping to think, she opened the door to the library, ran through, and shut it again. She was out the library door, across the portico, and hiding around the corner before she had her wits about her. Then she realized her mistake. There was no way she could get back in through the kitchen—Mr. Winslow was there. She was trapped outside until whoever she'd heard had left.

She leaned against the rough brick wall, berating herself. She should have paused to see where the voices were coming from and if they were headed her way. Now she was afraid to go back in. What if they were in the library? She would be caught. But out here, she could wait all night without knowing if they had left.

She counted to sixty ten times, then ten times again. Her socks soaked moisture from the damp grass, giving her shivers. She leaned against the wall, gazed at the stars overhead, and tried to count them until she couldn't wait any longer.

One of the steps of the porch creaked as she ascended, and she almost jumped. With a shaking hand, she opened the door and peeped in. Nothing. She stepped inside and closed the door softly behind her.

Her socked feet padded quietly across the room as she listened for any noises. She could hear voices again, but they were muted. She would go to the doors leading to the office and listen. Maybe then she could find out where they were, and if she could slip by.

When she was a few paces from the doors, they burst open. Brinnie leaped back as someone came in, holding up a lantern. Before Brinnie could hide, the person flicked on the solar lamp by the door, illuminating Ms. Tynsdale, standing directly in front of her. Brinnie froze.

But Ms. Tynsdale walked right past her, passing so close Brinnie had to jump out of the way. Ms. Tynsdale turned on more lights and strode across the room to the bookshelves. As soon as her back was turned, Brinnie darted into the office.

Brinnie thought she was safe until she saw the light under the door leading out of the office. But she could hear Ms. Tynsdale muttering to herself, coming back. She would just have to hope no one was on the other side. She slipped out the door and shut it behind her.

She sucked in a breath. Lights were lit everywhere. The front door stood open, and Uncle Merlin came through, supporting a limping man. Half a dozen other people sat on the steps or in chairs, while a handful more scurried about. Mrs. Winslow and Miss Burtle were among those on their feet, Mrs. Winslow in a robe and slippers, passing out mugs trailing steam. No one seemed to notice Brinnie as she stood gawking.

Something rammed into Brinnie from behind. "Oof!" She fell forward and landed on her hands and knees.

She looked over her shoulder. Ms. Tynsdale stood behind her, blinking and looking around wildly. Her gaze finally settled on Brinnie, but she continued to blink and squint. "Brynna? Is that you?"

"Uh, yes." Brinnie scrambled to her feet.

This seemed to break Ms. Tynsdale's bout of poor eyesight. Her sharp eyes focused. "How did you get here?"

"Um, I came down the stairs and through the kitchen and..."

"No, I mean what are you doing here?"

How many times had Mom told her to mind her own business, not get into trouble? "I'm really sorry, I didn't mean to pry. I'll go back to bed now." She began inching away.

She felt a hand on her shoulder and stiffened. She turned to see Uncle Merlin standing there, glaring at Ms. Tynsdale. "Did you bring her here?" Warning rumbled in his voice like distant thunder.

"What? No." Ms. Tynsdale crossed her arms. "I just found her standing here."

That piercing gaze redirected. "Brynna, is this true?"

She shrank back. "Y-yes, I'm sorry, I shouldn't have, I was really curious and so I thought I'd look, and..." She trailed off, her heart pounding.

"Brinnie." The hard lines of his face softened. "Are you afraid of me?"

She couldn't bring herself to make eye contact. "Maybe."

"Look at me." Haltingly, she met his gaze. Instead of piercing, his eyes seemed weary. "I'm not angry with you, and I would never hurt you. Everything I did was to protect you. Do you understand?"

Hesitantly, she nodded, but she didn't understand at all.

"I need you to go back to bed and stay there. I can't have you wandering around here. Soon, I'll answer your questions, but not tonight."

At least he was letting her off the hook. And not killing her off for discovering...whatever this was. "Okay."

"Mrs. Winslow?" Uncle Merlin called.

She was there in an instant. Brinnie had the feeling she had been watching the entire scene. "I'll make sure she gets to bed safely."

"Thank you." With that, he whirled away and through the front door again.

"Come, dear, I'll give you some hot cocoa before bed. That should help you sleep." Mrs. Winslow herded her toward the dining room.

Brinnie followed, but her heart clenched. "You—you lied to me."

Mrs. Winslow looked pained, and Brinnie immediately regretted her words. "No, dear, we never lied to you. It was true, what we said, but perhaps not in the way you took it to mean."

And though she knew secrets had been kept from her left and right, despite herself, Brinnie believed that much.

In the kitchen, Mr. Winslow still guarded the door with his rifle. When Brinnie came in, he raised his eyebrows. "How?"

Brinnie blushed. "You didn't see me." She gave Mrs. Winslow a smile that she suspected was more of a grimace. "I don't need hot cocoa. I'll go back to bed."

Mrs. Winslow opened her mouth, closed it again, and nodded. "Goodnight, dear."

Brinnie turned to the stairs, and Mrs. Winslow returned to the front of the house.

Her mind wandered as she trudged upstairs. What was everyone up to? She thought of possibilities—a group of foreign spies, a drug ring, a secret cult. At least she did know one thing—even though it was a secret, no one would hurt her if she found out.

At least not yet. What they did to her once she learned more—that remained to be seen.

Chapter Ten

As soon as Brinnie woke the next morning, she threw on clothes and hurried down the stairs. In the kitchen, a stranger sat asleep in Mr. Winslow's chair in the corner, his rifle in her lap.

Brinnie couldn't help but stare a bit. The woman looked like she could be a model, with long, golden hair and lovely features. Brinnie guessed she was in her thirties, but she could have been almost any age—she had that timeless look. She wore a simple purple top with gray pants and purple flats, but she still looked runway ready.

The woman's big blue eyes fluttered open and met Brinnie's. The woman jumped, and sitting in her place was Ms. Tynsdale, red hair, purple suit, and all. Brinnie shrieked.

"Hush!" Ms. Tynsdale exclaimed. "Don't wake the whole house."

"But—but I saw—I thought..."

"Saw that, did you? Well, don't go telling anyone." She got up, muttering under her breath, "Stupid magic. Doesn't work when you're sleeping, what good is it anyway?"

"Was that you?"

"It would be you, to catch me asleep. Yes, of course it was me. Who else would it be?"

Ms. Tynsdale began pulling things out of the cupboards as Brinnie's mind whirled. "You were beautiful," she heard herself say.

"Ha! That's my point exactly. Beautiful. Not efficient. Not smart. *Beautiful*. Cruel world, makes a woman look nice. Should've been born ugly. At least I can do something about it."

This was as alien to Brinnie as anything else she had seen and heard. She pulled out a chair and sat. "I think my head's going to explode."

"Try not to do that in the kitchen. Don't want brains in the cereal."

Brinnie looked up sharply, in time to see Ms. Tynsdale hide a smirk. "Did you say magic?"

Ms. Tynsdale raised an eyebrow. "Did I?"

"Yes."

"Then why are you asking me if you already know the answer?"

Brinnie couldn't help but smile. "Okay. But really, can't you tell me anything?"

"I can tell you I don't have much of an idea how to make pancakes." She had set out flour, milk, eggs, a mixing bowl, and a whisk. She frowned at them. "Do you know how?"

"Yes."

"Good." Ms Tysndale brushed her hands off. "Then you're in charge."

Brinnie hoisted herself to her feet, resigning herself to more fruitless wondering. "How many people are we feeding?"

"A lot."

She opened the flour. "Where's Mrs. Winslow?"

"Asleep. She was up all night and wouldn't go to bed until Merlin ordered her to."

"And Marcie?"

"Away on a family emergency."

Brinnie paused, measuring cup in hand. "What happened?"

"Nothing. I told her we had a call from her parents that something happened, and Mr. Winslow drove her to Lyle. That should keep her away for a few hours, at least."

"Why did you do that?" Marcie would be worried sick.

She showed no signs of remorse. "We needed her out of the house. There are too many people for her not to notice what's going on."

Brinnie dumped a cup of flour into the bowl. "What *is* going on?"

Ms. Tynsdale sighed dramatically. "You're making it very difficult to follow orders." Her tone changed. "Do you think you can handle this here? I need to help Edna Burtle with...things. Mrs. Winslow should be awake soon."

Whose orders? Probably Uncle Merlin's again. "Sure."

Brinnie loved making flapjacks, but her heart wasn't in it as she flipped the fluffy golden pancakes. She felt trapped in some sort of nightmare where everything was weird enough to be creepy but normal enough to make the creepiness scary.

Mrs. Winslow emerged as Brinnie poured the batter for the last pancake. "Oh, thank you, dear. I didn't know what I was going to do to feed everyone."

"No problem. It was Ms. Tynsdale's idea."

"I can finish up here if you wouldn't mind running out to get eggs for me. We can have scrambled eggs with our breakfast."

Brinnie strolled out into the bright, warm sunshine and down to the coop. It was a beautiful day, the sort of day that made everything seem fine. *A deceptive day.* Bruno loped along next to her, his tongue lolling out of his mouth. She didn't stop to chat with the chickens, just gathered the eggs and returned.

Back in the kitchen, Mrs. Winslow cracked the eggs into a bowl. "Beautiful pancakes you made, dear. Would you do me a favor and wipe down the dining room table?"

So now she was being told to go to the other side of the house? So much for being dangerous.

Soon, everything was ready. Mrs. Winslow roused the strange guests from where they slept in the library, in the parlor, and even on the floor. There were twelve in all once Miss Burtle and Ms. Tynsdale joined the strangers, Mrs. Winslow, and Brinnie. They sat at the table Brinnie had set and passed around the plate of pancakes, a dish of scrambled eggs, and jugs of orange juice and milk.

Brinnie finally had a chance to look at the visitors. There were four women and four men, and Brinnie didn't think any of them were the same as those she had seen last night. One man had a bandage around his head, while another limped into the room. The rest simply seemed exhausted. There was little conversation, besides weary thanks given to Mrs. Winslow.

Brinnie sat next to Mrs. Winslow after bringing in the last of the silverware, painfully aware that the strangers all kept stealing glances at her. It made her jumpy.

A slight movement across the table caught Brinnie's attention. A little green sprout had popped out of the pancake of the man sitting there. "Oops," he muttered, plucking it and sticking it in his pocket.

Brinnie's eyes nearly popped out of her head.

She dragged her gaze away. It was rude to stare. But she looked away in time to see the woman next to him suddenly become drenched in water that seemed to come from nowhere, her hair and clothes dripping. The woman gasped. Brinnie's heart gave a strange leap in her chest. *What is happening?*

The scene melted into chaos. A whirlwind spontaneously engulfed a man with crazy hair. A window burst open, and birds began circling one woman's head, while insects started crawling toward another. A tangle of ivy grew through the beard of the man with the sprout. But perhaps most disturbing was Ms. Tysndale. Where she had been sitting, a little girl in a purple sailor suit clutched a fork. Brinnie screamed and jumped up, knocking over her chair.

Mrs. Winslow scanned the room, brow furrowed. "All right, settle down, everyone. It's all right."

Miss Burtle flicked a beetle off her pancake and looked on with distaste.

"By George, Morgan, you're drowning me!" the sprout man told the dripping woman.

"Your ivy is trying to strangle me," she retorted.

Over the noise, Ms. Tynsdale pounded the table with her tiny fist. "Stop it! Who's doing this?" her childish voice squeaked. Her gaze swept the table and settled on Brinnie, standing with her mouth hanging open. "Brynna! You stop that right now."

"Stop what?" Panic rose inside her, and as if in response, Ms. Tynsdale became a stooped little old lady.

"That!"

Brinnie clutched the table. "I don't know what you're talking about."

The doors at the far end swung open, and Uncle Merlin stepped into the room. He took one look at the situation and commanded, "Brynna, control yourself."

Brinnie was about to retort that she wasn't the one destroying the place, but even as she thought it, the chaos around her spiked. The woman turned into a gushing fountain, and the whirlwind man blew away in his own storm and slammed into the wall. And ever so subtly, she was aware of a certain something in her that didn't feel quite right. *What* is *that?* It felt like an energy imbalance, or like her pounding heart was off by a millisecond. Brinnie tried to calm herself. She twitched, and it was gone.

At the same instant, the geyser shut off, the wind ceased, the ivy wilted, Ms. Tynsdale's wrinkles disappeared, and the birds flew out the window—after snatching a few of the escaping insects as a snack.

Uncle Merlin put a hand to his forehead and sighed. "Wonderful. Simply wonderful."

Brinnie slumped into her chair. "I'm dreaming."

"No, indeed. Merlin, how long are you going to keep this up?" Ms. Tynsdale demanded, a red-haired woman once more.

"Not for much longer. My apologies to all of you. Are you ready to return?"

As if nothing had occurred, the plant man nodded. "Yes, we were just waiting for you."

"Excellent. In that case, who's first?"

One by one, each of them left with Uncle Merlin. After a few seconds, Uncle Merlin would return with a different person, each of whom staggered from exhaustion. Brinnie stared as the first few came in, but Mrs. Winslow whispered to her, "Are you finished with your breakfast?"

She looked down at her soggy, half-eaten pancake. Who knew where that water had come from? "Yes."

"You can help me bring more food for the newcomers as they arrive, then. They must be starved."

Before Brinnie knew it, she was whisking dirty plates away from the table and setting down new ones. Soon, all the original people had left and new ones had taken their place. Mrs. Winslow set Brinnie to making more pancakes while she sliced apples. Brinnie periodically poked her head into the dining room. The faces inside kept changing. Even as she watched, Ms. Tysndale would escort one person in and one out. All of them looked exhausted and rumpled.

After a while, ingredients dwindled. Mrs. Winslow called into town, asking the owner of the gas station to tell Mr. Winslow to call her when he came to fill up so she could give him a grocery list. When she returned, she clapped her hands together. "Now for tea."

They heated a giant pot of water and made the tea, then Brinnie followed Mrs. Winslow through the dining room to the great hall, carrying a tray stacked with cups. In the hall, on the stairs, and in the parlor, a dozen people lay asleep, and Brinnie knew even more occupied the bedrooms and seating area upstairs. Half a dozen others sat staring into space, eyes half closed, heads drooping. Ms. Tynsdale bent over a woman with a gash on her forehead, dabbing it with a cloth.

Brinnie set up a tea dispensary on the steps while Mrs. Winslow took some upstairs. Every few minutes Uncle Merlin came through the door with another person and left with someone else. Brinnie's mind couldn't handle the oddness of it anymore, so she went on autopilot. Over the next several hours, she let her hands and feet do the chores without thinking—helping Mrs. Winslow cook, making tea, doling out food and water, washing dishes and then more dishes, tearing up sheets for bandages. It was all she could do to keep her mind from exploding with the things she didn't understand.

As Uncle Merlin came through the door yet again with a man bleeding from a gash on his arm, Mrs. Winslow caught him before he could leave. "Merlin, rest. You haven't stopped all night and day. Eat something, at least."

He shook his head, rubbing a hand over his face. From where Brinnie sat snipping an old sheet into strips, she could see the blood and dirt spattering his clothes and the heavy circles under his eyes. "I can't. There's no one else who can work the door."

Who can't open a door?

"Stay here. I'll be right back." Mrs. Winslow hurried away and returned with a glass of water and a slice of bread with cheese. "Have this, at least."

"Thank you." He gulped it all down and handed her the glass. "What would I do without you?"

"Starve yourself to death."

"Quite right." He grinned and turned to face a waiting lady. "Are you ready, Leonora?"

They linked arms and stepped through the doorway.

Leonora had shown up only two hours ago, slept like the dead on the sofa, and now she was leaving again. How was a trip to Wraithwood worthwhile for a two-hour nap?

After Brinnie finished snipping up the sheet, she went out back to cool off from the stifling summer heat inside. Her clothes clung to her, but the breeze lifted the humidity somewhat.

She heard a rumbling and saw the Model T coming toward the gate. She ran to open it, and Mr. Winslow parked the car in the garage.

"Where's Marcie?" Brinnie asked.

"Decided to stay in town with her folks, take her vacation day now." Mr. Winslow began unloading brown paper bags of groceries from the back seat. "Hope I got what Elsa wanted."

Brinnie helped him carry the food in and put it away as Mrs. Winslow began mixing up a giant pot of stew. The cycle of cooking and feeding and binding wounds lasted long into the night. Brinnie began to see familiar faces returning after a while, as if they were coming back in shifts. She still didn't understand why they would come so far out to Wraithwood.

Around midnight, Mrs. Winslow sent Brinnie to bed. "You're falling asleep on your feet, poor dear. Go get some good rest."

Only seconds after Brinnie's head hit the pillow, she was out.

Brinnie awoke late the next morning and squinted at her battery-powered clock. 9:30. She jumped out of bed. She never woke up this late at Wraithwood. Dressing quickly, she happened to glance out the window and saw someone unfamiliar entering the washroom.

Right. There are a bunch of strangers in the house.

When she opened the door to her room, a woman passed her in the hall and bobbed her head in a greeting. Downstairs, the kitchen bustled with activity. A woman she didn't recognize was helping Mrs. Winslow cook while another carried a crate full of dishes out to the washroom. Someone else passed through with a laundry basket full of bloodied rags.

"Good morning, dear." Mrs. Winslow had dark circles under her eyes, and she seemed ready to drop. Brinnie felt a pang of guilt for sleeping in.

"Good morning. What can I do to help?"

"There's oatmeal in the pot—you can have some of that. Then you can wash dishes."

Brinnie ate and brushed her teeth swiftly. She returned to the washroom and offered to help the woman washing dishes.

"I'd love that. You can dry and stack them and carry them back to the house." The raven-haired woman wiped her forehead with her arm and turned back to the sink. "Oh, I'm Belinda."

"I'm Brinnie."

As Belinda washed and Brinnie dried, Brinnie stole glances at her. She was of medium height with long, glossy black hair and big brown eyes. She had a soft, soothing, mothering voice, and she looked to be in her late twenties. She didn't seem like a spy, or a cult member, or...well, Brinnie wasn't even sure what she was looking for.

Before Brinnie could begin asking questions, Belinda started speaking. "Master Ludovic took me out of the front lines. My animals"—she winced—"were getting hurt too quickly. So I'm here, even though I'm not wounded."

"The front lines? Of what?"

"Oh, in front of Riverdell, by the bridge. Have you been there?"

"No."

"A beautiful place, especially the bridge. But what they've done to it—the trees themselves are twisted. The bridge looked ready to collapse when I left. I hope it doesn't. It's beautiful, all stone. But I'm sure you've heard of it before."

Brinnie accepted another plate Belinda handed to her. "Actually, no."

"What? Well, the river runs under it, you know, and there's ivy all over it. So many birds, and frogs, and fish. There was a crane—he was a noble creature. He aided us, but I sent him away when the fighting became too fierce." She sighed.

"Fighting who?"

At that moment Belinda's hand slipped and a plate clattered on the counter, drowning out Brinnie's words. *Was that an accident, or intentional to stop me from asking questions?*

Belinda handed Brinnie a crate of clean dishes. "Here. You can take these back in."

Not worth the risk if she's trying to hide something. On the way to the house, Brinnie passed another person carrying a basket of more bloody rags. Her eyes widened. *How many wounded are there?*

She put away the clean dishes. Mrs. Winslow was gone, but another woman stood in front of the lit fireplace tending a pot. With none of the usual Wraithwood folk around, Brinnie set down the empty crate and slipped through the dining room to the great hall.

An explosion of people filled the room. Blankets sprawled on the floor and furniture was dragged into strange places. The people lying here and there appeared to be wounded to some degree. One man nearest to her had no shirt on, only red-stained bandages wrapped around his torso, his breathing shallow. A woman near him was asleep, her arm in a crude splint. And so it was with all of them, around twenty in total. Brinnie's mind raced. There were ten people in the dining room, half a dozen more upstairs, and a few more scattered around the place. *What kind of fight is this?*

She returned to the kitchen and grabbed the crate. As she was about to open the door, it slammed open and a younger woman ran through. "Mrs. Winslow! Mrs. Winslow! Where is she?"

Brinnie heard footsteps on the stairs. "I'm here," Mrs. Winslow called, emerging. "What is it?"

"Anika is here!"

"Praise the Lord." Both of them rushed outside. Brinnie followed with her crate.

In the yard, a blonde young woman with a black bag stepped out of a dusty car. The driver stepped out too, and Brinnie waved. "Bert!"

He looked over and grinned. "Well, if it isn't Brinnie. Hello, there."

He said something to his passenger, tipped his cap, and she hurried away with Mrs. Winslow and the young woman.

"I'm so glad you're here," Mrs. Winslow said over her shoulder to the newcomer as the three passed Brinnie, hardly seeming to notice her. "I don't know what we would have done if you hadn't come."

Bert leaned against the door as Brinnie came down the steps. "How are you? Enjoying the country?"

"It's beautiful. A little strange around here, though." She froze. *This is my chance.* Bert could take her away. He could drive her to one of her relatives' houses. It would cost a lot of money, but her parents would be happy to pay if it meant she escaped...whatever it was she was escaping. She could run upstairs, grab her things, and be down in five minutes. No one would notice—they were all too busy. It was perfect. All she had to do was tell him.

But for some reason, she hesitated. She remembered Mrs. Winslow's patient instruction in cooking. She remembered Miss Burtle, after Brinnie had been dusting in the library, handing her a book and saying, "I think you might like this one. But be careful with it, you understand?" She remembered Mr. Winslow showing her which flowers were in bloom and Marcie reading Shakespeare with her in the garden. And she remembered Uncle Merlin's marvelous game of chess, and his lack of anger even after she had broken the rules and gone exploring in the front of the house. Mom would have been furious if she'd disobeyed.

As she refocused on the present, Bert was smiling and nodding. "A fine old house it is. Lucky girl. Well, I'd better get going. Good to see you again."

"You, too. Take care."

She watched as Bert climbed in, started the engine, gave a little wave, and drove away.

Brinnie Lane, you are absolutely insane. These people want to make sure you don't go home and the lot of them are probably dangerous criminals, and you gave up the perfect opportunity to escape.

But they're awfully nice dangerous criminals.

With that, she picked up her crate and returned to the washroom.

Chapter Eleven

AFTER BRINNIE FINISHED HELPING BELINDA, THEY returned to the house. They were greeted by an eerie quiet. A shiver ran down Brinnie's spine. "Where is everyone?" she whispered.

"I don't know. Maybe they're all sleeping."

As they passed through the empty dining room, Brinnie found herself tiptoeing and forced herself to stop. Half a dozen wounded occupied the great hall, and Anika bent over one of them. Other than that, the room was empty.

Belinda stepped forward and a floorboard creaked. Anika whirled around. "Oh." She relaxed.

"Where did everyone go?" Belinda asked.

"Ludovic gathered everyone who was able. The enemy was making an all-out assault."

So now Uncle Merlin is leading some sort of army?

Belinda's shoulders slumped. "What about me?"

"No one knew you were out there. I'm sorry."

Belinda scanned the room. "Where are the Wraithwooders? The Winslows, and Edna Burtle?"

"I sent them to rest. They've been up all night, and they're going to make themselves sick. I can handle things since it's only these few now." Anika expertly checked the bandages of the wounded man, nodded, then strode toward them. "Nothing to do but wait now."

"Wait...for what?" Belinda's voice trembled.

"For Ludovic to come back. They'll come back either victorious or in hasty retreat. But they will come back." Anika added the last bit as if reassuring herself.

"Any help from Castelon?"

Anika glanced back at the sleeping wounded. "They sent word to Artema. A dozen fighters were sent. But without enough portals, it would take too long for the Castelon people to get there. Ludovic transported the few who have been to both Wraithwood and Riverdell, but..." She shrugged.

"Is there any hope?" Belinda whispered.

"There's always hope until you're dead." Anika tightened her ponytail with finality. "Let's have a cup of tea."

The two women headed for the kitchen, and Brinnie followed. *I'm not even going to try to make sense of that.* Belinda put a kettle on.

While they waited, Anika ladled leftover stew into bowls. "I'll see if I can get a few of them to eat a bit. I'll be back."

She returned right after Brinnie started pouring tea into the cups. They sat, and Brinnie passed a cup to the physician.

Anika accepted it. "What's your name?"

"Brinnie."

"Pleasure. I'm Anika." She took a sip and tilted her head. "So, are you human?"

Brinnie almost choked on her tea. *Is that an insult? A compliment?* Anika looked serious. "Of course."

"I see." Anika nodded.

Brinnie tried to keep from raising an eyebrow. They finished their tea in silence. Belinda and Brinnie tidied up the kitchen, then Belinda went to nap in the great hall while awaiting Uncle Merlin's return. Anika resumed hovering over her patients. Brinnie waffled for a moment before deciding to attempt to read.

Hours passed, the atmosphere tense, waiting. Mrs. Winslow half-heartedly made dinner with Brinnie and Belinda's help, but her eyes kept wandering toward the front of the house. Miss Burtle was on the cell phone constantly. Every few calls she would punch in a number and then wait and wait, and the person wouldn't answer. "Nothing from Riverdell," she would mutter.

Mr. Winslow paced and got in the way until Mrs. Winslow sent him out to the garden. And still they waited.

By dark, everyone had gathered in the great hall. Brinnie wasn't sure what they were doing there. Everyone made a pretense of being busy, but they kept looking at the door. Mr. Winslow had been on the same page of the newspaper for ten minutes, and it was an edition from three weeks ago. Brinnie didn't know what she was supposed to do. No one sent her to bed, so she stayed.

When the door finally opened, the turning handle sounded like an explosion in the quiet house. Uncle Merlin pushed it open, leaning on it heavily. His right arm was linked with Ms. Tynsdale's as if they had been out skipping, but they both looked exhausted. They separated as soon as they were in the door, and Uncle Merlin turned to close it. As it clicked shut, his knees buckled, and he sank to the floor.

Anika rushed to his side. "Is he wounded?"

"Not much," Ms. Tynsdale said. "The problem is he worked too hard transporting everyone back and forth."

"I'm fine," Uncle Merlin said raggedly, his face gray. "Just tired."

Mr. Winslow supported him as Anika directed him to the parlor sofa. Mrs. Winslow scurried off to get food and drink for them.

Anika shook her head. "You did too much. You're not meant to be transporting so many others."

He smiled weakly. "I'd say it's better than losing Riverdell. I'll be fine in a moment."

"You must be dying to know." Ms. Tynsdale sank into a nearby chair. "We won."

"Oh, thank God," Belinda breathed.

Anika nodded. "I knew you would."

Mrs. Winslow bustled back in. "Here's water, and tea, and stew. Both of you eat."

Uncle Merlin took a cup. "Thank you." He sipped and sighed. "Won might not be the best word. They retreated, but our casualties are much higher than theirs." He looked at Anika. "Have you been to Riverdell?"

"Yes, once."

"Good. I can take you there, but I can't bring everyone back here." He struggled to his feet.

"Merlin," Mrs. Winslow began, right as Ms. Tynsdale said, "You *cannot* take her there. Last trip, you about got us lost in Kansas. Sit back down."

"Fine." He sat rigidly. "Miss Burtle, please call everyone and let them know Riverdell is safe for the moment."

"Of course."

"What needs to be done for the wounded here, Anika?"

"I put them in a deep sleep for the time being," she reported. "When they wake up—in a few hours, probably—they should be mostly healed."

"Excellent. Tom, everything is quiet here?"

"Yes. Haven't seen anything," Mr. Winslow affirmed.

"Good. Sounds like everything is under control. Anika, are you ready?"

"Merlin!" Ms. Tynsdale rolled her eyes.

"I won't be ready for another half hour while you rest," Anika said firmly. "We'll do no one any good stranded in Alaska."

He slumped back. "I see that none of you have any confidence in me whatsoever. Very well, then."

Brinnie watched the proceedings from a distance, as if watching a movie that had nothing to do with her. *Enough of this.* She slipped away.

In her room, she pulled out a pencil and paper and began to write.

Dear Dad and Mom,

Things have been really weird here. A lot of people have been in the house the last few days and some of them have pretty nasty wounds. Everyone keeps talking about enemies and fighting. I've been trying to figure out what's going on, but I can't. I know this will sound strange, but I keep seeing things that can't be possible. Ms. Tynsdale can make it look like she turns into different people, and a man turned into a tornado, literally. Mom, they've said some strange things about you, too. I don't know if you know what's going on, but if you do, I need help.

I'm going to put this letter in the pile to be taken to town. I'm going to try to find out the truth, and this way, if something happens to me, you'll know why. If everything is fine, I'll take it out of the pile before someone goes to town and throw it away.

I love you.

- Brinnie

She stuffed it in an envelope, sealed it, and scribbled the address. There wasn't any hope of them saving her if something went wrong, but she wanted them to know what had happened to her, just in case. *Even if they read it and think I went crazy.*

She took the stairs two at a time and threw the letter on the pile on the corner of the counter. Then she took a deep breath and stepped outside.

She circled the house to the front door. It had been almost half an hour, the time they had said they would wait. As she stood to one side, hidden in the shadows, she tried to speculate, but nothing made sense.

Her heart pounded. She should turn around and go back inside. No one would know. *I'm such an idiot. I should have left with Bert while I had a chance.*

But for some inexplicable reason, the thought of leaving Wraithwood made her heart squeeze.

On the one hand, she had been happier the last few weeks at Wraithwood than she could recall being in years. Her mind flashed back to when she had accidentally dropped half a dozen eggs on the floor. She'd immediately begun apologizing, but Mrs. Winslow had simply chuckled and helped her clean it up. "No worries, dear. The hens will lay more tomorrow."

Mom would have given me that look. The why-do-I-have-a-second-daughter look.

But when she was alone, she felt crazy for not wanting to leave. The facts showed that they had talked about preventing her from going home and were involved in violence.

She had to know. She couldn't leave Wraithwood without knowing. Somehow, she felt more at home in the creepy mansion than she had ever felt anywhere else, as if it was where she was supposed to be. If she ran away out of fear of what she didn't know, it would always haunt her.

So here she was, hiding in the shadows, waiting. Wherever Uncle Merlin went, she would follow him and find out the truth.

Just then, the door swung open, and two figures were silhouetted against the light. Uncle Merlin stood on the left with Anika on the right clutching her black bag, their arms linked. They stepped forward through the doorway. There was a sound like a gust of wind, and the door slammed shut.

Then, they were nowhere in sight.

Brinnie ran forward and stood in front of the door. They had stepped out right there. She had seen it. They weren't in the house. But they weren't outside, either. They had disappeared into thin air.

She sank to the ground with her back against the wall. She still didn't know where they were going or what they were doing, but one thing was clear. There was only one word for it, the word Ms. Tynsdale had muttered under her breath.

Magic.

Chapter Twelve

BRINNIE COULD ACCEPT IT MUCH MORE easily than she'd expected. After all, everyone knew magic wasn't real. Maybe she had read too many books. Maybe she was crazy. But she believed in magic.

She got up, dusted herself off, and went back around the house. In the kitchen, she grabbed her letter, tore it up, and threw it in the garbage. *I guess I'm not tracking anyone on a journey after all. As far as I know, I can't teleport.*

The dining room door swung open, and Mrs. Winslow walked in. "Oh! There you are, dear. I think it's about time we all went to bed."

Brinnie nodded, burning with her new knowledge. She wanted to say something like, *Oh, by the way, you don't have to keep secrets anymore. I know about the magic.* But she didn't. Not yet, until she had time to think. "Good night, then."

As she climbed in bed a while later, she kept turning the idea over in her mind. Magic. She had always loved books about it. When she was younger, she had often pretended she was a fairy or wizard or other such magical being. *Is this why Mom sent me here? Why Uncle Merlin visited?* Her heart beat faster. *Was that what happened in the dining hall? But I didn't make the plants and birds and things. Why did they blame me?*

Right about then, she hit a mental wall. Her mind couldn't handle the thought of actually doing magic herself.

She turned to the nightstand for a book to read to calm her mind, but there was only the one she had already finished. So she hopped out of bed to go get another. There was no way she would be able to sleep with so much swirling around in her brain.

Downstairs, the kitchen was empty. She started toward the back door when she realized she could just go through the front of the house. She was allowed there now.

She pushed open the door to the dining room and walked past the huge table. She was about to open the double doors at the other side when she heard voices coming from the great hall. She stopped and listened.

"It was quite a scene in the dining room—birds, water, plants, insects, even a whirlwind, and she saw it all."

Uncle Merlin's voice. He must have come back. Brinnie reached out to push through the door, unconcerned, when she heard another voice that stopped her dead in her tracks. "And you *let* her see it?"

Mom. But that was impossible. She was halfway across the world.

Uncle Merlin must have a telephone on speaker. But that was some awesome sound quality. *Since when can Mom make calls?* More lies, apparently.

"I wasn't there at the time," Uncle Merlin said. "I was a bit preoccupied at Riverdell. But it was only a matter of time before she saw such things, what with everyone who was here. Keeping her from noticing anything has been a much harder task than either of us expected it would be."

"Couldn't you have sent her to Lyle? Something?"

"She wouldn't be under protection in Lyle, and I wouldn't be there to keep watch. With things as they are, I think the only safe thing to do is to tell her what she is."

Brinnie clutched the doorknob. *What I am?*

"That's absolutely out of the question. If we need to, we can send her somewhere else, but she can't be told."

"Send her where?"

"Anywhere. Andrew's parents, his brother, his aunt. It doesn't matter. The important thing is that she doesn't get involved in any of this."

There were far more pressing concerns, but Brinnie could only think, *Please not Aunt Gertie. Anyone but her.*

Aunt Gertie was the only person in the world better at being disappointed in her than Mom. Dad's aunt detested her adopted nephew enough, and she always looked at Brinnie like she was Dad's horrific gremlin spawn. But her sense of duty would necessitate taking Brinnie in a pinch.

"Sending her anywhere would be very risky. Remember she only has a couple months before she turns fifteen. It's almost certain something would happen while she's with one of her relatives, and that would be dangerous. She needs to stay here."

Thank you, Uncle Merlin. Magic trumped Aunt Gertie anytime.

Mom sighed. "You're right." Her tone became stern. "But she must believe she's human."

Brinnie's eyes felt like they were about to bug out of her head. *I'm not human?* Maybe Aunt Gertie wasn't too far off with the gremlin idea after all.

"Eira, I strongly believe that for her safety, she must be told. The protection at Riverdell was completely down, and there was no explanation for it. With the enemy getting closer to Wraithwood all the time, she needs to know what to do if something goes wrong."

"No. Wraithwood has some of the best defenses of any estate. She'll be fine. She is *going* to come home this fall and everything is going to return to normal. She's here for you to find out what her ability is and for a safe place if it flares up. That's all. Once that's done with, she is never seeing Wraithwood again."

Brinnie heard Uncle Merlin sigh. "I believe you're making a mistake."

"Merlin, please. Promise you won't tell her."

"I can't do that. But I give you my word that unless her life depends on it, I will keep her in the dark as much as is possible."

"Thank you." A slight pause. "Wraithwood looks exactly the same, even after all these years."

Brinnie's eyes widened. *Looks?* She started to push the door open to peek, but stopped herself, remembering the loud squeak from her first foray into the front of the house. She would be caught eavesdropping.

His voice softened. "It may look the same, but it certainly feels different without you here."

"Remember sliding down the banisters?"

"Of course." He chuckled. "And Mother never did understand how we got such strange stains on our clothes."

"It was from that polish Eddie was always shining them with. What ever happened to him?"

103

"He moved on to Iriselie. Too many painful memories here."

"I know how he felt," Mom said softly.

There was a long pause and a sigh from Uncle Merlin. "But I believe the good memories outweigh the bad. And there are always more good memories to be made."

"Yes. But not here. Not in the middle of a war."

"We're all engaged in a war, no matter where we are. But because the war is invisible, we often forget it exists."

"I forgot about all your sayings that you think are so clever."

"Are you implying they're not?" His voice dripped with mock offense.

Mom laughed. "They're something, all right. Well," she said after a pause, "I should get back. Andrew will be out of his mind with worry if he finds out I'm missing."

"Of course. Shall we?"

As Brinnie heard the front door open, she threw open the dining room door. But she was too late. The front door was already swinging shut. She ran to the window and looked out.

As she had expected, the yard was empty.

Miss Burtle remained on the phone constantly the next day. Brinnie heard her say more than once, "No, Ludovic isn't here. If you want to talk to him directly, call Riverdell, for goodness's sake."

Ms. Tynsdale had a bounce in her step. "Didn't think we'd do it, but we won!" she declared. "So there, Artema. You can keep your trained fighters. Ha!"

Brinnie wandered into the great hall. The five people who had been wounded sat talking with Belinda and Mrs. Winslow. Some faces were pale, and others had dark circles under their eyes, but otherwise they looked none the worse, despite the blood Brinnie had seen just yesterday.

"Isn't that something else?" one exclaimed. "We beat them at Riverdell."

They were slapping each other on the back and laughing when the front door opened.

"Merlin." Mrs. Winslow jumped up.

"Hello, everyone." He nodded to the group. "All is well here?"

"Everything's fine. What about Riverdell?" Mrs. Winslow asked.

"Fairly well. Anika has her work cut out for her, but nothing too serious. The enemy is long gone."

"You look better," Mrs. Winslow commented.

He straightened his collar. "Feel better, as well. I caught a bit of sleep last night."

"Good. Now we have to get some food into you. Come along." She shooed him toward the kitchen.

He laughed and bowed slightly to the strangers. "If you'll excuse me. Oh, and Brinnie, please come with me."

Brinnie followed him through the dining room into the empty kitchen. Mrs. Winslow set a bowl of chicken noodle soup and a glass of lemonade on the table. "We've been making whatever can be made in bulk," she said apologetically.

"If you had a hand in it, I'm sure it will be wonderful. Thank you."

She waved off his flattery. "I think I'll see if our guests want any lemonade."

As she left, Uncle Merlin pulled out a chair. "Have a seat, Brinnie."

She sat across from him.

"Do you want anything?" he asked.

"No, thanks."

He nodded and took a spoonful of soup. He closed his eyes for a moment, savoring it. "She thinks I flatter her, but I mean every word." He opened his eyes. "I haven't been able to speak with you much lately. There was something I wanted to talk to you about."

"The magic?" Brinnie blurted.

He raised an eyebrow. "Have you been talking to Ms. Tynsdale?"

"No." She crumpled the tablecloth in her fist beneath the table. "Well, yes, but not about that."

"Hmm." He sat in silence for a moment, looking off into the distance. "The world is a strange place. Sometimes it's better not to ask too many questions. Some things are better not to be known."

"That's hardly fair." Magic was real and he expected her not to ask questions? "Aren't some things also good to know?"

He laughed. "Yes. Some things." Then he shook his head. "I'm sorry, Brynna, but I really can't explain anything to you. All I can say is this—enjoy Wraithwood for the place that it is, but when you go home at the end of the summer, you'll need to leave this behind. It has no place in the real world."

"Aren't we in the real world?"

His mouth turned up at the corners. "Perhaps."

And to her eternal frustration, he refused to say anything further on the subject.

Chapter Thirteen

UNCLE MERLIN AND MS. TYNSDALE WERE GONE for most of the rest of the day. When they came back, Uncle Merlin escorted the guests, now mostly recovered, out the door. Soon, only the usual Wraithwooders were left, plus Ms. Tynsdale.

Companionable silence graced the table after dinner, until Uncle Merlin said to Ms. Tynsdale, "You could stay the night if you would like and go home after church tomorrow morning."

She dropped her napkin. "Church!"

"We go to church every Sunday," he replied calmly.

She gaped. "Not at a time like this!"

"*Especially* at a time like this."

"Don't we have more pressing concerns?"

Brinnie's eyes ping-ponged from one to the other.

"If we let them intimidate us from living our lives," Uncle Merlin said, "they've already won, and we might as well stop fighting."

"Don't you think you're making too big a deal out of it?"

Uncle Merlin folded his hands. "I don't think it's possible to make too big a deal out of the God of the universe. The universe is fairly large."

She rolled her eyes. "Really, though. What difference does one Sunday make? Please, just this once have a little concern for safety."

Or we could just skip it because the people there think we're crazy.

Uncle Merlin stood and started stacking dinner plates. Mrs. Winslow rose to help him, and he passed her a stack. "Despite everything, even if one of them had to be away, my parents never let us miss a Sunday," he said quietly.

Mrs. Winslow accepted the plates and bit her lip. Those around the table sobered.

He didn't make eye contact. "I don't intend to start now."

Ms. Tynsdale sighed. "Fine. But I think you're making a mistake."

"The offerstands. Would you like to stay the night?"

"I suppose. But I'm still going to leave first thing in the morning."

No one spoke much the rest of the evening, and Brinnie tossed and turned that night. She couldn't stop thinking about her conversation with Uncle Merlin. And she never did ask about Mom's parents.

When she awoke the next morning, she felt like she hadn't slept at all. She slipped on her lavender dress and the white shoes. As she brushed her hair, she sighed. She couldn't weasel a thing out of him about magic. But why? And why didn't Mom want her to know? Since an answer was not forthcoming, Brinnie went downstairs.

Ms. Tynsdale stood in the kitchen wearing a dark purple outfit. "I decided I might as well stay," she said in answer to Brinnie's questioning look. "If Merlin's determined to get you all killed, at least I can be there to help—protect you, that is, not kill you."

Twenty minutes later, as they bounced along in the Model T, Brinnie watched gray clouds billowing in the overcast sky. They could expect rain soon.

They rounded the bend, and she thought she saw someone on the side of the road. Just as she was about to mention it, a man jumped out from the trees and threw something at the passenger side front tire. The car jolted and thudded. Another man leaped out from their left and threw what looked like a knife at the other front tire. The vehicle bounced and grated into the shoulder, sending Brinnie flying against the back of the seat in front of her.

"What did I tell you?" Ms. Tynsdale muttered to Uncle Merlin.

"Everyone be still," he directed, lips barely moving.

Nine men surrounded the vehicle, dressed in various shades of gray and brown. The tall figure directly in front of the car stepped forward, shrouded in a cloak. He pushed back the cowl, revealing the sharp angles of his face under dark hair. Too sharp, with sunken eye sockets, like a skeleton. Brinnie shuddered.

His voice was every bit as hard and chilling. "Merlin Ludovic. Lydia Tynsdale." His steel gray eyes flicked over the others in the car. "And human companions, of course."

"Excuse me, but we were on our way to church," Uncle Merlin said with complete calm.

Brinnie didn't know how he managed. Her heart thudded so hard she thought it would pop out of her chest.

The man's eyes narrowed. "I suggest you surrender now."

"I'm sorry, are you an officer of the law?"

So quickly Brinnie nearly missed it, the man reached into his cloak, grabbed a knife, and flicked his wrist. Brinnie screamed as it spun toward Uncle Merlin in the topless Model T. But just as fast, he disappeared and reappeared standing next to the car. The knife whizzed by harmlessly, almost hitting one of the man's comrades on the other side.

The man seemed unfazed by his miss. "You've given yourself away, Ludovic."

"Oh, very well." Uncle Merlin shrugged. *Shrugged.* After being almost impaled with a knife. "What do you want?"

"I want you and Tynsdale to come with us peacefully." His eyes flicked over the vehicle, and Brinnie clutched the seatback. "And I want all of these humans to be questioned—not harmed. We only want to visit your estate."

"Oh, I don't much care for visitors."

The gray-eyed man's hard gaze didn't waver. "The humans are our hostages. Do as we say, or they die." He motioned toward one of the other men—a man standing two steps away from Brinnie.

She didn't shrink away fast enough. His hand snaked out, grabbing her arm. She shrieked and tried to pull away, his large fingers digging into her skin.

"You horrible man!" Mrs. Winslow swung her pocketbook. It struck him in the ear and he grunted, but he batted it away and dragged Brinnie out of the car.

She stumbled, but he yanked her up. She twisted, trying to kick him, trying to wrench her arms free. "You put me down! I'll call the police! Let me go!" She heard a strange clicking sound and then a sharp, cold object pressed against her throat. A knife.

She went absolutely still. She could feel the blood pulsing at her throat, so close to that cool blade. Her head felt light.

Uncle Merlin glanced at her, and she briefly saw his eyes fill with pain and something deeper, something that resembled a haunted expression. But he hooked his thumbs in his pockets and resumed his indifferent demeanor. "Kill her, if you would like. She doesn't know."

He couldn't have. He said they would be safe. She thought he wanted to protect her.

"Unc—!" Brinnie began to gasp but was silenced by one warning look from him. *Oh.* It was some sort of twisted game of poker. She had no idea what, but in this moment, she had no choice. *You better know what you're doing.* She joined the game. "Mr. Ludovic, no, please!" she wailed.

"She doesn't know?" the leader asked. "Do you think I would believe that?"

"I'm telling you the truth. The girl doesn't know." The corner of Uncle Merlin's mouth turned up in a small smirk. "But go ahead. Kill her, and you'll see I wasn't lying."

The man scanned her from head to toe, not as if looking at a person, but as if she were an object. "Let her go."

The man restraining Brinnie pushed her away so hard that she fell and skinned her knees and the heel of one hand. "Get in the car and stay out of the way, girl," Uncle Merlin instructed in a distant tone.

She picked herself up and obeyed, though her legs felt like rubber. She shook so hard she was sure the milk she had with breakfast must be turning to butter in her stomach.

"So the girl doesn't know," the stranger said as Brinnie clambered into the car on wobbling legs. "The rest of them are your people, Ludovic. There's no reason they shouldn't die."

Brinnie collapsed on the seat. Mrs. Winslow put her arms around her and drew her close.

"Do you really want to do this?" Uncle Merlin asked the man mildly. "I don't quite feel like a battle today. I'd say we're fairly evenly matched. There will be a lot of bloodshed on both sides. I suggest we go our way, you go yours, and we'll all pretend we never even saw each other, no harm done."

"Indeed. Lead the way back to Wraithwood and all will be well."

"I don't know..." Uncle Merlin kept rambling as he made a sign behind his back. At the signal, Mr. Winslow reached down, grabbed what looked like a rifle, and pointed it at the man. Mrs. Winslow pushed

Brinnie down, and Mr. Winslow opened fire.

The scene erupted. Brinnie's ears rang from gunshots. She looked up to see a throwing knife embed itself in Mr. Winslow's arm. He dropped the gun, but Miss Burtle snatched it up and kept shooting.

Ms. Tynsdale had vacated the car. Brinnie didn't know where she was, but she didn't have time to wonder. A huge gust of wind buffeted the vehicle, and Brinnie almost fell out.

"Look out!" Mrs. Winslow grabbed Brinnie and jumped out of the car right as a tree toppled and smashed the seat where they had been sitting.

Brinnie rolled away from the scene of destruction and stumbled to her feet to see one of the attackers right behind Mrs. Winslow, about to stab her with a long, curving knife. Brinnie shrieked and punched him in the face. Her hand stung from the blow, but it did the trick, distracting him just long enough for Mrs. Winslow to brain him with her deadly pocketbook.

"You have to get away from here," Mrs. Winslow yelled to Brinnie.

One of the men charged them, knife drawn. Uncle Merlin appeared out of thin air in front and slightly to the side of the man, sticking out a foot. The attacker tripped, stabbing himself with his own knife.

A condensed whirlwind came up and knocked Uncle Merlin backward off his feet. A man stood behind it, pushing his arms forward as if directing its path. He put his arms down and the wind dispersed in all directions. Then he drew a knife and bore down on Uncle Merlin.

Brinnie could do nothing but watch in horror. She couldn't run— she was hemmed in on all sides by attackers. She couldn't help—she had no weapon.

Another man ran toward the first attacker as he raised his knife over Uncle Merlin. The attacker turned around and frowned, about to say something, but the newcomer promptly stabbed him. As the man keeled over, the stabber morphed back into the shape of Ms. Tynsdale and turned to combat another attacker.

Uncle Merlin jumped up as roots erupted from the ground around him, trying to grab him and pin him down. But Brinnie couldn't watch any longer—she had her own problems. A flock of birds swooped out of nowhere and began to dive-bomb Mrs. Winslow's head. Brinnie slapped at them, but they pecked and scratched her hands. Mrs. Winslow shielded her face with one arm and swung her pocketbook with the other. Mr. Winslow soon fought his way to Brinnie's side. He had pulled the knife out of his arm, and blood sprinkled the ground as he wielded a branch and smacked the birds out of the sky like baseballs.

Another attacker approached the group, throwing knives at ready, but he was brought down by a bullet to the shoulder. "Ha, ha!" Brinnie heard Miss Burtle crow. "Take that!"

Yet Brinnie could see they were losing the fight. Miss Burtle ran out of ammunition and began wielding the gun like a club. The birds and roots were after Miss Burtle and the Winslows, though they ignored Brinnie. *Why is no one attacking me?*

The ambushers ringed the sorry group. Ms. Tynsdale and Uncle Merlin slashed at birds, roots, and attackers but did little good. Wind blasted Uncle Merlin time and again, throwing him to the ground. Ms. Tynsdale was repeatedly doused with blasts of water the strength of a fire hose by one of the men, and both dodged tongues of flame thrown by another. An attacker almost snuck up behind Ms. Tynsdale to plant a knife in her ribs, but Uncle Merlin brought the hilt of his knife down on the attacker's skull. "Brinnie," he hissed. "Stop helping them."

"I have to!" she protested, kicking at the roots around Mrs. Winslow.

"Not them." He kicked an attacker and lowered his voice. "The enemy. Stop helping the enemy!"

"What? I'm not!"

Uncle Merlin turned and lashed out at a giant root that threatened to entangle him. "You are! Like in the dining room."

It was then Brinnie felt the imbalance again. She realized she had felt it the entire time, a sort of energy flowing outward, more like a vibration than a current. *Is this what magic feels like?* She gave a little jerk, and it was gone.

The giant root attacking Uncle Merlin drooped. The birds flapped erratically, drifting in dazed circles. The flame throwing man had fire dancing on his fingers, but his fireballs were now more like sparks.

The leader of the group who had first spoken with Uncle Merlin looked at Brinnie. Their eyes locked, and Brinnie felt that he truly saw her for the first time. Before, she had been scenery. Now she was a person. As her eyes remained transfixed by his, the sounds of battle faded away. He had not been fighting, she realized. Why not? And yet...for some reason she felt that he had.

Their gazes didn't falter. Brinnie got the feeling that his eyes were boring into hers, trying to reach her mind.

"Stop." His voice rung out over the battle, and remarkably, all paused. He strode toward Brinnie and stopped in front of her. All was silent. "What is your name, *liniad?*"

It felt like gray fog was clouding her mind, threatening to take over. But an alarm rang somewhere inside her. *I can't give in. I can't tell him.*

"None of your business." Then, with a tremendous effort, she broke the contact.

She thought she could feel the shockwave ripple away like from a stone dropped in water as she averted her eyes.

The man turned to Uncle Merlin. "You've been keeping a secret." He drew a shining knife the length of his forearm from his belt. The waved edges glinted. Grabbing Brinnie's arm, he held the blade to her throat. "Now there's no reason why I shouldn't kill her. Lead us to Wraithwood."

Chapter Fourteen

"IT WOULD HARDLY PROFIT YOU TO kill her." Uncle Merlin didn't move from where he stood. His voice remained steady, though his face was pale. "She's as valuable to you as to us."

"That's where you're mistaken." Brinnie's heart pounded as the man shifted the knife in his grasp. "You have so little, and we have so much. I would regret her death, yes, but I wouldn't hesitate to kill her. Lead us to Wraithwood and she will live."

"Do you think she's more important than Wraithwood?"

"It doesn't matter what I think." Brinnie could hear the smirk in the man's voice. "It's what you think."

Mrs. Winslow made a move as if to reach out for Brinnie, but the man pressed the knife closer against her throat. "Don't move," he commanded. Mrs. Winslow froze. "And don't try anything, Ludovic. The minute you disappear, she's dead."

"Fine, then. Follow me." Uncle Merlin started moving toward Lyle.

"Do you think me a fool? We came from that way, and you came from the opposite direction."

Brinnie couldn't tell what Uncle Merlin was thinking as he moved off in the right direction, back toward Wraithwood. The five other men who were still able to walk, though all wounded in various ways, surrounded the remaining Wraithwooders. They rounded up Miss Burtle, strangely enough, from under the car. The three attackers who had either been killed or severely wounded—Brinnie wasn't sure which—were left lying on the road.

The leader tied Brinnie's hands behind her back and kept tight hold of her, his strange blade hovering near her throat at all times. She concentrated on putting one foot in front of the other. So this was what Mom ran away from and what she didn't want Brinnie to know about.

Brinnie thought it was the best decision Mom could have made. Her pulse beat in her throat. Anyone in their right mind would run from these insane, bloodthirsty magicians. Especially this psychotic man in a cloak.

Her shoes had been lost during the struggle, though she hardly noticed the sharp rocks and sticks under her feet. She locked her eyes on the blade, intent on keeping her balance and not falling into it.

Uncle Merlin kept a few paces ahead, not going very fast, even though one of the attackers walked behind him, blade at the ready. When he slowed too much, the man poked him. "Move faster, Ludovic," Brinnie's captor said.

Brinnie glanced back once at the others, surrounded by the remaining attackers. Ms. Tynsdale scowled, while the Winslows looked worried to the point of fear. But for some reason, Miss Burtle wore what looked suspiciously like a smirk.

"Face forward," the man directed, and Brinnie did as she was told.

They walked for what felt like an hour but must have only been ten minutes. Then, Brinnie heard something wailing.

"Get off the road!" the leader commanded.

Brinnie obeyed. She had no choice, with a knife to her throat.

Uncle Merlin followed, though slowly.

But as the other attackers herded the rest of the group away, Miss Burtle tripped. As she fell, she grabbed Ms. Tynsdale and dragged her down with her. The attackers tried to pull them to their feet, but Miss Burtle proved difficult to help up for such a small woman.

The man shoved Brinnie into the undergrowth and pressed them both behind a tree, leaning out just enough that he could still see what was happening. Brinnie craned her neck to see as much as she dared.

The rumbling and wailing grew louder, and she recognized what the sounds meant—the police. The vehicles sped into view, lights flashing and sirens wailing. The attackers abandoned Miss Burtle on the road and hurried into the trees.

Two police cars screeched to a stop and four policemen jumped out, firearms in hand. An unmarked car pulled up behind them, and four more people emerged, also armed—but not in uniform. Were they police too?

Brinnie opened her mouth to shout. The man clapped his hand over her face. "Don't speak," he warned, pressing the knife closer to her neck.

She heard Miss Burtle yell something to the policemen about someone in the trees. Brinnie's captor pressed her back to the tree, his hand still over her mouth.

"They won this battle," the man hissed in her ear. "I could kill you now, but I would gain nothing." He grabbed her right arm, pushed up her sleeve, and slashed several times with his knife. She screamed and thrashed as it bit white-hot into her skin, but he kept her pinned. "Now you can't hide. We'll find you." Then he pushed her away. As she stumbled, he melted into the trees.

At the same time, all five of the other attackers ran off. The policemen shouted for them to stop, and the four strangers fired their weapons, but all their efforts failed to stop the attackers' escape. Brinnie hit the ground to avoid being shot. Above her head, the shots went wild. She didn't hear any shouts from the escaping attackers. Through the ferns, she thought she saw one of the strangers' weapons explode in his hand. The young man looked at it sheepishly and hid it behind his back.

Three officers gave chase, while one shouted, "Hold your fire!" at the mysterious newcomers.

Uncle Merlin ran to Brinnie. "Are you all right?"

She sat up slowly. "I...I think so." She put her hand to her arm and drew her fingers away, staring at the warm, red liquid. Blood. "He didn't kill me."

"No. He never wanted to." He helped her to her feet. As he did so, he looked at her arm and his face drained of color.

"What is it?"

"Nothing." But it was obviously something. He led her back onto the road.

"Agent Haberdash, FBI," one of the newcomers was saying. She flashed a badge at the police officer who had told them to hold their fire. "This is part of a federal investigation. We have been authorized to use whatever means necessary to capture the felons." She held up her weapon. "Tranquilizers."

"Apologies," the officer said. "We didn't know."

"That was to be expected."

The other officers returned from their chase. "We lost them, sir. No sign of them anywhere," one reported.

The officer in charge made a move to reach for his radio, but Agent Haberdash raised her hand. "We have the situation under control. Reinforcements are already on their way." She nodded to a nearby man, who tucked away an old model cell phone and nodded back. "In the meantime, the witnesses should be questioned."

Brinnie wasn't sure how questions were usually asked, but she got the feeling this wasn't the usual method. Agent Haberdash asked questions to the group at large, while one of the agents held a recording device.

"They slashed our tires and attacked us on the road. They wanted our money, so we were leading them back to our house," Miss Burtle told her.

"But there was a struggle?"

"Yes, we tried to defend ourselves. We couldn't, and that was when I called the police." Miss Burtle looked smug.

Understanding dawned. So that's what she had been doing under the car.

The agents asked many questions, but Brinnie didn't have to answer them. Miss Burtle and Uncle Merlin did most of the talking. They told the same story—they were attacked on the road, tried to fight off the attackers, and agreed to lead them to their home when Brinnie was held hostage. The attackers' sole interest, they said, was money. The Winslows confirmed the story. They hadn't witnessed the tree falling on the car, they all affirmed. It must have happened afterward.

One of the agents walked away to answer his phone. When he returned, he reported that the men had been apprehended three miles south. They were going to be taken to the county station.

Agent Haberdash nodded. "It seems everything is under control," she told the police officers. "We'll take care of the witnesses and the crime scene. No need for you to write up a report. We should be sending your department a full report shortly."

The officers seemed a bit uncomfortable with the situation, but they couldn't argue with the FBI, so they left.

As soon as the police cruisers were out of sight, Agent Haberdash brushed her hands together. "With any luck, they'll forget about the report. And if they don't, it will just stir up more of the usual animosity."

With these confusing words, everyone began smiling and shaking hands. "Excellently done," Uncle Merlin told Agent Haberdash. "To what do we owe this fortuitous rescue?"

She straightened her cuffs. "We were already on our way to Wraithwood when the call came in—in Lyle, in fact. We must have gotten it at about the same time as the police, so we followed them out."

"Call?" Uncle Merlin asked.

"You didn't think the police were the only ones I called, did you?" Miss Burtle smirked.

Uncle Merlin nodded. "Excellent thinking." He turned to the agents. "And I thank you as well. The last thing we needed was a police investigation."

"Trust me," Haberdash said, "we'd like it even less."

With that, the FBI agents turned into field medics. One of them bandaged Mr. Winslow's wound while Agent Haberdash brought out a first aid kit and cleaned up Brinnie's arm. "A clean cut. It should heal well, but it will leave a scar. A blade like that always does."

"A blade like what?" Brinnie asked, dazed.

"An enchanted blade."

Brinnie looked up at the woman as she closed the first aid kit and set it on the trunk of the car. She had seemed normal, with her straight dark hair in a bun and unremarkable features, though she appeared very professional while ordering the police around. Brinnie fought through the shock clouding her brain. "But you're from the FBI."

The woman's mouth quirked. "That would be news to them."

Brinnie stared after her as she walked away.

It wasn't far, so they walked back to Wraithwood together, including the strangers, except for one who drove their car. Brinnie stumbled along. It felt like her brain had decided to take a vacation. Mrs. Winslow gave her a hug. "Don't worry, dear. Everything's fine now. When we get back, I'll make a pot of soothing tea."

But it didn't feel like everything was fine. The FBI agents who weren't FBI agents arranged themselves around the group in formation as Uncle Merlin led the way. They looked ready for another attack. Each chirping bird and swaying branch was the gray-eyed man, come back to take vengeance.

The young man whose pistol had exploded marched dutifully next to Brinnie. But when they began to draw near to Wraithwood, he started weaving back and forth like a drunk and wandered toward the side of the path.

Uncle Merlin glanced back. "Oh." He stopped. "What is your name?"

"Quentin Morain."

"Quentin Morain, you are a welcome guest at Wraithwood Estate."

He immediately began walking in a straight line again. "Thank you, sir."

"I forgot," said not-Agent Haberdash. "He's an apprentice."

"Indeed." Uncle Merlin nodded, as if any of this made sense.

Brinnie looked around to see if anyone else found this strange. No one seemed to have noticed, but Ms. Tynsdale was giving Uncle Merlin a look that should have set him on fire.

When they got back to the house, the group began trooping inside, but Ms. Tynsdale pulled Uncle Merlin aside. "I *told* you we shouldn't go. Now will you listen to me when I tell you to stop taking risks like this? Look what happened! We almost gave away Wraithwood!"

"Do you think I'm not as upset as you are?" Uncle Merlin asked, his voice quiet and controlled—too controlled. "I almost lost my niece." He shook his head. "But we can't live our lives in fear."

As Brinnie stepped inside, she heard Ms. Tynsdale mutter, "You're impossible." Then both of them followed Brinnie in.

Brinnie's gaze flitted over the busy scene. Miss Burtle strode out of the room with a phone to her ear while Mrs. Winslow put a kettle on. One of the newcomers was running a long, thin wand over the walls of the kitchen, while another stood on a chair, using his wand to scan the ceiling. Mr. Winslow seemed to be warning the man standing on a chair that the chair had a bad leg, right when the bad leg gave out and sent the man crashing to the floor.

"Excuse me," Uncle Merlin asked, "but may I ask what is going on in here?"

Agent Haberdash tapped a pen on her clipboard. "After Riverdell, the DI sent out teams to conduct safety checks on all estates. We need to make sure everything is up to par."

"I could tell you myself that there's nothing wrong with the house and save you the trouble," Uncle Merlin said.

She shrugged. "Routine safety checks. It's standard. Although..." She looked at her clipboard. "It looks like Wraithwood is thirty years overdue."

At that moment a yell and the sound of a slamming door rang out from the front of the house. Brinnie jumped. Uncle Merlin looked at Agent Haberdash. "Did you tell your apprentice about the door?"

"I don't know. Why?"

"Because he just took an unexpected trip to Louisiana." Uncle Merlin turned and strode through the dining room door.

Brinnie leaned against the wall, trying to make the room stop spinning.

Agent Haberdash shook her head in exasperation and dug into her bag for an envelope. "While the house is being inspected, I have a message for Tynsdale from Castelon."

"Oh, wonderful," Ms. Tynsdale said wryly, taking the envelope from Agent Haberdash. She ripped it open and scanned the contents.

The man who had collapsed the chair had found another one and was scanning the ceiling again while Mr. Winslow started screwing the chair leg back into its socket.

"Oh, please. Haven't we gone over this?" Ms. Tynsdale rolled her eyes. "I told you all 'no' a month ago, and I haven't changed my mind. It's a suicide mission."

"You did so well last time..." Haberdash began.

"I almost got killed last time."

"It's a risk we all take."

"Except for the Council, sitting comfortably in Castelon, sending everyone else off."

Haberdash frowned ominously. "The Council is what keeps all of us alive."

"Of course, it is. What I'm saying is that I don't have to do their dirty work if I don't want to." Ms. Tynsdale tossed the envelope on the kitchen table. "Their plan is just plain stupid."

"I don't know about you, but where I come from cowards are frowned upon."

"Ha! Cowards. I don't mind risking my own skin. I've done it hundreds of times. But I do mind risking the rest of our skins."

Brinnie was distracted by a small drama playing out in the corner. The man standing on a chair wobbled on his toes on the very edge of the chair, stretching out to wave his wand above the cupboards. Predictably, the chair tipped and raised quite a clatter. Everyone stopped and looked at him. "Sorry," he muttered, clambering to his feet and setting it back up again.

Brinnie fought the urge to giggle maniacally. *I'm losing it.*

Agent Haberdash turned back to Ms. Tynsdale. "So, you're sure that's your decision?"

"Yep."

She frowned at her clipboard and pinched the bridge of her nose. "And what should I tell the Council?"

"Tell them to go boil their heads and see if it loosens up their brains."

"I don't understand." She shook her head. "You excelled at the Academy."

Brinnie blinked. *Like a military academy?*

"Look, I'm as much of a patriot as the next person, but this plan is idiotic. If they let me do it my way—"

"It's already been discussed." Agent Haberdash gave a long-suffering sigh. "It's too risky."

"Oh, yes, much more risky than *their* plan." Ms. Tynsdale snorted.

"Tea, anyone?" Mrs. Winslow interrupted.

Brinnie shuffled across the room and plopped into a chair, her fingers tracing the bandage around her arm. Tea. Maybe that would help her feel better. Maybe something would make sense. Mrs. Winslow gave her a sympathetic look as she poured a cup of tea and slid it in front of her. Brinnie could only manage a grateful half-smile.

She scalded her tongue when the dining room door slammed open, revealing Uncle Merlin and Quentin Morain. Mud caked Quentin up to his torso and Uncle Merlin's pants to the knee. Uncle Merlin's lips were pressed in a thin line.

Quentin bounced, eyes wide. "The front door leads to the bayou!"

Uncle Merlin simply looked at him for a moment. "Would you like a change of clothes?" he asked finally.

Quentin glanced at Agent Haberdash, who nodded. "Yes, please."

Miss Burtle walked in holding the phone. She handed it to Uncle Merlin. "It's Ravendal. He wants to talk to you."

"Oh, wonderful. An interrogation." He sighed. "Tom, could you please find something for Morain to wear?"

Mr. Winslow set aside the broken chair. "Sure will."

As Uncle Merlin walked away with the phone and Quentin and Mr. Winslow went off to find dry clothing, the wand men moved on to the dining room. Agent Haberdash turned hawklike attention to Brinnie. "And who are you?"

"Brynna. Brynna Lane."

She tapped her pen. "I suppose the better question is, what are you?"

"Um..." *I wish I knew.*

"Human," Ms. Tynsdale jumped in.

Agent Haberdash made a note. "From where?"

Brinnie saw Ms. Tynsdale and Mrs. Winslow flash each other a panicked look across the table. "Lyle," Ms. Tynsdale said.

"Arizona," Brinnie answered at the same time.

Ms. Tynsdale winced.

Haberdash looked up from her clipboard swiftly. "What?"

"She came from Arizona originally, then to Lyle," Ms. Tynsdale amended.

Brinnie tried to make eye contact. *What are you doing?*

"And how did you come to Wraithwood?" Agent Haberdash asked her.

"Summer job," Ms. Tynsdale replied before she could respond.

"Won't you let her speak? What's your position here, Brynna?"

"Uh." She glanced at Ms. Tynsdale and Mrs. Winslow. "General helper, I guess."

"Do you know?"

"Know...what?"

Brinnie looked over in time to see Ms. Tynsdale wince again.

"I knew it was a mistake to leave Wraithwood unattended," Haberdash commented. "This is a clear violation of policy. She needs to go back to Lyle immediately. We'll take her back with us and drop her off at home. She is not allowed back at Wraithwood under any circumstances."

Brinnie's mouth opened and closed. Mrs. Winslow and Ms. Tynsdale glanced at each other.

"That won't be necessary. We can—" Ms. Tynsdale started.

"Absolutely not. We will take care of it," Haberdash interrupted, making notes.

As she did, she knocked a wand like those the two men had off the top of her clipboard. It landed next to Brinnie and started wiggling. It reminded her of a lizard tail, so she scooted away, but it wriggled closer to her. Agent Haberdash looked up from her notes and raised an eyebrow. "What..." she began.

At that moment, one of the men walked in holding a cell phone. "Bad news. There was an attack on Iriselie."

"Oh, no!" Mrs. Winslow exclaimed.

Ms. Tynsdale half stood. "Is there anything we can do?"

The man shook his head. "The battle's over. They attacked a few hours ago, but they couldn't seem to get past the outskirts, so they burned a few houses and left."

Who did? Why? Brinnie felt a scream bubbling inside her.

"Any casualties?" asked Agent Haberdash.

"No dead. A few wounded."

She shook her head. "I need to check the boundaries as soon as possible. Where is Ludovic?"

"Here." Uncle Merlin entered with Miss Burtle, to whom he handed the phone. "I suppose you need to inspect the protection spell. I'll show you around the perimeter if you would like."

"That would be excellent." Haberdash grabbed her bag and they headed for the door.

Brinnie lingered for a moment and glanced around. All parties were either deep in conversation or otherwise engaged. She slipped out the door unobserved.

She stayed far enough behind not to be noticed as Uncle Merlin led the way down the path to the gate, then out past it. Brinnie stuck to the tree line. Uncle Merlin and Agent Haberdash followed the road, not speaking, until he stopped and pointed. "See that tall tree? That's a boundary marker."

He turned around then, and his eyes went straight to Brinnie. She caught her breath. *Don't see me, don't see me.* But he simply continued gazing in her direction, a puzzled expression on his face, before turning around again. Brinnie's breath escaped with a whoosh.

Agent Haberdash nodded. Muttering under her breath, she drew a circle on the ground, pulled a container out of her bag, and shook its powdery contents into her hand. She threw the bright pink powder straight up into the air. Some of it gravitated toward where Uncle Merlin was standing, but most of it lined the edge of the circle pointing farther down the road. Ms. Haberdash took four steps forward and repeated the process. This time the powder landed back the way she had come. She kept drawing circles and throwing powder in between her original circles until the powder she threw in the air floated down and landed directly in the middle of the circle. "Right here," she announced.

She pulled something that looked like a mini fire extinguisher out of her bag. Slowly, holding down the button, she sprayed from where the powder landed all the way up as high as she could reach. The device emitted a pink gas. Some of it drifted off, but most seemed to adhere to an invisible wall, forming a pink column.

She continued spraying until she had painted a wide section of wall. Then she leaned forward to examine the floating pink gas. She felt it with her fingers. After a long time, she nodded. "Strong. No defects in the spell. And since this is on a road, it should be the weakest part."

Uncle Merlin frowned. "I looked at the reports for Riverdell. The spell was checked only a week before Riverdell was attacked, and there was nothing wrong with it."

Ms. Haberdash focused with exaggerated intensity on taking notes. "Much can change in a week."

"And a whole spell can deteriorate completely?" He shook his head. "They have some sort of tool to break through the spell."

"No, no." She put away her clipboard. "Then we would be completely vulnerable."

"Just because we don't want it to be true, it isn't? The evidence is there. And as far as I know, there's only one way to get past a protection spell. The Master Key."

"Yes, as far as we know." She began waving a wand above her circles. The pink dust floated up and stuck to the wand, and she brushed it back into the container.

"Then they must have the Master Key."

She shook her head as she held the fire extinguisher device backward, sucking up the pink gas. "Castelon is not officially commenting on the Riverdell attack."

"Ah." Uncle Merlin paced slowly. "But, you see, I need to know everything to be able to lead wisely at Wraithwood. I know it's an embarrassment to lose something like the Master Key"—Ms. Haberdash made to cut in, but he kept talking—"but if they have the Key, we need to know."

Ms. Haberdash sighed, screwing the lid back on the container. "No one's contacted you?"

He raised an eyebrow. "I don't hear much from Castelon these days."

"Well..." She glanced around, as if checking for eavesdroppers. Brinnie ducked behind a tree. "You didn't hear this from me. The Master Key went missing a month ago—or at least, we noticed it was gone a month ago. No one knew where it went. We've had people out all over searching for it. But it wasn't until Riverdell that we got a clue."

"It was stolen by enemy agents," Uncle Merlin guessed.

"Yes, we think so."

He let out a long breath. "So nowhere is safe until we find the Master Key, is that it?"

"It might be a coincidence, but yes, I think that would be safe to assume."

"Any leads, then?"

"None. That's why we want Tynsdale."

"Ah." The two of them started walking back toward the house, and Brinnie followed. "She said no?"

"Yes."

He nodded. "Did you tell her why you needed her?"

"Of course not. She thinks it's routine."

"If you told her the truth, she might change her mind."

"We can't afford to do that."

Uncle Merlin stopped, and Brinnie pulled up short as well. "Don't you trust her?"

Ms. Haberdash hesitated. "Right now, we don't trust much of anyone. But really, would you trust her?"

"With my life," he asserted. He continued walking. "But seeing as Castelon suspects me of stealing the Master Key, I doubt they would take my word for it."

"What—what do you mean?" A guilty look crept over her face.

"Scans of the entire estate are not usual procedure, are they? They're searching for the Master Key."

Which is what?

She looked sheepish. "I assure you, you're not being singled out. Everyone is suspected."

"Hmm." His brows rose. "Except that Wraithwood was the first estate to be searched."

"It's hard to doubt your loyalty, but you have to realize that of anyone, it would be easiest for you to pull off a theft."

It would be easy for him to pull off anything, Brinnie realized. From what she had seen, he could appear anywhere, then disappear before anyone could catch him. A chill ran down her spine. How well did she really know him?

"Is that truly what they think?" he asked with a surprised laugh. "Even if I wanted to, I couldn't transport the Master Key."

"That's not all. You were in Castelon for the first time in ten years a month and a half ago, right before the Key went missing. You have to admit that seems a little suspicious."

He waved a hand. "There's an easy explanation for that. The only time I'm obligated to come to Castelon is for the Decennial Masters Council, which, as you might recall, was a month and a half ago. But why are you telling me this?"

"Because quite honestly, I think the idea of your stealing the Master Key is ridiculous, and we should be asking for your help in finding it, not suspecting you of hiding it." She shrugged. "But my opinion isn't worth much in Castelon. I'm only following orders here, whether I agree with them or not. And you do have a number of violations."

"I do?"

They stopped outside the kitchen door. Brinnie remained hidden around the side of the washroom. "That girl, for one. You can't keep an uninformed human here."

"Hmm." Brinnie peeked around the corner to see Uncle Merlin gazing straight toward her. She ducked back, her heart pounding. "She needed a place to stay. Just for the summer."

"You can't do that. She needs to go. I suppose her being here means that the people of Lyle know about Wraithwood?"

"Everyone here has been friendly with the people of Lyle for decades."

She shook her head. "That's completely out of keeping with policy."

"Indeed."

She looked to the sky as if for patience. "As soon as all this other business is cleared up..." She didn't finish her sentence. Instead, she pulled another envelope from her bag and handed it to Uncle Merlin. "I hate to be the bearer of bad news."

He didn't open it. "What is it?"

"An order from Castelon. A spellcaster is coming within twenty-four hours. Everyone capable of transport is being ordered to forfeit their magic to a restraining spell."

"What! For what purpose?"

"They're hoping to slow down the thief and any accomplices, if they are among our ranks."

"But the enemy already has the Key."

"It isn't likely to have reached Mordizan yet, or all defenses would

127

be down. So it must still be in translation."

He sighed. "I understand. Shall we go in?"

They both went inside. Brinnie waited a moment, then slipped in after them.

"I let them in the library," Miss Burtle was informing Uncle Merlin. She stood in the kitchen with Uncle Merlin, Ms. Haberdash, and Ms. Tynsdale. "But they haven't gotten to the third floor of it yet."

"Good. That will need supervision." Uncle Merlin turned to Ms. Haberdash. "I assume you'll be on to the next estate once you're finished with this one?"

"Yes, as quickly as possible."

"Would you like to travel by door?"

She shook her head. "Thank you for the offer, but we have a lot of equipment in the car. Besides, it's not too far to Habrin."

"In that case, would you mind giving the Winslows a ride out to our vehicle? We should take care of the battle scene before anyone finds it. I'll meet you there."

"We need to bring Brynna back to Lyle as well, remember," Ms. Haberdash said.

Brinnie didn't much like the idea of being dumped off in Lyle. "Um, I'd rather go tomorrow or something," she piped up. "I need to pack and stuff."

Ms. Haberdash sighed. "All right. We don't have time to waste. But Ludovic." She pointed her pen at him. "Make sure you send her home."

He made eye contact with Brinnie. "That is my full intention."

She sensed his warning. *"Behave yourself. I'm sending you home to your mother at the end of the summer in one piece."* He raised an eyebrow at her, and she knew he was perfectly aware she had been watching everything. Her cheeks heated.

Ms. Haberdash pulled out the wand from her clipboard. "If you don't mind, I'll start inspecting upstairs to get this over with more quickly."

"Of course." Uncle Merlin gestured toward the door. "Go right ahead."

He waited until the door swung shut behind her, then looked at Miss Burtle. "What are the Winslows doing in the dining room?"

"Trying to catch the chairs."

"What?"

Ms. Tynsdale smirked. "A bit of levitation gone wrong."

He shook his head. "We'll take care of that later. For now, we need to gather everyone together. Including you, Brynna. Unfortunately, you'll be needed if this is going to work."

"About time," Miss Burtle muttered.

He turned to Ms. Tynsdale. "I believe you will enjoy this, Lydia." He smiled slightly. "We have a bit of plotting to do."

Chapter Fifteen

UNCLE MERLIN LED MISS BURTLE, MS. TYNSDALE, and Brinnie into the dining room.

Brinnie stared.

The heavy dining room chairs floated around the room, some near the ceiling and others drifting just out of reach. Mr. Winslow clung for dear life to the leg of one of the chairs that was floating in circles about fifteen feet up, while Mrs. Winslow tried to snag it with a broom, even though her broomstick didn't reach. "Hold on, dear!"

He yanked downward. "Reckon the magic can't last much longer."

Uncle Merlin shook his head. "Well. This is inconvenient, to say the least."

Ms. Tynsdale sighed. "I suppose there's nothing for it." She morphed into a seven-foot-tall man wearing a purple basketball jersey. She strode over to where Mr. Winslow was flying, jumped like she was about to make a slam dunk, and grabbed him by the ankle. With much pulling, she heaved both him and the chair back to earth, although he had to release it once he reached the ground. It went floating away again.

Ms. Tynsdale changed back into her normal form.

"Thank you," Mr. Winslow said. Then, with a twinkle in his eye, "You ever thought about trying out for the—"

"No," she said shortly, although Brinnie caught a hint of a smile.

"Thank you, Lydia," Uncle Merlin said, then addressed the entire group. "We have more pressing concerns than the chairs at the moment, and we don't have long to discuss. I need to outline the plan before our guests finish their work."

Ms. Tynsdale perched on the edge of the table, ignoring Miss Burtle's disapproving look. "What's going on?"

"The Master Key has been stolen."

Everyone's eyes widened. Miss Burtle sucked in a sharp gasp.

"They noticed it was missing about a month ago," he continued, "and after the Riverdell attack, it's thought the enemy has it. Unfortunately, Castelon believes I'm the one who stole it."

Ms. Tynsdale slapped the table. "That pack of dunderheads!"

If nothing else, her annoyance was a comforting confirmation that whatever else Brinnie's uncle was, he didn't seem to be a thief. Some sort of magical knife-wielding fighter, but not a thief. *Small blessings.*

"In any case, they're searching the house for it now." Uncle Merlin's nose wrinkled in distaste. "And a spellcaster is coming within twenty-four hours to put a restraining spell on me."

"We can't let that happen!" Mrs. Winslow exclaimed.

"Precisely. Which is why I've come up with a plan. The investigators have agreed to take you two," he nodded to the Winslows, "to the battle scene to take care of it. I've told them I will meet you there. Tom, I'll need you to replace the tires and do what you can to get the car running again. I'm sure our levitating friend Morain will help you with the tree."

At this, everyone's eyes went to the floating chairs.

"I advise you to stand back for that bit. That might be the worst part of this plan," Uncle Merlin conceded. "Call when you arrive, and Lydia and I will come to help. Once the investigators are out of sight, you and Lydia will go to Lyle. We'll need enough supplies to last at least a week or two, so get whatever you think we'll need for a siege."

"A siege?" Mrs. Winslow repeated.

"Indeed. I will return here, but call if you run into any trouble, and I will come. Lydia, you will be in charge of protecting them until I arrive if something does arise."

She smirked and twirled a knife. *Where did she pull that from?* "Got it."

"Good. Edna, Brynna, you will assist me in the library."

"In the library? Doing what?" Miss Burtle asked.

"Sifting through the Wraithwood Scrolls. I'm going to raise the Maze."

Silence.

Then Ms. Tynsdale exclaimed, "Are you crazy?" at the same time

Mrs. Winslow gasped, "Why, you can't do that!"

Mr. Winslow held up his hands. "No need to be hasty."

"You can't go raising the Maze for no reason." Miss Burtle shook her head.

Uncle Merlin waited out the exclamations. "On the contrary, it is quite necessary. The Master Key is missing. That means for the time being, we can consider the protection spell useless. And once Lydia and I depart, that would leave you completely vulnerable."

"Depart? Where are you going?" Mrs. Winslow asked.

"To find the Master Key, of course." Ms. Tynsdale turned to Uncle Merlin. "Am I right?"

"Quite right," he agreed. "And though Wraithwood certainly isn't the largest estate, if the enemy has any sense, it will be their next target. Think what they could do with the Scrolls."

Mrs. Winslow shuddered. "But there must be a better way. Raising the Maze..."

If even Mrs. Winslow was afraid, this Maze didn't sound appealing. But Uncle Merlin remained stoic. "All will be well. By the time you return, we will have found the scroll we need, and I will be ready to raise the defenses. As long as you remain in the house and on the grounds, you will be completely safe, and the enemy will be incapable of reaching you. That will leave Lydia and me to search without worrying if Wraithwood is under attack."

"Castelon isn't going to be happy," Miss Burtle remarked.

"Ha!" Ms. Tynsdale laughed. "That's the best part of this crazy scheme." She sobered. "Well, I have to admit the Maze is the only chance we've got. Let's do it."

The Winslows exchanged a look, then nodded.

"Fine," Miss Burtle sighed.

Brinnie finally had the chance to speak. "What's the Maze?"

Uncle Merlin looked grim. "You'll see soon enough."

Brinnie scowled. *Descriptive.*

He turned to Mr. Winslow. "Is there anything you'll need to bring to make repairs?"

"If we're done with the planning, I'll go pack a toolbox now."

"Excellent. I believe I should go oversee the inspectors in the library. They shouldn't be left unattended."

Miss Burtle looked up at the floating chairs. "Agreed. What are we going to do about these?"

Uncle Merlin frowned. "The magic should wear off eventually. But we could ask Morain to reverse it."

"Not a good idea," Ms. Tynsdale advised.

Uncle Merlin's moustache twitched. "Then I suppose we'll have to be patient."

Everyone scattered to their various tasks. Mr. Winslow went out to the shed and Mrs. Winslow headed off to write a grocery list. Miss Burtle and Uncle Merlin left for the library, leaving Brinnie standing awkwardly, wondering what she was supposed to be doing.

Ms. Tynsdale hopped down from the table. "Do you know where I could find a large mirror?"

"There's one in my room you could use."

"Perfect. Lead on."

Brinnie pushed open the door to her room. Silly as it was, the familiar surroundings felt odd. Mom, Dad, and Anna smiled at them from the picture frame Brinnie had set on the dresser, their expressions vacant and oblivious to the magical woman trailing her. Her shoes in the corner with soles perpetually stained with red Arizona dirt, a favorite pair of jeans tossed on the bed in anticipation of her return, seemed ridiculously incongruous to whatever was going on downstairs.

Ms. Tynsdale made a beeline for the mirror. "Hmm. Let's see." Her red hair melted into dark brown and grew until it hung a couple of inches past her shoulders. Her eyes changed from blue to brown with slight wrinkles at the edges, and her face elongated. She stretched taller and slimmer. Her purple suit became a dark purple T-shirt with jeans, and her pumps turned into sneakers. She frowned at herself and her skin darkened slightly. In the end, she looked like someone in her late forties. "Now for a voice." She proceeded to utter nonsense phrases over and over in slightly different voices until she hit upon one that she repeated twice. She turned to Brinnie. "What do you think?"

Brinnie blinked. "Um...good?"

She turned back to the mirror. "What's wrong with it?"

What's wrong is that you change into random people. That's not normal. "Nothing. I just don't know what look you were going for."

"I need to blend in. In Lyle. Do I look normal?"

"I think so."

"Good. I don't usually do normal very well."

Brinnie raised an eyebrow and suppressed a snort. *Understatement.*

Ms. Tynsdale glanced over her shoulder. "You know, you could do with a bit of an appearance change as well."

Brinnie looked down at her dirty, torn dress and bare feet. "Oh. Yeah, probably."

As Brinnie pulled open a dresser drawer, Ms. Tynsdale examined herself in the mirror, twisting and moving. "So, what's my name?"

Brinnie paused in her quest for a clean T-shirt. "Um, Cindy, uh..."

"Johnson. Generic." She nodded. "I'm Cindy Johnson, I'm forty-eight, and I live on a farm with my husband, two teenage daughters, and one son."

"Cool. But why?"

"If I'm going into town with the Winslows, I don't want any of the townspeople informing the enemy I was there. I need a different identity. And I like getting fully into character."

Brinnie clutched the clean shirt. "I thought they got arrested."

"So did the police. That was the point."

"So...they didn't?"

"Of course not. Fake FBI, fake arrest."

"Oh." *This feels like a fever dream.*

She nodded at herself in the mirror. "I've got this one down. I think I should be able to change into it again fairly easily." With that, she morphed into her usual form.

Brinnie tried to distract herself from the fact that all of the attackers on the road were still at large. "Do you have a, you know, normal self? Like, a true form or something?"

"Yes, of course. Thank you for the use of your mirror." She strode toward the door.

"No problem." Brinnie wasn't about to let it go that easily, though.

Her curiosity was piqued. "Are you in your, uh, true form, right now?"

"Of course not." She stopped and fluffed her bob. "Do you think this hair color is natural? It took me a while to figure out how to grow it. Someone must have it, but I haven't seen it yet. I'll see you downstairs." She turned again to leave.

"But how do you know what you really look like? How do you know you're not in another form?"

She sighed, pausing in the doorway. "I *know* what I really look like. And if I ever forgot, all I would have to do is fall asleep."

"Fall asleep?" Brinnie remembered Ms. Tynsdale muttering something about that before. *Stupid magic. Doesn't work when you're sleeping.*

"I revert to my birth form when I fall asleep, since I'm not awake to keep the magic going."

"So..."

"Yes, yes, that was my true form you saw in the kitchen the other day, and no, I *don't* think I should stay in it more often, and before you ask, I'm actually the same age as your mother." She put a hand on her hip. "Did I answer all your questions?"

Brinnie realized her mouth was hanging open and snapped it shut. "Do you read minds, too?"

"No." She raised an eyebrow. "And yes, I knew your mother very well."

"You do read minds!"

She laughed. "I anticipate obvious questions." She waved. "Thanks, again. I'm going to see what Haberdash is up to. Probably making a mess of the testing rooms."

Brinnie would rather ask more questions—preferably about the Master Key, the Maze, and magic—but she didn't. Instead, she changed into jeans and a T-shirt. She looked in the mirror. *I look like a dumpster fire.* She ran a brush through her hair and glanced at the bandage around her right arm. She realized it didn't hurt anymore. Curious, she unwound the bandage and peeled off the gauze.

Her breath caught. Instead of revealing a bloody wound, the lines were closed and slightly raised. They were silvery in color and almost seemed to glow. The largest slash ran in a straight line about four inches down her upper arm. On either side, two lines sloped down slightly from a place nearer the top of the line, from which two more lines came down. It looked like either a sword or a cross with the crosspiece broken—or both.

She traced it with her finger, to make sure it was really there. She remembered what Ms. Haberdash had said about an enchanted blade. No ordinary knife would make a mark like that.

Brinnie sat on the edge of her bed and stared at herself in the mirror. She didn't look any different, besides the scar. No sign she had almost been killed in a magical battle and now seemed to be participating in some sort of plot against what appeared to be magical police. There was magic everywhere—floating chairs, magic wands, shapeshifting, disappearing, spells. She didn't know what was more difficult to accept—the terror of the battle or the strangeness of the magic.

There was still so much she didn't understand, and that was becoming an increasingly dangerous position to find herself in. Who was the enemy, and why were they at war? How on earth did no one know that magic was real? Why did Mom run away? What was the Master Key? Which secrets were worth keeping, and from whom?

She got up and lifted the picture from her dresser, running her fingers over the frame. Anna, the smart one, would be better at this. In the picture, Mom's arm around Anna was loose and comfortable, her smile easy, mouth slightly open as if she'd been laughing.

Mom never looked like that around her second daughter.

Brinnie purposely brought a picture she wasn't in, one where she wouldn't have to see Mom's tight hand on her shoulder or forced smile, always ready for Brinnie to do...something. Mess up somehow. Brinnie wasn't even sure what she might do, but Mom was always there to make sure it *didn't* happen, that Brinnie was always perfectly behaved and composed.

But Mom wasn't here to make those decisions. Brinnie took stock. Whatever the Master Key was, it was important, and Uncle Merlin needed to get it back. And judging by what happened on the road, his enemies were some nasty people. She'd rather be helping Uncle Merlin than them.

She replaced the picture and wrapped her arm again as best she could with one hand. The bandage wasn't necessary anymore, but at least it covered the strange mark. *I guess I'll be wearing longer sleeves until it heals up.* On the other hand, it could be a pretty cool tattoo. She bit back a rebellious smirk at the idea and headed out the door.

In the library, investigators Morain and Thomas swept the second level, waving their wands over the bookshelves. Miss Burtle watched anxiously, wincing as Thomas put his feet on a shelf to reach higher. Uncle Merlin was nowhere to be seen.

Miss Burtle noticed Brinnie and came down the stairs. "Where's Tynsdale?"

"She said she went to check on Ms. Haberdash."

Miss Burtle nodded. "They've almost finished the entire house. Stay close. We'll need you soon."

Uncle Merlin, Ms. Tynsdale, and Ms. Haberdash entered from the main doors. "I'm sure it will be a nightmare," Ms. Haberdash was saying. Her eyes locked on Brinnie. "Ah! Exactly what I need. A human stabilizer. Come with us, please."

Brinnie exchanged a glance with Uncle Merlin. His lips twitched, but he nodded. "Okay." She followed Ms. Haberdash and Uncle Merlin up to the third level of the library.

Her eyes widened when they reached the top of the stairs. Bookshelves lined the walls, but not all of them held books. Many held scrolls, while others were piled with strange objects like rings, staffs, medallions, and even a broomstick. *A broomstick? You've got to be kidding me.* A diagram covered an open space on the wall, what looked like the floorplan of a four-story house and a map of the surrounding area. Small dots roamed the diagram. *Oh. It's a picture of Wraithwood.* Sure enough, most of the little dots were moving around in what had to be the library. *They must represent people.* It was a magical blueprint.

"This is going to be impossible," Ms. Haberdash muttered, looking down at the wand in her hand. It shook and wiggled like a squirming snake.

"I would have to agree with you," Uncle Merlin said. "Can you search up here at all?"

"Yes, but I'll have to do it manually." She put her wand away and instead closed her eyes, holding her hands out palms downward, like someone wading in the ocean running their hands along the waves. After a moment, she opened her eyes and looked at Uncle Merlin. "I don't think all of these are registered with Castelon." She waved to the strange assortment.

He put his hands in his pockets. "Probably not," he agreed.

She shook her head and resumed her odd search. She paced in front of the bookshelves with furrowed brow and pursed lips, touching things, often pausing and closing her eyes. She reached out toward a medallion.

"Don't touch that!" Uncle Merlin warned.

She snatched her hand away and raised an eyebrow. "Why do you have a cursed medallion?"

He shrugged. "Once I acquired it, I couldn't very well get rid of it. I wouldn't want it to fall into the wrong hands."

"Are there any other things I should know about?" she asked drily.

"Hmm." He pointed. "The black box releases a whirlwind, the blue ring will suck your magic, the red stone is called solid fire for a reason, the black stone causes amnesia, and the staff summons lightning."

Holy cow. Brinnie took a step back.

Ms. Haberdash pressed her lips together. "And you didn't think to tell me this before I started searching."

"My apologies." He looked genuinely sheepish. "I thought you would have known."

She shook her head. "Not immediately. I have to investigate each piece individually to determine specifics."

Her search continued. Brinnie kept her arms clapped to her sides but watched in fascination. How could Ms. Haberdash feel magic?

It took a while for her to make it all the way around the level. Brinnie debated the danger for several minutes before she sat in a chair, which luckily didn't turn her into a duck or incinerate her. *Why am I even up here?* She itched to explore the strange objects, but she wasn't in the mood to die.

Uncle Merlin pulled out his pocket watch to check the time. When Ms. Haberdash finally finished, he looked relieved.

"The Master Key, as I'm sure you're aware, is not here," she announced.

"Indeed."

"But there are many other very interesting objects that are certainly not registered."

"I've picked up a few things in my travels, I must admit. I bring them here to keep them from doing harm."

She narrowed her eyes. "They need to be registered. The magic up here is very unstable, even with a human stabilizer."

For some reason that made him smile slightly.

Probably because I'm apparently not *human, even if no one will tell me what I am.*

Maybe I'm a unicorn.

Brinnie snorted, and the two looked at her quizzically. She reddened. "Sorry." *I'm getting slap happy from stress. I need to get a grip.*

Uncle Merlin proceeded as if nothing had happened. "I shall register them at the earliest logical opportunity, I assure you."

Brinnie followed them back down the stairs. Ms. Haberdash gathered the other investigators, and the Wraithwooders and Ms. Tynsdale joined them in the kitchen. Brinnie saw them all giving each other meaningful looks and nods behind the backs of the investigators. Soon enough, the car pulled away, and the Winslows left with the investigators.

As soon as they were out of sight, Uncle Merlin said, "We must hurry. Come."

Brinnie, Miss Burtle, and Ms. Tynsdale followed him to the library and up, once again, to the third floor. Uncle Merlin led them to a section of the shelves devoted to scrolls that took up almost half the space. "It has no name on the ribbon, but the scroll we need is all about Wraithwood. It should be a smaller scroll. I'll start at the left end, Miss Burtle, you start at the right, and Lydia and Brinnie, you can start from the middle and work out toward us. Oh, and Brinnie." He reached into his pocket and pulled out what looked like a magnifying glass without the handle. "Use this to read."

"Um, thanks." Why was she the only one who needed a magnifying glass?

"Wouldn't it be easiest to find it alphabetically by author and title?" Ms. Tynsdale asked. "I thought that was how everything was usually organized in here."

Miss Burtle pursed her lips. "Everything on the first two levels. I don't dare come up here on my own."

Ms. Tynsdale's gaze ran over the strange objects. "I see. Probably wise."

They set to work. Brinnie skipped over the scrolls with names on the ribbons without pausing to read what they said. She pulled out one with no name and carefully unrolled it, holding onto the wooden handles that made the scroll look like two rolling pins covered in yellowed paper. Handwritten script in black ink flowed across the page. Brinnie squinted to make out the words *Historia Roma.* It didn't appear to be in English, but she was still pretty sure that meant "History of Rome." She put it back.

The next scroll she pulled out wasn't written in English either. In fact, the letters themselves were unrecognizable. "What language is this?"

Ms. Tynsdale leaned over. "The ancient language. You can use the translator stone to read it."

"What?"

"The glass," Uncle Merlin explained without looking up, one scroll in his hands and another tucked under his arm. "It works best if you hold it a few inches from the writing."

I don't think enlarging it is going to help me understand. Nevertheless, she held it over the first line.

A Guide to Casting Protection Spells, read the words under the glass.

Brinnie's eyebrows shot up. She pulled the glass away. There at the top of the page were a series of unrecognizable characters. Slowly, she slid the glass over them once again. Under the glass, the words were clear and understandable. Everywhere else, the characters remained the same. *Magic. Duh.* Though she was curious how protection spells were cast, this was not the scroll they needed, so she put it back.

All but a few of the unnamed scrolls were in what Brinnie assumed was the ancient language, since she had to use the glass to read. They had interesting titles, such as *The Founding of Castelon*; *Egyptian Wizards; The Case of the Master Key;* and *Advanced Spellcasting*, but none seemed to be about Wraithwood.

Finally, she came across one that didn't have a title even on the inside. She began to read. *"Wraithwood Estate has always been one of the most powerful estates, though not one of the most populated. However, it has always been somewhat shrouded in mystery. I, Dafydd, current Master of Wraithwood, undertake to record the various attributes and workings of the estate for the benefit of my sons and their sons thereafter."*

"I think I found it," she announced.

The other three gathered around. She handed Uncle Merlin the scroll and he looked it over. "Yes, indeed. Well done. Thank you, Brynna."

He took it to a table and spread it out. Miss Burtle and Ms. Tynsdale hovered on either side. "Hmm. The gardens, the Gate—the Gate is part of the Maze, I would think. Nothing, though."

Miss Burtle pointed. "The woods?"

There was silence for a moment as they all squinted at the scroll. "No. Dafydd was a notoriously unorganized record keeper, if I remember correctly." Uncle Merlin rolled the scroll to a new section. "No, this is all about the library."

Brinnie didn't know what to do now, so she stood and watched.

"The cellar? I didn't know Wraithwood had a cellar," Ms. Tynsdale remarked a moment later.

"Terrible place. It was closed off decades ago," Uncle Merlin said absentmindedly. He rolled the scroll once again. "Hmm. Defenses. Should be here."

"Nope. That man!" Ms. Tynsdale snorted. "He got distracted and started talking about the roof."

"Perhaps it's under streams and waterways," Miss Burtle said dryly.

Ms. Tynsdale smiled, scanning again. Then she stabbed her finger at the beginning of a line and broke into a laugh. "Ha! It is."

Miss Burtle shook her head with a disapproving frown. "Of all places."

Uncle Merlin's brow furrowed in concentration as he read. "Interesting. I'll need to study this. The instructions aren't exactly clear."

Ms. Tynsdale rolled her eyes. "Imagine that."

A phone rang, and Miss Burtle pulled out her cell. Just as she was about to flip it open, it started making chirping noises. She shook her head. "Too much magic up here."

"Surprised it's working at all," Ms. Tynsdale said.

Miss Burtle went downstairs. Ms. Tynsdale continued to lean over the scroll, her lips moving as she read. Uncle Merlin pointed to something and seemed to read it out loud, since whatever he said wasn't English. She shook her head and pointed to another line, reciting whatever it said there.

Brinnie tried to piece together what the "ancient language" might be. It didn't sound like Greek or Latin, which would have been her first guesses. Fascination bloomed as she realized that if magic was real, it might be a language entirely unknown to humankind.

Miss Burtle returned a few minutes later. "They're ready for you."

"Good." Uncle Merlin rolled up the scroll. He tilted his head, indicating Brinnie. "The safest place for you two will be on the second or third floor. Lock all the doors, the front included, and if anyone comes, let them believe the house is empty. We'll be back as soon as we can."

Miss Burtle nodded, her jaw set in a firm line.

Uncle Merlin looked at Brinnie for a moment as if he wanted to say something, but he didn't. Instead, he turned to Ms. Tynsdale. "Shall we?"

She nodded. All of them went downstairs to the great hall, where Uncle Merlin and Ms. Tynsdale linked arms and stepped through the door. Once they were through, Miss Burtle locked it behind them.

"How will Uncle Merlin get back in?"

"He doesn't need to come through a door," Miss Burtle replied, as if this was something obvious.

Which, Brinnie supposed, it should have been, considering all the teleporting she'd been seeing him doing. *Magic—remember, that thing that exists now? Right.*

"Come on." Miss Burtle went first to the library and locked that door, then to the kitchen. After locking the kitchen door as well, she picked up two large pokers from the fireplace and handed one to Brinnie. "Just in case." Then, without another word, she led the way to the third floor.

Miss Burtle positioned herself in front of one of the windows in the sitting area and stared out toward the road to Lyle, eyes steely.

Brinnie clutched her fire poker. "What would happen if those men did come here?"

"Nothing." She didn't peel her gaze from the window. "We would hide until your uncle returned."

Oh, joy. Then we can all die. "What good could he do by himself against them all?"

She did glance Brinnie's way for a moment at that. "What good? A lot, I would say. Attacking on the road is one thing, but only a fool would face a Master on his own estate."

"Oh." *That literally means nothing to me.* None of it did. "What if they come before he gets back, and they find us? What would they do?"

"I don't know. Stop asking so many questions."

Brinnie tried to keep the quaver out of her voice. "Would they kill us?"

Miss Burtle sighed. "You sound as if you think killing us is the worst thing they could do."

Brinnie's eyes widened. That was far from comforting. She gripped the poker tighter and turned her gaze to the stairs. She doubted anyone could sneak past Miss Burtle's watchful eye, but she wasn't taking any chances.

Chapter Sixteen

FOR WHAT FELT LIKE HOURS, THOUGH couldn't have been more than fifteen minutes, Miss Burtle stared out the window and Brinnie watched the stairs, her ears pricked for any noise. When thunder rumbled, she nearly jumped out of her skin. The overcast sky grew darker.

Suddenly, someone appeared at the top of the stairs. Brinnie screeched and raised her fire poker before she relaxed.

Miss Burtle whirled around, her own poker at the ready. When she saw it was only Uncle Merlin, she shook her finger at Brinnie and exclaimed, "Brynna Gwynneth Lane! If you ever scream like that again, so help me, I'll..." She seemed unable even to state what exactly she would do.

Brinnie grimaced. "Sorry."

"My apologies." Uncle Merlin looked at his pocket watch. "I wanted to let you know I've returned and repairs are well under way. It was agreed it would be foolish to leave the two of you alone, so I've returned earlier than expected."

"Good." Miss Burtle still looked a bit shaken.

"If you'll excuse me, I must return to studying the scroll." With that, he disappeared.

Brinnie let the poker hang loose in her grip. If Uncle Merlin could refrain from startling her, she might even feel safe enough to return the poker to the fireplace now that he had returned. "Where did he go?"

"To the library, of course." Miss Burtle sighed. "I suppose we should see if we can help."

The two of them made their way down the stairs and around to the library. When they ascended to the third level, they found Uncle Merlin with the scroll in his hands, glancing from it to the blueprint on the wall. "The problem is, I don't know where the Wraith Wand is," he said over his shoulder.

Miss Burtle pursed her lips. "I may have mentioned it before..."

"Yes, I agree that I need to organize. I simply never have the time." He set the scroll down and began rifling through the shelves. "Unfortunately, I never saw my father use the wand, and I don't recall him ever telling me where it was."

Miss Burtle frowned in thought. "I would think it would be kept in a special place."

"Indeed." He pushed aside a pile of books. "However, the very informative yet rather disorganized Dafydd does not mention where that would be, only that it is needed."

"We'll help you look." Miss Burtle wagged her finger at Brinnie. "But you be very careful."

"Noted." Brinnie touched nothing as she peered behind shelves. Her eyes wandered to the blueprint on the wall. *It's too cliché.* "What about behind the map?"

Uncle Merlin grasped both sides of the huge frame holding the parchment and lifted it off the wall, exposing a rectangle of the wall a different color than that surrounding it, showing just how long it had hung there. But most importantly, the central wooden panel featured a prominent knot.

Uncle Merlin pushed on the knot. It sank in until it clicked, and he stepped back as the panels swung outward, revealing a glass case. Inside, standing up vertically, was a thin wood wand about two and a half feet long.

All those books with hidden doors behind paintings were right. *See, Mom—those mystery novels were good for something.*

"Excellent thinking, Brynna" Uncle Merlin opened the case and pulled out the wand before closing it and shutting the panels back in place. He set it next to the scroll and squinted at the text. "Now that I have it, I'll need to memorize what this says. It doesn't look like the raising of the Maze can be done in steps—and I don't want to ruin the scroll by taking it outside."

"Is there anything we can do in the meantime?" Miss Burtle asked. "Any supplies to gather?"

He ran a finger along the handwriting and shook his head. "The instructions are difficult to understand, but I don't think so. I'll let you know if I come across any. However..." He paused and glanced at Brinnie, then back at Miss Burtle. "If you would like to do something to occupy your time until the others return, I would appreciate it if you and Brynna ran some, ahem, experiments."

You're not sneaky.

"Me?" Miss Burtle exclaimed.

"You know how. I would rest easier when it comes time to depart if there was, ah, data."

Brinnie resisted rolling her eyes. Did he really think she didn't know what those "experiments" were at this point?

"Oh." Miss Burtle fidgeted with her skirt. "I suppose."

"Thank you." He was already half lost in his reading and hardly looked up. "I will let you know when they return, or if there is a situation you should be aware of."

Brinnie followed Miss Burtle back down the stairs, leaving Uncle Merlin to study the scroll. She glanced at the library door. "Shouldn't we be, you know, keeping watch or something?"

"We don't need to do that."

"But how will we know if the enemy is coming?"

She gave a flick of her hand. "Mr. Ludovic will tell us."

"Um...Isn't he studying?"

"Yes."

They passed through the great hall and began ascending the grand staircase. "Then how will *he* know?"

"So many questions," Miss Burtle snapped. "He would just know, of course."

Brinnie pondered for a moment. "Oh! The parchment. He would see them coming on there, wouldn't he?"

Miss Burtle ran a hand along the banister and then rubbed her fingers together, frowning at whatever invisible dust she'd found. "If he wanted to. But he doesn't need a magical parchment. He's the Master. He knows where everyone is on the estate when he chooses to."

Brinnie was getting the feeling "master" meant something more than just the owner of the property. "Like Santa," she blurted.

Miss Burtle stopped halfway up the stairs leading to the third floor. "What on earth do you mean?"

Brinnie's face heated. "You know. 'He sees you when you're sleeping and knows when you're awake.'"

"Santa isn't real." She turned and kept going. "And that is a most disturbing idea. Merlin doesn't *see* you, for goodness's sake. He simply knows where you are."

"And that's magic."

"Yes."

"Can you do magic?"

"No," she said shortly.

"Why not?"

"Most can't."

"But how come some people can?"

She stopped and put her hands on her hips. "Because they're wizards. Now stop with the questions. You aren't supposed to be asking them."

She couldn't help herself. "Why not?" she asked like a three-year-old.

"Because Merlin said so. Now come."

Miss Burtle opened one of the doors on the third floor. Inside, the floor and walls were covered in metal, and several fire extinguishers hung around the room.

But Brinnie was only sidetracked for a moment. She had stayed quiet long enough. If she could survive the battle on the road, she could survive Miss Burtle's glares. "Why does he say so? Why doesn't anyone want me to know anything?"

Miss Burtle's mouth set in a thin line. "Shall we begin the experiments?"

"Please." She heard Mom's voice. *For goodness' sake, don't whine, Brynna.* She adjusted her tone. "I'm sorry, but I don't understand anything. I don't know why people are fighting, or what the deal is with magic, or why we're trying to fool those FBI people who aren't FBI people, or why my mom didn't tell me about Wraithwood, or any of this. Is there anything you *can* tell me?"

"Are you done ranting?"

Brinnie scowled. "Yes."

"All the secrecy is for your own good." She jabbed a finger at

Brinnie. "Everyone is trying to keep you safe. Magic can be fascinating, but it can be extremely dangerous to be a wizard or even to be associated with wizards, especially right now. Your mother is determined that you will live life as a normal human, and Merlin has promised to abide by her decisions, and you should as well. That means not asking questions. Now, can we finally move on?"

"Just one question, please. Uncle Merlin is a wizard. Is my mom a wizard?"

"I never said that."

"But she is, isn't she?"

"I said nothing of the sort." Her footsteps echoed on the metal floor.

"But Mom and Uncle Merlin did."

The footsteps stopped. "When?"

"Um..." She had strayed into dangerous territory.

"Hmph. It doesn't matter. We have things to do." Miss Burtle strode to the single window and pulled aside heavy metal shutters. Outside, the sky loomed dark and ominous. "Now. For this experiment, you need to burn this." She pulled a scrap of paper from her skirt pocket and handed it to Brinnie.

"This is ordinary paper, right?"

"Yes."

I'm done playing these stupid games. "So, what are we trying to determine by burning a piece of paper?"

"You have to burn it with only the supplies you find in this room."

Brinnie looked around. "There's nothing in this room."

"I'll be in the safety booth." She retreated into a small, closed off room in the corner that Brinnie hadn't noticed before and shut the metal door. There seemed to be a small window through which she could see, but Brinnie couldn't see her through it.

"So, the only solution is magic?" Brinnie called after her. But Miss Burtle didn't seem to hear.

She thought back to the other two experiments. The only way she could have made it from one lighted square to another across the grid was to disappear and appear there, like Uncle Merlin. The only way she could have kept all of the papers in the air would be to create a whirlwind, like the man in the dining room. And the only way she could burn this piece of paper was to summon fire. *No one around here is half as sneaky as they think they are.* They weren't experiments at all. They were tests, the tests Mom and Uncle Merlin had talked about.

With that, she stared at the paper and thought about it catching on fire. She thought about heat, and flames, and the process of burning. She stared at it as hard as she could. When that didn't work, she tried squinting, then closing her eyes, imagining the paper bursting into flame.

Nothing happened. Evidently fire was not her talent.

"I don't think I'm a fire person," she called, looking at the booth.

Miss Burtle stepped out. "What?"

"A fire wizard. I'm not a fire wizard."

"Who said anything about fire wizards? I said burn the paper." She shook her head. "I think we're done with this experiment. Enough data gathered. Come." She strode out the door and into the hallway.

Brinnie followed down the hall and into another room dominated by a huge glass aquarium tank three quarters full of water. A metal ladder went up the outside and down into it.

"There are two different experiments we could do." Miss Burtle hardly looked at her. "Either you can see how long you can hold your breath, or you can try to fill that bucket in the corner with water from the tank without touching the bucket or the water."

"The second option sounds impossible."

"It isn't. But it's your choice."

Brinnie was sick of supposedly possible tasks. "How about holding my breath?"

"Then climb the ladder and get in the tank."

"In my clothes?"

"Well, I would prefer you kept them on."

No thank you. "How about option number two, then?"

"Go ahead."

Brinnie forced herself not to glare at Miss Burtle's grumpiness. Instead she looked from the bucket to the water. There really was no way to put water in the bucket without magic. She wondered how someone would go about performing this sort of magic. She thought back to what she knew about water from science class. But she couldn't think of anything that would produce the effect she wanted without manipulating several other factors, such as heat and air pressure. Then she had to laugh at herself. Of course, there wouldn't be a scientifically viable way. It was magic, after all.

Instead, she tried what she had tried before with fire. She thought about the water moving. She thought about it sloshing over the side of the tank, across the floor, and into the bucket. But no matter how many ways or how hard she thought about it, nothing happened. She even tried making hand motions, though she knew she must look ridiculous. But still, the water didn't move.

"I give up."

Miss Burtle crossed her arms. "You haven't tried for very long."

"Nothing's working. I can't think of anything else to try."

"You have to try for more than five minutes, at least."

Just as Brinnie was about to point out that there was no reason to try longer since there was nothing else to try, Uncle Merlin appeared in the doorway. She jumped. *Still getting used to his spontaneous arrivals.*

"They're back from Lyle."

"Good." Miss Burtle's tense shoulders relaxed slightly. "All three?"

"Yes. Plus two more."

"Two more? Who?"

He frowned. "Marcie and Quentin Morain."

"What! Why on earth..."

"My question exactly. I suppose we should go find out."

The three of them departed. *Finally.* Why was Miss Burtle so cranky about the tests?

Of course, she's almost always grumpy.

Outside, Mr. Winslow was pulling the car into the garage. A few seconds later, Ms. Tynsdale in her assumed form came jogging toward them. "We have a problem."

"So I've noticed." Uncle Merlin squinted past her. "What are they doing here?"

She heaved a dramatic sigh. "Morain has been sent to keep an eye on you and report your activities to Castelon."

His moustache twitched at her reaction. "Well, that makes things more difficult, though I did wonder why they didn't think of that before. You know how to handle that."

"And Marcie?" Miss Burtle asked.

"That's more complicated." Ms. Tynsdale glanced over her shoulder. "She saw us in town, said she was ready to come back to Wraithwood. She didn't recognize me, of course. The Winslows told her she could stay home for a while longer, but she didn't want to. She said some men had been in town, asking if anyone had been to Wraithwood. Apparently, she managed to evade them, but they're supposedly watching her house, waiting for her."

Miss Burtle sighed this time. "And you couldn't have tried a little harder to persuade her?"

Ms. Tynsdale crossed her arms and raised an eyebrow. Yes, Miss Burtle was *definitely* crankier than usual if she was going to pick a fight with Ms. Tynsdale.

"She said they gave her a bad feeling. *I* imagine they were probably agents of our enemy. We couldn't leave her in Lyle. Who knows what they might do to her?"

Uncle Merlin gave Miss Burtle a warning glance. "Unfortunate as it is, there does seem to be no alternative. She'll have to stay here, at least for now."

Miss Burtle's hackles seemed to lower as she processed logistics. "How are we going to keep her from seeing the Maze?"

Uncle Merlin frowned. "That, I don't know."

They went to help unload the groceries. As Miss Burtle pulled ahead, Uncle Merlin said under his breath to Brinnie, "Forgive her if she was less than pleasant earlier. She doesn't have the best of memories with the experiments."

Brinnie glanced at Miss Burtle's rigid back. "Why?"

He hesitated for a moment. "She was never able to complete any of the tasks."

He veered away, leaving Brinnie to ponder that. But she didn't have much time to think as Marcie jumped down from the car and waved at her. "Hey, there!"

"Hey!" She forced a smile. "Glad you're back."

Brinnie noticed a series of meaningful glances pass between Uncle Merlin and the Winslows. Uncle Merlin looked pointedly from Marcie, to the garage, to Quentin, to the outside.

"Oh, my!" Mrs. Winslow exclaimed. "I seem to have lost my earring somewhere in here."

"I'll help you find it," Marcie offered.

As Marcie moved toward the front of the vehicle, farther into the garage, Mr. Winslow began closing the barn doors. "I'll close this up before it rains. We can use the side door."

Brinnie stepped out of the way as the doors swung shut, leaving the Winslows and Marcie on the inside and everyone else outside.

Quentin nodded to Uncle Merlin. "Excuse me, sir, but I've been ordered to shadow you until the spellcaster arrives."

"Yes, so you have," Uncle Merlin agreed. "Unfortunately, I can't afford to be shadowed at the moment."

Ms. Tynsdale stepped behind Quentin and snagged the phone from his pocket, then stepped out of reach before he could react.

His mouth dropped open. "But...I...I thought you were innocent."

"I am." Uncle Merlin grimaced. "Which is why I need Castelon out of my hair for the time being."

Quentin snatched for the phone, but a swirl of dirt erupted from the ground and grabbed his arm as if in a giant fist. When Quentin tried to pull away, Brinnie saw Uncle Merlin flick his hand, and another column of dirt grasped Quentin's other arm.

Brinnie's jumped back, staring at Uncle Merlin. Her heart thumped. *That one's new.*

Quentin yanked against his unmoving restraints, eyes wide. "You can't get away with this. I'm supposed to call every hour and report. When I don't call, they'll know."

"I don't think we have a problem there." He looked at Ms. Tynsdale.

Smiling, she morphed from Cindy Johnson into an exact duplicate of Quentin Morain. "Hello, Department of Intelligence? This is Quentin Morain, reporting on Merlin Ludovic."

Quentin paled at the sound of her voice, exactly like his.

"You have three options," Uncle Merlin told him. "You can leave here and walk to Lyle where you can report me, by which time Wraithwood will be inaccessible. You can stay here as a hostage until we succeed in our venture, which may take a few weeks. Or, you can help us."

"I would never help you!"

"You wouldn't help find the Master Key?"

His brow knitted. "What?"

"Lydia and I are going to try to retrieve the Master Key from the enemy."

Quentin craned his neck toward Ms. Tynsdale as if for confirmation, and she nodded. He turned back to Uncle Merlin. "But you can't. The Council has ordered that you stay here."

"Sometimes authorities make mistakes, and obeying laws, in this case, could lead to all of our deaths. Now, can we please speak civilly without this?"

The dirt began to fall away. As soon as it was thin enough, Quentin made a grab for his phone. Grass shot up and entwined around his legs up to the knees, preventing him from moving. Uncle Merlin sighed. "It seems not."

Grass, too. What *didn't* Uncle Merlin control with magic? Quentin's resistance seemed increasingly ridiculous.

Quentin clenched his fists. "You can't win against Castelon. They'll stop you."

"I don't believe they can stop me if they don't know I need to be stopped. But my intentions are to help Castelon and all of the other estates." He pulled out his pocket watch. "But you really must make a choice. I haven't much time."

Instead of an answer from Quentin, a rock picked itself up off the ground and bobbed toward Uncle Merlin.

Uncle Merlin raised an eyebrow at it. "Is that supposed to have hit me? That would have been uncalled for." He plucked it out of the air and dropped it on the ground.

Quentin burned red in what seemed to be an equal measure of embarrassment and anger. "I know what you're doing! You stole the

Key and this is all an act. Well, Castelon is going to find out and—"

"Why on earth would I want to steal the Key?" Uncle Merlin said. "Now, make a decision or I will be forced to make one for you. You can serve Castelon better by assisting us than by trying to keep us from helping."

"It's for power! That's why you're stealing the Key. I won't help you—"

His eyebrows rose in amusement. "Indeed. My insatiable appetite for power is why I've avoided becoming a Council member for decades."

Ms. Tynsdale snorted.

Miss Burtle sighed. "How long are we going to drag this along?"

"Fair point. Time has run out." Uncle Merlin stepped forward.

Quentin flinched back. "What are you going to do to me? No—" His sentence cut off as Uncle Merlin put a hand on his shoulder and they both disappeared.

Brinnie looked at Ms. Tynsdale. "Where did they go?"

"Through the door, first, of course." She slipped Quentin's phone into her pocket. "After that, I have no idea. Somewhere we can keep Morain until the Maze is up."

"But he won't be hurt?"

"Morain? Of course not. Just held captive for a while."

Miss Burtle shook her head with a frown. "Well, that was dramatic. Nothing like flaunting orders, obstructing the law, and kidnapping to add to the day's excitement. We're becoming criminals around here."

Ms. Tynsdale laughed and morphed back into Cindy Johnson. "We never have toed the line very well. Let's go find that imaginary earring."

Inside the garage, Mr. Winslow tinkered with the car. It was heavily scraped and dented from the falling tree, but it appeared to be functional. He waved when he saw them walk in. "Lots to bring in."

Brinnie picked up a bag in each arm, and Miss Burtle and Ms. Tynsdale did the same. "Oh," Mrs. Winslow called from the front of the car, "here it is!" She held up the "missing" earring.

"Oh, good!" Marcie straightened. "I thought we'd never find it."

They made a procession to the house, carrying the supplies. Marcie looked around in puzzlement. "Where did Mr. Ludovic and Quentin go?"

"They had some business to take care of," Ms. Tynsdale—or Mrs. Johnson—replied.

"Oh." Marcie nodded, but continued eyeing Ms. Tynsdale quizzically. Evidently, no one had yet given her an explanation of what this strange lady was doing at Wraithwood.

The wind began picking up as they went inside, though the long-threatened deluge was not yet forthcoming. Mrs. Winslow directed the putting away of the various items in cupboards and sending others out to the refrigerator in the washhouse. As Brinnie made a trip out to put away the milk and orange juice, the boom of thunder made her jolt. *Chill out, jumpy.* She deposited the items with Marcie and left her to organize the fridge, then ran back to the house, head ducked to avoid the whipping wind.

"Brinnie, please put the flour and sugar in the cupboard over there," Mrs. Winslow directed back in the kitchen while stacking cans on another shelf.

As Brinnie pulled the flour out of a bag, Uncle Merlin appeared near the dining room door. He wore a cloak and high boots, a wand in his hand. It was the outfit the dark figure had been wearing Brinnie's first night at Wraithwood.

"It's time," he announced. "Can you keep Marcie distracted here?"

Ms. Tynsdale gave a thumbs-up. "No problem."

"Good. With this weather, she shouldn't be able to see anything, but we can't be too careful." His gaze passed over them all and settled on the Winslows and Miss Burtle. "Once I raise the Maze, there will be no leaving Wraithwood. Is there any reason you might need to leave?"

They shook their heads. "We have everything we need," Mrs. Winslow said, "including supplies in case we lose water and electricity."

He nodded. "Good. I suggest that everyone stay inside until the Maze is complete. I don't know what the effects might be."

Ms. Tynsdale and Miss Burtle exchanged a look. Mr. Winslow squeezed his wife's shoulder.

"These are strange times." Mrs. Winslow shook her head. "The Master Key stolen, the Maze going up. Be careful, Merlin."

"Indeed. If you need me, I'll be at the Gate."

Then he disappeared.

Mrs. Winslow turned back to the groceries and took a deep breath. "Here's the chicken. Ah, and the broccoli. Brinnie, can you take these bags out to the washhouse? Then you and Marcie come straight back."

She nodded and took the packages. Outside, lightning flashed, but strangely there still was no rain. She brought the items to Marcie, who organized them in the freezer. "There. That's that. Let's go see what needs doing in the kitchen."

"You go ahead," Brinnie replied. "I'll be there in a minute."

As soon as Marcie was inside the kitchen door, Brinnie darted around the side of the house.

If no one would tell her what the Maze was, she would find out herself.

Chapter Seventeen

BRINNIE SHIVERED IN THE WIND. SHE wished she had put on a jacket, but she couldn't go back now.

She slunk around the side of the house and kept to the gardens instead of the drive. Following the road, she soon came to the gate. Uncle Merlin stood in front of it with his back to her, his cloak flapping in the wind. She stopped behind a hedge to his right far enough away that she wouldn't be noticed.

She paused. Miss Burtle had said Uncle Merlin knew where everyone was on the estate. That meant he would know she was here.

But that didn't make sense. When she had explored the front of the house, he had been surprised to see her. And when she had followed him this morning, he had seemed confused at first. She tried to remember exactly what Miss Burtle had said. *"He knows where everyone is on the estate when he chooses to."* Ah. If he only knew where people were when he chose to, he probably wasn't paying attention sometimes. She hoped now was one of those times.

He didn't look up from the scroll he held in front of him, reading. He didn't appear to notice her.

With a nod, he rolled up the scroll and tucked it inside his cloak. Then he stepped forward and took hold of the padlock on the gate. At his touch, it clicked open and the chains fell away.

Brinnie added magical lockpicking to the ever-growing list of his talents.

He raised the bolt but didn't open the gates. He hesitated a moment with his hands in position, ready to push them open. Slowly, Brinnie crept closer, still hidden, until she could see his face.

His brow was furrowed, his lips pressed together. His haunted eyes stared, as if seeing something long ago. Then his features hardened with resolve. He gave the gates a shove, and they swung outward ponderously until they spread to their full width with a clang.

A shiver ran down Brinnie's spine. At the same moment, lightning flashed, and a roll of thunder followed shortly after, like an echo of the gate's ominous clang. The gate was open, and she couldn't see anything outside of it from this position. That didn't sit well with her, so she crept back to her original hiding spot.

Uncle Merlin knelt on one knee and placed his hand on the ground at the place where the two gates had met. He bowed his head in concentration, and the ground rumbled. Brinnie gasped and barely kept herself from stumbling. About seven feet outside of the gate, thick tendrils erupted from the ground and raced upward. Smaller tendrils grew out from them, until Brinnie saw them for what they were— branches. The branches intertwined into walls as Uncle Merlin slowly stood, arms outstretched, and the branches sprouted dense foliage, forming impenetrable hedges about fifteen feet high. He raised one arm, and the hedges Brinnie had once attempted to claw her way through grew another five feet in height until they matched the hedges outside the gate. Then he gestured toward the ground, and it rumbled as roots shot outward and downward. He made a spreading motion and a thick mist billowed outward from the gate until it blanketed the strange new hedges. Finally, he pulled the wand out of his cloak, held it up vertically, and drove it straight down into the ground so that it stood upright where the gates had once met. It glowed with a pale-yellow light.

Lightning flashed, thunder boomed, and the clouds finally burst with driving rain. Uncle Merlin sagged against the gate.

Brinnie turned in a circle. As far as she could see, tall, monstrous hedges surrounded Wraithwood. Except for the gate, it was completely closed in.

"Brynna." She jumped and whirled around to see Uncle Merlin standing behind her, frowning. "What are you doing here?"

She scrambled for words. "I, uh—I was just—"

"Didn't you hear me say that everyone should stay inside?"

"Yes."

His gaze bored into her. "And you came out anyway?"

His voice almost sounded like Mom's. *"Come on, Brynna, can't you do* anything *without making it more difficult than it needs to be?"*

She wilted as he frowned at her from his far greater height. "I'm really sorry."

"When I say to stay inside, it means that you must stay inside. That was dangerous. I didn't know what would happen. Anything could've gone wrong, and something terrible could have happened to you."

"I'm sorry," Brinnie said, hoping to ease his penetrating glare. She bit her lip and forced herself to meet his gaze. "But nothing bad did happen. If there's magic everywhere, I should know about it, but no one will tell me, and..." She looked down, her momentary bravery spent. "Sorry."

He sighed, and the anger left his eyes. "Enough standing in the rain. You're shivering. You must be freezing without a jacket. Here." He took off his cloak and put it around her shoulders.

She gasped, instantly warm and dry. "Thank you. Is this magic?"

"Yes. Now let's go inside." He led the way back to the house. He shook his head. "I suppose it's natural to be curious. But Brynna, magic can be very dangerous, especially if you don't understand it, and especially if it's something like the Maze. I'm trying to keep you safe."

She nodded, scowling. "That's what everyone keeps telling me. But what exactly is the Maze?"

"Just that—a maze. An unnavigable maze that no one can ever find their way through, unless they have the enchanted parchment—or, I suppose, unless they're me." He stepped over a particularly large puddle, and Brinnie skirted around it. "The hedges are impenetrable, the roots make it impossible to dig underneath them, and the mist obscures any view one might have by looking over the hedges."

She searched for a response. "Wow."

"It's the perfect defense." He gave her a hard look. "But it's unpredictable, dangerous. Anyone who wanders into it from either side without the parchment has little hope of ever returning. No one knows what is really hidden inside the Maze."

Brinnie shuddered, then scolded herself. *Get a grip.* "But it's just a maze going through the woods, the same woods that have always been there."

"Yes, but also no."

By this time, they had arrived at the back door. "Yes and no?"

He paused. "It's not quite the same woods. There's a reason the gate has always been shut. It is the same woods you came through to get here, but it's also more."

Brinnie blinked at him. "I don't get it."

"Think of it like the front door of the house. To come to the door from the outside, you pass through the yard. But if you open it from the inside..." He trailed off, musing. "Of course, the Maze makes little sense in that respect. It's both here and there."

What was that supposed to mean? "Mrs. Winslow opened the gate for us to come through when I first got here. It didn't seem to be special then."

"Oh? Hmm. An example of the Reverse Gate Theory when exposed to outside anchors, I would think." He must have noticed her blank look. "In any case, the important thing to remember is that you must not, under any circumstances, go into the Maze."

Brinnie nodded. That was one thing she understood perfectly well. "I won't."

They went inside. Marcie and Mrs. Winslow were cooking something that smelled wonderful, reminding Brinnie that she had skipped lunch.

"Brinnie, there you are!" Mrs. Winslow rushed over from where she was stirring a pot on the stove. "We were worried when you didn't come back. And look at you! You're both soaked. Go change out of those wet things, dear, and bring them down to dry."

No questioning or scolding? Brinnie glanced at Marcie, chopping vegetables. *Oh. Secrets. As usual.* She nodded. "Thanks for letting me use this." She handed Uncle Merlin his cloak.

"You're quite welcome. I think I could use a change of clothes as well."

They both exited the kitchen, and Brinnie trailed her uncle up the stairs, puzzling over how exactly the Maze and Gate worked. *At the very least, they'll keep us safe from the enemy.* "Uncle Merlin, who are the enemy?"

He looked over his shoulder at her with a slight smile. "You're full of questions today."

"There's a lot I don't know."

"Hmm."

He didn't seem as though he was going to answer. "So..."

"Well." He rubbed the back of his neck. "We're in a bit of a conflict with some people who want to destroy us, and so we call them the enemy."

"People? Like, wizards, people?"

"Yes."

They paused at the top of the stairs. "Why do they want to destroy you?"

"A difference of opinion, you might say."

She wanted to shake him for answers. "So there's a bunch of wizards who are trying to kill you because they disagree about something?"

"It's a bit more complicated than that, but yes, essentially."

"What do you disagree about?"

"Whether humans should be annihilated." He nodded to her. "I'll see you downstairs." Then he disappeared.

Brinnie stared at the spot where he had stood, her mouth open. "Can I assume you're on the 'not' side?"

Predictably, the air didn't answer her.

She stomped to her room. "You can't say something like that and then disappear," she muttered to herself. She pulled out a dry shirt and jeans. "No, we aren't telling you anything. Okay, now we are. Wait, now we're not again." She shivered as she wriggled out of her wet clothes, dug out a towel, and started drying her hair.

The bandage around her arm was soaked, so she took it off and put on a hoodie. *Because we have to hide my new magical scar from Marcie, because Marcie can't know about magic. Because...reasons.* She glowered.

Downstairs, Brinnie found Ms. Tynsdale and all the

Wraithwooders minus Marcie in conversation. "Morain is in the fire room," Uncle Merlin was saying. "After we leave, you might want to let him free. Of course, if he seems inclined to make a nuisance of himself and go running through the Maze..."

"We'll take care of him," Mrs. Winslow assured him.

"Very good." He nodded a greeting to Brinnie, then turned back to the rest of the group.

"I have one question about the Morain situation," Ms. Tynsdale said. "Why don't you take him somewhere through the door where he can get back to Castelon and we don't have to worry about him?"

"To buy us some time. In the interest of fairness, I offered to let him leave initially, but now I would rather keep him here. If he tells Castelon we're off to find the Master Key, they'll waste time looking for us instead of the Key. This way, Castelon won't know about the Maze until the spellcaster arrives, and then you, Lydia, in the guise of Morain, will inform Castelon that I have shut myself up here both to protect Wraithwood and to retain my abilities. As long as 'Morain' keeps reporting to Castelon that I haven't left Wraithwood, though they will be rather upset, they won't divert anyone from searching for the Key."

"You're way too good at this devious plotting," Ms. Tynsdale commented.

He offered a slight bow. "Speaking of which, I tried to cast an illusion spell over the Maze so that it would be difficult to see from the house, but I'm not sure how effective it was. The Maze doesn't respond well to magic, even mine."

Ms. Tynsdale smirked. "It's the fault of the Maze, huh?"

"I've gotten *better* at spellcasting, thank you very much." He made a face at her, and she snickered. "In any case, it would be best to keep Marcie as close to the house as possible."

"I don't think it's possible to keep her in the dark anymore," Miss Burtle put in.

You think?

"Perhaps not, but we must try, at least. Anything less would be unfair to her." He stopped. "Here she comes."

Brinnie had to hold back a laugh as everyone scrambled to look busy. Marcie walked in from outside holding an umbrella and lemons. "Ah, thank you, dear," Mrs. Winslow said, taking the lemons. "Nothing like hot tea with lemon on a cold, rainy day. The potato and bacon soup should be ready soon."

Brinnie looked at the bubbling pot, and her stomach rumbled. The savory smell filled the room in a most tantalizing manner.

"So I hear there were some strange doings in Lyle," Uncle Merlin said to Marcie as she folded the umbrella.

"Uh, yes." She fiddled with the umbrella stand.

"What happened, exactly?"

"Would you like me to tell the whole story, or just..."

"The whole story would be excellent." He waved toward the table. "Come take a seat."

"Okay." She pulled out a chair and sat with a sigh. "It all started when I went to the store to pick up a few things for my mom after church, and I overheard Mr. Benson talking to a stranger. I was in the next aisle over, but I had seen them both when I walked past, and something about that man..." She folded her hands on the table and shuddered. "I don't know, it gave me the creeps. But anyway, the stranger was asking about Wraithwood, so I was curious and started listening."

She stopped, shrinking at the six pairs of eyes on her, but Uncle Merlin nodded encouragingly.

She took a deep breath. "He was asking a lot of questions about who lived there and what the estate was like, but Mr. Benson didn't know much about it. Then the man asked if anyone in town had ever been there, and Mr. Benson told him just me, as far as he knew."

"Way to throw her under the bus," Ms. Tynsdale muttered. Mrs. Winslow waved a hand to silence her.

Marcie twisted her hands in her lap. "He ended up giving the man directions out to my parents' place. I guess he didn't know I was in the store. I bought what I needed and went home, but when I got there, a car already sat in the drive and that man and a few others were talking to my parents. I don't know why, but that scared me so much I turned right around before they could see me and left. I stayed in town for a while, but when I started to come back, the same car was sitting on the

163

side of the road where it turned off toward home, so I went past it instead of turning."

"Did you catch the make and model?" Miss Burtle interrupted.

"Oh. I'm not very good with cars. It was black, I think. A car with four doors."

Miss Burtle pressed her lips together. "Proceed."

Marcie hesitated, but moved on from Miss Burtle's irritation at the unhelpful answer. "I had just returned to the store again when I saw the Winslows, and I figured that Ma could come and get her groceries, but I needed to go to Wraithwood until those men left. I called and told her. She was a little upset, but she said the men seemed strange to her, too, and that something about them wasn't quite right, so it was probably best. So that's what happened." Her mouth quirked up. "I guess it's a little silly. I could have just talked to them and answered their questions."

Uncle Merlin shook his head. "No, you did the best thing you could have done. I would recommend that you stay here until they're definitely gone. Better to be safe than sorry."

"You think they really were dangerous?" Marcie's knuckles whitened.

He sank back, looking too tired to come up with anything. "As I said, better to be safe than sorry."

"And as I always say, nothing like hot soup on a rainy day," Mrs. Winslow said with forced cheer. "It's ready!"

They all sat down with bowls of creamy soup and cups of tea. Brinnie almost burned her tongue in her eager hunger. No one seemed much inclined to talk. Uncle Merlin looked barely able to lift the spoon to his lips, his face gray. Whatever he had done to raise the Maze seemed to have drained his energy along with his color.

She looked around while she ate and noticed that Mr. Winslow had rolled down his sleeves so they covered his bandaged arm. She began to realize how much work it took to keep someone from finding out the truth about Wraithwood, with all the little details that had to be attended to with care. *How many clues did I miss before I knew? Probably hundreds.*

After dinner was over and everything tidied up, they sat sipping tea in the warm glow of the fire. Ms. Tynsdale excused herself—Brinnie assumed it was to make her hourly check-in as Quentin Morain. Brinnie yawned, her eyelids heavy. "What time is it?"

Uncle Merlin pulled out his pocket watch. "Hmm. Almost six."

"It feels like ten."

"At least," Ms. Tynsdale agreed, reentering the room at that moment. She raised an eyebrow at Uncle Merlin. "Or seven?"

He nodded. "Seven."

Brinnie looked from one to the other. *Oh. Code.*

Brinnie grew so sleepy she decided to get ready for bed. As she came upstairs after brushing her teeth, she saw Ms. Tynsdale in the hall in Morain form talking on his phone, Uncle Merlin standing next to her. "Right, sir, he just put it up," she was saying. "I couldn't stop him, sir. He says it's only to keep Wraithwood safe...Yes, sir. Would you like to talk to him? Of course, sir."

She held the phone for a moment and winked at Brinnie. Brinnie waved goodnight to them both and went into her room. Outside, she could hear Uncle Merlin say, "Hello? Yes, the Maze...These are dangerous times. I wanted Wraithwood to be protected...No. As I'm sure Morain has told you, I haven't left the estate. It would be very difficult to take it down and put it up again, even to let you in. But Morain is shadowing me, so I don't think the spell is necessary...I come there? How would I return here after the spell was cast? Exactly...No need to get upset. I don't see why a restraining spell is wise in the first place. I could be of help in the search...Right. Yes, I'm a suspect. That is unfortunate. I'm sorry, but I'm quite firm. The Maze shall stay up. Good night to you."

Brinnie heard Ms. Tynsdale's Quentin voice again as she slipped into her pajamas. "I'm sorry, sir. There's really nothing I can think to do...I'll watch him like a hawk, sir. The second he disappears, you'll hear about it...Yes, sir. I understand, sir. Goodbye." Ms. Tynsdale's ordinary, non-Quentin, non-Mrs. Johnson laugh came from the other side of the door. "They're all going to go crazy."

"Yes. I hope not too crazy to search for the Master Key, though."

"Speaking of which—see you at two-thirty."

"Indeed."

Brinnie was lying in bed, starting to drift off, when someone knocked on the door. She sat up slowly. "Come in."

Uncle Merlin poked his head in and squinted. "Brinnie?"

"Yes?"

"I wanted to let you know that Ms. Tynsdale and I will be leaving at two-thirty this morning. We'll be coming back every hour for her to make calls—we can't bring a phone through the door without ruining it—but you will likely not see us."

"Will you be gone a long time?"

"I don't know. I would guess a few days, at the very least."

"Oh." *They're going to be facing the enemy, alone.* An enemy like that man on the road. Uncle Merlin certainly had magic, but how much did the enemy have? "Are you a—a very powerful wizard?"

"Do you mind if we have some light?"

She shook her head, then realized it was too dark in the room for him to see. "No."

He made a scooping motion with his hand, and a small ball of soft white light appeared in his palm. He tossed it toward the ceiling where it floated, glowing gently. "Much better. In answer, yes, as far as wizards go. Why do you ask?"

"It makes me feel better to know that, if the enemy..."

His expression softened. "I see. Not to worry. We won't be facing anyone in battle if we can help it. And if we run into trouble, we can always come back here."

"By teleporting?"

"Er, yes, if by such you mean instant travel."

She nodded.

"In any case, I simply wanted to let you know. If you stay away from the Maze and the door, you will be perfectly safe here—safer, in fact, than anyplace else on earth, at the moment."

Is that supposed to be comforting? "I will."

"Good. Well, good night."

"Good night. And good luck."

"It will not be luck we need so much as a miracle." He nodded to her. "Keep us in your prayers." Then he closed the door, and the magic light went out.

Brinnie rolled over and set her alarm for quarter after two. She wanted to be there for the departure.

Her alarm blared what seemed only minutes later. She turned it off and lay wondering for a moment why on earth she had set it for such an unreasonable time. Then she remembered. They were leaving to find the Master Key.

Quietly, she hurried down the hall, through the doors, and down the grand staircase to where everyone had gathered in front of the door.

Miss Burtle held a lantern while Mrs. Winslow handed Uncle Merlin and Ms. Tynsdale each a sack. "You'll need to eat," she explained.

"Thank you." Uncle Merlin glanced at Brinnie where she stood at the foot of the stairs. He gave a half-smile. "You might as well come over here."

She joined them without a word. Closer, she could see that both he and Ms. Tynsdale had undergone transformations. Uncle Merlin no longer had a moustache, and his hair was much shorter and darker. Instead of his usual Victorian attire, he wore a black T-shirt and jeans. He looked like an ordinary man—something he never would have been able to pass for before.

Ms. Tynsdale also had changed. She seemed to be around forty, with long black hair and a hard expression—except for the smirking quirk of her lip. Her attire, unlike Uncle Merlin's, had become more bizarre. She wore a black dress or robe that made her look very much like a witch.

"No purple?" Brinnie asked.

She grimaced. "Purple underwear was the best I could do, given the circumstances."

If Brinnie hadn't known better, she would have thought she saw Uncle Merlin's face redden. "Are we ready?" he asked.

"As we'll ever be, Mr. Human-who-looks-an-awful-lot-like-Merlin," Ms. Tynsdale said with an unintentionally sinister smile.

Mrs. Winslow's brow knit in worry. "Stay safe." She gave each of them a hug.

"The same to you all." Uncle Merlin looked at each of them.

"We'll try not to have too much fun without you," Ms. Tynsdale cackled. Then she paused, grinned evilly, and cackled again. "I outdid myself on this one, if I do say so myself."

"We'll be popping back every hour, even if you don't see us," Uncle Merlin said as Mrs. Winslow released him from a hug. "You need not worry too much."

"Don't tell her that," Mr. Winslow said. "She won't leave the door."

She gave him a playful shove. With a few goodbyes and waves, Uncle Merlin and Ms. Tynsdale linked arms, stepped through the door, and disappeared.

Chapter Eighteen

THE NEXT MORNING, BRINNIE WOKE SLOWLY. She reached over and scratched her right arm, then froze when her fingers hit the smooth, raised skin of a scar.

My uncle is a wizard, magic is real, and I'm living in a magical house. She almost snorted at the absurdity of it. Then she frowned. *Of course, I almost got killed by wizard wackos and apparently they're out to destroy humanity.* That was slightly less exciting.

She threw on some clothes and went downstairs to the kitchen. Mrs. Winslow was cracking eggs into a skillet.

"Good morning." Brinnie stepped across the threshold.

"Good morning, dear." Mrs. Winslow turned around with a smile, then gasped as her gaze fell to Brinnie's arm. "Oh!"

Oops. She had forgotten to cover it. "Yeah. It healed quick. But I probably shouldn't let Marcie see it. I wouldn't be able to explain it very well."

Mrs. Winslow just looked at it for a moment, her hand in front of her mouth. She quickly turned away, back to the eggs. "Yes, dear, find something to cover it with."

"Is it that bad?"

She glanced back, her lips pressed together. "No..."

"What's wrong?" The man had hinted at a meaning behind the scar. But what?

The dining room door swung open as Miss Burtle walked in from the front of the house. Brinnie turned toward her, and her eyes went to Brinnie's arm. "That's not good," she said with a grim expression.

"What?" Brinnie tried to look at the scar more closely. "It looks like it's healing great."

"Eira is going to kill Merlin," Miss Burtle stated.

"Brinnie, that's a mark. A mark of...the enemy," Mrs. Winslow said slowly, wiping her hands on a rag. "It doesn't go away."

"Like, ever?"

"Never. It will look like that the rest of your life," Miss Burtle said bluntly.

Um...no thanks. "Even if I put Vitamin E on it every day?"

"It was an enchanted blade. A mark made by an enchanted blade—it doesn't fade," Mrs. Winslow explained.

To distract herself from the fact that she was likely stuck with an unwanted tattoo forever, she asked a different question. "So Mr. Winslow will have a weird scar like this too? Was that an enchanted blade?"

They looked at each other. "It was, but no, he won't," Miss Burtle said finally.

"So I *can* get rid of it?"

"No. You can't, dear." Mrs. Winslow's expression was so sympathetic it made Brinnie worried. "But you should hurry and do something about it before Marcie comes in here."

"Okay. I don't understand, though."

"Keep it covered or the enemy will see it and kill you. That's basically what you need to know," Miss Burtle said.

"Edna!" Mrs. Winslow shook her head. "You'll be fine, dear. But hurry along, now."

Brinnie went back upstairs and changed into a long-sleeved shirt. *If I were planning on getting a tattoo, I'd get something cooler than this. And something a little less deadly.* She tried not to think about it. She was sure the enemy had better things to do than track down teenage girls and kill them. She would be fine.

She hoped.

Downstairs, breakfast was ready. Marcie didn't question that Uncle Merlin was away on business again, and that the others had left early that morning, but she glanced at Brinnie's attire. "Are you cold today?"

There was no way she could keep up that ruse as the temperature rose. "I need to do laundry." It wasn't a lie, technically—most of her clothes were dirty.

She laughed. "Ah. A day-before-laundry-day outfit."

Brinnie just smiled.

After breakfast and tidying up, Miss Burtle tapped her on the shoulder. "Brinnie, would you like to join me in the library?"

"Sure."

She followed Miss Burtle outside, around the house, and to the library. "You spend a lot of time here anyway, so we thought you would be the best one for the job." Miss Burtle's brisk pace forced Brinnie into almost a trot. "We need someone to watch the parchment and let us know if anyone goes into the Maze."

"Why would anyone do that?"

"The enemy might try it." Miss Burtle pulled open the door, ushering Brinnie inside. "It would be foolish, but if they do, it would be good to know."

"But it's impossible to get through."

She frowned. "Yes. Merlin's convinced of that. But to be safe...I don't like to put too much faith in magic."

A chill ran down Brinnie's spine. "Okay. I should look for moving dots in the Maze?"

"Exactly. If you check every few hours, that will be fine."

"No problem."

"Good."

Miss Burtle left, and Brinnie went upstairs to look at the yellowed parchment. Now that there weren't any distractions, she could examine it more closely.

The lines of the diagram were drawn in black ink, but several differently colored dots roamed the surface. A green dot moved in the garden, another came toward the kitchen door, and another was in the kitchen, while a yellow dot moved down the hall on the second floor. Looking at the library on the parchment, Brinnie saw a blue dot that had to be herself. Another blue dot on the third floor perplexed her, until she realized it had to be Quentin. The Maze surrounded the house and grounds with its many paths. To her relief, no dots were there.

She went back downstairs, careful not to touch any of the objects on the third floor. Her next order of business, she decided, was to figure out how she was going to hide her scar. She refused to wear long sleeves for the rest of her life, especially once she went home to the desert.

Extra clothes in upwards of one-hundred-degree heat? *No thank you.*

She went to her room to see what she could do. First, she dug through her belongings until she pulled out an unused bottle of makeup. It was a darker shade than her skin—it was near impossible to find any light enough to match—but that hadn't been the intention of this purchase. Mom had the idea recently that Brinnie should start wearing it to darken her skin. Out of some sense of rebellion, she refused to do it unless Mom specifically asked her. Just another way to try to hide the weird daughter, the disappointment daughter. *At least this will finally be good for something.* She pushed her sleeve off her shoulder, pumped out a generous amount, and slathered it on.

It did absolutely nothing.

Three coats later, the mark remained prominent as ever. Brinnie huffed. So much for that.

She frowned at herself in the mirror. What could she do? Perpetually wearing a bandage wasn't an option either—scratches only lasted so long.

All sorts of possibilities ran through her head, from using facial putty on her arm to painting it with industrial paint, but none seemed like viable options. Maybe she could have the scar surgically removed. Was that possible? She didn't know, but it wasn't feasible at the moment.

Finally, she wondered if magic could erase the scar. She wasn't sure how spells actually worked, or if she was even capable of doing them, but she figured it was worth a shot.

"Abracadabra, mark, disappear!" Nothing. Maybe rhyme? "Mark, mark, be gone as in dark." Nope. Brinnie sighed. She doubted spells used words anyway.

Instead, she thought about what she wanted. She wanted no one to be able to see the mark. She wanted it to be, if not gone, at least invisible. She thought about how badly she wanted it to remain unseen. She glared at it, willing it to disappear, but nothing happened. With a huff, she looked back at the mirror. And shrieked.

In the mirror she saw the bed, the wall, the nightstand—everything but what should be in the foreground.

Herself.

She waved her arms in front of the mirror, and suddenly there she was again, which surprised her so much that she yelled again.

Footsteps pounded down the hall. Brinnie quickly thought about being invisible again as Marcie flung the door open. "Brinnie? Was that you?"

Brinnie watched in silence as Marcie scanned the room, her concerned look morphing into one of puzzlement. "Brinnie? Are you in here? Are you okay?"

Brinnie stood perfectly still while Marcie checked on the other side of the bed and looked out the window with a baffled expression. "Okay, then. Crazy old house." Marcie left, closing the door behind her.

Brinnie looked down at herself. She could see her hands, arms, legs—everything was visible. But when she looked in the mirror, she saw nothing at all.

She consciously stopped desiring to be invisible, and she appeared once again in the mirror. Goosebumps broke out on her skin. "No way."

Focusing on invisibility again, she sat on the edge of the bed and watched in the mirror as the covers developed a dent where she should have been sitting. *So weird.* It didn't feel like what she had expected magic to be. She had expected surges of energy and dramatic spells—instead, it felt natural.

Well, wizard confirmed. Her heart thumped. It was all her childhood fantasies come true. It was a strange, mind-boggling thought, that she could actually be anything other than average, ordinary, disappointing, second-daughter Brynna.

She turned visible again. *I should probably tell someone I've figured out what I am. Mrs. Winslow?*

She hopped off the bed, adjusted her sleeve, and went down to the kitchen. She didn't find Mrs. Winslow there, but she did find her out in the vegetable garden.

"Hi!" Brinnie waved. "Can I help?"

"I'd appreciate it, dear." Mrs. Winslow brushed off her hands and pointed to the patch she was working on. "The weeds are terrible in the lettuce."

Brinnie knelt and began pulling weeds from in between the heads and throwing them in the basket. "Can I talk to you about something?"

"Of course. What is it?"

"Well..." She paused. "Are there wizards, who, you know, turn invisible?"

"I should think so. I don't know any personally." Her brow wrinkled and she stopped with a weed in her hand. "I think they call it shadow walking. Merlin explained it once. He said it wasn't invisibility so much as blending in with the shadows, but they seem to become invisible. Why do you ask?"

Brinnie wiped away sweat beading on her brow from the sun and her warm clothing. "Maybe I should just show you." With that, Brinnie thought about being invisible.

Before Mrs. Winslow looked up, the kitchen door opened, and Brinnie snapped back to complete visibility as Marcie stepped out. "Hello!" Marcie called. "I was wondering if you had anything else for me to do."

Nope. Nothing. Please go away.

"You could help us in the garden if you would like, dear," Mrs. Winslow replied.

Brinnie suppressed a sigh.

"Absolutely!" Marcie came over and knelt on the other side of Brinnie. "Weeding, I'm guessing?"

"Exactly." She forced a smile. "The more the merrier."

They chatted for a while, with no mention made of their earlier conversation. Brinnie kept worrying she would randomly turn invisible and give everything away. She concentrated on thinking about being very, very visible.

After they finished weeding, it was time to prepare lunch, which Marcie helped with, so Brinnie didn't get a chance to bring up invisibility then, either. After that came lunch itself, then cleanup, at which point Brinnie gave up for the moment. She wasn't going to be able to talk with Mrs. Winslow anytime soon, and she needed to check the parchment again.

In the library, she climbed the steps, avoided the magical objects, and examined the parchment. Nothing moved in the Maze, only the Mr.

Winslow dot in the rose garden. There was her blue dot in the library, Quentin upstairs, and the green dot in the office was most likely Miss Burtle. The yellow and green dots in the kitchen had to be Marcie and Mrs. Winslow. But as she watched, two new dots, one blue and one red, blinked into existence in the great hall.

Her heart leaped in her throat. She turned, ran down the stairs, and burst into the office where Miss Burtle sat at the desk, shuffling through papers.

She frowned at Brinnie. "What...?"

"Intruders!"

She stood. "Where?"

"In the hall, by the front door."

Miss Burtle looked at her for a moment, then slowly smirked. "Two dots, blue and red?"

"Yes!"

She strode toward the door. "That's Merlin and Tynsdale."

"Oh." She tried to calm her racing heart. *Idiot.* Of course. They had to come back every hour.

She followed Miss Burtle into the great hall, where sure enough, Ms. Tynsdale in Quentin form was on the phone, while Uncle Merlin sat on a step, waiting. He stood and turned around toward Miss Burtle and Brinnie before he could have seen them, reminding Brinnie of his uncanny abilities. His eyes twinkled. "Startled you, did we?"

Brinnie smiled sheepishly. Of course he would know about her mad descent. "A little."

"How is it going?" Miss Burtle asked.

He sobered. "As well as can be expected. Lydia is welcome at many of the dark estates. I, on the other hand, am most emphatically not, which causes a bit of difficulty." He wrinkled his nose. "We may have to move on to other strategies."

"She can't go in alone?"

"She could, I suppose, but besides the fact that she would be without escape if things went badly and would be unable to come here to enact her impersonation, she's not a Master, which would make it much more difficult."

Miss Burtle paused for a moment. "Why must she be a Master?"

"Oh, I must have neglected to explain. Masters can detect the Key.

Which, of course, makes the search much more difficult, since most Masters have large estates to watch over and are unable to go treasure hunting." He grimaced. "I have no such impediments."

She frowned and admitted, "I was unaware of that."

Uncle Merlin chuckled at her sour expression. "It isn't common knowledge. Don't feel too badly."

"I'll accept an instance of ignorance." She smiled slightly. "But only one."

Ms. Tynsdale joined them, back in her creepy-witch-lady form. "Done with that, finally. You'd think I could just make a quick report, 'Everything's the same.'" She held out an arm to Uncle Merlin. "Shall we go?"

"Indeed." He turned to Miss Burtle. "All is well here, I assume?"

"Yes."

"Good. We'll check in again soon."

"Behave yourselves," Ms. Tysndale said with an evil grin.

Then the two of them stepped through the door.

By that evening after dinner, Brinnie stewed in impatience. She had been unable to get Mrs. Winslow alone, so her newfound skill remained a secret.

As they tidied up, Mrs. Winslow slipped Brinnie something wrapped in a cloth, put her finger to her lips, and looked pointedly upstairs. Brinnie didn't understand at first. She hid the large package behind her back until Marcie turned around, then brought it out again to look at it quizzically. It wasn't until Mrs. Winslow coughed what suspiciously sounded like "Quen-tin" that Brinnie understood. "Oh. Uh, I'll be right back," she said, heading for the stairs.

Sneaky, Brinnie. Real sneaky. She must have gotten her sneakiness abilities from her father.

She remembered from the parchment that Quentin was in the room covered in metal, so she climbed the stairs to the third floor.

Before she opened the door, she examined the package in her hand. It contained a serving of the dinner they'd had and a bottle of water.

The door was locked from the outside, so she hesitated before opening it. What if he tried to attack her to get away? But Mrs. Winslow wouldn't send her up if it wasn't safe.

She pushed it open and her gaze swept an empty room. She frowned. He had been in here not long before. Had he escaped?

"In here!" she heard a muffled voice call. She turned toward the safety booth, where a hand waved out from a tiny window in the door. She came around and saw Quentin standing on the other side, cheeks flushed. "They're holding me captive!" He gripped the window ledge. "Are you coming to set me free?"

"Um, no. Sorry. But I did bring dinner."

He slapped a hand to his sweaty forehead. "Do you realize this is wrong? And illegal?"

"Yeah, I picked up on the illegal part."

"If you help them, you're breaking the law, too."

Brinnie's eyes widened. *Didn't think about that.*

"Exactly. The right thing to do is unlock this door and let me out of here."

She may not have had a handle on how the magical world worked, but she didn't think releasing an imprisoned wizard was a good idea. "I'm sure Unc—er, Mr. Ludovic has a good reason for this. They're planning to let you go eventually."

"After they get away with what they're doing, which is wrong!" He paced in his small space. "I know you don't know exactly what's going on here, but I am an official, and these people are breaking the law left and right."

"Do you want some dinner?" Brinnie asked peaceably.

He waved his arms. "They're deceiving you. They seem nice, but they aren't. If you let me go, I'll—"

"I'm sorry, but do you want food or not?" She put a hand on her hip. "If not, I have other things to do."

He opened his mouth as if about to say something else, but he stopped and sighed. "Yes. Thank you."

Brinnie passed him the package. He pulled out the water first and gulped it down. "It's awfully hot in here."

"Yeah. I can ask. Maybe they'll move you somewhere else," Brinnie offered. *Not his fault. He's just trying to do his job.*

He shook his head. "They won't."

"Why not? They're nice people. They feel bad about doing this to you, but they have to."

"This is the only safe room, I would think. I might escape from the other ones."

She cocked her head.

He banged on the wall. "Metal. Can't break through. Believe me, I've tried."

"Oh. Sorry about that, then."

"I guess it's fitting. I've always been a failure of a...ahem." He turned his attention to the food, shoving a forkful in his mouth. "Mmm. This is really good."

"Mrs. Winslow is the best cook I know. Just don't tell my mom," she joked.

He paused. "Aren't you supposed to be in Lyle?"

Oops. "Yeah. I will be, soon. But with everything that's going on..."

"What do you mean, everything?"

"Uh..." *Why can't you keep your mouth shut, Brinnie?* She wasn't supposed to be there, as far as the DI was concerned, let alone know anything. "You know. Angry robbers. Kidnapping you. That sort of thing."

He looked at her as if he didn't believe a word she was saying. *He's clumsy, mistaken about the Master Key situation, and always seems to end up where he's not supposed to be, but he's still a wizard,* Brinnie reminded herself. She had to be more careful.

"Did that blade leave a scar?"

"What?" Brinnie snapped back to the present.

"That man. I saw him cut you. Did it leave a scar?"

Brinnie saw where he was going with this. She'd had a suspicion ever since they said Mr. Winslow's wound wouldn't leave a scar like hers. If she was correct, only wizards were left with magical scars. *Play it cool.* "Well, usually when you get cut it leaves a mark for at least a little while."

"It was a strangely shaped cut, wasn't it?"

"Different, I guess." She tried to divert his attention. "Your dinner is getting cold."

"It's kind of hot for long sleeves, don't you think?"

"I need to do laundry."

"No bandage?"

"Huh?"

"You don't have your arm wrapped up. Why not?"

"How can you tell whether it is or not?" She mentally composed herself. *Distract, don't debate.* "I need to get going. Are you done?"

"Can I see the wound?"

"What? No! Ew. Who wants to see that?"

"I do." He took another swig. "I think you're hiding something."

"Like what, a gross bloody mess?" She tried to smile as if the whole conversation was in fun.

"If you let me see, I'll stop asking you about it, I promise."

"No." *There is no saving this.* "I'll come back for the dishes later." She started to walk away.

"I think you're hiding the fact that you're a wizard."

She turned around slowly. "A *wizard*?" she forced herself to ask incredulously. "Are you feeling okay?"

"Yes. Why are you hiding it?"

"Um...wizards are in fairy tales."

"You can stop pretending. I *know* you're a wizard."

She crossed her arms. "I'm going now. Maybe Mrs. Winslow will know what to do. Are you *really* sure you feel okay?"

"I can levitate humans—well, hair, or a limb, or something, at least. I've been trying to do that to you for the past five minutes and it hasn't worked. It doesn't work on wizards."

Brinnie tried to ignore the goosebumps that rose in spite of the heat. "Goodbye."

"Did you even know? Did they tell you you're a wizard? Or have they been lying to you?"

His questions followed her out the door as she shut it and locked it behind her. *Hopefully it isn't too important that those wizard detectives don't find out who I am, because I think they just did.*

179

Chapter Nineteen

BRINNIE SCANNED THE PARCHMENT FOR ANYTHING unusual. Nothing.

Quentin seemed to be pacing upstairs, his dot moving back and forth in tiny increments. *He doesn't have much space in there.*

Last night, she hadn't said anything to anyone about her conversation with Quentin. She told Mrs. Winslow it had gone well and that she had left the contents of the package with Quentin.

At that, Mrs. Winslow paused. "He can't be left with anything, dear. He'll use it to escape."

She called Mr. Winslow, and the three of them hurried upstairs. Inside the metal room, they found a bowl hovering over the lock on the door to the safety booth, repetitively hitting the latch without enough force to actually unlock it. Mr. Winslow seized the bowl.

"We're here to take everything for you, dear," Mrs. Winslow commanded.

Quentin opened his mouth to protest, but then he sighed and handed out the cloth, the water bottle, and the spoon.

"Thank you," Mrs. Winslow said in a much friendlier tone. "Is there anything else you need?"

"No," he replied sullenly.

"Good night, then, dear."

Brinnie smiled as she remembered Mrs. Winslow's command. No one could say no to Mrs. Winslow.

She returned to the kitchen. Inside, Mrs. Winslow was putting together another package wrapped in a cloth.

"Hello, dear. You said you had no problems with Quentin last time?"

"Um, no."

"Would you mind taking this up to him, then?"

Are you sending me because Quentin used his powers on you? But you know he can't do anything to me? "Sure."

When she came around to the door of the safety booth, Quentin was waiting for her. "They sent you back up again?"

"Yes. With this for you." She handed him the package.

"Thanks. You didn't tell them what I said, did you?" It was more of an observation than a question. "Otherwise they wouldn't want you talking to me." She didn't answer, and he smiled. "I didn't think so. What's your name?"

She had already told Ms. Haberdash her name before she realized the need for secrecy. Now he would go back to the DI, tell them she was a wizard, and they would know exactly who she was. *No harm in it now.* "Everyone calls me Brinnie."

"Nice to meet you. I'm Quentin."

She narrowed her eyes. "Are you going to ask me to free you again?"

"Would you?"

"No."

"Then I won't waste my time." He opened the package and pulled out a sandwich. "Best prison fare I've ever had. Not that I've ever been in prison before. But I don't think this is usual." He looked back at Brinnie. "What kind of wizard are you?"

"Um, the pink happy friendship magic kind?" she offered with a grin. "Why do you keep talking about wizards?"

His expression grew grave. "There are dark wizards out there who might have the power to destroy the world in their hands at this very minute. Every moment I spend in here is a moment I'm *not* helping to stop them!" He waved an arm and almost dropped his sandwich. "And Ludovic and the rest of them are hindering those of us loyal to Castelon from finding the Key before it's too late."

"They're helping look for the Key, you know." Brinnie kept her tone placating. "And for all anyone knows, Mr. Ludovic is still here right now. I'm sure it will all be okay."

"It will not be okay! You don't understand!"

"You could explain it to me."

It wasn't until after she said it that Brinnie realized what she could stand to gain.

At the same time, he seemed to realize he might benefit from the bargain. "You don't know anything?"

"Not really."

He pointed his sandwich at her. "What if I explained everything to you, and in return, you did something for me?"

"Like what?" she asked warily.

"Let me go."

She shook her head. "Even if I did, you couldn't go anywhere. The Maze is up."

"I could go through the door."

For a moment, she considered it. What harm could he do if he got dumped off in some random place by the door? Then she shook her head. "I can't do that."

"Fine. How's this. I'll explain everything, and you let me go. I'll promise not to contact Castelon for twenty-four hours before I report the situation."

"Why would I believe you?"

He looked offended. "Because I gave my word."

I could do it...But how can I trust him? And what would happen to me? I shouldn't get involved in this dispute. She wanted to know what was happening, but she couldn't get involved until she knew more. "No. I don't need to know."

"Let me know if you change your mind." He took a bite of his sandwich. "By the way, why were you trying to hide that you're a wizard? It's not like I'm a human who can't know."

"I'm still not sure we're on the same page about that."

"Where do you actually live? Who are your parents?"

She rolled her eyes. "Why do you think I don't actually live in Lyle?"

"Because there aren't any wizards in Lyle. What estate are your parents from?"

"Um...they're not from an estate."

"Well, they can't just live in a human city." He laughed.

"Why wouldn't my parents be humans?"

"Because you're a wizard. You have to have at least one magical parent."

Interesting. So magic was hereditary? "Then I must not be a wizard."

He slapped his forehead with his palm. "Why are you being so evasive?"

"Why are you being so interested?"

"Because you're being evasive."

She had to laugh. "Are you done with your lunch yet?"

"No." He looked at her for a moment, head tilted. "You have a lot of the Drakon look."

"Excuse me?"

"Family of dark wizards. Lydia Tynsdale's father was a Drakon— the Master of Dirklon, actually. Are you related?"

"I don't think so."

He scratched his chin. "You look a lot like a Ludovic, too."

Her heart gave a thump. "Huh. Interesting."

"Are you related to Merlin Ludovic?"

"Could be." She shrugged. "Who would know?"

"Are you registered with Castelon?"

"Um, I don't think so."

"That's illegal, you know. All wizards have to be registered."

"I didn't know."

"How do you not know these things?"

"Uh..."

"As an official, I'm asking you to name your parents."

"And as the one who is *not* inside a cell, I'm asking you to eat your food so I can get out of this super-hot room." Brinnie fanned her face.

He wasn't distracted. "You're a Ludovic," he stated.

"No. My last name is Lane."

"Hmm. Were you adopted?"

Sometimes it feels like it. "No. My parents are perfectly normal people, I definitely was not adopted, and my last name is definitely Lane."

"What was your mother's maiden name?"

Brinnie sighed. "It was Dover." That should make him stop prying. Then she paused. Dover? Why wasn't it Ludovic?

"Oh." He squinted at her. "Are you lying?"

She opened her mouth to give a frustrated retort, but instead she laughed. "If I was lying, why would I tell the truth about it?"

He laughed as well. "Silly question, I guess. I suppose we're at a stalemate."

"I suppose so."

"All right, then. I guess I'll eat so you can go."

A few minutes later, Brinnie headed downstairs. In the kitchen, Mrs. Winslow said, "Thank you, dear. How did it go?"

"Fine. He talks a lot."

She laughed. "Was he trying to persuade you we're all wrong and you need to let him free?"

"Something like that."

"Poor young man. It's too bad we have to keep him that way, but there's nothing for it."

After putting away the cloth and other things from the package, Brinnie went out to gather the eggs. Bruno joined her on the path to the coop. As if through a haze, she could see the hedges circling the property. That was probably the result of Uncle Merlin's spell.

The chickens were skittish, squawking as she opened the gate. "What's wrong with you? You don't like the Maze, do you?"

After they had plenty of food and water, Brinnie and Bruno left. Bruno trotted along with his tongue lolling out, seeming unaffected. Brinnie laughed. "You're such a dog." He panted up at her.

Her next stop was in the library. She went up the stairs to check the parchment. She didn't expect to see anything unusual—the thump that her heart gave every time she looked at it had ceased.

Her eyes roamed over the parchment until they rested on an unfamiliar sight—several dots moving in the Maze near the road that led to Lyle. The enemy were coming.

She rushed downstairs and through the office and hall, not stopping to think about what Marcie might think. She flew through the dining room and burst into the kitchen, where Miss Burtle and Mrs. Winslow appeared to be in conversation. "People in the Maze!" she announced.

They exchanged concerned glances. "What color?" Miss Burtle asked.

"A lot of red and one yellow."

Mrs. Winslow put a hand to her mouth. "Oh, my."

"Not the DI, that's for sure," Miss Burtle said grimly. "Why yellow?"

"A hostage?" Mrs. Winslow suggested.

"Or a guide. Merlin allows humans who don't know."

"I'll get Tom."

Mrs. Winslow left, and Miss Burtle nodded in the direction of the library. "I want to see that parchment."

On the third floor, Brinnie and Miss Burtle watched the group of dots continue along one of the paths near the outside of the Maze.

"It's not a super hard maze." Brinnie traced a path through.

"Not when you can see the diagram. When you're in the Maze, it doesn't look anything like this." Miss Burtle crossed her arms, frowning. "No one has ever made it through before without the parchment. We aren't in any danger." But she sounded as if she were trying to convince herself.

"Can Uncle Merlin make the Maze kick them out or something?"

"I don't know." She pressed her lips together. "They haven't been here in three hours."

"Did the checking-in-every-hour thing change?"

"No."

Brinnie's heart skipped a beat. "Do you think something happened to them?"

She hesitated. "There are a lot of things that could have happened. Not all bad. They could be in a situation where they would be noticed if they left. Or they may even have found the Master Key—Merlin can't transport it by magic." She dropped her arms. "In any case, we should return."

Back in the kitchen, Mr. Winslow held his rifle. "Think I've got an old shotgun somewhere, too. Don't know if it works or not."

He and Mrs. Winslow turned when Brinnie and Miss Burtle entered. "It looks like we have two firearms if we need them," Mrs. Winslow said. "And, well, I have a lot of kitchen knives." She winced. "But there's no reason to think it will come to that."

"I think it's safe to say the protection spell is down if they're in the Maze," Miss Burtle observed. "If they have the Master Key, we don't know if any magic can stop them."

"Do you think they have it?" Brinnie asked.

"Impossible to know."

"And Castelon can't help, because anyone they send would get lost in the Maze," Mrs. Winslow mused.

"When Merlin and Tynsdale come back, Merlin can bring reinforcements here by door. Then they can take the parchment with them and find out," Miss Burtle suggested.

Mr. Winslow set the rifle by the door. "Better keep watch for 'em, then."

A phone rang. Miss Burtle pulled it out of her pocket and sighed. "Castelon again. They haven't stopped calling since Tynsdale missed the first call. If they don't come back in a few hours, I'm going to have to explain everything."

"They will, I'm sure." Mrs. Winslow frowned.

Miss Burtle stuck the phone back in her pocket. "I'll take first watch."

With that, the meeting broke up, leaving Brinnie with a knot in her stomach.

Chapter Twenty

"GOOD NEWS. OR AT LEAST, NO more bad news," Miss Burtle announced the next morning.

Brinnie sat up straight in the Watching Chair, as she had mentally dubbed the chair they had set up facing the front door after the dots entered the Maze. She'd offered to take a turn at the monotonous job of watching nothing. Mrs. Winslow had arrived to take her shift when Miss Burtle came out of the office.

"What is it?" Mrs. Winslow asked.

"Castelon is absolutely furious with all of us, demands the release of Quentin, and has declared that Merlin and Lydia are facing charges of treason, but—" Here she paused dramatically. "They considered it of less importance to search for them or to try to break through the Maze than to search for the Master Key, what with even more protection spells that have gone down at several estates in the past twenty-four hours, so they will not be attempting to do either."

Mrs. Winslow clapped her hands together. "That's wonderful!"

Brinnie raised an eyebrow. *Yes. Treason charges. Always wonderful.*

"The best that could be hoped for. Of course, I hate to inform you that we're all facing charges as well. Kidnapping DI agents and aiding and abetting 'traitors' appears to be frowned upon."

Mrs. Winslow brushed off her apron, as if brushing away her concerns. "Well, there's nothing we can do about it."

Miss Burtle frowned. "With all this mess, I'll be happy if Castelon is ever in a position to arrest us."

"We'll pray that we all make it through safely to be put under arrest," Mrs. Winslow agreed with an ironic smile. She patted Brinnie's shoulder. "Thank you for your help, dear. I can take over watching now. Oh, and if you wouldn't mind, would you go explain to Quentin that he's free now? Tom will come up to release him in a bit."

"Sure." Brinnie was certain now—Quentin had been causing trouble levitating people. Miss Burtle had brought him dinner the night before and breakfast this morning and came back extraordinarily grumpy. So, Brinnie seemed to be the designated Quentin-handler.

She ascended the grand staircase, then turned invisible in case Marcie happened to come upstairs. As she changed from visibility, she felt as if she were melting into something, or drawing something over her. She remembered Mrs. Winslow's earlier words. *Shadows. I'm hiding in shadows.*

She ascended the stairs to the third floor and changed back to visibility. She recognized a feeling now of emerging, as if from water, or of throwing off a covering. But it was so slight she had to concentrate to notice it.

Inside the metal room, Quentin again waited at the door. "Hello." He took in her empty hands. "Have you come to talk?"

"I came to let you know that you're going to be set free today."

"You're freeing me? In broad daylight?"

"No," she laughed. "Castelon knows everything now, so there's no reason to keep you here. Mr. Winslow is coming up in a little bit to let you out. I just came to tell you."

He grinned and pumped an arm. "Yes!" Then he sobered. "Did they find the Key?"

"No." The smile melted off Brinnie's face. "Actually, things have gotten worse, I think. But I don't know much."

"Then how does Castelon know everything?"

"Mr. Ludovic and Ms. Tynsdale haven't come back for a whole day. We don't know why." She tried to keep the worry out of her voice. "Miss Burtle had to answer the calls from Castelon eventually."

"Oh." He paused for a moment. "That's not good."

Understatement. "Yeah. What is Castelon, anyway?"

"Who are your parents?"

Brinnie scowled. He wouldn't even answer such a simple question. Well, there was no sense in hiding who her parents were. A simple internet search of her name would bring that up. "Andrew and Eira Lane. And Castelon?"

His eyebrows rose. "Eira? That's an uncommon name."

She shrugged. "I guess. So is Castelon."

"Castelon is...well, world headquarters, I guess. It's the largest estate, and it's where the Council meets, where the DI is headquartered, and the Academy, and that sort of thing."

"That sounds like more than one estate."

"Oh. Estate means something different in wizard society. It's an area enclosed by a protection spell and under the authority of a Master, so that could be a whole city."

"Huh." Interesting. "Where is it?"

"Who were your mother's parents?"

She sighed. "Really?"

He smirked. "Yes."

"I don't know what their names were."

"Are you lying?" he asked, then quickly said, "Dumb question. Her maiden name was Dover. Are they gone? What was their last name?"

"Um, yes, they're gone, and to tell you that I would have to make assumptions. So, where is Castelon?"

"I can't tell you exactly. It's in Great Britain."

"You don't have an accent."

"I didn't grow up there."

"Oh."

The door opened, and Brinnie startled.

Mr. Winslow stepped in. "Howdy."

Brinnie waved, and he came around to the door to the safety booth.

"Came to let you out. Sorry about all this. Hope it wasn't too bad."

"Could have been worse." Quentin watched as Mr. Winslow unlocked the door. "You're all going to be facing serious charges, you know."

"Reckon so." He pulled the door open.

Quentin stepped out quickly, as if afraid the door would slam shut again.

Downstairs, Mrs. Winslow waited in the great hall. "There you are." She turned to Quentin. "So very sorry about this, dear. If you ever come this way again, it will be as an honored guest, not a prisoner."

He blinked. "Um, thank you."

"Feel free to open the door until you find where you want to go. We would take you to town, but the Maze..."

"Okay. No problem."

Brinnie hid a smile at the rather absurd conversation between captor and former captive. Quentin went to the front door. As he took hold of the handle, his eyes rested on the rifle standing upright against the wall. "Are you expecting, uh, trouble?"

"Dark wizards in the Maze. We can't be too cautious," Mrs. Winslow explained.

He stopped and turned around. "The protection spell is gone?"

"We would assume."

He shook his head. "You can't leave an estate without a registered wizard guarding it, especially without a protection spell. It isn't safe."

"We have no choice, dear."

"I do." He straightened his thin shoulders with sudden resolve. "I can't leave you here alone. For your protection and the protection of the estate, I'll stay until the danger is past."

Miss Burtle walked out of the office and overheard his statement. "Absolutely not!" she exclaimed, coming over to join the conversation. "Completely unnecessary."

The Winslows looked at each other. "You don't have to do that, dear," Mrs. Winslow said. "The Maze will keep them out."

"The protection spell didn't keep them out, so the Maze might not either." He grimaced a bit, as if he had frightened himself with the thought. "Besides, it's against the rules to leave an estate wizardless."

Why is he doing this? Didn't he want to leave?

"I'm sure we'll be all right, dear. Thank you, though."

He shook his head. "I insist. For the sake of laws and safety."

"And perhaps your reputation, too?" Mrs. Winslow asked gently. "Something to balance out the hostage incident?"

He turned red. "That, too."

She looked over at Mr. Winslow, and they seemed to have a conversation with their eyes. Then she glanced at Miss Burtle. Even Brinnie could understand the emphatic "no" coming from Miss Burtle's expression. But Mrs. Winslow said, "We'll think about it. You can stay for now."

Miss Burtle raised an eyebrow. "Will an improvement in your reputation cause an improvement in your report about us to Castelon?"

"Huh? Oh! Um, yes, probably."

She nodded. "Might be worth it. If you leave our dining room chairs alone."

His cheeks flamed again. "Yes, sorry about that."

"Marcie is still here," Mrs. Winslow told him. "You remember her from the ride here? She doesn't know anything, so you're still Merlin's relative as long as you're with us."

"Yes, ma'am."

"Good. Brinnie, would you like to show Quentin around while we talk?" Mrs. Winslow asked.

Brinnie looked at her for a minute. He had already seen the house when the DI agents searched it. *Oh.* They wanted to talk about him, so they wanted her to distract him. "Sure. Uh, this way."

She led him into the dining room. The chairs had sunk lower and lower, but they still floated at least a couple feet off the ground, some spinning slowly, others circling the room. "Oops," Quentin said. "Why can't I do things like this when I actually want to?"

"It could actually be fun. Watch." She waited until a chair drifted by, then hopped on. It spun at the same time that it circled the room, reminding her of a ride at an amusement park. She laughed. "I'm not sure if I want them to go back to normal."

He stood frowning, watching the chairs with shoulders slumped. She hopped off. "I'll let you ride the best chair."

He looked as if he were about to protest, but instead he shrugged. "All right. Why not?" When it came around again, he jumped on and went spinning away.

The sight of Quentin's lanky legs spinning in circles on a floating chair sent Brinnie into giggles as she jumped on another chair. This one she stood on and put her arms out like a surfer as it floated in circles. She could almost hear her mother scolding her. *"Brynna! Stop drawing attention to yourself. Get down."*

"Okay." Quentin grinned. "I'll admit this is fun."

But Mom isn't here. Brinnie smirked. "Know what would be even more fun?"

"What?"

"If you made them go faster."

"Well..."

"Just a little bit?"

"I'll try, but I don't know if I can." He closed his eyes to concentrate.

As he did, Brinnie's chair passed close to his. She felt something, like a spark, and all of a sudden, the chair almost zoomed out from under her. "Whoa!"

She grabbed the back of the chair and held on for dear life as it zipped around the room. *Oh, no.* Another chair sat right in her path, on track for a collision.

She covered her head with one arm, but at the last possible second the chair she was riding zipped up and over it. Uncurling from her defensive position, she breathed a sigh of relief.

She glanced around and saw Quentin gripping his seat with white knuckles, leaning forward with an expression of shock. "I changed that chair's direction! I've never been able to do anything like that!"

"*You* did that? Thank you!"

"Yup." He leaned to the side, steering around another floating chair. "You can steer by leaning."

She tried it and laughed. "This is fantastic! Go-karts, flying edition."

"You could have all sorts of fun with these." Quentin swooped low and scooped up an unlit candle from the table. "Catch!"

He threw it over a chair flying in between them, and Brinnie caught it barely in time to avoid a collision with another chair. "Yes!"

She flew low and threw it up to him as he flew overhead. He reached out and snatched it. "This should be a new sport. Chair riding."

"Definitely." They continued to throw the candle back and forth. Looking at Quentin's grin, Brinnie realized he was a lot younger than she'd first thought. In fact, he probably wasn't any older than nineteen. No wonder he didn't seem as competent as the other agents.

She zipped low past the door leading to the kitchen and reached out to grab the candle when she saw that the door was open and someone stood in the doorway, staring openmouthed. She dropped the candle. "Oh, shoot."

Marcie stared at her as she whizzed by. "Brinnie? What in the..."

"Un-levitating!" Quentin announced, and Brinnie's chair abruptly slowed, lowered, and came to a stop on the floor.

Brinnie hopped off. "Um...hi."

Marcie rubbed her eye. "Were you riding a flying chair?"

"Uh..."

Quentin hurried over from where his chair had landed. "Flying? Not flying. That would mean wings. I think."

Marcie's brow furrowed. "When did you get here?"

"Not extremely long ago."

She gazed around at the dining room and the chairs strewn everywhere. "Are there always flying chairs in here?"

"No..." Brinnie wasn't sure what else to say.

"How did you make them fly?"

Brinnie gestured to Quentin. "He did it."

"Yes, well, it's just, physics, really, and...thermodynamics." He nodded as if that settled the matter.

Marcie looked from one to the other. "Why are you in the dangerous part of the house?"

"The dining room isn't *that* dangerous." Brinnie shrugged while Quentin's head bobbled in agreement.

Her gaze wandered to the chairs again. "I'm confused."

"Maybe we should, um, go get a drink," Brinnie suggested. "Or something. To be less confused. Because, you know, water is good for you."

Now both Quentin and Marcie looked at Brinnie strangely. *I am terrible at this.*

She raised her eyebrows at Quentin. He straightened. "Oh! Right. Good idea. Let's go do that."

Brinnie half herded, half led Marcie into the kitchen. "Water." She got out three cups and filled them. Downing a large swig, she exclaimed, "Mmm. I was thirsty."

Marcie held the glass Brinnie had thrust into her hand without drinking from it. "Brinnie, what are you doing?"

She felt her cheeks flush. "Huh? Nothing. What have you been up to this morning?"

Marcie shook her head. "I think you should explain."

Brinnie's mouth opened and closed. "Well, uh..."

"There's nothing she can explain," Quentin stated.

"I think there is. There's something going on in this house, and at this point, I believe I should know about it." She looked at Brinnie. "I've ignored a lot of weird things lately, but this is getting ridiculous. Strange men coming to my house and asking questions, and now flying chairs! If you've figured out what's going on, why haven't you told me?"

"Well," Brinnie said slowly, "the truth is—"

At that moment, the outside door opened and Miss Burtle stepped in. Her sharp eyes pierced each of them as they froze. "Hello." She turned to Marcie. "Quentin will be staying with us for a while. Would you mind preparing one of the rooms for him?"

"Sure." But she didn't move. Miss Burtle continued to look at her with a raised eyebrow. "Um, yes, I'll go do that." She turned and left hesitantly.

Once she was out of sight, Miss Burtle turned to Quentin. "You can stay. You might be helpful if things go badly." She looked from one to the other of them with an unreadable expression. "Your recent levitation feats in the dining room convinced us."

"How do you know about that?" Brinnie blurted.

"We were watching the parchment." Her eyebrows raised. "But we expect a good report to Castelon."

He nodded. "You'll get one."

"Good." She exited through the dining room door, only to return seconds later. "You two might want to clean up these chairs."

"Yes, ma'am."

As soon as she left, Brinnie and Quentin looked at each other and burst into laughter. *What am I going to tell Marcie?*

"They've gone down the same path four times in a row." Brinnie leaned over the parchment.

Mrs. Winslow's knitting needles clicked. "That's good news for us."

As they sat in the hall, Mrs. Winslow knitted while Brinnie alternated between flipping through an old newspaper and watching the parchment. "It doesn't make much sense. It looks like they keep coming out, turning around, and going right back to the dead end."

"I don't think you can tell which direction you're going in the Maze."

Brinnie nodded and watched Marcie walk up the stairs. It amused her to see the dot blip from the first floor to the second.

Mrs. Winslow yawned. "It's late, dear. Don't you want to go to bed?"

Her eys followed Marcie's dot, still moving, and she shook her head. "I'm not really tired. But if you are, you can go. I don't mind staying here until Mr. Winslow comes."

"Are you sure?"

"No problem. It's only a few minutes."

"In that case, I will. Good night, dear." Her eyes softened. "You're such a sweet girl. Just like your mother always was."

Brinnie smiled, her cheeks warm. "Good night."

The thought of Mom as a "sweet girl" felt strange. The mom she knew had a will of steel and the emotional range of a toaster oven. *What changed?*

On the parchment, Brinnie watched Mr. Winslow come walking down the path from the chicken coop. The gate had fallen off its hinges that evening when Brinnie went to feed them, so he had been fixing it.

Brinnie's long visit to the chickens had been an attempt to avoid Marcie, something she had succeeded in doing since that morning. She didn't know if she could bring herself to lie to Marcie anymore, so she stuck to avoidance.

As she waited, she picked up the newspaper Mr. Winslow had left near the chair. It was two weeks old, but it would stave off boredom. She flipped to a random page. "NASA Scientist Dr. Nathaniel Morton Still Missing Three Months after Disappearance," read the headline. She remembered hearing about him before she came to Wraithwood. It felt strange to think of the world outside, still going as it always did, while she was wrapped up in concerns of magic.

She heard a door open and set the newspaper aside as Mr. Winslow came in. "Hi."

"Howdy."

"Is the gate all fixed?"

"Should be." The front door swung shut behind him. "Won't be any chickens in the rose garden tonight."

She laughed. "Oh, good."

He came over and looked at the parchment. "Not much to see."

"They're just going in circles." She stood. "I think I'll go to bed now."

He nodded and pointed. "Marcie's coming downstairs. I'd go around outside."

"Okay. Good night."

She went through the library and out the door. She had thought about going through the dining room anyway, even though Marcie was there, and simply turning invisible, but then she would have had to explain everything to Mr. Winslow, and that was a conversation for another time.

Outside, she saw something moving out of the corner of her eye. She turned to see Bruno sniffing furiously with his nose to the ground, tail high in the air, following a trail. "Do you think you're a bloodhound?" she teased.

He barely glanced at her, continuing on the scent. What could have him so riled up? She followed out of curiosity.

He followed the trail around to the front of the house, zigging and zagging as if unsure exactly where the trail was. Past the circular drive and partway down the road, he suddenly charged at a bush, and a rabbit came leaping out. Brinnie laughed as he streaked after it, tongue hanging out of the side of his mouth. He would never be able to catch it. But he didn't give up the pursuit as the distance between him and the rabbit lengthened—and the distance between him and the gate shortened.

The rabbit was heading straight for the entrance to the Maze, and Bruno was intent on following it.

"No! Bruno, stop!" She took off running after him. "Come here, boy. Leave it!" But he didn't listen. *Please turn, please turn,* Brinnie thought to the rabbit, but it didn't, pelting straight through the gate and into the Maze. "No! Bad dog. Stop!" Bruno followed right after the rabbit. *Stupid dog.* Brinnie charged after him.

Past the gate, a hedge rose immediately, and Brinnie turned to the right, just as Bruno had. She kept running down the straight path in between the hedges. "Bruno! Come here. Stop."

She turned a corner and skidded to a halt. Bruno sniffed back and forth, whining at a fork in the path. "Bruno!" She fell to her knees and hugged him around the neck. She felt like her heart was able to beat again. "You bad dog, don't you ever do that again," she scolded while rubbing his ears. "You scared me. Come on, let's get out of here."

She stood and called him after her. He looked back at the fork and whined. "No, come on." She patted her leg. "Let's go!"

With one final look, he trotted after her. "Good boy."

She turned her attention to the way out. She had turned right and then left to get there, which meant all she had to do was turn right and then left to get out. "It's a good thing you didn't go very far," she told Bruno.

As planned, she turned right first. She walked down a straight path for a while, looking to the left for the obvious huge gate. But she never saw it. Instead, they came to a hedge wall blocking the path, with the path continuing only after taking a right turn.

Brinnie stared at it for a moment, her heart giving a little *thump-thump* of fear. Why was the hedge there? She looked down at Bruno and his lolling tongue. "I must have missed it. Let's look again."

She turned around, Bruno following. She walked the same path again, staring very carefully at the right wall. After walking for a much longer time than she remembered walking before, she still hadn't found it. "I didn't take a wrong turn," she muttered out loud. "I went right and then left, which means I had to go right and then left. It's simple. I didn't do it wrong. Maybe it only seems longer."

She passed three paths leading off to the left. She didn't remember passing any before. She thought she would have noticed, having gone by them twice. Logically, then, the first one had to be the one she had turned down. But she still hadn't come across the gate.

She kept walking until she came to a dead end. She stared at it uncomprehendingly.

Unnavigable...no one can ever find their way through...little hope of ever returning...No one knows what is really hidden inside the Maze.

"No." She bit out the word. She pushed and yanked at the branches of the right wall. When that didn't work, she tried to wriggle through them, but they wouldn't give. She scrambled to climb up them, but they wouldn't hold her. "Dig, Bruno, dig!" She scraped at the ground, but several minutes and broken nails later, she discovered only an impenetrable root system. She sat back, panting from the exertion. She knew it. She had known it already. Uncle Merlin had told her, and he had been right.

She was lost in the impossible Maze.

Chapter Twenty-One

"HELP!" BRINNIE YELLED UNTIL HER VOICE was hoarse, listening for an answering voice on the other side of the hedge, but none came. As her cracked voice pleaded, she came to a horrible conclusion. There was no way she could even know this wall was the one closest to Wraithwood. The other walls and paths had moved. It was equally likely that the only thing on the other side of this hedge was another path.

The walls seemed to mock her with their simplicity. They were just branches, just bushes. But she was trapped.

She sank to the ground. "No." The held-back tears exploded now that the dam of hope had been breached. She hugged her knees. "No, no, no..."

Bruno nudged her and tried to lick the tears off her face. She hugged his neck and cried into his fur. *Mom should never have sent me here. We'll never get out.* With a new rush of tears, she let go of him. "You stupid dog! Why did you chase that rabbit?" Then she hugged him again. "No, it's not your fault. You didn't know about the Maze."

Patiently, Bruno let her hug him and occasionally licked her face. Finally, she had no more tears left and her sobs gave way to shuddering breaths. She wiped at her tears before she realized she still had dirt all over her hands. "Now I'm a mess, too."

She sat, exhausted, leaning on her knees. Bruno lay next to her and she curled up with her head resting on him. He didn't seem to mind, giving her a quick lick before laying his head down again. There was nothing she could do right now. Maybe, in the morning, she would have better ideas.

It occurred to her that the dark wizards were in the Maze somewhere, and they shouldn't find her while she was sleeping. It took her a couple of attempts, but she pulled a shadow over herself like a blanket and relaxed in her safe invisibility, the darkness lulling her to sleep.

She woke up shivering. She was glad she was wearing long sleeves and jeans, even if she had been sweltering the day before. The mist hanging over everything made it cold and damp.

Mist? She sat up face-to-face with a wall of leaves and her heart plummeted. Still lost in the Maze. It took several deep breaths before she felt calm enough to think.

The mist made it hard to tell, but she thought it was early morning. Bruno stretched next to her but didn't open his eyes more than a slit. Brinnie felt the invisibility still wrapping her, more like a thin gauze now than a blanket, and shook it off.

Okay. What should I do? Last night, she had been terrified and upset, but now she was determined. She would escape the Maze. It was only a matter of careful thought and planning.

The idea came to her that Mr. Winslow had been watching the parchment. He would have seen her go into the Maze, and so of course, someone would come to rescue her. They just had to follow the parchment to find her and get back out again.

"We're getting out of here today, Bruno. I'm sure of it."

He lifted his head and looked at her with eyes still half closed.

"It's only a matter of time. All we have to do is stay here, and they'll come get us." She grinned and let out a sigh of relief. To think she had been so worked up last night. They would be fine.

They didn't move from their spot in the dead end. Brinnie thought several hours passed, but she couldn't tell. The mist obscured everything. She played fetch with Bruno with a stick she found lying on the ground, but after he got tired, she couldn't think of anything else to do. Her stomach started to grumble eventually, and her mouth was dry, but she ignored it. Soon, she would be rescued.

As she waited, she tried to dig through the roots with her stick, but it was like trying to chip at a boulder with a blade of grass. *That's fine. Someone will come soon, anyway.*

It wasn't until dusk began to fall, closing the long, thirsty, boring day, that she began to worry. *They should have found me by now.* Almost twenty-four hours had passed since she first entered the Maze. There was no reason it should have taken that long.

She fought to stay awake, staring down the path, but eventually, boredom and tiredness overtook her, and she fell asleep.

She awoke the next morning from a dream about being given sand to drink, only for the feeling to follow her into wakefulness. Her mouth felt like a desert. She rolled over and looked at Bruno, still sound asleep. "They didn't rescue us," she murmured, her heart feeling like a millstone.

She sat up, and her head pounded. She winced. Crying like that on the first night hadn't been a good idea. She was dehydrated. More concerning, it had been a day and a half, and she still hadn't been found.

Why not? She knew they wouldn't waste a moment coming to find her...if they knew she was lost. What if they didn't know? Or worse, what if something had happened to them, and they couldn't help her?

"I don't know. I hope nothing bad happened."

Bruno blinked up at her and whined.

"Well, boy, I don't think they're going to rescue us. We're going to have to find a way out ourselves." She stood slowly, sharp pain stabbing her skull. "Or at least, we need to find some water."

Using her stick, she made an X in the ground. Then she started walking. Bruno heaved himself to his feet and followed her. Every few steps, she made another X. At least she would know if she passed the same way twice.

She turned right down the first path she came to, for lack of a better plan. The mist obscured everything more than twenty feet away, and the hedges rose around her like ominous specters, branches like crooked fingers reaching toward her. *It's morning. The sun's out, somewhere. They're bushes. Just bushes.*

They walked for what she thought was a few hours. They took more turns than she could remember, but at forks, she always took the path on the right. She never came across any of her X's, but she wasn't sure if that was a good or a bad thing.

Finally, she sat down at a fork with a groan. "You've got to be kidding me. All these paths look exactly the same!"

Bruno plopped beside her, his tongue hanging out of his mouth.

Brinnie pressed her fingers to her temples, closing her eyes. This was a nightmare. She couldn't think of anything she could do, other than keep walking and hope she would blindly stumble upon an exit—the very thing the Maze was supposed to prevent.

She opened her eyes. No miraculous spring of water had sprung from the ground during her despair, and no gate had opened before her. She sighed. "Well, we definitely won't find it if we keep sitting here." She got up. Bruno gave her a longsuffering look and followed. Making X's and choosing the right forks, she continued onward.

Eventually, they came to a path that split three ways. Brinnie was about to take the right fork, as always, but for some reason she hesitated. She looked down the left path. It seemed narrower and less appealing than the other two. But she wondered if she had it wrong, going down the right path. It was getting her nowhere. *Just stick with the plan,* she thought, at the same time she told Bruno, "We're trying something new."

Down the left path they went. It continued, curving and twisting, without any paths branching off of it, for a long time. Brinnie started to wonder if they should go back, but she kept on until suddenly they turned a corner and emerged in a wide-open space.

Her heart leaped before falling again. It wasn't an exit. Instead, she had reached a small clearing with paths branching off it like uneven spokes on a wheel. But she grew excited again when she saw what shimmered at the center of the clearing—water.

She hurried to it and knelt at its edge. The water in the small pool looked clear enough. Bruno was already beside her taking great gulps. She was too thirsty to think too much about bacteria and pollution. She was soon gulping it down as well.

She splashed water over her face. If nothing else, they weren't going to die of dehydration. That alone made everything ten times less terrible.

After enjoying the water, she began to plan again. She wasn't sure what time of day it was, but they had been walking a long time, so she decided it was time for a rest. Besides, it would be silly to walk away from a water source as soon as they found it.

She began searching the clearing for something to hold water. She found grass, sticks, and rocks, but nothing that looked promising. Bruno sniffed around the clearing, presumably for food. She spent an hour trying to weave grasses into a watertight basket, but the water inevitably seeped through.

"Argh!" She threw it down. That was a waste of time.

Bruno came over to sniff it, then looked at her as if to ask, *Why is this not food?*

"Here's the plan, Bruno. We'll camp here tonight. Tomorrow morning, we'll set out."

She lay next to the pool and turned invisible.

Night three in the Maze.

The next morning, Brinnie gulped water until her stomach felt distended. Then she picked up her stick and set about deciding a course.

Since she had been wandering around in the clearing, she had lost track of which of the eight paths she'd come from. They all looked the same. Not daring to venture too far, she checked the entrance to each for one of her X's. But none of them bore a mark.

"That means one of two things, Bruno. Either I forgot to make an X, or the Maze is getting rid of my X's." She paused. "Or both."

Lacking direction, she chose a random path and struck out, carefully making X marks along the way.

This path was different than the ones she had been going down. Within a few minutes, it widened, and trees began to spring up in it. She recognized them as the kind of trees that grew all around Wraithwood, some spiny with pine-like needles, others with gray, smooth trunks, still more with dark, scaly bark and leaves like hands with pudgy fingers. But most importantly, some boasted sturdy branches almost within reach. "Yes! Stay here, Bruno."

She had never been the best at climbing trees—there weren't many to climb back home in Arizona—but she began to clamber up the trunk of one with many branches. The rough bark offered enough traction until she could reach the lowest branch. She pulled herself up awkwardly, swinging for a moment like a sloth before managing to right herself. The next branch was a few feet higher than the first, which she managed with no major difficulties. But after that, the nearest branch that looked strong enough to support her was several feet out as well as a foot or two above her head. "Oh, boy."

Bruno barked at her from below. She made the mistake of looking down at him and shuddered. She was not a fan of heights. That was way too far to fall.

Paralyzed, not willing to go forward, but also afraid to go back, she stood clinging to the tree. *You're being silly. You are* not *that high.* But it seemed like a pretty long drop. She looked at the next branch again. *All I have to do is jump. I'll catch it.* She bit her lip. *But what if I miss? Ouch.*

She weighed her options. She could go back down and keep wandering aimlessly. Or she could climb this tree and get a view of where she needed to go. *Duh. Not a hard choice.* She took a deep breath, chanced one last look, and leaped.

Her hands grasped the branch, but her forward momentum kept her body swinging, making her palms scrape against the rough bark. She hissed, but held on tightly and swung her legs up, clambering onto the branch itself. "I made it, Bruno!"

He barked and wagged his tail.

From her vantage point, she looked around. She knew she was above the hedges, but she saw...nothing. The mist obscured everything more than a few feet in front of her.

Unwilling that her daring acrobatic feat should have been in vain, she looked upward, but the mist continued that way as well. Even if she climbed higher, she still wouldn't be able to see. She sighed. The Maze wouldn't let anyone get away with something that easily.

Now the problem remained how to get down. She had reached this branch, but how was she supposed to get back down to the other one? *Idiot. Why didn't I think of that?* She repented of ever thinking the cats that got stuck in trees were stupid.

Wiping her scraped hands on her jeans, she took hold of the branch and lowered herself to a swinging position. There was no way she could launch herself and land on the branch with her feet. Instead, she reached out with one arm and grabbed a branch halfway between the two. She tugged on it. It gave, but she hoped it would hold her for a few seconds. There was another branch on the other side of it. If she could swing from one to the other like a monkey, she would be in position to drop down on the branch she had been on before.

She let go of the first branch and swung forward to grab the third, but as she did, she heard a horrible cracking noise. The branch she held snapped at the base, and it went swinging downward. Clinging to the branch, she smacked into the trunk of the tree. The force dislodged her grip, and she fell with a shriek.

She landed on her wrist, hard. She gasped at the pain, tears welling unbidden. Bruno came to sniff her as she sat up, holding her wrist. "Ow, ow, ow!"

She let go long enough to look at it. She didn't think it was broken, but she didn't know how to tell if it was. She tried to bend it, but it hurt too much, so she stopped. An injured wrist. Yet another thing to add to their list of problems.

She wanted to sit there and cry, but that wouldn't help anything. Instead, she stood, cradling her wrist. "Come on, boy. Let's keep walking." Her voice hardened. "This Maze is not going to win."

Chapter Twenty-Two

THE MAZE GREW STRANGER AND STRANGER. Sometimes it was hard to see the hedges with so many trees. The mist swirled around them, obscuring everything farther than a few feet away.

Brinnie didn't know whether it was day or night. She couldn't base her judgment off whether she could see or not, since her night vision had grown just as good as her vision in the light. By now, she was pretty sure it was linked to her powers of invisibility.

She noticed a light ahead. She squinted.

Am I seeing that right?

She followed the glow until she ended up in a small clearing, about thirty feet in diameter, ringed with trees. Right in the middle squatted a small dwelling, more of a hut than a house. A light shone through the open door.

There's a house in the Maze? Had it already been there, and the Maze grew up around it, or was it part of the grand delusion? She hesitated, standing just inside the ring of trees. If someone lived there, maybe they could help her. On the other hand, this seemed like the perfect place for a witch to have her lair.

Don't be ridiculous. Witches aren't real—at least not that kind.

She paused. But a few weeks ago, she would have said wizards weren't real, either. It was impossible to know.

She turned invisible, layering on extra shadows for good measure. *Layering on shadows. Because that's something people do.* She gathered them from around her, as if shadows were a real thing, instead of an absence of light. Then she tiptoed to the door.

Inside, an old woman stirred something in a big iron pot over a fire. No, "old" didn't do her justice. She was ancient. Her hair hung long and white, and her wrinkles had wrinkles. She wore a dress and shawl that looked as ancient as she was.

Well. She's old. Like a witch. But she isn't wearing black. Or a pointy hat. Brinnie mentally shook her head. *But I'm not wearing a robe with stars and moons on it, carrying a staff, and wearing a wizard's hat. And I don't have a long white beard, either.*

The old woman looked up toward the door. Though she was ancient, her bright blue eyes were still piercing. "Hello, there," she said in a voice that was strangely clear.

Brinnie jolted. Had the woman seen her? But then she felt something thwacking her leg and looked down to see Bruno right beside her, wagging his tail. No, she had only seen Bruno.

"Where did you come from?"

A cat jumped down from the small table in the middle of the room and hissed. "Now, now, be civil to our guest," the old woman admonished. She walked over to the doorway and Brinnie stepped back. The woman patted Bruno's head. "Hungry, are we? Let's see what I have for you."

She opened a tall basket standing on the floor and pulled out a loaf of bread. Brinnie's mouth watered. The woman cut off a piece and gave it to Bruno. "That should help fill your stomach."

His tail wagging, he gulped down the bread.

"Been a long time since you ate, eh? Your friend hasn't been feeding you. It's not her fault, though, is it? Not much to eat when you're lost in the Maze."

Brinnie's mouth dropped open. The woman looked toward the door. "I can't see you, but there's a strange collection of shadows over there. Care to show yourself?"

"How did you know?" Brinnie blurted.

The woman laughed, a sound like dry leaves blowing in the wind. "Your friend told me. I won't hurt you, child. I imagine you're as hungry as he was."

Brinnie wasn't about to let down her guard so easily. "Who are you?"

She smiled. "A strange question, don't you think? Do you mean, what am I? Or what is my name? People mean so many different things when they ask that question."

"I think I mean both."

"I'm a wizard, like yourself, though of an older order. And as for my name, I am called many things. You can call me Chevska."

Cool. You have a name. But I'm still not becoming visible. "Do you live here?"

"Yes. It's not much, but I like it that way." She cocked her head. "Why don't you come in and have a bite to eat?"

Brinnie looked at Bruno. He didn't seem poisoned. The cat sat atop one of the many baskets lining the walls, pretending to be disinterested. Chevska looked too old to do any harm. But that was the trouble with magic. One couldn't tell from appearances.

The woman shuffled back to the fireplace and stirred the pot. "The Maze hasn't been active for decades. There must be something important going on in the world for that to happen."

Brinnie nodded, then realized Chevska couldn't see her. "Yes."

The old woman reached into one of the baskets and pulled out two wooden bowls. "I don't know much of what happens, these days. Ever since the tragedy, no one comes to see me."

"The tragedy?"

"The invasion of Wraithwood." She ladled what looked like a chunky stew into the two bowls. "You're the first since Merlin came to ask me if I wanted to leave before he shut the Gate." She chuckled. "As you might have guessed, I didn't."

Brinnie didn't know what she was talking about. But she did know that stew smelled wonderful. Subconsciously, she drifted closer.

Chevska looked in her general direction. "Come, have a seat, child. There's plenty for two."

Brinnie hesitated. If she sat in one of the rickety wooden chairs, Chevska would know exactly where she was, and it would be harder for her to run. On the other hand, the old woman had given her no reason to fear, and her stomach was growling.

Warily, she let the shadows slip away.

Chevska's eyes twinkled. "Ah. A Ludovic child. You're doubly welcome here. Sit!"

Chevska sat on one side of the rough wooden table and Brinnie sat on the other. "How did you know I was a Ludovic?"

She laughed. "How did I know? How wouldn't I know? I can tell by looking at you."

"So you know my uncle Merlin?"

"Yes, of course. Though as I said, the last time I saw him was some three decades ago." She pushed one of the bowls in front of Brinnie and handed her a wooden spoon. "Eat, child."

"Thank you."

Brinnie didn't say much for the next few minutes, too busy digging into the vegetable stew. At that moment, it was the best meal she had ever tasted, steaming and savory, even without meat. Finally, she set down the spoon with a sigh of satisfaction. "That was delicious. Thank you."

The old woman chuckled. "You would think it was delicious if I gave you a raw potato." She sat back. "Tell me, how did you get lost in the Maze?"

"It was three days ago, I think. Bruno—the dog—was chasing a rabbit. He chased it into the Maze. I went after him like an idiot so he wouldn't get lost, and, well, I got lost."

"Why is the Maze up?" Her lips quirked. "I walked out one morning, and my vegetable patch was gone behind a hedge."

Brinnie wasn't sure how much she should say. But almost everyone knew about the Master Key by now. It couldn't hurt. "The Master Key is missing, and the protection spells are going down. Wraithwood's is down right now."

Chevska shook her head slowly. "Missing? Stolen, you mean?"

"That's what everyone thinks. Some people think Uncle Merlin stole it."

"You don't agree with them?"

"No. He's looking for it right now."

She tapped a finger on the table. "If it isn't found soon, thousands of lives are at risk."

Brinnie's skin prickled. "What do you mean?"

"The protection spells around the estates are the only things keeping the dark wizards from attacking them. If they go down, there's nothing to keep the dark armies from attacking innocent people in the streets." Her expression grew grim. "And if any humans happen upon one of the estates..." She trailed off. "But surely you know that."

"I don't know much of anything, actually." Brinnie fiddled with her spoon. "The whole magic, wizard thing is kind of new to me."

Chevska's head tilted. "Would you care to explain, child?"

Before Brinnie knew it, she was spilling the entire story, everything from when she came to Wraithwood, to her eventual discovery of the existence of magic, to the battle on the road, to getting lost in the Maze. She paused only for water. She wasn't sure what made her speak so openly to a random stranger in a hut in the forest, but there was something about Chevska that seemed to invite it. When Chevska heard about her fall, she pulled out some rags from one of her many baskets to bind Brinnie's wrist. Finally, the tale was done, and Brinnie sat holding her arm out as Chevska gently but firmly wrapped the injured wrist with thin, deft fingers.

"That was quite the tale," Chevska said softly. "Times have changed since I was a part of the world. Especially at Wraithwood." She finished wrapping Brinnie's wrist. "There. I have no healing abilities, or I would help you more."

"Thank you. It feels better already."

"Good." Her voice changed and seemed to grow far away. "I've lived here half a century. Before then, I was a defender, but I grew too old for such work." She gazed off. "I've seen a lot of things, my dear, but I have the feeling times are changing. I was already a remnant of an old order, but I believe the current times are giving way to a new one." Her eyes grew focused and piercing once again. "I think you're part of that new era."

Brinnie inexplicably shuddered.

"But will it be an era of chaos or renewal? It remains to be seen." She folded her hands together in a businesslike manner. "Well, child, we can't have you wandering through the world of magic without knowing what you're doing. It's a recipe for disaster, especially at a time like this."

"Thank goodness." Finally, someone smart enough to stop letting her muddle around in the dark.

"I think you already know you're a wizard. In your case, you are a Ludovic, which, by nature, should make you a wizard with rather strong magic."

"Why?"

"Magic is hereditary, and some wizard families have stronger magic than others. As a Masters family, Ludovics are naturally more gifted. Now, you, child, are a helper, as your mother suspected. You strengthen the magic of others—without meaning to, sometimes, as you did for the wizards in the dining room and on the road. I suspect this is why your uncle inexplicably disappeared and appeared in front of you before you knew about magic. Your magic rendered his stronger than he anticipated."

Brinnie's eyes widened. All of those times, it really had been her. "But I'm not just a helper."

"You're right. You must want to know about your most obvious ability, the one your family hasn't guessed. You're a shadow walker. I doubt they found that out in any of their tests, since they wouldn't be looking for it."

"That sounds a little...creepy."

She gave a small chuckle. "It is. As far as anyone knew, only dark wizards are shadow walkers."

Brinnie fidgeted with her bandages. "Um, are you saying I'm a dark wizard?"

She laughed. "Of course not, child! I'm saying you're a strange and interesting exception."

An exception. She was never exceptional at anything. Not like Anna. Anna was good at everything. "What do shadow walkers do, exactly?"

"That's a good question. They manipulate shadows. They can hide in the shadows and see in the dark. Other than that, not much is known for sure about them." Chevska leaned forward. "They're rare, you see, and generally secretive. There are tales—very, very old tales—of shadow walkers who could call shadow armies to do their bidding. They're said to see things that others can't. Some have said they can enter dreams, but I wouldn't put much faith in such tales."

Brinnie shifted uncomfortably. It sounded more than creepy, maybe even a bit evil. "I don't know if I like that."

Chevska nodded once. "Before I tell you any more, child, I must warn you. You have lived a comfortable life in the world of humans. You won't find that in the world of magic. The odds are against you. You're a Ludovic, a shadow walker, and an enchantment wizard. It won't be easy."

"I've heard a lot about the dangers of magic lately."

"Ludovic was once a respected name—it's still greatly respected, in some ways, but Wraithwood and Castelon are often at odds. People will look at you differently because of it. More suspicion will be cast on you, especially now after what your uncle has done. It was the right thing, but that will mean little to them." She fixed Brinnie with a hard look. "But at least they won't try to kill you—as an enchantment wizard against the dark wizards, you will be up against a force that will do anything to destroy you. And as a shadow walker...even if all else could be forgiven, people will fear you for what you are. It's a gift, but most won't see it that way."

Brinnie stared. Finally, she could muster the words, "That's depressing."

"Do you still want to know?"

"Yes."

"Good." She smiled. "I'll tell you everything—why we're fighting, how wizardry works, and all of that—but not now. Now, it's time to sleep."

"Wait, what?"

She stood. "It's far too late for such discussions. Now, where did I put it?" She looked around the room with a finger to her chin.

Brinnie stood as well. "Put what?"

"The bedroom. Hmm." She turned to the cat. "Do you remember where I put it, Ami?"

It looked at her out of the corner of its eye with disdain.

"Ah, yes. In the blanket. Thought I was clever, didn't I?" She reached into one of the baskets and pulled out a folded blanket. She shook it out. "There."

Brinnie wasn't sure if she had blinked, but she now stood in another room, exactly like the other one, except that the baskets, table, and chairs were gone and had been replaced by two simple pallets on the floor. The cat had landed on its feet when the basket disappeared but looked none too happy about it. Bruno, on the other hand, simply sniffed the air, then laid his head back down.

"I always keep one for guests." Chevska gestured to one of the pallets. "Make yourself at home, child."

Brinnie was about to voice some sort of protest, or maybe an expression of gratitude, but she was hit with an overwhelming sleepiness. She could barely mumble, "Thank you," before she sank under the weight of her tiredness, collapsing on the pallet. Her last conscious thought was, *This is a spell. I'm being influenced by magic.*

Chapter Twenty-Three

BRINNIE'S EYES OPENED INCREMENTALLY AND SHE took in the small room. As soon as she saw the rough walls and the two pallets, she bolted upright and looked around. *She put a spell on me!*

Chevska was gone, as were Bruno and the cat. Brinnie stumbled outside.

In the mist-filled clearing, Chevska put something in a basket on her arm while the cat lay on a rock and Bruno gamboled about trying to get it to play. Chevska looked up and smiled. "Good morning, child."

Brinnie let out a breath. "Good morning."

Chevska continued to wander around the trees, stooping here and there to pick something up and put it in her basket. Finally, Brinnie asked, "What are you doing?"

"Gathering mushrooms. I can't seem to find my vegetable garden, so mushrooms it is."

"Oh." Brinnie continued to watch for a moment. She wondered if she should ask the question burning in her mind. "Why did you put a spell on me?"

Chevska straightened and looked at her in askance. "A spell?"

"A sleeping spell."

"Ah!" She chuckled and drew closer. "I did not put a spell on you. The sleeping room is designed for sleep. Naturally, you would become sleepy."

"Oh." Brinnie looked back at the hut. It was clearly the same hut she had entered last night, when it had been a kitchen of sorts, but now it was most definitely a place to sleep. *That's strange even for magic.*

Chevska shuffled past her and into the hut. "Where did I put it? Ah, yes." She picked up a bowl and turned it over, and suddenly, the room from the night before returned. A shadow passed over her face then, and she shuddered, putting a hand to her eyes.

"Are you okay?"

She turned slowly. "I'm not as young as I used to be. We must speak, while there is still time." She sat. "Come. I'll tell you what you need to know."

Brinnie entered and sat across the table from her. She'd barely taken a seat when Chevska began, "There is evil in the world."

She stopped, as if this was some great point. Brinnie wasn't sure what was needed for her to continue, so she nodded. "I know."

"Do you?" Those eyes were suddenly difficult to meet. "You do not. It is great, so much greater than you think. You are young, child. You cannot know. You don't know its subtleties, its power. There is the evil of death, of war, of suffering, of the human heart and human cruelties—and these are great. But there is more." She brought a hand down on the table. "There's darkness outside of the human heart. And unlike the human heart, it can't be won over to the light with love or truth but will forever oppose it. Those who serve it...those are who we fight against."

Brinnie shuddered.

"Ah. But I must start at the beginning." She looked into the distance. "Thousands of years ago, wizards could do whatever they pleased. It was easy to subdue the humans and make them slaves, since none could stand against their magic. In those days, many fell prey to pride and lust for power. They considered humans inferior and wanted to eradicate humankind from the earth and create a world entirely for themselves. They wanted to be gods."

The cat jumped into Chevska's lap. She stroked its fur, eyes downcast. Brinnie's skin prickled, words echoing through her skull in the brief silence. *Eradicate humankind...become gods.* Could they actually do that?

"They conquered many and killed many. They were well on their way to achieving their goal, and none of the humans could stop them. But the remnant of wizards who still walked in the light wanted to put an end to the ruthless schemes of the others. So a group of the most powerful of them came together to cast a spell."

The cat jumped down, and Chevska's eyes returned to Brinnie, her gaze piercing once more. "We call this spell the Enchantment. It is the most powerful piece of magic ever enacted. It took decades, even centuries of work and hundreds of wizards. Because of the Enchantment, if a wizard killed a human, the wizard would die instantly the moment that human died. Of course, this put an end to the dark wizards' domination. Wizards were forced to hide, and humans could live without fear of them."

"Then why are they still fighting?" Brinnie asked.

Chevska sighed. "The Enchantment had its flaws. Once a human knew about wizards and wizardry, the Enchantment no longer protected that human, and a wizard could kill him with impunity. Also, it did not prevent wizards from killing one another. But perhaps most important of all, the Enchantment had to attach itself to wizards. It stayed inside them, since it needed the magic to keep its power. But it is possible to cast out the Enchantment, and if all those who still have the Enchantment die or willingly give it up, it will be gone forever, and the dark wizards may do whatever they please once again.

"Throughout the centuries, the Enchantment has been passed down from generation to generation along with the gift of magic. But the dark wizards have never given up. They still want to eradicate humans from the earth. They can't kill humans until the Enchantment is gone, and to get rid of the Enchantment, they either must persuade the others to give it up willingly, or put them to death. And so, throughout history, the dark wizards have attacked those who still possess the Enchantment, and we have continued to fight back."

Brinnie blinked. Her mouth opened and then closed once before she could say, "That's insane." She shook her head. If she believed in magic, why not throw in a completely new twist on history? "Why not just tell everyone? The humans, I mean. Then they could round up the dark wizards and throw them in jail or something."

Chevksa smiled slightly and shook her head. "If the humans know, they can be killed by the dark wizards. They would die."

"In that case, why don't the dark wizards make a worldwide announcement and then kill everyone?"

"That would be much more difficult than you think. How could they be sure they had reached everyone? And how could they be certain everyone believed what they heard? Hearing and believing are two entirely different things." She tapped her fingers. "Besides, there are billions of people in the world. These people would have to be told that the dark wizards were intending to destroy them before the wizards would be able to do so. This would give them a chance to prepare. Governments would be able to raise their armies. What the outcome of such a worldwide war would be is uncertain. The humans would be just as likely to win as the wizards. Millions would die. The dark wizards would prefer to surprise the world by attacking after the Enchantment is gone."

Brinnie had to admit that her points were valid. She rested her forehead on her hand. "This is nuts."

"It's what?"

"Crazy. Hard to wrap my mind around." She shook her head. "I can't do this. I can't be a part of this. If someone should be here fighting dark wizards, it should be Anna, not me. I can't believe this is happening. My life has been normal. I've always been normal..."

Chevska reached out and took Brinnie's hand. She stared fiercely into her eyes. "There is no such thing as normal, yet the world is ever changed by people who are 'normal.' And that is not a curse. It's a blessing." Suddenly, she stiffened. "Do you hear that?"

Very, very faintly, Brinnie thought she heard...voices. Her heart lifted. "Do you think they've found me?"

"Perhaps." Chevska's eyes narrowed. "Or perhaps it is the dark wizards."

The balloon of hope popped, replaced by a sinking feeling of dread. "What should we do?"

"You should hide. They shouldn't have any interest in me." She opened one of the baskets. "In here."

Brinnie clambered in, struggling to fit. Crouching in an awkward position, she managed to get her head just low enough for Chevska to put the lid back on.

Pressing her face to the wall of the basket, she could see through the weave. Chevska looked out the doorway. "Are they coming?" Brinnie asked.

"Yes. It is the dark wizards. They're at the edge of the clearing." She strode to the fireplace and busied herself about the pot. "Lord in Heaven help us."

Please let them just go away, please don't let them find me, please let it be okay.

A shadow fell across the floor. Brinnie had to stifle a gasp.

Standing in the doorway was the man who had given her the scar.

Chapter Twenty-Four

THE MAN'S COLD EYES SCANNED THE room as Chevska turned around. When she saw him, the polite smile froze on her face. Her eyes widened. Then she regained her composure. "Hello."

"Do you live here?" The simple words seemed to diffuse a menacing darkness into the atmosphere. Brinnie sensed a power to him, a power she had only caught a glimpse of on the road during the battle.

Chevska was unfazed. She put one hand on her hip, holding her ladle out with the other. "What do you think?"

"Who are you?"

"It seems I should be asking that of you, as you have come to my door."

He ignored the implied question. "I need to find my way through the Maze. Do you know its ways?"

She shook her head. "It's as much a mystery to me as to anyone else."

He was silent for a moment as his hard eyes bored into her. "You are of the old order."

She nodded. "That I am."

His eyes slowly widened. "The Lady of the Forest," he stated.

Her lips pressed together. Brinnie could see her throat bob. "It's been a long time since I heard that name."

"You should be dead," he breathed.

"And so should you."

They gazed at one another for a moment, each with a strange expression.

"I'm looking for a girl," the man said finally. "Have you seen one?"

"A girl? Of course. I've seen many."

He glowered. "Have you seen one in the Maze? She has dark hair, pale skin."

Brinnie's heart pounded. How did he know she was in the Maze?

"I live alone."

Brinnie noticed a faint coolness on her arm. She glanced down to see the outline of her scar glowing slightly through her shirt. Her mouth dropped open.

"I know she is close by." He pulled his enchanted blade from a sheath at his side. It glowed with a bright silver light.

In response, Brinnie's arm suddenly felt like ice and light pierced through her sleeve. She tried to move her hand around to cover it, but she was wedged too tightly in the basket.

"Ah. I see." Chevska nodded. "You may not have heard. I'm neutral. I no longer fight in the war."

He laughed, a harsh sound. "You have never been neutral."

"Times change."

"If you are truly neutral, will you allow me to search for the girl?"

"Then I would be aiding you."

"But if you do not allow me, you will be aiding the girl."

She turned her full attention to the pot. "I have nothing further to say. Do as you will. I neither aid nor oppose you."

He waved over his shoulder and two other men entered the hut. The three of them began tossing lids off the baskets. Brinnie quickly turned invisible. Her heart pounded. She watched as the men peered into each basket, reaching in and feeling around. Even if they couldn't see her, they were going to feel her. Her heart beat even faster. They pulled out pieces of cloth, bowls, and other odds and ends from the baskets, throwing them on the floor. Brinnie winced as the man from the road poked his knife into one basket. Soon, one of the men had made his way around the room and was searching the basket right next to her. She was on the verge of panic when suddenly, the basket around her disappeared and they were in the sleeping room.

"What did you do?" the man not two feet from Brinnie growled.

Chevska looked over her shoulder and raised an eyebrow. "I did nothing. You moved that blanket. I was keeping the bedroom in it."

The man from the road looked down at his blade. It shone brightly. "She is still in this room." His eyes traveled from wall to wall. "Block the door," he commanded the man next to Brinnie.

She jumped to her feet and tried to run past him, but she was too late. His broad shoulders and wide stance in the small doorway made it impossible for her to slip through. The other man came to stand beside him, completely blocking the doorway.

"I know you are here," the blade man called. "Show yourself. I don't desire to kill you."

Brinnie stood perfectly still.

"If you don't care for your own safety, perhaps you care about an old woman." He stepped closer to Chevska. "Show yourself, or I will kill her."

Chevska shook her head, turning to face him. "You wouldn't kill me."

"Would I not?" He snapped his arm up, the point of the blade under her chin. "You certainly deserve it." His eyes traveled the room. "Come out, girl."

Brinnie remained invisible. Would he really kill Chevska? Or was he bluffing?

"Mordred." Chevska's eyes beseeched him, not in fear, but with pain. "You're better than this."

His face contorted in a snarl. "*I'm* better than this? Oh, Morgana. How far you've fallen."

With that, he thrust his blade into her chest.

Brinnie screamed. "No!"

A flash of bright light burst from Chevska, but a flash of dark from Mordred overwhelmed it. Mordred yanked the blade out of her chest, and Chevska fell, clutching the wound.

He turned and looked at Brinnie.

"How could you?" Her voice cracked. "What did she ever do to you?"

His eyes grew even harder. "More than you would ever know." He glared back at Chevska. "But now, you will die knowing that finally, we have everything that we need to win. The world will fall. And you— you are the one who made it possible."

Her expression calm beneath the pain, she pressed a hand to her chest. "You are wrong, Mordred. What you have done has only set the prophecy into motion. You are bringing about your own doom."

"Silence!" He threw out his arm and she flew back, as if struck by a powerful force. Then he turned fully to Brinnie, striding toward her. "Now for you."

"No." The word came from behind him, softly but firmly. Brinnie stumbled back, away from Mordred, as Chevska struggled to her feet, her gaze directed at him. He began to turn around, but Chevska thrust both hands outward.

Something like a force rippled out from her and struck him. Before he could react, he froze into place.

Chevska collapsed. Brinnie ran to her, falling to her knees. "What can I do? Bandages? Something?"

"No," Chevska gasped. She grasped Brinnie's wrist with one bloodied hand. "You don't have long. It took the last of my strength to petrify him, and it won't hold."

"Then we have to hurry." Tears blurred her vision. "I'll grab some cloth, we'll bind you up, and we'll run."

"No, child. My time upon this earth is done."

"Don't say that." Brinnie's eyes cast around the room, searching for something to help. "We'll get you fixed up."

"Listen. You must escape. You must stop Mordred."

"Me? I can't do that. Let's get to safety, and we can find Uncle Merlin, and—"

"Focus!" Chevska squeezed Brinnie's wrist, hard. "There is a prophecy in Mordizan. If you find it, it will tell you how to defeat Mordred." She coughed, and blood stained her lips. "Go. He will be free soon."

"But—"

"Go!"

Brinnie stood and stumbled back. Tears ran down her face. "Chevska..."

The old woman's expression softened. "Don't worry. I am going to my eternal home. Now it is your turn to protect this one." Her eyelids fluttered. "I can rest at last."

Brinnie nodded, unable to speak.

The woman's eyes glazed over.

Brinnie stepped backward. "No. No, no, no." She stood, frozen in horror. In front of her, Mordred's finger twitched. She jumped—time was running out. She wriggled her way between the frozen men blocking the door and burst outside.

In the clearing, several men milled around or sat under the trees. She stopped, and for a moment they stared at her while she stared back at them. Then one yelled, "The girl!"

They leaped into action. Brinnie took off, pursued by the men. She heard a whooshing sound and barely ducked out of the way of a ball of fire. *You idiot!* She yanked shadows over herself. She heard exclamations of surprise behind her but didn't slow. She darted into a gap in the hedges and continued running until her breath came in ragged gasps.

She collapsed to her knees at a fork in the Maze, panting. She stared at the ground, uncomprehending.

She should have stayed. Surely, she could have done something to save Chevska. The old woman had died protecting her.

This is insane! She was trapped in a magical maze, pursued by evil wizards who had killed the kindly old woman who had taken her in. Brinnie wished she could have done something. She was a wizard, after all. She pounded a fist into the earth. *What use am I as a wizard if I let people die?* She should have been able to stop him.

A new and horrible thought struck her. Where was Bruno? He had been outside when the evil wizards came. Where had he gone? Had they hurt him?

Tears ran down her face. *What now?* Even if she had wanted to, she couldn't go back. The Maze would never let her. And besides, Mordred would capture her. She had to continue trying to find a way out of the Maze. If she could make it back to Wraithwood, they would know what to do.

With that, she stood. For no reason, she decided to take the right path. Reason and logic seemed useless in navigating the Maze. She dropped the shadows covering her, wiped her eyes with her sleeve, and strode forward.

This path seemed narrower than most of those she had been down before. She could touch both walls without stretching her arms out more than a few inches from her body. She imagined the hedges squeezing in to crush her. The mist made it difficult to see, and the hedges looming through it gave her the chills. For the first time, she was truly and completely alone, without even a dog for company. And this time, she knew evil wizards were out there somewhere, trying to capture her.

With these pleasant thoughts, she picked up her pace.

Chapter Twenty-Five

AS IT GREW COLDER, BRINNIE ASSUMED night was approaching. Her feet dragged, but she hated to stop in the narrow, twisting part of the Maze she'd been stuck in all day. She had to come across a clearing of some sort eventually.

She checked her scar. No unusual glowing or feelings of cold. Mordred and his cronies weren't near.

Her chest ached. Every day, a rescue became less and less likely. Before, she could have put it down to delays. Now, she feared the only reason it could be taking so long was because something terrible had happened. Images of Mordred's blade and Chevska's blood flashed through her mind.

Not paying attention to where she placed her feet, she tripped and fell. "Oof!" She looked back to see a protruding root in the path. That was new. Maybe different terrain lay ahead.

She scrambled to her feet and resumed with a much quicker pace. Not two minutes later, she emerged into a wide-open area.

Open wasn't quite the right word. There were trees and underbrush everywhere, but it felt spacious after the narrow corridors of the Maze. She stumbled out into the trees and took in a deep breath. She knew she was still in the Maze, but she felt like she could breathe without the looming hedges surrounding her.

Though exhausted, her first order of business was to try to find water. She pushed through the dense underbrush, searching the ground for signs of small rivulets running to a larger stream.

She had searched for a few minutes without any luck when, out of the corner of her eye, she saw something halfway hidden under the ferns and covered in leaves. Something blue. She brushed the leaves away and pulled it out.

What on earth?

She held a grime-covered doll in a faded blue dress. She wasn't sure what the body was made out of, but it looked like sanded wood. A matching blue bow adorned the doll's dirty hair, and where the paint hadn't peeled off, Brinnie could see the remnants of a sweet smile, rosy cheeks, and brown eyes. *And who did you belong to?*

She put it back where she had found it. It wasn't water. She continued, but only a few seconds later she came across what looked like a baseball. *Odd.*

The trees began to thin. She looked up, but mist still obscured the sky, blocking a possible view of the moon and stars. The underbrush came to consist more and more of scraggly, weed-like plants, and the ground crunched under her feet. She stooped to investigate. The earth seemed unusually smooth, and when she brushed away some of the dirt, she saw what looked like brick paving.

Now that she knew about the paving, she could see where the road led. A clear difference existed between the surrounding trees and the weeds and saplings that grew from the path. She followed it.

Within a few moments, she saw something ahead, covered in weeds and grass. She picked up the pace and soon found herself in the middle of an eerie scene.

Greenery sprouted from the charred remains of what had once been buildings, now only foundations and crumbling bricks. The buildings that had once lined the street were now half hidden in vegetation. As Brinnie drifted along the road, she passed more and more burned structures. They continued, some of the foundations suggesting large buildings, others small. She was now in a wide clearing, with only grass, weeds, and saplings, but to her horror, she could see the telltale piles of brick peeking through the underbrush all the way across. It looked as if an entire town had burned to the ground.

What happened here? And when? She continued walking, taking in the destruction. She came to what she thought was a large boulder in the path, but she soon realized it was the basin of what had once been a fountain. The crumbled remains of whatever statue had decorated the center littered the interior. It didn't seem like it had slowly crumbled— the large chunks suggested intentional destruction.

A wide circle of road surrounded the fountain, with charred

remains of buildings around it and four roads leading out from the circle. She guessed she was in what had once been the town center.

As she continued, the foundations and piles of brick became spaced farther apart, and the trees grew taller. She could barely discern the road. It led up an incline until a wrought iron gate rose from the mist at the top of the hill. It reached about chest height, set in a fence of the same wrought iron. Over the gate, she could see that there were no trees on the hill. Instead, rows of stone slabs stood upright.

A graveyard.

She shuddered. It didn't matter if she could see perfectly well—the idea of being in a graveyard alone at night horrified her. She turned invisible. *Yes, Brinnie, because if you were visible the invisible ghosts would get you. Great logic.* She took a deep breath. *Ghosts aren't real. People don't hang around after they die. You know that.*

Her heart beating a rapid staccato, she put her hand to the latch and pulled upward. It creaked loudly, and she winced. She pushed the gate, and it swung open with a long squeak.

She knelt before the first grave she came to, hoping it would shed light on the identity of the former inhabitants of the deserted town. Her gaze passed over the name and epitaph and came to rest on the dates. They were recent. In fact, the date of death was only about thirty years ago.

Her skin prickled. She moved on to the next headstone.

The date of birth was twenty years before that of the other, but the date of death was exactly the same. Her brow wrinkled.

She walked along the entire row, and as she did, her disturbance grew. Every single date of death was the same—a day about thirty years ago.

Row after row of headstones listed the names of children, adults, and the elderly. Some epitaphs cited the person's family and whom they were buried alongside, while others had no epitaphs at all. But each headstone was of the same stone and cut, and each cited the same date of death. Her stomach turned sour.

At the very back of the graveyard, under a spreading tree, two headstones stood apart, larger and more ornate than the others. Brinnie knelt in front of them and read first one, then the other.

Ieuan Ludovic
Master of Wraithwood
beloved father of Merlin and Eira
He gave his life to save those he loved.

Elaine Ludovic
Wife of Ieuan Ludovic, Master of Wraithwood
beloved mother of Merlin and Eira
She gave her life to defend those she loved.

The death dates were the same as all the others.

Brinnie rocked back. What awful thing had happened here? Not only had all of those people died, so had her grandparents. Had they died in the fire too?

Trying to process the horror, Brinnie began to realize why Mom didn't want to talk about her childhood. Whoever the people in the town had been, they had likely been her friends and neighbors. In one day, she had lost them all, and her parents as well.

But what happened? She thought she remembered Chevska saying something about a tragedy that had happened three decades ago. *What did she call it? The invasion of Wraithwood?*

Chills ran down Brinnie's spine. Invasions were made by people. This was no accident. It was a massacre.

Chapter Twenty-Six

BRINNIE GENTLY TRACED THE LETTERS OF the names on the headstones. Her grandparents were buried here, the grandparents she had never known and never would know, at least not on this earth. She tried to imagine how she would feel if she lost both her parents and all of her friends and neighbors in one day.

She would be shattered.

Shattered enough to run away from home? To leave her sibling and everything she knew behind?

If her old way of life had caused the horrible tragedy, then yes. She would flee as far as she could.

Slowly, she began to understand her mother. She understood why she had fled from magic—the fighting had killed everyone. She understood why her mother didn't want her family to have anything to do with magic—she didn't want to lose them, too. And finally, she understood why Mom had called her a mistake. Why she always worried that Brinnie would mess something up, act out, cause problems. After all Mom's hard work to escape magic and create a safe family, Brinnie had come along and threatened everything.

Brinnie felt tears forming in her eyes. Now, she was making Mom's worst fears come true. She was trapped in a maze with evil wizards after her, with little hope of rescue or escape. Quentin knew her identity, knew she was a wizard. He would tell the others, and with a little digging, they would find Mom, Dad, and Anna. A tear hit her grandmother's gravestone and rolled downward. *She was right. I am a mistake.*

But it didn't really matter. The dark wizards already had the Master Key, Uncle Merlin was missing, something terrible must have happened to the Wraithwooders for them not to have come for her, and soon the dark wizards would take over the estates, and then the world.

Then they would all be dead anyway. She clutched her arms over her chest.

She reread her grandmother's epitaph. *She gave her life to defend those she loved.* Whom exactly had she defended? The entire town had burned to the ground.

She stood and kicked the grass with a huff.

But Wraithwood still stands. And Mom, and Uncle Merlin, and the Winslows and Miss Burtle...all of them survived. Elaine Ludovic died, but somehow, she and her husband had defended Wraithwood itself.

And now Brinnie was alone, and everyone, not just Chevksa, might be captured or dead for all she knew. "Fantastic," she muttered aloud. "You saved them, and I managed to screw it up."

"Brinnie?"

She screamed and stumbled backwards. She hit the headstone behind her and flipped over it, landing on her back with her legs in the air. She wriggled frantically, trying to get to her feet. *Ghosts. Graveyard. Night. Run!*

"Brinnie! Are you there?"

She finally gained her feet, poised to fight. Then she recognized the voice. "Quentin?"

Quentin stood somewhat to the left of her grandparents' graves under the spreading tree, looking around in confusion and squinting. "Yes, it's me."

"Quentin!" *He's not dead. Are they all not dead?* She darted forward and grabbed his shoulders. "Are you okay? Is everyone all right?"

"Agh!" He jerked and struggled. "Something's got me! Brinnie, where are you?"

She quickly let go and stood back. "Oh!" She let out a sharp laugh and turned visible. "I'm sorry! I completely forgot I was invisible."

He jumped when she returned to visibility. "You turn invisible?"

"Yes."

He pressed a hand to his chest. "You almost gave me a heart attack."

"*I* almost gave *you* a heart attack? I did *not* expect a gravestone to talk back to me." She glanced at her grandmother's headstone, then returned to grilling him. "How did you get here? Are the others here? Is everyone okay? What's going on?"

He held his hands up. "Slow down. Let's see." He ticked off answers on his fingers. "I was sleeping under that tree for the night when I heard your voice, I'm here alone, as far as I know they're fine, and I'm here to rescue you."

Her knees wobbled in relief. "I thought something terrible had happened to all of you when you didn't come. But...everyone's okay. And all we have to do is find Bruno and get out of here and everything will be fine and—" She thought her cheeks might split from her widening grin. All was well. Soon she would be safe, the evil wizards would be left wandering in the Maze, and...

He rubbed the back of his neck. "About that. It's not quite that simple."

"What do you mean?" Her grin started to fade at his sober expression.

He glanced around and shuffled his feet. "I don't have the parchment."

"You...don't have it?" Brinnie took a deep breath. "I thought you could only get through with the parchment."

"Um, yes, that's true."

"Then why didn't you bring it?"

"I did." He looked at the ground, then back up at her sheepishly. "But I lost it."

It took Brinnie a moment to comprehend. She struggled for words. "You lost the parchment."

"Yes."

"Our only way out."

"Yes."

"So you're just as lost as I am."

He looked up at the sky as if pleading for death. "Yes."

She let out her breath with a whoosh. "How? How did you lose it?"

"I don't know!" He rubbed his forehead. "I set it right next to me when I went to sleep, and when I woke up, it was gone."

She put her head in her hands. "You didn't put it somewhere safe?"

"It's really old. I was afraid if I rolled it up, I'd destroy it." He jutted his chin. "I couldn't do anything else with it."

"So you left it unrolled on the ground?"

"Yes!" He threw his hands up. "I don't know what happened to it. I didn't hear anyone come by. It must be the magic of the Maze."

She gaped at him. "I'm pretty sure it wasn't magic. You put a giant piece of paper on the ground, outside. What did you think would happen?"

"Excuse me?"

"Obviously, *it blew away!*"

He slowly lowered his hands that he had raised along with his voice. "Oh."

Brinnie sighed and turned away. *Stay calm. Anger doesn't help anything. It can't be changed now. Forgive and move on.*

"So now what?"

Despite her resolve, the look she gave him was anything but forgiving. "More of the same. Wandering around lost. But now, we get to enjoy each other's company."

Brinnie rolled over and winced as a stick poked her in the back. She pulled it out from under her and threw it aside. "Quentin?" she whispered.

Nothing. She sighed. She didn't know how he could sleep.

They were still in the graveyard, bedded down in the tall grass on either side of the tree. Brinnie didn't know if sleeping in a graveyard was disrespectful to the dead, but, she reasoned, they were dead, so they didn't care.

Quentin had confirmed that it was night—at least she could count on him for that. He had also informed her of a small brook on the other side of the fence from the graveyard. The water didn't taste quite right, but she drank it anyway. They concluded there was no sense in beginning their aimless wandering at night while Quentin could hardly see, and Brinnie felt ready to keel over from exhaustion, so Quentin returned to his previous state of rest while Brinnie tossed and turned.

Her mind still spun from the events of the day—Chevska's sacrifice, all she had learned about herself, discovering the burned town.

But finally, her mind settled on her earlier conversation with Quentin.

They had been sitting on the ground as Quentin pulled provisions from a knapsack. Mrs. Winslow had provided him with plenty of food and two bottles of water. The water had run out long ago, leaving Quentin to fill them with questionable brook water, but her "snacks" had been more than plentiful.

"Have Mr. Ludovic and Ms. Tynsdale come back yet?" Brinnie asked, biting into a peanut butter sandwich.

Quentin zipped up the bag. "They hadn't when I was there, but I only left the day after you did. They might have word from them by now."

"Oh." She couldn't decide if that was heartening or not. "How were you chosen to be the one to come rescue me?"

He shrugged. "I volunteered."

"You did?"

"Of course. I wasn't doing much good sitting around at the house. And..." He fiddled with a strap of the knapsack. "It was partially my fault to begin with."

"What do you mean?" Brinnie took a swig of weird-tasting water. "You're not the one who went chasing a rabbit into the Maze."

"What?"

"That's why I came in here in the first place. Bruno was chasing a rabbit, and I went after him. I thought if I caught him before he got too far, we could get back out easily." She grimaced. "I didn't realize that the Maze shifts."

"Oh. We wondered how you ended up in here." He stalled, unzipping the bag and rooting around until he pulled out an apple. "I accidently did something to the sink in the washhouse, I'm not sure what, but there was water spraying everywhere. By the time Mr. Winslow got it fixed, it was the middle of the night, and I felt bad, so I offered to watch the parchment and the door. I noticed there was one dot by itself in the Maze, but I didn't think much of it. But when you didn't show up to breakfast, we turned the place upside-down before I put two and two together and pointed out the lone dot in the Maze. And here I am."

"Oh." Brinnie cocked her head. "But I didn't go anywhere for that whole first day. How come you didn't find me?"

"Even with the parchment, it's still a maze." He drew a stick in circles. "I had to go around the house at least four times to get to where you were, not counting all the switchbacks and loops. It got too dark for me to see, so I stopped for the night. The next morning, I started out again, but you were moving all over the place. I spent the whole day trying to chase you down. I lost the parchment that night."

Brinnie slapped a hand to her forehead and leaned on her knees. "If I had been patient for one more day we would have been out of here by now." *Stupid, impatient, reckless.* "I—I'm sorry I got upset with you about losing the parchment. Thank you for coming after me."

He shrugged, fidgeting with the apple. "Honest mistakes. I'm just glad I found you...or, I guess, glad we stumbled upon each other. Now all we have to do is find our way out of here."

She shook her head and echoed his words from earlier. "It's not quite that simple." She sighed. "Mordred knows I'm here. He's after me."

"Who?"

"The dark wizard. I think I'd better explain." She popped a last bite into her mouth and washed the peanut butter down with another swig of dank water. *I'm going to get sick from this.* "And I should probably start at the beginning."

As she began explaining about Chevska, Quentin interrupted her. "The Lady of the Forest? You saw her?"

"I haven't gotten to that part yet," Brinnie protested.

"It was her?"

"Yes, but you have to let me get there."

Quentin leaned forward. "Do you realize who she is?"

Brinnie frowned. "I don't know. She called herself Chevska, but then Mordred called her Morgana..."

"Exactly! She's *Morgana le Fey!*"

Brinnie's brow wrinkled. "Excuse me?"

"Morgana le Fey. Arguably the most famous wizard ever, behind Myrddin, of course. Even humans know about her."

"Myrddin? You mean Merlin?"

"Yes, but Merlin wasn't his actual name. It's a variation of

Myrddin. But you know who I'm talking about now, right?"

"Of course. From Arthurian legend." She shook her head. "But that's impossible. It's a myth. Besides, she would have to be like, what, a thousand years old?"

"More than that."

Brinnie tried to wrap her mind around that. Chevska's ancient appearance made that much more sense.

"Everyone wondered what happened to her after the invasion of Wraithwood," Quentin mused. "She hasn't been heard from in decades. So she's still alive."

"Well." Brinnie looked at her hands. "Not anymore."

As Brinnie told all about Chevska and Mordred—all, of course, except what Chevska had told her about Brinnie and her family— Quentin's frown deepened. "And after wandering around for a long time, I ended up here," she finished.

Quentin scratched his chin. "This Mordred—do you know anything else about him?"

"Nothing. I just know he's the man from the battle on the road."

His brow furrowed. "Morgana was old. She couldn't have had much strength left. But still, it would take a very powerful wizard to kill her."

"What do you think he meant, when he said she had wronged him?"

"Who knows?" He chucked his apple core over the fence, into the woods. "Most dark wizards respected her neutral status since she used to be a dark wizard, but a lot of them still think she's a traitor, and she was quite the warrior for our side for a while."

Brinnie decided not to try to understand that explanation at the moment. "What should we do?"

"Avoid Mordred at all costs, I guess. At least your scar is a good early-warning sign."

"For him as well as us," Brinnie reminded him.

"True." Then he grinned. "I told you that you were a wizard, didn't I?"

"Okay, okay."

"Turning invisible is pretty handy. Is there anything else you can do?"

"See in the dark. That's about it, as far as I know. Quentin..." Her gaze swept the graves. "What happened here? What was the invasion of Wraithwood?"

"You don't know?"

She shook her head. "I pretty much know nothing, remember?"

"Oh." He pressed his mouth into a line. "It's not a nice story. It happened a long time ago, probably about thirty years ago. Do you want the detailed version, or the quick version?"

Brinnie settled herself in the grass. "Detailed."

"Okay." He sat back and looked up at the branches stretching across the milky sky. "I might not have it exactly right, since most of what I've heard is gossip, but the story goes like this. Veronica Tynsdale—"

"Veronica?"

He gave her a look. "You're interrupting already?"

"Sorry. But, is she any relation to Lydia Tynsdale?"

"Yes. She was Lydia Tynsdale's mother."

Brinnie folded her arms around her knees. A Ms. Tynsdale origin story. Interesting. "Continue."

"*Anyway*, she came and told Master Ludovic—not Merlin Ludovic, but his father—that there were people wandering around outside the border of the protection spell, and one of them looked hurt. Somehow the whole family ended up going out there—Elaine Ludovic, and Merlin and Eira—and Master Ludovic invited the people in. There were six men, I think, and it turned out it was a trap. Somehow, they maneuvered it so Master Ludovic ended up outside the protection spell, where his Master's powers were useless, and they started fighting."

Brinnie snapped her fingers. "A Master's powers are useless outside the protection spell. What could the, uh, current Master of Wraithwood do beyond the protection spell?"

"You really do know nothing." He put his hands up when Brinnie glared at him. "Just an observation! He would be able to use the magic he was born with—traveling, or instant transport. But that would be it."

Hence the reason he didn't use the magic she'd seen him use on Quentin at the skirmish on the road. Her stomach clenched. That also meant wherever he was right now, he didn't have any of those powers either. "Okay. Go on, please."

He sighed. "I guess once they were outside the protection spell, more dark wizards showed up to help fight. Merlin went back to get help—by instant transport, you know—but when he went out from the house with reinforcements, he left the Gate open, and some of the enemy men went through it to get to the rest of the estate, and—" He rolled his eyes when Brinnie raised her hand. "Yes?"

"What are you talking about, with the gate?"

He rubbed his temples. "How do I explain Gates? I guess I'll have to explain protection spells, too. It's not that complicated, really, but it's hard to explain." He picked up the stick he'd discarded earlier and drew a circle. "So, the protection spell goes around the estate, right? And you can only get through the protection spell if you're invited by the Master—or if it's a blanket invite, where a Master might say, 'All humans who don't know can come through,' or something like that. Which is what Master Ludovic did for those six men—invited them in. But for most estates, you can't actually get to the towns or cities of the estate by just walking through the protection spell." He stabbed a leaf in the center of his circle. "You have to go to the house, or castle, or whatever's at the head of the estate. Then you turn back around and exit the house and grounds through the Gate"—he set a twig near the leaf—"whatever that may be for that particular estate, and you can access the double-space. That's where most wizards live."

Brinnie blinked. "Explain that to me again."

"Okay, for example, you get through the protection spell at Wraithwood, right? But even if you went to this exact spot where we're sitting, this graveyard would not be here. To get here, you have to go to the house, turn back around, and go through the Gate." He tapped the twig. "It's like a portal that only opens from the inside. Then you can get to the destroyed town back there, and this cemetery. Even if you can instant transport, you still can't get to it except by Gate."

"So...we're in a different world or something right now?"

"No, it's the same world. The topography is identical to what you would see if you didn't go through the Gate, except for what people have changed. That's why it's called the double-space. It exists twice."

"I didn't expect a lesson in theoretical physics." She rubbed her face. "I think Mr. Ludovic said something about it before. Something about a Reverse Gate Theory?"

"Right." Quentin sat up straighter. He seemed in his element, explaining wizard theory. Brinnie couldn't help thinking he belonged in a classroom, not in the field as a special agent. "The Reverse Gate Theory states that if someone from the outside—not from the double-space—comes to the Gate, it can be opened to allow them into the estate and thereby accesses the outside, rather than the magical double, due to the presence of these people acting as outside anchors."

"And that's why Mrs. Winslow could let Bert in. Got it. I'll let you continue the story now."

He rubbed his hands together, relishing the lesson in magic theory far more than Brinnie. "Okay, where was I? So, Merlin Ludovic went through the Gate with reinforcements, but he left it open, and some of the dark wizards—the ones Master Ludovic had invited—left the battle, came through the open Gate, then went back through it to get to the double-space. Basically, the townspeople didn't know what hit them. I guess Merlin realized what must have happened when he saw the six dark wizards were missing from the battle, because he sent the reinforcements back to save the town. Merlin went ahead, with instant transport, so he got to the town first, but it was already in flames. With the reinforcements gone, Master Ludovic and his wife were overwhelmed, and they were cut off from getting past the protection spell, so Master Ludovic couldn't rescind the invitation to keep the six men from massacring the entire estate. Oh, that's because a Master has to be on the estate grounds to do all that stuff. So, he let himself be killed."

"What!" Brinnie grabbed her knees. "Why?"

"I haven't gotten to that part yet." Quentin waved her off impatiently. "When he died, Merlin became the Master. And since Merlin was on the estate—"

"He could rescind the invitation," Brinnie breathed.

"Exactly. So he did, which meant the six wizards started wandering around in a daze in the general direction of the protection spell. He transported back to the battle scene, but it was too late. His mother had been killed, too. But he transported Eira back to the house by door—because, you know, he can transport other people by door, now that he's a Master. Weird quirk of Wraithwood. I'm not sure how he knew he could do that, but"—he shrugged—"no one really understands Masters. Anyway, all the other attackers were thereby stuck outside the protection spell. For some reason he didn't kill the six wizards while they were vulnerable—I guess he was too busy trying to make sure everyone was safe. It was too late for the town, though. Everyone was killed. Of course, Veronica Tynsdale was imprisoned at Castelon—"

"Wait, why?"

"Because she was the one who told the Ludovics about the wizards. She must have been in on it."

Brinnie didn't know why she was getting defensive of someone she didn't know, but she crossed her arms. "How do you know that? Isn't it just as likely that she just happened to see them?"

"No. Because the leader was Goran Drakon—Lydia's father and Veronica's ex-husband."

Brinnie pinched the bridge of her nose. Ms. Tynsdale's father was responsible for the deaths of Brinnie's grandparents? "But why would Veronica be in league with her ex?"

"It was all an elaborate plot. She pretended to turn away from the dark wizards so the trap could be sprung."

"So that's why Castelon doesn't trust Ms. Tynsdale," Brinnie mused. She rested her head on her knees. "They lost everyone, all in one day." She lifted her head, mind spinning. "How did they ever get over that?"

Quentin fiddled with his stick. "This is all just gossip, but most people say they never did. Merlin Ludovic pulled away from association with other estates, especially Castelon. He still continued fighting against the dark wizards, but usually in coordination with individuals, not heads of estates. Some say he still blames himself for the attack. And Eira Ludovic...Merlin spread the story that she died in an encounter with dark wizards, but most people don't believe that."

"What do they think happened to her?" Brinnie asked.

He hesitated, then shook his head. "Never mind. It's idle speculation."

"Do they think she's still alive?"

"No. They think she...couldn't quite handle the trauma."

"Oh." She understood now. She rubbed her forehead. "Is this, you know, normal for the wizard world? All this war and death?"

"Well..." He looked down, an unreadable expression on his face. "It's not rare." He stood. "It's really late. We should go to sleep."

Quentin's soft snores brought Brinnie's mind back to the present. She rolled over and sighed. Everything was messed up. How did wizards live with it? How did they deal with a whole way of life that revolved around war?

I don't know how they do it. But I do know one thing. This wizard is not going to live like that. This fighting has to end.

Chapter Twenty-Seven

WHEN MORNING CAME, BRINNIE WASN'T SURE if she had slept or not. In fact, she wasn't even certain it was morning. But Quentin was up and moving around. He approached with two water bottles in his hands, both filled with liquid of a questionable color.

"Is that the same water we drank last night?" Brinnie asked, sitting up.

"It looks a lot worse in a bottle." He looked at the water skeptically. "It's better than nothing. Hopefully we'll find something cleaner."

"Yuck." She stood and brushed herself off, picking a wayward leaf from her hair. *I must look awful.* "What's our plan? How are we going to get out of here?"

"I've been thinking." He began pulling everything out of the knapsack and reorganizing its contents. "The Maze can't be up forever. If we wait, eventually it will be taken down."

"But Uncle Merlin's missing."

Quentin stopped, forearms buried in the knapsack. "*Uncle* Merlin?"

Brinnie cursed internally. She wanted to bang her head against a tree. Of all the things to let slip. "You know, but, *uh,* Merlin is missing."

He stared at her. "Master Ludovic is your uncle?"

She felt her mouth opening and closing like a fish. "That would be ridiculous, since..." She trailed off.

"Since Eira Ludovic is supposed to be dead," Quentin said slowly. "But she's not. You said your mother's name was Eira. She's Eira Ludovic, isn't she?"

"Well..."

He pointed at her, a grin spreading across his face. "I said you looked like a Ludovic!"

"Quentin—"

"I knew it!"

"Quentin, listen." Her fists clenched. "You told me what happened here. You know what my mom went through. You have to understand why she left. You can't tell *anyone.*"

His surprise seemed genuine. "I have to tell Castelon. Unregistered wizards are against the rules."

"Enough with the rules. Castelon has stupid rules." When he still looked unconvinced, she tried to redirect. "Anyway, none of that really matters right now. What matters is getting out of this Maze without getting caught by Mordred. Do you have any plans?"

"Okay, Brinnie *Ludovic.* Like I said, we could wait it out."

I'm going to murder him. "And as I said, Uncle Merlin is missing."

"But he has to come back eventually. Or." He hesitated. "If he doesn't, I would think you would inherit the Mastership, and you could get us out of here."

She stiffened. Inheriting the Mastership. Someone had to, someday. Was there no escaping it? Would she be sucked back, eventually? Could anyone in her family truly leave Wraithwood?

She shut down the runaway freight train of thought. "Okay, let's not even go there. The problem with waiting for him to come back is that we don't have the supplies to last that long."

"All right, do you have any ideas?"

She frowned. "No. But we can't just sit here and subsist on nasty water and a couple apples for what could end up being weeks—or, if they're being held captive or something, even months."

He paled. "Aren't you optimistic."

"I'd rather at least try to get out of here. Any ideas on how to navigate? I've tried making marks or only left turns and all that sort of thing, but it was pointless. The Maze moves, and I could swear it erases my marks."

He closed the knapsack and rested his chin on his fist. "I could try to levitate something, like maybe a branch, and you could sit on it, so you can scout it out."

"Already climbed a tree. The mist gets thicker the higher you go up." She sat back. "Unless you could just levitate us both over the Maze and keep going in a random direction. Then we'd have to come out eventually."

"Well, I tried the levitating branch thing myself, and I completely lost all concept of up and down and crashed exactly where I started. Even if I sent you off alone in some random direction, I wouldn't know when to stop levitating you, and I doubt that I could, anyway."

"All right, not that then."

He stood and started pacing.

Brinnie lay back, picked up a pebble, and began tossing it in the air and catching it. There had to be some trick. But she was drawing a complete blank.

"I got it!"

Brinnie startled and forgot to catch the rock. It came down and hit her in the nose. "Ow!" She sat up. "What is it?"

"Remember the parchment? Mordred has a human with him."

"How do you know that?"

"Because the parchment shows humans and wizards and dark wizards as different colors. But that's not the point. They have a human!"

Color coding. *That makes so much more sense.* "And..."

"Humans aren't as affected by magic as we are. I would think that's why Mordred has a human with him—as a guide. The Maze confuses us with magic, but a human wouldn't be nearly as affected. So, if we find Mordred, we can follow them, and we'll have a much better chance of getting out of here."

Brinnie wrinkled her brow. "One problem. How do we find them?"

"We'll use your scar. We can wander around until it starts to glow, then we'll follow it as it gets brighter."

Brinnie's heart lifted, then sank again. "But he'll know we're there. The blade will tell him."

Quentin grinned. "Not if he doesn't have the blade."

Her heart gave a thump. "You don't mean..."

"We'll wait until night. Then, you'll turn invisible, sneak into their camp, and steal the blade."

"That's insane. There's no way that would work."

"Do we really have a choice?"

The cold glint in Mordred's eye flashed through her mind, a ruthless thrust, a bloody blade. More than anything, she wanted to avoid him at all costs. "Okay, here's the deal. We'll start wandering around. If we get close enough that my scar starts glowing—and that's a big if—then we'll do it."

"No time to waste, I guess." He slung the knapsack over his shoulder. "We've got lots of wandering to do."

"Your turn to choose—left or right?"

"Right."

As they turned down the path, Brinnie held in a sigh. They had been wandering for several hours, and her scar had yet to glow. She blew out a puff of air. They really weren't doing anything different than what she had been doing all along—wandering around and hoping for the best.

"Does it seem brighter down this path to you?" Quentin asked.

Brinnie raised a brow. "You're asking the girl who can't tell day from night?"

"Oh. Right." He shifted the knapsack on his back. "I'm just trying to notice something different. Every path for the last few hours has looked exactly the same."

"I saw a stick down that last one. That was new."

He gave her a look and she smirked.

"Anything?" he asked.

She pushed up her sleeve and showed him. "Nothing."

"I think we're going in circles."

She frowned as they rounded a bend. "What should we..."

Right then, the path opened into a wide, roughly circular space about the size of a football field. At the far side was an opening in the hedge.

Squish! Brinnie lifted her foot and looked down. "Ew! What is that?"

Quentin kept walking. *Squish, squish, squish.* "Finally, something new." He stopped and looked back. "Coming?"

Brinnie regarded the ground skeptically. "What is this stuff?"

"It's *mud.*"

"It feels...weird." She looked up. "Are you sure it's safe to step on?"

He laughed. "As far as I know, mud isn't vicious."

Brinnie scowled. The mud didn't seem right, even to a desert girl. Instead of being squelchy and slick on top, with hard ground underneath, it looked like solid dirt until she stepped on it—then it felt like she had stepped on a giant cake. "You don't think it's a little weird that it hasn't rained in days, but it's all muddy here? And only right here? Look!" She pointed behind them. "It was completely dry back there."

He looked at his feet. The mud had only come halfway up his shoes. "I think it's just mud."

"Maybe we should turn around."

"And keep wandering in the same place over and over again? Maybe if we cross this mud, we'll finally get somewhere new."

He had a point. *Okay, Brinnie. It's only wet dirt. Don't be silly.* "Okay."

She took slow, careful steps, easing from one foot to the other. Each time, she felt as if the ground wouldn't hold her, and she was going to fall through. The mud gave more and more with every step she took, but she didn't dare stand in once place too long for fear of sinking.

"Slow down!" she called to Quentin. He splatted along far ahead in the middle of the mud plain, his feet making sucking noises as he strode carelessly.

He turned and grinned when he saw Brinnie's mincing steps. "Are you afraid of a little mud?"

"Weirdest mud I've ever seen," she muttered. She looked up from the careful placement of her feet and gasped. "Quentin! You're sinking!"

With a great *squoo-elch!* he pulled out one leg and then the other. Mud covered his legs to the shin. Finally, he looked as concerned as Brinnie felt. "It's fine. We just have to keep moving." With that, he turned, took a step, and fell through the mud.

"Quentin!" Brinnie ran forward. Her feet made strange slapping noises against the ground. Then, only feet from Quentin, her foot plunged through.

She cried out as she fell. She tried to push herself up with the foot that was free, but the force plunged it down into the mud as well, leaving her up to her thighs in the strange, clay-like mud. She wriggled, reaching with her feet for solid ground under the mud to push off from, but found none. In front of her, Quentin struggled madly, somehow having sunk chest-deep in the mire.

A tingle ran up her arm—something cold. "Oh, no." Sure enough, light began to shine through her sleeve.

"Quentin." She tried to keep her voice low. "Quentin, stop!"

He paused in his struggle and craned his neck to look at her. "What?"

"They're nearby. My scar is glowing."

His eyes widened. "We have to get out of here."

She cast about for an idea. "Don't move. I'm going to try something."

Slowly, she lay backward and spread her upper body out over the surface of the mud. She had read that in quicksand, struggling made a person sink faster. Maybe it was the same with mud. Then, with her arms spread out and her weight dispersed as evenly as possible, she pushed herself backward with her arms. The mud resisted. Holding on with her upper body, she pulled her left leg up with all her might. Her shoe was sucked off, and then her sock, but with one final squelch, her entire leg sprang free. She spread it out over the surface of the mud, grabbed her upper right leg with both hands, and pulled. With the combined pulling strength of her arms and her leg, it, too, came free. "Got it."

Barefoot and covered in clay, she army-crawled over to Quentin. She sat up slowly. "Give me your hands."

Without question, he grabbed them. She tightened her hold, took a deep breath, then pulled with all her might, throwing herself backward as if rowing a boat.

"Agh!" She barely muffled her cry of pain. She'd forgotten about her injured wrist. She fell, back, clutching it, as pain streaked up her arm. "Ow, ow, ow."

"Are you all right?"

She clenched her teeth, and her scar burned colder. "I'm fine. Just hurry! Do what I did."

She had pulled him up far enough that most of his upper half was free, but it seemed to take him a painfully long time to pull himself out of the mud. As soon as he had broken free, lying spread-eagled and panting, Brinnie started pulling herself toward the other side of the mud field with one arm. "Hurry, come on!"

Quentin crawled much faster using two arms. When he reached the point where the mud would hold them, he stood and waved to Brinnie. "You can do it!"

She tried to get to her feet, but she took one step and sank into the mud. Too soon. Quentin came running back toward her, but a few yards from her, both his feet sank in the mud. His eyes fixed over her shoulder and his mouth opened. "They're here."

Brinnie turned. On the other side, at the entrance to the path they had come from, several figures stood watching them. She wasn't close enough to see their faces, but she recognized the one in front—Mordred.

Heart pounding in her chest, Brinnie lay back and yanked her feet out of the mud. She rolled over and scrambled forward on her stomach.

Quentin did the same. Side by side, they crawled furiously for the exit.

Brinnie chanced a glance behind and gasped. "They're a lot smarter than us. Hurry!"

Mordred's men darted around the edge of the field, close to the hedges, where the ground was the firmest. They were swiftly gaining.

Brinnie scrambled forward, trying to use both arms to crawl, but her wrist wouldn't hold. She realized Quentin was still right beside her, though he could move much faster. "What are you doing? Hurry!"

"I'm sticking with you."

Panting and clawing at the mud, she gritted out, "No. I'm not fast enough to get away. Go!"

He gave her a stubborn look. "I'm not leaving you."

"You have to!" She stopped talking to gasp for breath. "I'm getting captured no matter what. But if you escape, you can come back and save me." *Ideally.*

No response came for a minute, other than panting from exertion. "I guess I'll have to do the nighttime sneaking."

"Exactly."

He sped up. Soon, he was on his feet and running. Then he disappeared into the Maze.

Only seconds after Quentin escaped, Mordred's men reached the exit. Brinnie stopped her mad crawl. A few began to run into the Maze after him, but Brinnie heard Mordred call, "Stay. You'll only get lost chasing him."

Mordred himself strode forward and stood in front of the exit, the shining blade in his hand. "It seems we meet again."

Brinnie turned to go the other way, but his men blocked that entrance as well. She was trapped.

"You have nowhere to go. Do not make this difficult. Come here."

"No."

He regarded her with a maddeningly calm expression. "Don't be foolish. If I intended to hurt you, I would have done so already. But if you continue to be obstinate, I will. Come. You have no other choice."

Brinnie's mind raced. She couldn't turn invisible—they would all see her footprints on the mud and know exactly where she was. She couldn't fake anything...or could she?

She turned around and began crawling in the other direction, back toward the middle of the field.

"As you can see, you are indeed surrounded," Mordred called.

"Thanks. Saw that."

"You can't stay out there forever. If you continue to waste our time, I will send someone after you."

"That's nice."

"Stop!"

"Okay." She turned around, got to her feet, and stomped each foot into the mud. Slowly, she began sinking. "You said I don't have a choice. But I do. I'm not going with you dark wizards. I'd rather drown in this mud field!"

One of the men next to Mordred started to step forward, but Mordred held out an arm to stop him. "You wouldn't do something so foolish."

"I would and I am. I'm not going with you."

She heard one of the men say something, but Mordred shook his head. She didn't catch what he said in return. Then he turned back to her. "If you would rather die, that is your choice."

She wriggled her feet, and the mud reached her waist. "I'd rather drown in mud at fourteen than live to be old and evil like you."

"Very well."

Brinnie stared back at him defiantly, trying to keep from shaking. This was not going as she had hoped.

The mud reached her chest. "Still intent on death?" Mordred asked. "Yes."

"Please, continue."

The idea had been that the men would come rushing to save her. In the chaos, she would turn invisible, faking having been sucked into the mud to her death, and crawl away while they searched through the mud for her. Instead, there was no chaos. They all simply watched.

The mud reached her neck. Only her head and arms remained above ground. She was almost beyond the point of no return.

"Ah!" She screamed, threw her hands in the air, then cut the scream short as she turned invisible. She smacked her arms against the mud to fake the sound of being suddenly sucked down into the mud.

"Now get her," Mordred said.

As three men made their way across the mud, Brinnie began trying to pull herself up, only to reach a horrifying conclusion—she couldn't get out. She was too deep in the mud to lie back or push up with her arms, and when she tried to push with her hands, not only did her wrist flare with pain, but both of her hands sank in the muck. She tried desperately to pull her legs upward, but she couldn't fight the thick mud. She continued to sink.

No. No, no, no. The mud reached her chin as she struggled. She tried to keep her head above ground as it crept toward her mouth. The men were drawing closer, but she was completely stuck. *I'm actually going to drown.*

She changed back to visibility. "Help!" She only managed to gasp a quick breath before the mud closed over her mouth, then nose. She struggled, but as she closed her eyes and the mud rolled over her head, she could only hold her arms up in the desperate hope that her enemies would rescue her.

Chapter Twenty-Eight

THE FIRST THINGS SHE WAS AWARE of were her burning nose and the gritty taste in her mouth.

Next, the horrible pain in her wrist.

She groaned and opened her eyes. Little brown and gray dots danced everywhere—no wait, that was something caked to her eyelashes. And something red and orange—a campfire.

She glanced to the side and shrieked when she saw someone next to her. Or at least, she tried to shriek. Instead, she emitted a rasping noise that made her cough.

"Hush. I worked hard enough to save your life once. I don't want to have to do it again."

Brinnie blinked as the figure came into focus, a man with gray hair and a long beard to match. "Who..."

"Dolphus. Healing wizard. Knew I'd be useful on an expedition like this, though I didn't think I'd be healing enchantment wizards."

Brinnie closed her eyes again. He was one of the bad guys. She must be in their camp.

She gathered her strength, then in one quick burst, she opened her eyes, leaped to her feet, and turned invisible. Or rather, that was the plan. Instead, she opened her eyes, turned invisible, and fell on her face.

"Now you stop that. You're in no condition for such things."

"I'm sure it had nothing to do with the fact that I'm tied up hand and foot," she rasped, rolling over and returning to visibility.

He chuckled and helped her sit up against a tree. "There, now. Behave yourself."

She coughed and spat out a mouthful of grit. She grimaced. "I'm disgusting."

"I won't argue," he said with another chuckle. "I'll go get some water."

After Dolphus left, Brinnie looked around. On the other side of the campfire, several forms lay on the ground under blankets, apparently sleeping. She looked down. Not only were ropes tied around her hands and feet, but one end of a rope wrapped around the tree, with the other end attached to her feet. She wasn't going anywhere.

"Hsst. Brinnie."

She jumped, eyes darting for the source.

"Don't look," a voice breathed, "but I'm behind the tree. Once that old man is asleep, I'll get you out of here."

"Quentin?" Brinnie whispered in amazement. "How...?"

"Shh. He's coming back."

She heard a slight rustling behind her. Dolphus came from the other direction, bearing a canteen. "Here we are," he said as he returned. "Thirsty?"

She narrowed her eyes at the canteen. "Is that poisoned?"

"Why would we have gone to the trouble of saving you just to poison you? Open."

Brinnie tilted her head back and opened her mouth, feeling like a baby bird. She spluttered and choked as Dolphus dumped the water all over her face. "Why?" she gasped.

"Quit complaining. It's only water."

"Wouldn't it be easier to untie my hands?"

He snorted and screwed the lid back on the canteen. "'Untie my hands,' the invisibility wizard says. 'I won't escape.'"

"Point taken."

"Now, I'd much rather rest than watch an indecisively suicidal ninny, so if you're sure you won't die, I'm going to sleep." He fixed her with a hard stare, eyebrows raised.

Her lips twitched in spite of her. "I'll try not to die."

"Good." He settled his belt. "I'm holding you to it."

Brinnie watched as he waddled on bowed legs to the other side of the fire and unrolled some blankets.

He was about to lie down when Mordred strode from the other side of the sleeping men. "What are you doing?" Mordred asked.

Dolphus plopped down. "Going to sleep."

"And leaving the girl unattended?"

"She isn't going anywhere. She can turn invisible as much as she wants. It won't get her out of those ropes."

Mordred's cold gaze fixed upon Brinnie, and a chill ran down her spine. "Don't underestimate her."

He stepped around Dolphus and strode toward her. His hands clasped behind his back, he loomed over her like an ominous specter. "I see you're alive."

She wanted to say something snarky, but no sarcastic replies came to her. A layer of ice seemed to slip over her mind in his presence. "Yep."

He turned sideways as if viewing some distant sight. "I believe we may have met under inconvenient circumstances."

She said nothing, simultaneously trying to hide her trembling and wanting to smack the imperturbably sinister expression off his face.

He turned his gaze back to her. "You're angry with me."

She scowled. That broke the barrier on her snark. "No, really. First you kill my friend, then you try to kill me, and now you have me tied to a tree."

He resumed his distant look. "You're new to wizardry, are you not?"

What was he driving at? "I don't know."

"No one bothered to tell you much, did they?" She remained silent as he slowly paced. "Yet, you have been staying at Wraithwood. With Merlin. It's not a wonder, then, that you have been deceived."

"What do you mean?" she blurted. Then she bit her lip. *Don't ask questions. That's what he wants you to do.*

"I suppose you think Merlin and his allies are the good ones, and we're evil."

"It seems pretty obvious."

"Obvious? Hm. Perhaps if you have only heard their lies."

She snorted, then coughed, her throat still gritty. "No, obvious because you attacked us, you held a knife to my throat, you gave me this scar, you killed Chevska, and you've hunted me down. That's bad guy stuff."

"Is it?" He looked at her sideways. "Yet, I seem to remember Merlin fighting in many battles. Do you think he has never attacked or killed anyone?"

For a moment, Brinnie paused. Had Uncle Merlin killed anyone? *No. Stop. He's getting in your head.* "If he did, it was to protect the world against dark wizards like you."

"Protect it? Don't you know we're trying to make the world a better place?"

She raised an eyebrow. "By murdering all humans?"

"Is that what so-called Chevska told you?" He barked a dry laugh. "This has nothing to do with wiping out the human race. Think about it. Wizards have a wonderful amount of power. The things humans have done in the last few centuries with their technology? Wizards have been doing them for millennia. It isn't right that we have to hide in the shadows, in obscure corners of the world, simply because we have been made defenseless against humans."

His jaw clenched, his cloak flapping as he paced. "We should be free. And with our freedom, we would not only live better lives, but think what we could do for the world. With our power, there would be no more famine or drought. Our healing wizards could cure those with incurable diseases. Our magic could defend against any weapon." He turned to face her completely, his eyes burning with a cold fire. "Wizards are the rightful rulers of the world."

Her head started to hurt. "You're power hungry."

"No." He knelt in front of her, and she shrank back. "The idiots in Castelon are power hungry. They want to regulate us all, confine us to hidden lives of no meaning. People like Merlin aren't protecting the world. It's their fault people are dying every day. It's their fault we all have to hide. Wouldn't you like to be able to let the world see you for what you are? Without lies? Without deception?"

She couldn't argue with his logic yet, but she knew he couldn't be right. "No. If you're the good guy here, why are you acting like such a bad guy?"

"You don't understand. Everything we did was for good." His gray eyes bored into hers, and she averted her eyes, avoiding his gaze. "I gave you that mark so I could find you and help you. The woman you call Chevska—she was one of the worst of the oppressors. Anything she told you was a lie. I had to stop her. I wouldn't have you tied you up here, if it weren't the only way to reach you. You must listen to me. The people of Wraithwood—they're using you. I'm here to free you."

"You're lying."

"Am I?" He stood and tucked his hands behind his back again. "Think. Search your heart."

*Using me...*Ridiculous. Uncle Merlin. The Winslows. Even fiery Ms. Tynsdale and the ever-prickly Miss Burtle. They all had shown kindness to her in their own ways, tried to protect her from magic. She glared at Mordred as he continued his slow, hypnotic pacing. "You can't claim that the dark wizards are good. Your people wiped out that entire town in the attack on Wraithwood—even the kids! They were innocent. Good people don't do that."

He stopped and placed his fingertips together in front of him. "You were told that the dark wizards burnt down that town?"

"Yes."

"You were told wrong. It was Merlin."

It took her a moment to respond. "Come on. That doesn't even make sense. Why would he murder his own friends?"

He resumed pacing. "Ah. You see, Merlin was ever a tempestuous young man. The 'attack,' as you call it, was an attempt at peace." He pressed his thin lips together. "But at the first sign of our people, the Ludovics attacked. Merlin's father was killed as the messengers of peace tried to defend themselves. Some of our men fled to the town to beg for help in making their plea for peace, but Merlin pursued them. It was not they who consumed Wraithwood with fire. It was he. In his passion to destroy them, he set everything ablaze with his newfound power. I doubt he meant to kill his own people—but then, the thought didn't seem to deter him either."

"You're lying! You twisted, sick-minded..." she broke off. *Don't listen, they're lies, they aren't true.*

His features arranged themselves into a semblance of compassion as he knelt in front of her. "I know it is difficult to hear these things. But you are not to blame. How could you have known? I'm sorry to tell you that all they want you for is your power."

She shook her head and wrinkled her nose at him. "And now I know for sure you're lying. I don't have any special sort of power. Turning invisible is cool, but it's not like I throw fire or anything like that."

He nodded. "Once again, they have deceived you. I doubt they wanted you to know. You are far more special than you believe. Don't let them use you. Come with me. I'll train you to use your power. Together, we can bring about the world that should be."

ALYSSA ROAT

She looked into those cold, gray eyes and she began to believe him. It made sense. Why else would they lie to her and hide things from her? Why...

Then the tender face of Mrs. Winslow flashed before her eyes, the laugh of Ms. Tynsdale rang in her ears, and she saw Uncle Merlin smiling at her as they bent over the chess board, creating an outrageous story. She snapped back to alertness. "No."

For one brief second, she saw a burning rage in his eyes that made her fear for her life. But it was immediately gone. "Very well. But think about it."

He stood and walked away. As she watched him awaken one of the men, she wondered about what he had said. How much was true? *Is it all a misunderstanding?*

Quentin's voice was barely audible. "Brinnie! Is he gone?"

"Yes," she whispered. "But he's still awake. Wait, he's coming back. Don't make a sound."

Mordred returned, a man with dark, heavy brows following him. "I understand that you do not yet believe me," Mordred said to her, "But for your safety, we must be certain that we can find you if you run off." He nodded to the other man. "This is Atherus the spellcaster."

Brinnie narrowed her eyes in suspicion. "What exactly are you going to do?"

Mordred didn't answer. Instead, Atherus stepped toward her and pulled out a knife. She flinched away as he reached for her arm, and when the knife slashed down, she cringed. She opened her eyes to see that she hadn't been harmed. Rather, he'd cut off her sleeve to expose her scar.

Mordred nodded in approval. He pulled his blade out of its scabbard and handed it to Atherus. Immediately, Brinnie's scar flared with intense cold, radiating light. Atherus directed the tip at Brinnie's scar, then with a quick motion slashed upward. She hissed in pain, trying to jerk away. But Atherus was unmoved. He held the weapon to the cut he had made along her scar as blood trickled down the blade. He waved a hand over the area and muttered something to himself that Brinnie didn't catch. She wasn't sure what he had done, but before her eyes, her blood took on the same silvery hue of her scar and the blade. The blade and her scar glowed even brighter, and the silver blood

252

running down the blade seemed to be absorbed into it.

At that, he removed the blade, waved his hand over it once more, and presented it to Mordred.

"Excellent." Mordred turned it over in his hands. "Let us see if it works."

He set the knife on the ground, the point facing away from Brinnie, and let go of the hilt. Slowly, as if pulled by an invisible force, it rotated until the tip pointed directly at her.

"What did you just do?" she demanded.

Mordred's small smile made her shudder. "Before, as you must have noticed, the blade would glow more brightly the closer it came to you. But now, not only will it glow, but since it is enchanted with your blood, it will point to you as a compass points north. No matter where you go, or how far you run, I will always find you."

Chills ran down Brinnie's spine. *This can't be happening.*

"Excuse me," Atherus broke in. "It isn't quite that simple."

Mordred turned an icy gaze upon him. "Explain."

"It won't always point to the girl. It has to be within range."

Brinnie wouldn't want to be on the receiving end of that look. "And how close would that be?"

Atherus fidgeted with his knife. "That would probably be around a hundred leagues."

Mordred nodded. "Far more distance than we need." He turned to Brinnie. "Even the Maze can't hide you."

She tried to still her racing heart. *Now what?*

"Atherus, tell Lupus to guard her." His gaze turned back to Brinnie. "In the morning, she will help lead us to Wraithwood."

Brinnie watched his receding form and clenched her jaw. Somehow, she had to escape.

Chapter Twenty-Nine

THE MAN NAMED LUPUS STOOD GUARD over her all night. His broad shoulders never sagged, and his gaze remained sharp. His bright eyes and thick, wild hair reminded Brinnie of his namesake, the wolf. She began to wonder if werewolves existed in the wizard world.

For hours, she waited for a chance, but no opportunity arose for any attempt at a rescue. As her eyelids began to droop, she heard a faint rustle behind her. She assumed Quentin had left.

His decision was wise—within moments, the dark wizards were stirring and the camp came alive. She tried to count the men as they packed things away, ate breakfast, and put out the campfire. Including herself, there seemed to be ten people altogether.

One of the figures milling about caught her attention with long, sleek black hair. As the person turned around, Brinnie saw it was a woman. The woman pulled bread out of her pack and gave it a disdainful look. She set it aside and instead pointed to the ground. Where she pointed, a seedling popped up. The plant grew until it branched out, and small green orbs formed. The orbs merged from green, to orange, to red, and Brinnie finally realized they were tomatoes. The woman pulled out a knife, cut off a piece of bread, and sliced the tomatoes onto it.

"Can you grow us a chicken tree?" one of the men asked her. "What I wouldn't do for some roasted chicken."

Her incredulous stare would have melted a smarter man into a puddle of shame. "Have you ever seen a chicken tree before?"

"Well, no, but..."

She tossed her head and sliced off another piece of bread. Getting to her feet, she sauntered over to where Brinnie sat, guarded by Lupus. "What are you doing?" Lupus asked.

"Bringing food for the prisoner. Excuse me, I mean 'guest.'" She made air quotes. "Mordred is too busy talking to the idiot to think of it."

Brinnie glanced toward the other end of the camp. Mordred was indeed speaking with one of the men, a lean, scruffy-looking fellow. He seemed strangely familiar.

Lupus's voice drew her back to the present situation. "I think you should ask him first."

"Please." The woman rolled her eyes. "The girl was half-dead. It'd be a shame if she starved to death now."

He shrugged. "All right, ma'am. But I don't want to take the blame if something goes wrong."

She waved a dismissive hand at him. "Hold this." She shoved the bread at him, then knelt and untied Brinnie's hands. "Don't try anything or you're dead, got it?"

"Okay."

Once her hands were untied, Brinnie stood slowly, the dried mud on her clothes chafing against her skin. She accepted the bread with one grimy hand. "Thanks."

The woman looked her up and down. "This is unacceptable. She's covered in dirt and blood, with no shoes, and..." She looked at Brinnie's one limp arm. "What's wrong with your hand?"

"I hurt my wrist."

"It figures Dolphus wouldn't even notice. Well, if no one else is going to do anything about this mess, I will."

"Nimue."

Brinnie jumped at Mordred's voice. She hadn't even seen him approach.

The woman turned around. "This girl is a disaster."

"I'm aware."

"It's barely dawn. I'll take her, get her cleaned up, and bring her back here before we need to set out."

He looked at Brinnie calculatingly. "It isn't worth the risk."

"Are you saying I can't handle her?" The woman put her hands on her hips.

"Nimue."

Brinnie flinched. She would be shaking if she heard Mordred say her name that way.

But Nimue remained unfazed. "What are you going to do? Leave me in a cave for a thousand years?"

His expression was unreadable, but his jaw twitched. "Fine," he conceded. "Be back in ten minutes."

As he strode away, Brinnie regarded Nimue with a mixture of respect and concern. If this lady could change Mordred's mind, she was someone to be reckoned with.

"Lupus," Nimue directed, "will you hobble her please?"

Brinnie wasn't sure what he did exactly, but before she knew it, instead of being bound together, her ankles were tied to each other with just enough length of rope for her to take small, waddling steps.

Nimue pulled a knife with waved edges from a sheath at her hip and started twirling it around in her fingers. "Here's the deal. I'm being nice by doing this. So I don't want you trying to run away, got it? I'll be watching you, and the minute you turn invisible is the minute I throw this knife."

Brinnie nodded. "Understood."

"Good. This way."

As Brinnie shuffled along, Nimue directed her to a wide stream. Once there, Nimue tied a rope around Brinnie's good wrist. "Okay, jump in and get that mud off. Remember, if I can't see you, I still have this rope, and I'm throwing a knife where it ends."

Brinnie couldn't think of any way she could escape without being skewered, so instead she tried to appreciate the opportunity to clean up. She knelt and began to splash water over her face.

Nimue snorted. "That's going to take forever. Here." She gave Brinnie a shove.

Brinnie fell into the cold water with a splash and came up spluttering. "Hey!"

Nimue crossed her arms and raised a brow. "Come on. You can't tell me that doesn't feel good."

Brinnie dunked her head under the water once more and came up again. "It does," she admitted.

Brinnie continued to splash and dunk until the water downstream no longer ran brown. Then she sloshed out, water running off her in rivulets. She began squeezing her hair with one hand.

Nimue frowned. "Here." She moved behind Brinnie and wrung out her hair with a few deft twists.

"Thanks." Brinnie eyed her. "Why are you being nice to me?"

She shrugged. "Because I'm a halfway decent person. Now." She leaned against a tree and crossed her arms. "Who are you and what does Mordred want with you?"

Apparently, Mordred wasn't very good at sharing his evil plans. "I'm not sure what he wants with me, to be honest. I guess he wants to turn me to the dark side or something."

Nimue gave a short laugh. "The dark side." She stuck out her hand. "Nimue Drakon."

"Drakon?" Why did that sound familiar?

"Yeah, yeah, my father was the Master of Dirklon. I thought he was as much of a jerk as everyone else does." She rolled her eyes.

"Wait, are you related to Lydia Tynsdale?"

"Half-sister. Unfortunately. So anyway, who are you?"

Nimue's father had led the attack on Wraithwood that caused Brinnie's grandparents' deaths, as well as the deaths of all the townspeople. Of course, he had been Ms. Tynsdale's father, too, and Ms. Tynsdale was no mass murderer. Was Nimue?

She mentally shook herself. Nimue had asked a question. "It's, uh, Brittney."

"If you didn't want to give me your name, you could have said so." She stood up straight. "Come on. I don't want Mordred giving me the icy death stare for being gone too long."

When they arrived back at camp, Mordred motioned to the scruffy man he had been talking to earlier. As the man hurried over, Mordred addressed him and Brinnie. "You two will be at the front. You," he pointed to the man, "will continue to choose the path, but hopefully she will make it easier."

Brinnie crossed her arms. "I'm not doing anything for you."

"You don't have to do anything willingly. You entered the Maze on the Wraithwood side, so if you are to exit the Maze, it will most likely direct you to that side."

That hasn't exactly been working for me. But she didn't voice that thought. Instead, she looked at the scruffy man more closely. "Wait— Jerry?"

He squinted at her. "Do I know you?"

"No. But I know you're Marcie's husband. What are you doing here?"

"Enough," Mordred broke in. "Time to go."

Nimue pushed Brinnie toward the front, and the group set out, following Jerry.

Brinnie looked over at him. "Do you know where you're going?"

"Not a clue." He grinned. "But they wanted a 'human,' and they were willing to pay. And they promised they'd take care of that old miser Marcie's been working for to boot."

"What? Don't you realize what you're doing? These people are evil! They—"

She stopped as the scar on her arm burned cold. She looked over her shoulder to see Mordred gazing at her, testing the point of the enchanted blade.

She got the message. Shut up and walk. So she did.

Chapter Thirty

BY NIGHTFALL, BRINNIE WAS MISERABLE. HER feet hurt from walking all day with no shoes, she shivered in her damp clothes, and the ropes had begun to rub her skin raw. They had wandered all day to no avail. Apparently, Mordred's plan wasn't working.

"I can't see a thing," Jerry complained. "We should stop."

"Keep going," Mordred ordered.

"But I can't—"

"I'm not paying you to complain," Mordred snapped. "Keep going."

Muttering, Jerry continued. Brinnie tried to keep up, but every step was painful. Now, she wasn't thinking about escape. She could only think about rest.

What felt like decades later, Mordred finally ordered a halt in a place where the Maze widened to accommodate four pathways. Trying to maneuver without being obvious, Brinnie worked her way toward the path they had come from. She barely made it to the entrance before she collapsed in a heap, exhausted. If Quentin was going to rescue her, he would be coming from that direction. But at the moment, sitting near it was all she could do to assist him.

Lupus followed her and bound her ankles tightly together once more. As the group started to set up camp, Nimue came and untied Brinnie's hands. She handed her bread and a canteen. "Here. Drink sparingly. No water source tonight."

Brinnie tried to take small sips, though she wanted to drink the whole thing. "Thank you."

Nimue nodded and turned to Lupus. "Who's watching her tonight?"

He shrugged.

"I'll go find someone."

As Brinnie gnawed on the piece of bread, she wondered how to communicate with Quentin. She wasn't even sure if he had been able to follow them. Without the benefit of invisibility, it would be difficult to stay close enough not to be separated by the movements of the Maze, yet far enough away not to be seen.

Another man came to relieve Lupus and tied Brinnie's hands once more. He, too, watched her with an eagle eye. She fought to keep her eyes open. She needed to be ready for rescue. But slowly, her head began to bob. She woke slightly when she tipped over and ended up lying down, but it was momentary. Soon, she was fast asleep.

Something woke her in the middle of the night. She listened, but she heard no sound except the crackling of a campfire and the soft breathing of those who slept. The man guarding her still sat alert a few feet from her, whittling at a stick.

Then she heard it again—a soft hooting sound, like an owl. *Quentin!* She stole a glance at her guard, then quietly gave her best impression of an owl.

The guard grinned. "It's a bird. Saw it fly over a while ago."

"I'm just practicing my owl call."

He shook his head, returning to his whittling. "Uh-huh."

She strained her ears, but she didn't hear the noise again. Quentin didn't seem like the type of person who would have perfected bird calls anyway.

The night dragged on. She tried to stay alert for opportunities, but she spent half the time asleep. The guard whittled his stick down to a tiny nub before he was replaced by someone else. Escape wasn't possible tonight.

The next morning, Brinnie wanted to sink into the ground and never move again. Her arms and legs ached from being tied together. Lupus returned and rearranged her bonds into a hobble once again, and Nimue gave her food and water. With little ado, they set out once more.

The wandering seemed even worse than that of her previous days. The Maze remained maddeningly constant, without break from the twisting, turning paths between the hedges. Brinnie tried to keep her mind elsewhere, replaying some of her favorite books in her head. She could have sworn they walked a hundred miles, but that night, they stopped in a place that looked eerily similar to their camp from the night before.

More exhausted than she could remember ever being, Brinnie remained determined that tonight, she would escape. She closed her eyes, leaving only a slit open, and pretended to be asleep in hopes that it would lull her guard into a false sense of security. The trouble was staying awake herself. Over and over in her head, she sang the most obnoxious songs she could think of, recited multiplication tables, and made up ridiculous rhymes. Maddeningly, her guard remained alert, alternating between staring at her and surveying the surroundings.

Finally, she noticed his shoulders begin to sag. Every muscle tense, she watched as they slowly drooped lower and his head began to bob. *Come on. Sleep.*

After what seemed like an eternity, his eyes finally closed. She seized her chance. Quickly, she turned invisible, struggled to her feet, and began to hop away.

Just as she reached the entrance, her guard sent up a shout. She hopped faster into the Maze. "Quentin! Quentin, where are you?" She turned visible so that he could see her. "Quentin, hurry!"

No response. With her night vision, she saw that the path was empty. He had lost them.

Footsteps pounded behind her and her guard grabbed her by the arms. "How far did you think you could hop?" He laughed and shoved her back toward the camp. "Let's go."

At the campsite, Mordred stood with his arms folded.

"Caught her," Brinnie's guard announced, swaggering forward.

Mordred's expression was impassive. "And how did you lose her in the first place?"

"She turned invisible and ran off." The guard yanked at Brinnie's arm. She stumbled, wincing. "But she didn't go far."

"You mean to tell me it took you all that time to catch her after she disappeared right in front of you?"

Finally, the man realized he was in trouble. "Well, it's hard to find someone when they're invisible," he defended.

Mordred's eyes bored into him. Brinnie could almost feel the guard withering like a plant under the desert sun. "This will not happen again."

"No, sir."

As Mordred turned and walked away, Brinnie's guard pushed her to the ground. "Now stay put."

She sat, slumped. *Quentin's not here. I'm going to have to escape by myself.*

All night she tossed and turned as much as her bonds would allow. The next day found her hobbling beside Jerry once again. She glanced over her shoulder, then whispered to him, "These people aren't what you think."

"This again?" he grumped.

"Listen. If you help them, you're endangering hundreds of people. Maybe millions."

He snorted. "As if either of us is actually helping them do anything. They're crazy, but they pay."

"They might be crazy, but they're dangerous." She chanced another glance back. "Haven't you seen what they can do?"

"You mean their little magic tricks?" He laughed.

"Yes!"

"Sad thing is, they actually seem to think it's real."

Brinnie gaped at him. "You don't think it is?"

"Course not. They're all as cracked as Ludovic."

Her eyes burned. "This is serious—"

"I'm getting sick of this. I'm going to tell Mr. Knife back there that you won't shut up."

Her mouth snapped shut and she glared at him. *Fine, then. Don't be part of my master escape plan.*

"Look at me!" Jerry swaggered. "I'm making a left turn, because I'm a special human and I know where I'm going. It doesn't matter that I don't get anywhere, I still lead the way. I'm so—what's that?"

Brinnie looked up the path and saw what looked like a large piece of yellowish-brown paper blown against the side of a hedge. Her eyes widened. *Oh, no.* "It's just a piece of trash," she said quickly.

"I'll go grab it."

"No!" she hissed. She glanced over her shoulder. No one seemed to be paying any attention to her conversation.

"You know what it is?"

She hesitated.

He took in her agonized expression and grinned. "Is it something I could get paid a lot for?"

"Jerry, no. You can't. They'll kill everyone."

"Hey, I found something!" he called over his shoulder.

"No!" Brinnie protested. "Take it back. Pretend like it's nothing."

"What would that be?" Mordred asked, coming to the front.

"Nothing." Brinnie glared at Jerry. "A piece of garbage."

"I think it's something important," Jerry said helpfully.

Mordred gave him a skeptical look, but he strode over and picked it up anyway. As his eyes moved over the parchment, his lips curled into a smile. "Something important indeed. A map leading us straight to Wraithwood."

Chapter Thirty-One

MORDRED TURNED TO JERRY. "WELL DONE."

"My pleasure." He winked at Brinnie.

She held back tears. This couldn't be happening. Eight wizards against four unsuspecting humans. They would be destroyed.

Mordred studied the parchment. "Yes, so simple. Follow me." He set off, looking down at the parchment.

"What about me?" Jerry asked.

Mordred didn't slow. "What about you?"

"I'd guess that map is worth a lot to you." He grinned.

Mordred stopped and looked up at him. "Yes. And now you are worthless to me." He waved his hand and Lupus stepped forward, drawing out a long knife that could properly be called a sword.

Jerry paled. "We had an agreement."

"I don't make deals with humans."

As Lupus raised his sword, Jerry threw up his arms and cowered. "Wait! I can still help you!"

Mordred motioned for Lupus to hold. "How?"

"If you let me live, I'll do whatever you want. Just name it. All I want is to see my wife again."

Mordred regarded him calculatingly. "You would do anything."

"Yes." He trembled. "Anything at all."

"Would you kill whoever I instructed you to?"

He hesitated. Mordred started to wave Lupus on. "Wait! Yes, I would. I'd do it."

Mordred nodded. "Fine. You can live. For now." Lupus put away his sword. "Now come."

Mordred led the way, his eyes glued to the parchment. Brinnie's forced her faltering steps forward. *What now?* What would he do to them once they got to Wraithwood?

Now that they walked with purpose, Brinnie could barely keep up. The trek continued through the morning and into the afternoon until Mordred finally called a halt and summoned Lupus and another man to him. "The boy who was with our guest is just around the bend. Take him. He might be of use."

As they rounded the corner, there indeed was Quentin walking straight toward them. His eyes widened and Brinnie yelled, "Run!" But it was too late. Two men grabbed him and quickly tied him as they had Brinnie.

"Give me one reason why I shouldn't kill you," Mordred said as Lupus dragged him toward the group, kicking and wriggling.

"Traitor! Evildoer!" Quentin struggled, trying to wrench his arm free of Lupus's grasp.

Mordred's nose wrinkled. "Lupus, dispatch him."

"Wait!" Brinnie blurted. As Mordred glanced at her, she struggled to come up with something. "He's human. If you kill him, you'll die."

"Very well." Mordred pointed to Jerry. "You, human."

"Yeah?"

"You said you would kill anyone. I want you to kill him."

Brinnie gasped.

Jerry's face went slack. "Oh, uh..."

"I'm a wizard!" Quentin interjected. "A wizard."

"Good." Mordred nodded. "I can kill you myself."

"No!" Brinnie thrust herself forward. "You can't."

Mordred turned to her. "More lies from you? And why shouldn't I? Remember, he and his kind are the ones keeping us from freedom."

"That's not true." She cast about wildly for a reason he might accept. "You shouldn't because—because he works for the DI!"

Quentin winced and Brinnie inwardly cringed. *I just made this a million times worse.* Who knew what Mordred would be willing to do to Quentin to extract Castelon's secrets?

Mordred raised an eyebrow. "Interesting." He waved a hand at his men. "Bring him along. But if he tries anything, kill him."

At least he's still alive. Brinnie let out a breath as Lupus pushed Quentin into line. Out of the corner of her eye, she saw Jerry gazing from her to Quentin with a dazed expression. A small part of her took perverse satisfaction in his rude awakening to what he had promised. Maybe he would reconsider his loyalties.

As they began to move, Brinnie tried to stealthily make her way toward Quentin, but Nimue blocked her. "Yeah, I don't think so."

As they continued and Brinnie hobbled along as quickly as she could, the paths grew broader. She wracked her mind for a solution. *We could...or Quentin could...or I could...*

She had zero ideas.

Her legs threatened to give out by the time they halted. She looked up, only for her heart to plummet. A glowing wand stood upright in a wide gap in the hedge flanked by wrought iron gates. Beyond, sunlight shone on a red brick mansion free of the Maze's perpetual mist.

They had arrived at Wraithwood.

Nimue steered Brinnie to the front beside Mordred. Brinnie took advantage of her chance. "You can't attack the house. There are humans inside who don't know."

His expression was unreadable. "I would suggest you stop making threats, if you do not want the young man to die."

Am I getting to him? "He could tell you all sorts of stuff about your enemy. You won't kill him." She smirked. "And you can't threaten to kill Jerry either, because if you kill him, you'll die. Should I tell him that he's pretty much invincible?"

To her annoyance, Mordred didn't seem to care that his threats had been foiled. Instead, he pulled out the enchanted blade. "If there are such humans in the house, I must resort to using you. As I have said, I don't desire to kill you, but your friends should submit quietly once they see a knife at your throat." In one smooth motion, he grasped her by the hair at the nape of her neck, pulled her head back, and pointed the blade at her throat. "Now walk."

Mordred pushed Brinnie ahead of him up the familiar path with Nimue to the right. As they crunched over the gravel through the gardens, Brinnie gave it one last attempt. "This is a bad idea. You're going to walk up and face a Master on his own estate?"

"Ludovic isn't here. Only four humans."

"How...?" Brinnie paused. *The parchment.* It showed exactly where everyone was, and the colors of the dots even showed what they were. *I am an idiot.* "You knew Qu—the young man—was a wizard. And you already know who's in the house."

"That is true."

"Why didn't you call my bluff?"

She could hear the smirk in his voice. "Your confidence was amusing."

Brinnie's eyes widened. He didn't mind when she got the better of him because she didn't get the better of him at all. She suspected her current emotions were his intention—she was off-balance, unsure of herself or any plans she thought she might have.

"Besides," he added, "as you can see, I have a tool I can use against any human threat."

Jerry. But how far would Jerry go? Would he actually kill for Mordred?

They circled the drive. Brinnie climbed the front steps carefully, trying not to trip and fall into the blade. Mordred's fingers twisted in her hair, and she winced. At the door, Nimue lifted the knocker and let it drop.

As the agonizing seconds ticked by, Brinnie's heart pounded in her ears. Then rattling sounded from the other side and the door swung open. Mrs. Winslow took a step back and gasped.

"Good afternoon," Mordred greeted her, pressing the blade against Brinnie's throat. "Mind if we come in?"

Chapter Thirty-Two

"WHAT'S GOING ON?" MRS. WINSLOW DEMANDED. "You let her go!"

"As you can see, I'm not hurting her," Mordred replied. "I only intend to do that if you decide to act rashly."

Her gaze darted from Brinnie to Mordred. "What do you want?"

"We only want to come in."

Brinnie stared back at Mrs. Winslow. She wished there was something she could say, but she had no idea what Mordred had planned.

Mrs. Winslow stepped aside, her hand trembling on the doorknob. "Come in, then."

Mordred nudged Brinnie forward. She shivered when her dirty feet hit the cool, polished wood. One by one, the entire group filed into the great hall.

"What's going on?" A door swung open and Miss Burtle stepped out of the office. She halted. "What is this?"

"We have some visitors," Mrs. Winslow replied tightly.

"I am glad you are here," Mordred addressed Miss Burtle. "Assemble the household."

Miss Burtle glared. "I don't take orders from you."

Mordred slowly pressed the knife against Brinnie's neck until she held her chin high in the air, not daring to breathe. "Assemble the household."

She looked down her nose at him. "Fine."

Miss Burtle left, and Mordred addressed Lupus, who held Quentin's arm. "Tie him to that railing," he instructed.

As Lupus tied Quentin to the post at the foot of the stairs, Mordred turned back to Mrs. Winslow. "Your Master isn't home?"

Mrs. Winslow's voice remained even, but her hands fidgeted with her apron. "You know he isn't."

"Where is he?"

"I don't believe that's any of your concern."

"Is he dead?"

Brinnie watched with rapt attention, hoping to glean the answer, as Mrs. Winslow crumpled her apron in her hands, not saying a word.

"Is he?"

"He's away on business." Her gaze darted toward Brinnie. "He could be back at any moment."

"I see. And when was he here last?"

Nothing. Mrs. Winslow blinked rapidly.

"Ah. He has gone missing. How exceptionally fortunate."

Miss Burtle came in through the dining room door, Mr. Winslow and Marcie in tow. Marcie gasped. "Brinnie!" Then her eyes settled beyond Brinnie, and she stopped. "Jerry."

"Good." Mordred's grip readjusted on the blade. "All of you are here. Listen carefully. I don't desire to harm any of you—my conflict is strictly with the Master of this estate. If you do not make nuisances of yourselves, no harm will come to you. We intend to stay here for an indefinite amount of time. You all have a choice—will you accept these terms?"

"What's going on?" Marcie's voice trembled. "I don't understand."

"All you need to know is that I want nothing from the four of you except that you do not hinder me." His voice oozed sickly sweet. "If you cooperate, all will be well."

"What about these two?" Mrs. Winslow gestured to Brinnie and Quentin.

"My deal is only with you."

"So you'll kill them," Miss Burtle stated flatly.

Marcie gasped, hands flying to her mouth.

Morded traced the blade along Brinnie's jugular, and she held her breath. "Perhaps. Perhaps not."

Mr. Winslow hooked his thumbs in his belt loops and scowled. "Then I don't see how we can agree."

"Think carefully about what you're doing," Mordred advised.

"We have, and we're not going to let you waltz in and take over." Miss Burtle frowned ominously. "Get out."

"Very well. Take them."

Mordred's men stepped forward. The struggle was brief. Mr. Winslow put up a fight the longest and managed to land a few blows, but soon he lay pinned to the floor with his hands behind his back.

Mordred glanced at Nimue. "See if you can find something to bind them with."

She nodded and disappeared through the dining room door.

Mordred sheathed his blade and handed Brinnie over to Lupus, who tightened her bonds and bound her to the stairs on the other side of Quentin. Mordred began to pace in front of the prisoners. "Now, which of you knows the most about the library?"

"You did all this for a book?" Miss Burtle twisted against the knee planted in her spine and raised an eyebrow.

He regarded her from above like an eagle eyeing a beetle. "Who would know?"

"I would."

"Excellent. Does Wraithwood's library house a large collection of scrolls, by chance?"

A mocking smirk. "It is a library."

"Are you familiar with the scrolls?"

Deadpan. "No."

His boots thumped on the wood as he paced. "You know nothing at all of them?"

"No."

"I find that I don't quite believe you."

Nimue returned with a roll of duct tape. "This should work."

Mordred quit pacing, a crease furrowing his brow. "Is it enchanted?"

Nimue's lips twitched. "It's tape."

Brinnie looked at Mordred curiously as Nimue proceeded to bind the Wraithwooders' wrists and ankles. *How does he not know that?* She knew wizards lived a little differently, but tape?

Once they were bound, Mordred turned to Marcie. "Now, you.

Your husband tells me you've worked here for a while. So you know who she is?" He gestured to Brinnie.

"Don't say anything," Miss Burtle interjected.

"It's a simple question." He stepped closer to Miss Burtle, the threat implied. Then he turned a serene expression back toward Marcie. "No harm in it." He pointed at Brinnie. "Who is the girl?"

Marcie's eyes darted between Miss Burtle and Mordred. "Don't answer, dear," Mrs. Winslow instructed.

"It isn't a difficult question." Mordred pulled out a knife and ran it between his fingers. "I wouldn't want to make it difficult to answer."

Brinnie mentally scrambled for a solution, something to say—

"Lucy."

Brinnie swiveled her head toward Mr. Winslow in surprise. He nodded. "Name's Lucy. No need to go hurting anyone."

Mordred looked at Marcie. "Is that true?"

Marcie's mouth opened and she hesitated. "Uh, y-yes, it is."

Mordred fixed Brinnie with his icy stare. "Hm." Then he turned to his men. "We will interrogate them further later. For now, you three, watch them. The rest of you, follow me. And you." He stopped and gave Jerry a look of distaste. "Tie him up as well."

Mordred led the way to the library, as Jerry protested, "Wait, we're on the same side!"

Despite Jerry's insistent protests, Lupus bound him hand and foot, the same as the rest, and then left to join Mordred in the library. The three men assigned to watch the prisoners waited just long enough for Mordred to exit the room, then proceeded to haggle over who would stay while the others scoped out the house for food.

"How did you two get into this mess?" Miss Burtle hissed at Brinnie and Quentin as the men argued.

"It's a long story. Basically, Quentin lost the parchment, but then we ran into each other, but we got captured by those guys, who happened to find the parchment, so we ended up here," Brinnie explained.

"You lost the parchment." Miss Burtle's look could have fried an egg.

It appeared to be working judging by the redness of Quentin's face.

271

"Well, uh, not intentionally."

"More importantly, dears," Mrs. Winslow put in before Miss Burtle could commence berating him, "what do these people want?"

"I'm not sure exactly." Brinnie frowned. "On the grand scheme, Mordred—the guy in charge—wants to get rid of the Enchantment, of course, but I don't know why they're particularly interested in Wraithwood, or what he wants from the library."

"How do you know about the Enchantment?" Mrs. Winslow asked.

"Um, long story. For now, consider me informed."

"Mordred..." Miss Burtle mused. "Mordred what?"

"I don't know. Just Mordred."

"Edna," Mrs. Winslow asked, "is there any particular scroll you think he might want?"

"I have my ideas, but I don't trust that one." Miss Burtle nodded toward Jerry.

"Jerry, what are you doing here?" Marcie asked, her eyes wide with fear. "What's going on?"

"Nothing to be worried about, Mars." Brinnie imagined he intended to give a reassuring smile, but it looked more like a grimace. "They just needed someone to lead them here, and I wanted to see you. They promised they wouldn't hurt you."

"And you know how well they keep their deals." Brinnie fixed him with a pointed glare.

Miss Burtle glanced up. "Shh, they're coming."

The three men seemed to have made up their minds. One of them held Quentin down while the other removed the rope from his ankles and replaced it with duct tape. They repeated the process for his hands, did the same for Brinnie, then used the rope to tie the other prisoners conveniently to the banister. "Don't try anything, or you're all dead," one of them warned. Then all three went off to forage.

"Can anyone reach the knots?" Mr. Winslow asked.

For a few moments, all was silent as each captive tried to wriggle into position, but ultimately it proved fruitless. The knots were unreachable, and the duct tape made it almost impossible to move.

"They must be used to tying people up," Brinnie observed.

"What about Master Ludovic? Any word?" Quentin asked.

Miss Burtle looked at Jerry. "Once again, I don't trust that one."

"Trust me, I don't like them any more than you." He leaned around them to address Marcie. "I did this so I could see you. They said if I got them here, they'd take care of Ludovic, so I could go after my wife." His expression softened, pleading. "That's all I want, Mars, is you to come home."

Marcie recoiled. "So we're all tied up by a bunch of lunatics because of you?"

He hastily backtracked. "No, I—"

"Doesn't matter," Brinnie interrupted. "Jerry, you've seen how Mordred is. You can't trust him, and he's using you. There's no neutral—what side are you on?"

"That depends." He glanced at Marcie. "What side do you want me on?"

"This side," Marcie said quickly. "Please don't do anything for those people."

"Guess I'm on this side, then."

"I'm less than convinced," Miss Burtle said. "How do we know he isn't a spy?"

Brinnie studied him for a long moment. His motives were straightforward—win back Marcie—and Marcie had made her desires clear. And she didn't think he was sly enough to double-cross. "I don't think we can trust him completely, but he's not a spy. I think it's safe to talk in front of him."

Miss Burtle glared at him. "Fine." Her voice lowered. "But if he decides to betray us, I will personally rip—"

"Edna!" Mrs. Winslow scolded sharply.

Jerry paled, evidently filling in the blanks. "Understood, ma'am."

Miss Burtle leaned back, satisfied. "We haven't heard anything since you two left, Brynna. They're still missing."

"So, no rescue." Quentin frowned.

"Probably not."

"What are they after?" Mr. Winslow nodded toward the library.

"I don't know," Miss Burtle said. "There are a lot of valuable scrolls, but there are only a few that I know of that would be of any interest to a dark—ahem—person." She glanced at Marcie. "There are some spell books, but I would think he would be after *The Case of the Master Key.*"

"What's that?" Mrs. Winslow asked.

"I'm not sure exactly. I don't go up there often, so I've only looked at it once. It's in the ancient language and full of ideas I admit were beyond me, but considering the circumstances, it might have information they need about the Master Key."

Brinnie nodded. "That makes sense."

"But it sounded like Mordred wanted to go after Master Ludovic, as well," Quentin pointed out. "Why? It would be suicide to face a Master on his own estate."

"Excuse me, but what on earth are you all talking about?" Marcie's eyes shone with tears.

Brinnie's eyebrows rose. "She still doesn't know? Where did you tell her Quentin and I had gone?"

Mrs. Winslow looked sheepish. "We had to stretch the truth a bit, dear."

"Can someone please explain?" Marcie asked.

"It's best we don't, dear. We can't tell you why, but you're a good deal safer this way."

"Any case," Mr. Winslow said, "how are we going to escape?"

In the middle of his question, the dining room doors opened, and the three men tromped through, looking quite pleased with themselves as they carried in a large pot of stew and started dishing it into bowls. "Oh, dear," Mrs. Winslow fretted. "That isn't supposed to be ready for another few hours."

Miss Burtle raised an eyebrow. "We'll just have to wait for an opportunity to present itself."

Night had fallen, or so Quentin informed Brinnie. Mordred and his minions had been moving about the house all day, doing who knew what. Now, they passed by with lanterns and candles.

Brinnie's back ached from the awkward position, but she was still about to nod off when she heard a purposeful stride coming their way.

She raised her head to see Mordred holding a scroll, looking pleased with himself. He motioned to the guards. "Go. Find someone to relieve you for the night." As they left, he turned to the prisoners. "I will need each of you for questioning. Starting with you." He pointed to Marcie.

"M-me? I don't know anything!"

"Exactly." As three new men entered the room, he motioned for one of them to untie Marcie from the banister. "Bring her with me," he instructed, turning toward the library.

As they led her off, Marcie turned and looked back at them, eyes shining with fear. Brinnie tried to give her a hopeful smile but doubted she succeeded.

"Did you see that scroll?" Quentin whispered. "Do you think it was *The Case of the Master Key*?"

Miss Burtle frowned. "It's quite likely."

One of the guards scowled at them. "Keep quiet."

Brinnie's mind raced. What did Mordred want with Marcie? What information could she give? The only thing she knew that Mordred didn't was Brinnie's true identity. But what did that matter? He wasn't exactly going to communicate it to the DI. Not to mention the fact that Quentin already knew anyway. Mordred would be after her no matter who he thought she was. Unless...

"Miss Burtle," Brinnie whispered. "Can you think of any reason why Mordred would have a specific hatred for Uncle Merlin?"

She glanced toward the guards. "No. I don't know who he is, and neither did Merlin. After that skirmish on the road, he said he didn't recognize him. Is there anything at all that you know about him?"

Brinnie racked her mind to find everything she knew about Mordred. Finally, something clicked. "Chevska—I mean, Morgana— she knew him."

Miss Burtle looked like a bird who had hit a window. "You met Morgana?"

"Yes, in the Maze. She helped me, but Mordred killed her."

She inhaled sharply. "That's impossible. She's of the old order."

"Well, he did. Right before Morgana died, she said..." She tried to remember the exact words. "She said there's a prophecy in Mordizan that would tell me how to defeat Mordred." When Brinnie's focus returned to Miss Burtle's gaping face, her heart thumped. "What? What is it?"

Miss Burtle's mouth snapped shut. "Listen very carefully," she hissed. "There is no information more important to keep from Mordred than your identity. If he finds out who you are, he will kill you immediately."

Her heart pounded. "What? Why? He's been trying to turn me to his side, not kill me."

"That will change the moment he finds out you're a Ludovic." Her eyes darted toward where Marcie and Mordred had disappeared. "We need to figure out a way for you to escape, now. When Marcie tells him who you are..."

"You think she will?"

"Of course she will. She doesn't know why it's important, and she doesn't know that Mordred can't kill her. We need to think of something."

"Hold on. Who is Mordred, really? Why will he want me dead?"

She shook her head. "No time. But no matter what happens, you have to live, understand?"

"Um, okay, but..."

"I've got it. Tell them you have to use the bathroom."

Brinnie's mouth opened and shut again. "Oh. *Oh.*" She nodded. "Got it."

As Brinnie was about to voice her request, a strange sound startled her.

"What is that?" one of the guards growled.

"It's a phone." Another looked around before his eyes fixed on Miss Burtle. He glanced at the remaining guard. "Get Mordred."

As he ran off, the other two searched Miss Burtle until they found the phone in her pocket. As one held it up, it stopped ringing. "Don't touch it!" the other reprimanded him. "You'll break it."

He gingerly set it down and the two stared at it like it was some sort of strange creature. When it rang again, one of them visibly jumped.

Miss Burtle snorted and rolled her eyes. "Some people clearly haven't ventured much beyond the double-space."

Mordred swept into the room. He nodded to Miss Burtle. "Untie her hands, quickly." He drew his blade and pointed it at the group. "Operate it as if all is normal, or every one of you will die." As Miss Burtle slowly reached for the phone, he said, "Now. And make sure to use it in the way that all can hear."

"Speaker phone," Nimue translated, striding into the room. She smirked at Mordred. "Remember that from our English lessons? It was in that section on human tech."

He shot her a withering glare.

English lessons? Who exactly was Mordred?

Miss Burtle hesitated but flipped open the phone and pressed a few buttons. "Hello?"

"Edna! We have it. We're on our way home."

Brinnie felt her eyes widen in horror and saw her expression mirrored on the faces of her fellow prisoners.

The voice was Uncle Merlin's.

Chapter Thirty-Three

"You have the book?" Miss Burtle asked.

Mordred glared at Miss Burtle and prodded Quentin with his blade.

There was a short pause on the other end. "Er, no. The Key, of course."

Miss Burtle winced visibly, while Mordred's lips turned up in a smirk. "That's wonderful!" she said. "You're both all right?"

"Yes, splendid, in fact. It took quite a while, but in the end, we found out the enemy never had the Key after all. They had the Case, but only as a decoy."

Everyone looked at each other, and Brinnie guessed they were wondering the same thing—then who did have the Key?

"How strange."

"Yes. Do you remember that scientist in the paper who went missing from NASA? It seems he had the Key. We found him experimenting on it, and it appears his experiments were responsible for the fluctuations in the protection spells. We couldn't retrieve the Case from Mordizan, of course, but we have the Key, and we've called a team from Artema to take care of the man. We're bringing the Key back to Wraithwood now. It can't come to Castelon, seeing as there's no Case to keep it from disabling protection spells, but at Wraithwood we have the Maze. Hopefully once it's back on an estate, the spells will return to normal."

"Yes." Her jaw clenched. "Such wonderful news."

"Indeed. I apologize for our unexpected break in communication. Once inside, it was impossible to get away without detection, and now that we have the Key, cell phones don't work at all. I hope you didn't worry too much."

"There were moments," Miss Burtle replied.

"How is everyone there? Are you all safe?"

Miss Burtle gritted her teeth as Mordred pressed his blade against

Quentin's neck. "We do have the Maze."

"I suppose you had to explain to Castelon?"

"Yes. We're all facing charges of treason."

"That's to be expected. I apologize for that. In any case, we should be there within a couple days, since I can't use instant transport with the Key."

Miss Burtle closed her eyes with a pained expression. "How nice."

"Are you all right?"

"Yes, of course. It's excellent news. We're so glad you're safe."

"And I'm glad you all are, as well. How is Brynna faring, with all of this?"

Brinnie's heart thumped. Miss Burtle glanced at her, then quickly away. "Very well. All is well. I think the phone is dying, so I'll let you go. Don't want to...*hold you prisoner.*"

"Of course. The pay phone is running out, anyway. We'll check in later."

"Goodbye."

As Miss Burtle hung up, Mordred gave her an icy look. "You're lucky I didn't kill anyone for that."

Instead of responding, she glared at him.

"Tie her up again," he instructed the guards, "and keep the cellular device away from her."

They nodded and did his bidding. He returned to Miss Burtle. "Who's Brynna?"

"The dog."

He raised an eyebrow. "He's concerned about a dog."

"She hasn't been doing well," Miss Burtle explained. "She's old. Wet weather is difficult for her."

"I see." He smirked. "No matter. Within a few days, both Ludovic and the Key will be mine." He turned and left the room.

"Um, excuse me," Brinnie piped up. The guards and Nimue turned to look at her. "I need to use the restroom."

The guards looked at each other, then at Nimue. She rolled her eyes. "I'll take her. But remember, kid, you try anything, you're dead."

Nimue untied Brinnie from the banister and pushed her along with one hand while holding a knife in the other. They passed through the dining room and into the kitchen, then outside to the washroom.

Brinnie's whole body quivered, her heart pounding, as she waited for the perfect moment.

As they stepped into the washroom, the door shut before Nimue could flick on the lights. Brinnie seized her chance. She wrenched her shoulder out of Nimue's grasp and dropped to the floor to avoid Nimue's blind swipe. "I warned you!" Nimue shouted, fumbling along the wall for the light switch.

Using her night vision to her advantage, Brinnie kicked Nimue's legs, causing her to stumble away from the light switch. As Nimue reached for the door, Brinnie wriggled to her feet and threw the latch, locking them in. Nimue swiped with her knife again, and Brinnie leapt backwards out of the way. She hobbled as quickly as her bound ankles would let her to the sink. Luckily, a knife sat on the drying rack. She turned around so she could grab it with her bound hands. She held it between her back and the counter and began furiously trying to cut through her bonds, wincing at the pain it caused her wrist.

At that moment, Nimue managed to find the light switch. Brinnie heard a *flick* and looked up to see Nimue scanning the room warily. Completely invisible, she continued to work feverishly at her bonds.

Nimue held her blade at ready. "I don't want to hurt you. Show yourself, and I won't even mention this to Mordred."

Brinnie kept sawing.

Nimue's eyes roamed the room. "You can't get past me. You're just trapping yourself in here."

The knife started to slip, and Brinnie pushed it back into an upright position. Nimue's gaze snapped to where Brinnie was standing. She held up her blade. "I know where you are. Please don't make me do this."

Almost there. With a few final desperate sawing motions, Brinnie's hands snapped free.

At the same moment, Nimue threw the knife. Brinnie dove to the floor as it whizzed by and stuck in the wall right behind where she had been standing. As Nimue darted toward the knife, Brinnie snapped herself out of staring at the blade in shock. She grabbed Nimue's leg and pulled, bringing her crashing to the floor. Nimue grabbed Brinnie's arm as she fell. "Got you!"

With all the force she could muster, Brinnie kicked Nimue away and wrenched her arm free. She reached for anything she could use as a weapon, but all she came up with was a cast iron skillet.

Nimue wrenched her knife out of the wall and slowly advanced toward what Brinnie assumed she saw as a floating frying pan. "Please." She drew nearer. "I don't want to hurt you, but I will."

"I really don't want to hurt you either. But I have to." As Nimue slashed forward with the knife, Brinnie swung with the pan, hitting Nimue in the hand and sending the knife spinning. Before Nimue could properly react, Brinnie brought the pan down on her head.

Nimue collapsed, and Brinnie dropped the pan and untied her ankles. Groggy, Nimue tried to grab her, but Brinnie was already halfway out the door. She latched it behind her. It wouldn't hold Nimue for long, but it might be just long enough.

She darted outside and around the house to the library. As she peered in, she saw Dolphus and Atherus sitting in chairs at the conference table playing cards, the parchment spread out at the opposite end. If she was going to have any chance of staying free and sneaking around to help free the others, she needed that parchment. Otherwise, even her invisibility wouldn't be able to hide her whereabouts.

Slowly, she turned the handle and eased open the door.

As it swung open, Atherus's head snapped up. "How did that open?"

Dolphus shrugged. "The wind?"

As Atherus stood to investigate, Brinnie took the opportunity to dash to where the parchment sat.

Atherus looked out with a puzzled expression. "There's no wind."

Slowly, keeping an eye on both men to make sure they were distracted, Brinnie began to roll up the parchment.

Dolphus stood and joined Atherus. "Then how did that happen?"

Brinnie tucked the parchment inside her shirt and began to tiptoe toward the door.

Atherus shrugged and closed the door. "Who knows. It's the Ludovic estate, after all."

The two turned and started back toward the table, but Dolphus stopped. "What happened to the parchment?"

They seemed frozen in disbelief for a moment, then Atherus exclaimed, "The shadow walker!"

They turned to barricade the door, but they were too late. Brinnie threw it open and darted outside. She didn't wait to see what they would do. Instead, she pounded around the house, down the path, the gravel biting into her feet. Lungs burning, she charged through the gate and lost herself in the twisting paths of the Maze.

Heaving in great gulps of air, she finally stopped to pull out the parchment. Dots milled all over the house and the grounds, but soon enough all but a few of the red dots had congregated near the hedges that surrounded the grounds, directly across from Brinnie's own dot in the Maze. *The blade must have pointed them to me.* She smirked in satisfaction. *But they can't come after me.* They would only get lost in the Maze.

She scanned the parchment. Now she simply had to follow it to the entrance to the Maze and warn Uncle Merlin and Ms. Tynsdale. She didn't have a plan beyond that—they would be able to figure everything out. She positioned herself in accordance with the parchment, then started off.

Within a few moments, she faced a fork in the path. She frowned. There hadn't been a fork on the parchment. She looked down at it again. Where she stood, the path was supposed to be straight. She looked up. There were clearly two diverging paths in front of her. Unsure what to do, she started down the path to the left.

When she looked down again, her brow furrowed. Where her dot had been, there was nothing. She scanned the Maze until she saw a blue dot, several inches away on another path. Staring at the parchment, she started walking forward. The dot moved as well. It was clearly her.

Once again, she positioned herself in accordance with the parchment, then looked up and began walking forward. This time, she came to a dead end, though on the parchment, a path clearly led off to the right. She looked between the Maze and the parchment. There was no path in real life.

She went to the hedge on the right side and put out a hand. Her fingers met leaves and branches. It wasn't an illusion. She tried to push her way through, but the hedge didn't give. She huffed in frustration.

"So you work for Mordred but not for me?" she asked the parchment. "Great. Thanks a lot." She stepped back from the wall and held the parchment out in front of her. "Watch this. I'm going to walk right down the path that's supposedly right here. Let's see what happens. I'm walking forward, and I'm walking forward, and I..." She trailed off.

And I'm not running into a wall.

She turned around. Right where the hedge should have been, the hedge that she hadn't been able to so much as make a dent in, was the path she had been on, with a second path leading nicely off to the right—just as shown on the parchment.

She looked from the parchment to the Maze. Then her mouth snapped shut and she felt exceptionally dim. The parchment only worked if the user was looking at it, and not at the Maze itself.

She held the parchment in front of her face and set off along the path that was marked. Eventually, she stopped bracing for impact every time she made a turn. Occasionally, she would peer around the parchment and see that she was headed straight for a wall, or a fork in the road, then would look back down at the parchment and marvel as she traveled down a smooth, straight path.

She wasn't sure how long she walked, since she couldn't tell day from night, but her legs felt like noodles by the time she reached the other entrance to the Maze. She had been lucky that in her initial parchment-less wandering, she had somehow ended up more than halfway there to begin with. Stumbling along, she reached the entrance and gazed at the trees outside. A few more steps, and she exited the Maze entirely. She looked up and saw the sun hanging low in the sky to what she thought was the west. It must have taken her most of a night and day of travel to get there.

Feeling freer than she could remember feeling in a long time, she sprawled out right on the road in front of the entrance to the Maze, gazing at the sky. Within an instant, she fell asleep.

She awoke to the sound of gravelly footsteps crunching on the road. She jumped up. "Uncle Merlin!"

But the smile melted off her face as her joyful expression was met with malevolent scowls from the dozens of armed men in front of her.

Chapter Thirty-Four

TWO MEN IN FRONT GRABBED HER arms before she could react. Another man with a large, bald forehead and broad shoulders stood in front of her and sneered. "Who are you, and what are you doing here?"

She cast about for a story. "I was just hiking, and I decided to take a nap. I'll get going—"

"What's this?" Before she could stop him, he snatched the parchment out of her hand and unrolled it. He slowly revealed large teeth. "A wizard girl. What are you doing guarding the Maze?"

That depends. Whose side are you on? "What are *you* doing here?" She straightened her shoulders. "And why am I being held like a prisoner?"

"We received word that Wraithwood is under new ownership. Is that true?"

"No, but Mordred is holding captives on the estate." She eyed them. Their reactions to such news might indicate whether they were friend or foe.

He grinned broadly. "Sounds like new ownership to me. Tell me, where is Ludovic?"

Foe. Great. "I don't know."

He leaned forward. "Do you know why we're here?"

She kept her mouth shut.

"We're here because Mordred, as you call him, sent for us. We're here because he has everything in place to kill Ludovic." He held up the parchment. "Except this. So tell me—were you sent to lead us to Wraithwood, or did you steal this?"

Brinnie's mind worked furiously. If they didn't know what side she was on, she could use that to her advantage. "Mordred sent me. I'm supposed to lead you through the Maze."

"I see." He nodded slowly. "And would you care to explain why he would trust an enchantment wizard?"

Brinnie's mouth opened and shut.

"Look!" He turned the parchment around and thrust it in her face. "You're blue. Why do you have the Enchantment?"

So there are colors for alignment *too?* "I—"

"You were waiting for Ludovic, weren't you?"

"N-no, I wasn't, I..."

"Silence!" He held up a hand. "Either give me a reason to spare your miserable life, or we'll leave your body here as a calling card to Ludovic."

Brinnie heard a few chuckles from behind the man. With a glare, she turned invisible.

The men on either side of her yelled at her disappearance and clung to her arms as she struggled to free herself from their grasp. She kicked and wriggled while other men came to the aid of the first two.

Just as she thought she might squirm free, a searing pain scorched her side and she gasped for air, losing her invisibility.

The men let go of her arms and let her fall. She looked up to see their leader standing before her with a bloody knife. He scowled at his men. "Fools! The only thing to do with a shadow walker is kill it. Strike while it thinks it's invincible." He leered at Brinnie. "Not so invincible now, are you?"

With the last of her strength, Brinnie turned invisible and stumbled away, just out of reach. The men started to go after her, but their leader stopped them. "We have better things to do than chase a dead girl."

The man led the way off into the Maze, the rest of the fighters following him. Brinnie collapsed on her side next to the hedges, pressing a hand to her wound. Blood flowed too quickly between her fingers. She tried to do something—stand up, go after the parchment, anything—but she could only gasp in pain and try not to throw up.

Instead, she fainted.

Brinnie shivered. Her eyes opened, then snapped shut again. Pain. She raised her hand from her side and felt both the stickiness of new blood and the dried-paint sensation of old blood covering her fingers. Her eyes flickered open again. There, standing next to her, was Mom.

"Mom!" she gasped, reaching up with a bloody hand. "How?" But as she reached out, her mother disappeared.

"Wait! No..."

As she sank in and out of consciousness, she was aware of many forms around her, some familiar, some not. A bird flew overhead, and a wolflike creature sat at her feet. Strange imaginings ran rampant through her mind, but at the same time, she wasn't sure they were imaginings, as the figures from her dream danced across reality.

I need to get up. I'm going crazy.

Instead, she slipped into darkness.

"Merlin!"

From afar, she heard the voices.

"Brynna!" Footsteps, running. Strong fingers feeling for her pulse. "Is she alive?"

"Yes. She must have passed out from shock." Something being pressed to her wound. "Brynna, can you hear me?"

She wanted to say something, but her lips wouldn't move. *You tell them.*

The shadow felt reluctant, as if some outside force was quickly draining Brinnie's hold. But from somewhere outside of her, her voice said, "I hear you."

A female exclamation. "What are you? What have you done to her?"

"I'm just a shadow. I've done nothing. She was attacked. Dark wizards have taken over Wraithwood."

A man's voice. "And are you from these dark wizards, 'shadow'?"

"No. I'm not real." The voice began to waver. "I was created by the shadowmaster."

"Who is that?"

But the shadow had fallen from her grasp. "It's me," Brinnie croaked.

She managed to open her eyes and look up at Uncle Merlin through a fog. Brinnie blinked once, then fell unconscious in his arms.

She woke to a cool rag being applied to her forehead. Her eyes fluttered open.

"Brynna." Uncle Merlin set down the rag. "How do you feel?"

She blinked. "Not the best." Then she sat bolt upright, pain streaking through her side. She gasped but kept going. "You can't go to Wraithwood—Mordred's taken over!"

"Relax. Lie back." He helped her ease against the backpack propped behind her. "We're outside the Maze. There's no danger. Start from the beginning."

She fought against spots dancing across her vision. "Wraithwood has been taken over by dark wizards. We were all taken prisoner, but I escaped. When you called, Mordred made Miss Burtle answer like nothing was wrong, so now he knows you're coming."

Uncle Merlin nodded, much calmer than Brinnie would have been in the same situation. "And who is Mordred?"

"The man from the road, the one who gave me the scar."

He nodded again. "How many men does he have?"

"He did have around eight, but when I was waiting for you, even more came—probably thirty more."

"Those ones are probably lost in the Maze by now," Brinnie heard a voice say.

She glanced over to see a beautiful blonde woman sitting nearby. She looked vaguely familiar. "Do I know you?"

She laughed. "It's me. Tynsdale."

Right. Her true form. She focused back on the matter at hand. "Actually, they're probably at the house by now. They stole the parchment from me."

Ms. Tynsdale grimaced. "Great. Any idea whether they were humans or wizards?"

"No, sorry."

"Either way, we're outnumbered more than five to one," Uncle Merlin observed.

"Good thing you're a Master," Brinnie said confidently.

He frowned. "That I may be, but I have no power. The Key has robbed us both of any magic we possessed."

Brinnie closed her eyes briefly. *Of course it would.* "Permanently?"

"No. Only as long as we have it."

"What are we going to do?"

"First, we're going to take care of you." The worry in his eyes warmed her heart. She felt a surge of anger toward Mordred for even suggesting such horrible things of Uncle Merlin. "What happened?"

"I was waiting in front of the Maze to warn you when the reinforcements came. I got away, but not before one of them got me." She reached for the wound.

"Don't touch," he instructed. "We don't want it to get infected."

Ms. Tynsdale snorted. "Because everything we used to patch her up was so sterile."

"Wait, what?"

"It's fine." Uncle Merlin gave Ms. Tynsdale a look. "I'm no expert, but you should make a full recovery." He spoke with confidence, but she sensed he was trying to convince himself.

She wouldn't let on and make him worry more. "Good." She looked around, taking in the trees and lack of mist. "Where are we?"

"We're outside the Maze still, at least until we come up with a plan."

"So they can't see us on the parchment."

"No. For now, we're safe."

"Of course," Ms. Tynsdale put in, "any other information you can give us would be very handy."

"Indeed," Uncle Merlin agreed. "How they managed to get through the Maze in the first place, for example."

She rubbed her forehead. The raw pain in her side made it difficult to think. "It's pretty complicated. I guess the best thing I can do is tell you what happened since we lost contact."

As succinctly as possible, Brinnie explained how the invaders had shown up on the parchment and how she had gotten lost in the Maze. She told how Quentin had gone after her but lost the parchment, then explained about meeting Morgana, Mordred's attack, and Morgana's death.

"Wait," Uncle Merlin stopped her. His shoulders tensed, as if bracing for impact. "She was killed?"

"Yes. By Mordred."

He stood and looked away from her. "You're sure?"

"Yes. She told me to let her go to her eternal home."

She couldn't see his face as he remained silent for a moment. "But they knew each other." His voice was strained, but he didn't turn back toward her. "She knew Mordred."

"Yes. She seemed shocked to see him."

Ms. Tynsdale looked at him in alarm. "Merlin..."

"What happened next?" he asked.

Brinnie explained how she and Quentin ran into each other, though she left out finding the graves. She told about her capture and how the blade was paired to point toward her within a radius of a hundred leagues, about Jerry, about the parchment, and about Quentin's capture. She explained how Wraithwood was taken over and told them Miss Burtle's suspicions about *The Case of the Master Key*. When she explained how she overpowered Nimue to escape, Ms. Tynsdale rolled her eyes. "Of course, she had to be here, too."

"So you are sisters?"

"Half," she corrected. "And a more stuck up, annoying—"

"In any case," Uncle Merlin interrupted. "You were saying?"

"Well, I stole the parchment and got out of there. I couldn't hang around, since Mordred's blade would point them right to me, but I thought if I could get to you in time, you would be able to do something."

"Thank you, Brinnie." He smiled at her, a break in the grave expression that had dominated his features throughout the conversation, and the warmth reached his eyes. "You've been incredibly brave. I'm proud of you."

She felt herself blush. "Now what?"

"You rest. You must be exhausted. We'll try to figure out what to do."

She liked the sound of that. Uncle Merlin and Ms. Tynsdale would figure it out. She knew they would. But she was too tired to think at all.

Brinnie's eyelids fluttered. Voices had woken her. Not far away, Uncle Merlin and Ms. Tynsdale sat perched on a pair of moss-covered rocks, talking in hushed tones.

"I'm sorry, Merlin. I know she meant a lot to you."

He took a deep breath. "Not only that. After all she's been through, for centuries...it's hard to believe she's gone. She was like a grandmother to me."

"To many of us."

Through half-closed eyes, Brinnie saw him take her hand. "I know. I'm sorry. You knew her, too."

"More like she knew me, and I tried to avoid her as much as possible. You know how I was."

He laughed softly. "I certainly do."

"Merlin," she asked, withdrawing her hand, "what are we going to do?"

He sighed. "I don't know."

"Do you think it really is Mordred? As in, *Mordred,* Mordred?"

"As much as I hate to say it, who else could kill Morgana? And who else would be the subject of prophecies in Mordizan?"

"He's been virtually dead for fifteen hundred years. Something would have had to happen to awaken him. Wouldn't someone at Arthrys notice if he woke up one day and waltzed out of the crypt?"

"Perhaps. Perhaps not. No one ever dares go near the crypt itself."

She blew out a breath of air. "Wonderful. So the ancient evil has awoken. But why is he here? Why Wraithwood?"

"You heard Brinnie. He wants me dead. If he couldn't kill Arthur..."

"He'll want to kill Arthur's descendants." A dark scowl puckered her absurdly beautiful face. "Great. Edna must have come to the same conclusion. By now Marcie's probably spilled the beans and he'll be after Brinnie's blood, too."

"Our biggest concern at the moment is getting the Key to Wraithwood. Until we do that, all the estates are in danger. If Mordred was able to send for more men, he certainly was able to alert all of our enemies that the protection spells have eroded."

"We need reinforcements. Maybe if we phone from Lyle..."

"There's no time. By the time help arrives, the estates will be overrun."

"What are we going to do, then? Take on dozens of enemies *and* Mordred, only the two of us? With no magic?"

Brinnie's side throbbed just thinking about it.

"What choice do we have? The Key must be properly stored for the spells to work again."

Ms. Tynsdale glanced toward Brinnie, and she snapped her eyes all the way shut. "And Brinnie?"

"She can't come with us."

"Of course not. For goodness' sake, we're going to our deaths. But what are we going to do with her?"

Brinnie chanced opening her eyes enough to see Uncle Merlin rub the bridge of his nose. "I suppose we'll have to send her home, or at least to some of her father's family."

"I'm not sure that will go over well. 'Here's your daughter. She's marked for death, has a stab wound, and oh, she's also a shadowmaster.'"

"That was indeed an unexpected development."

"Unexpected? It should be impossible. She's a Ludovic, not a Drakon."

"Quite. But the more pressing matter here is keeping everyone alive. How do we get in undetected if they have the parchment?"

"Maybe I could help," Brinnie piped up.

"Stars above!" Uncle Merlin exclaimed. "How long have you been awake?"

"Long enough." Gingerly, she pushed herself into a sitting position. "I'm a shadow walker, after all. They might see me on the parchment but being invisible might be enough to help me get in anyway."

"I appreciate that, but unfortunately, you wouldn't be able to turn invisible," Uncle Merlin said.

"Why not?"

"The Key," Ms. Tynsdale explained. "It will neutralize your powers, the same as ours."

Of course. She sighed.

"Wait," Uncle Merlin said slowly, tapping a finger on his knee in thought. "That's it! The Key neutralizes our magic. They won't see us coming."

Ms. Tynsdale raised a brow. "Please explain."

"The parchment works by detecting the Enchantment's magic, whether it applies to a wizard or a human. But the Key neutralizes magic. So..."

Ms. Tynsdale leaned forward. "Hypothetically, the parchment wouldn't be able to detect us as long as we have the Key." She snapped her fingers. "It seems a little crazy, but if we're understanding all of this right, it should work."

"Of course, once we actually get to the house, it will be quite a bit harder." He rubbed his chin, much scruffier than last time Brinnie had seen him. "The Key should stabilize once it's on an estate, but it will also start tearing down all of Wraithwood's magic, including the Maze. We'll have to hurry."

"So how will you keep it from taking down the Maze?" Brinnie asked.

"There's a place in the cellar. It's not nearly as effective as the Key's Case, but it should contain the Key sufficiently to keep Wraithwood's magic intact and regain our own."

Brinnie thought about that for a moment. "Don't I remember you saying something about the cellar being a terrible place, so it got closed off?"

"Yes, unfortunately I did." He grimaced. "At one point a couple centuries ago, Wraithwood was taken over by dark wizards and the cellar was converted into a dungeon. Luckily, it was important to the torturers to construct a room that would contain the magical effects of wizards in agony."

She didn't care to imagine that. "Disturbing, but handy. When are we going?"

"You are not," Uncle Merlin said flatly.

"But you said it yourself. I'll make a full recovery."

"This isn't about you being hurt. There's every chance that something will go wrong. It isn't safe for you here anymore. You need to leave."

And it was safe for her before? She almost laughed. "And go where? I can't exactly walk home."

"No, but you can go to Lyle. Lydia, you take Brinnie to Lyle and see her off. Contact her family, call a cab. I'll take the Key to Wraithwood."

"Have you lost your mind?" Ms. Tynsdale exclaimed. "You can't go alone."

"It's for the best." He stood. "I'll get the Key into the cellar, then my magic will return, and the enemy will be forced to leave."

"You're forgetting something." She stood as well, hands on hips. "It will take time for your magic to come back, time you won't have. Once you put the Key away, they'll see you on the parchment."

"I'll be fine."

"Fine? Mordred will kill you!"

"Perhaps. Perhaps not." A corner of his lips quirked, but the mirth didn't reach his eyes. "I'll take a page out of my father's book. Once I'm gone, the Mastership will go to Eira. If nothing else, I'll be able to keep them from the Key long enough for the protection spell to function again and drive them out."

She glared at him. "You don't get to be the martyr. I'm coming with you."

"No. I need you to protect Brinnie. Get her to safety. After me, Mordred will be after her."

"Um, I'm right here," Brinnie tried to put in.

Ms. Tynsdale didn't even glance at her. "Absolutely not. I'm not going to stand by and let you die."

"Mordred has to be kept from the Key at all costs." His tone remained carefully even. "I'm counting on you to alert Castelon that he has returned. Once he's driven out, he has to be stopped before he regains his full power."

"And we'll need you to help us do that."

His voice rose to match hers. "Lydia, it's the only way. Either I die or all three of us die."

Tears spilled from her enormous blue eyes. "Don't do this, Merlin."

"I have to. If we're going to save the estates, there's no getting around it."

Her mouth opened and closed as if she was going to say something, but all that came out was, "Argh!" She turned and stormed away.

Brinnie looked from one to the other, and she started to formulate a plan.

Chapter Thirty-Five

IT WASN'T LONG BEFORE UNCLE MERLIN was ready to go. Ms. Tynsdale helped him relegate the necessary supplies to his pack without saying a word.

"Well. It's time," Uncle Merlin said.

Brinnie rose to her feet, though it took a great effort and quite a lot of inward groaning. "Kick Mordred's butt."

"I'll see what I can do." He embraced her gently to avoid hurting her. "Tell your mother I love her...and that I'm sorry."

She nodded.

He turned to Ms. Tynsdale, his expression pained as he met her red-rimmed eyes. "Lydia. Please, let's not part like this."

She bit her lip, then threw her arms around his neck. His eyes widened for a moment before he embraced her back. He held her tight, and Brinnie glanced away, feeling like she was intruding on a personal moment. "It will be all right," he assured her.

She stepped back and nodded, jaw firm. "Yes. It will be."

He hesitated for a moment, then he nodded to them both one last time and walked away.

As soon as he was out of sight, Brinnie turned to Ms. Tynsdale. "You're not going to listen to him, are you?"

"Of course not." She slung a backpack over her shoulder. "And you won't listen to me if I tell you not to follow me, will you?"

She grinned. "Of course not."

"Then let's go. We can't lose sight of him in the Maze."

One hand holding her side, Brinnie followed Ms. Tynsdale, trying to ignore the pain. She couldn't see Uncle Merlin, but she assumed Ms. Tynsdale knew where she was going. They came through the trees just in time to see Uncle Merlin entering the Maze.

Ms. Tynsdale gestured rapidly and put a finger to her lips. Brinnie gritted her teeth and followed her in a sort of tiptoeing run, hurrying after him.

They entered the Maze as Uncle Merlin rounded a bend. Brinnie was sure at any moment he would look back and see them, but he didn't. They followed him through several twists and turns until Brinnie realized they hadn't come to any forks in the road.

Just to be sure, she waited a while to make certain her theory was correct. They didn't encounter a single fork. The Maze was not a maze.

She motioned for Ms. Tynsdale to stop. Ms. Tynsdale gave her a look that said, *Are you crazy?* Brinnie motioned anyway. Ms. Tynsdale stopped and hissed, "What is it?"

"The Key has taken away the magic of the Maze. It isn't a maze anymore."

"What do you mean?"

"This path hasn't had any forks. It's a straight shot through. We don't have to worry about sticking close to Uncle Merlin."

Ms. Tynsdale looked about with pursed lips. "You're right. But we still have to stay close. The Key is what's keeping them from seeing us on the parchment."

"Can you do magic?"

She paused and concentrated. Then she shook her head. "No. As long as that remains the same, we should be safe."

"Then maybe we could walk a little slower?"

She looked at Brinnie for a moment, then realization seemed to dawn on her. "Oh! I'm sorry. How is it?"

Brinnie pulled her hand away from her side and showed Ms. Tynsdale the new blood that stained her fingers. "Not the best."

"For Pete's sake, why didn't you say something earlier? Let me see."

As she lifted her shirt, Brinnie fought nausea at the sight of the blood seeping through the cloth wound around her middle.

Ms. Tynsdale's expression didn't make her feel any better. "That's not good."

Brinnie looked up so she wouldn't see the blood. "I'm fine. Can you do something to make it stop?"

"Maybe if I had a needle and thread instead of duct tape and rags."

Brinnie shuddered. "I'm kind of glad you don't."

Ms. Tynsdale's brow furrowed. "You really do need medical attention."

"I'm fine. Really."

She shook her head. "I should have listened to Merlin. If

something happens to you, he'll kill me. We have to go back."

"What? No! He won't be able to kill you because he'll be *dead*." She squared her shoulders. "He needs us. After his magic returns, he can take me anywhere. I'm not going to die, but he will."

Ms. Tynsdale stood back and looked her up and down. Brinnie watched her resolve crack. "What happened to the scared little girl I met hiding in the library?"

Brinnie grinned. "Turns out she's a wizard."

They added a new layer to the bandages around Brinnie's middle from Ms. Tynsdale's pack, then continued.

"What's our plan when we get there?" Brinnie asked.

"Distraction. I'll keep them busy until Merlin regains his powers."

"But they'll see him on the parchment."

"That's why they're not going to have the parchment." She raised her eyebrows. "You stole it once. How do you feel about stealing it again?"

Brinnie smirked. "I'd love to."

"Good. You'll go first and get the parchment. Once you find it, you'll come back, and I'll stage an attack to try to buy Merlin enough time to get in, place the Key, and get out."

"But...how will I go first if Uncle Merlin doesn't know about our plan?"

"He will." They turned a corner. "We'll catch up to him, and he won't be able to send us away, since we'd only get lost in the Maze."

Brinnie laughed. "You're good at this."

She shrugged and smiled. "It's my job."

Brinnie sobered. "But even you can't take on that many at once."

"I know." She kept her gaze straight ahead. "Also part of my job."

Brinnie put a hand to her side, still throbbing from her wound. "And your job is to protect the world from dark wizards?"

"Pretty much."

"Do they..." Brinnie looked down, watching the leaves crunch under her feet, weighing her next words. "Do they really want to destroy humanity?"

"Of course. That's what this is all about."

Brinnie hesitated. "That's not what Mordred said."

Ms. Tynsdale scowled. "And what did he say?"

"He said they aren't interested in destroying humanity. They're only fighting against the wizards with the Enchantment because they want to be free. He said we could use our powers to help people, cure diseases, that sort of thing." She watched for Ms. Tynsdale's reaction.

Her eyes darkened. "How familiar are you with Arthurian legend?"

"Pretty familiar. At least, I thought I was." Meeting the real—and not evil—Morgana had been a bit of a shock.

"Well, back during the days of Arthur, wizards were much more powerful. Now, we all have specific abilities—I'm a shapeshifter, you're a shadowmaster, Merlin's a traveler, that sort of thing. But back then, one wizard could be all of those things and more. Not all of them were, of course, but it was possible. The Enchantment was already there, but most people in Arthur's time knew about wizards—druids, they called them—so they were still greatly feared, and because of that, they were hated and to be killed if discovered."

Brinnie winced.

"Mordred was born during that time. His father, Myrddin, was the most powerful wizard ever to live. Myrddin believed that Arthur would bring about a time when dark wizards would be gone forever, the Enchantment would be broken, and wizards and humans would live together in peace, a time he called the Golden Age of Albion. But Mordred's mother, Morgana—"

"His mother!" The two had clearly shared a history, but she would never have guessed this was it. "He killed his own mother?"

"Yes. If you'll let me finish, you'll see why that's not exactly shocking."

Brinnie frowned. "Okay. I think I know enough about the legends to know where this is going."

"Morgana believed at the time that the only way wizards could live free was to destroy Arthur and establish wizards over humans. She raised her son to think the same way. To make a long story short, Morgana changed her mind, but Mordred didn't. He killed Myrddin and Arthur, but not before Myrddin cast the spells that created the estate system and limited all future wizards' powers." She gave a small smile. "This is taking me back to my primary school days. I was terrible at history."

Brinnie snorted at that, imagining learning these legends as history.

"Before Arthur died, though, he wounded Mordred with the

enchanted blade Excalibur. Mordred would have died, but to save his own life, he cast a spell on himself that trapped him in a long sleep. No one was able to actually kill him, so he's been kept in a crypt at Arthrys in Britain for over a thousand years."

"But was he right?" Brinnie hurried to explain. "I mean, was Mordred's point valid? Would we be better without the Enchantment? Was Arthur the true villain of the story?"

Ms. Tynsdale sighed. "During his time, Mordred did nothing but kill and destroy. He didn't use his powers to help people. In fact, he believed he was the rightful king, and he was bent on exterminating any humans that he could. Myrddin, on the other hand, gave his life to protect the people from Mordred, and left behind a legacy meant to protect humans and wizards alike. So who do you think actually has the world's best interests in mind?"

The itching turmoil in the back of her mind, planted by Mordred, subsided. Relief washed through her. "We can't be trusted, can we? If we had unlimited power like wizards used to have, and no Enchantment to stop us, some of us might do the right thing, but it's just as likely that people like Mordred would try to take over the world and be impossible to stop."

"Exactly."

"But now he's back." Brinnie shook her head. "After all these years."

"It appears so. Obviously he still wants all that crazy 'world domination'"—she wiggled her fingers mockingly—"but he's also out for revenge, if I'm not mistaken. He wants Ludovic blood."

Any relief she'd been feeling evaporated with a chill. "Why?"

"The Ludovics are the direct and only descendants of Arthur, Mordred's hated enemy."

Brinnie realized that her mouth had fallen open and snapped it shut. "We're descended from *King Arthur*?"

"Yes." Ms. Tynsdale laughed. "Don't sound so shocked. Seems like you would have learned by now that the world isn't exactly what you thought it was."

"No kidding." A new thought struck her. "If Mordred is so powerful, why is he sneaking around and using other people to do his dirty work?"

Ms. Tynsdale blew out a puff of air. "It's times like these that I wish I had paid more attention in the Academy. Magic worked differently back then. I think he used all his power to cast the sleeping curse that kept him alive. Chances are, he's still restoring his strength."

"That's good. That means Uncle Merlin might be able to defeat him, right?"

"Maybe. If we make it to that point."

They continued in silence. Without the Maze's maze-like qualities, it took far less time to pass through. Soon, the gates of Wraithwood rose before them.

Brinnie looked around. "Where is he?"

"If I were one of Mordred's men, you would both be dead."

Brinnie jumped and whirled to see Uncle Merlin standing behind them, arms crossed. "What are you two doing here?"

Ms. Tynsdale put her hands on her hips. "You think I would just let you prance off to your death? Your plan stinks."

"My plan was that you and Brinnie would be safe. Instead, you took it upon yourself to drag my wounded niece into the heart of enemy territory."

"She couldn't make me stay behind," Brinnie said. "I would have followed her anyway. But we're here now, so you can't send us back, or we'll get lost."

His stern gaze melted her backbone of defiance. Facing Mordred almost would have been easier. "Sorry," she amended.

To her relief, he sighed. "Unfortunately, you have a point. Both of you will have to stay in front of the entrance. By the time they notice you on the parchment, hopefully it will be too late for them to do anything."

"Actually," Brinnie said, "I think Ms. Tynsdale has a better plan."

"I get the feeling that I'm not going to like this plan, am I?"

Ms. Tynsdale grinned. "Nope. But here's what we're going to do."

Chapter Thirty-Six

BRINNIE SLIPPED BEHIND ONE OF THE hedges, trying to calm her ragged breathing. She winced at every intake of breath. Only a few yards away, one of Mordred's men stood watch.

Moments before, Uncle Merlin and Ms. Tynsdale had been arguing over the plan. "That's a terrible idea." He had scowled, one hand rubbing his chin. "Once Brinnie leaves the influence of the Key, they'll be able to see her on the parchment before she can take it."

"That's why she'll be invisible. She'll be awfully hard to catch, even with the parchment."

"No. Absolutely not. Far too many things could go wrong."

As Brinnie's eyes bounced from one to the other as if watching a tennis match, she made up her mind. "Okay, glad we all agree. I'm off."

With that, she had darted through the gates and onto the estate before she could hear the protests behind her.

Now she prepared herself and then dashed from the cover of one bush to another. For once, under the influence of the Key, she understood why everyone was so clumsy at night. It was difficult to see. But though difficult, it wasn't impossible. The guard might still spot her.

Safely out of sight, she grimaced and clutched her side. Her goal was the library. The parchment would most likely be there, the room Mordred had taken over as his command center.

Again, she darted out over the open space, then back into cover. She continued her stealthy dashes until she stood right outside the library.

A large, burly man stood in front of the door. *Great.* Tentatively, she reached out for the shadows around her. She felt them. The Key's influence was wearing off. She dragged the reluctant shadows over her and turned invisible.

She tiptoed up the steps of the portico. The man completely blocked the door, and he was sure to notice if it swung open. Reaching out, she found some stray shadows and sent them floating across the lattice on the other side of the portico.

The man turned and looked at the lattice warily. Ever so slightly, Brinnie set the shadows to swaying. As the man went to investigate the strange sight, she eased open the door and slipped through.

Inside, Mordred was gathered with a group standing around the conference table, eyes trained on something on the table. Brinnie's heart thudded when she realized what they were looking at—the parchment.

Mordred looked up and his eyes locked on her position. "Get her."

Brinnie ducked under their charge, avoiding humming blades, and rolled under the table. Feet leapt on top of the table as Mordred's minions pursued her blip on the parchment. "Block the door!" she heard Mordred direct. She rolled out again, ducked under a wild swing, and snagged the corner of the parchment. She tried to pull it with her, but Mordred held the other side. "Capture her now!"

A circle began to form around her. Brinnie's wild gaze locked onto the parchment. Grabbing it with two hands, she pulled it apart.

RIIIIIIP! Brinnie continued to tear until the parchment hung in two pieces. The dots faded and melted away, then the ink lines, and then the entire parchment crumbled.

For a moment, no one moved. Brinnie stared at the crumbled remnants, as surprised at what she had done as anyone else could be. Then she looked up at Mordred's shocked expression. She turned visible for a brief second and offered a cocky grin. "Your move."

Instantly, everything dissolved into chaos once again. Brinnie turned invisible and ducked the grasping clutches of her would-be captors. She dove through an opening, rolled, and jumped up, ignoring the wetness seeping through her shirt. The door to the outside was blocked, but the doors leading to the rest of the house weren't. She darted through them.

She burst through the office and parlor. In the great hall, two sleepy guards stood watch over the captives. Brinnie slipped behind one of them and slid the knife from his belt. As the man spun, confused, she knelt beside Mr. Winslow and whispered, "It's me, Brinnie. Take this and cut yourselves free. You'll know when the time is right." She pressed the handle of the knife into his bound hands.

His eyes widened, but he nodded.

Mordred's men burst through the office door. Brinnie jumped up and ran through the dining room. Soon she was through the kitchen, out the door, and running for the gate.

She stumbled up to where Uncle Merlin and Ms. Tynsdale waited, just outside the gate, her breath coming in ragged gasps that made her side feel like fire. "I destroyed the parchment. You're clear."

"You're in huge trouble, young lady," Uncle Merlin said, then he was gone into the night.

Ms. Tynsdale clapped Brinnie on the shoulder. "Well done. Stay here."

"No way! I'm coming."

"Look at you. You're a bloody mess."

"Doesn't matter." She shook off Ms. Tynsdale's hand. "They're after me, one way or another. It wasn't exactly a clean getaway. But I gave Mr. Winslow a knife to cut everyone loose. If we attack the front, they can back us up."

"Okay, I'm impressed." She heaved a sigh. "I don't have time to argue with you. Let's go."

As they ran down the path toward the house, Ms. Tynsdale said, "If we both attack the front, they'll know we're only a distraction. I'll attack the front, and you go around through the library. If we hit them from both sides, maybe we can keep them out of the kitchen. The entrance to the cellar is under the stairwell. We have to keep them out of there."

"Got it."

"Here. Take this." Ms. Tynsdale reached into the pack on her back and pulled out a blade the length of Brinnie's forearm.

"Seriously?"

"Just try not to hurt yourself. Go!"

Brinnie rounded the front of the house and ascended the steps of the portico.

The guard was waiting for her. He swung at her with a long blade and she jumped back. He thrust his hand toward her, then looked at it in confusion. He repeated the motion, and a tiny spark fizzled down toward the ground.

Uncle Merlin must be in the house. The Master Key was negating all powers.

She ducked around the confused guard and reached for the door. He recovered and raised his blade above his head, ready to strike. Just in time, Brinnie turned the handle and tumbled into the library.

She jumped up to see a group of men staring at her.

"Um. Attack!" She charged toward the doors leading to the rest of the house, blade held aloft.

To her surprise, no one stopped her. She threw them open and within seconds she reached the great hall.

Now she understood why they had let her through. The great hall was filled with Mordred's men, all armed and ready.

Mordred himself stood at the foot of the stairs in front of the prisoners. "Back already?" he asked.

"Yes." She tried to use her best intimidating voice. "Get out of here, or else!"

Chuckles rose from around the room. Mordred sneered. "Put the knife down. You will only hurt yourself."

"Well, I can't, because, um..."

At that moment, the front door flew open and Ms. Tynsdale barreled through. In an instant she had taken down the man closest to her and was parrying blows from several more.

"Because this is an attack!" Brinnie finished.

The prisoners jumped up. Mr. Winslow swung at Mordred with his knife and Mordred leaped out of the way. He held his hand out toward Mr. Winslow, but nothing happened. "The Key is here!" he shouted. "Find Merlin."

The ground shook and the house shuddered. The men running to find Uncle Merlin stumbled. "If it loses all magic, the house is going to collapse!" Ms. Tynsdale called out.

Mordred's men recovered. They dispersed in all directions, and a few ran toward the doors to the dining room.

Brinnie ran after them, but she was too late to stop them. She pursued them through the dining room and into the kitchen. They began throwing open cupboards and kicking things around. One threw the door open to the Winslows' room, while another started for the room that housed the staircase.

Brinnie darted toward the latter, blade at ready, but he spun around and blocked her swing. Her blade went spinning across the floor, so she grabbed the first thing her hand touched—a plate. She ducked under his swing and threw the plate at his head like a discus. He yelled as it hit him in the nose before falling and smashing on the ground. Soon four men were on top of her, grabbing her arms and pinning her down.

Brinnie heard a loud *thwack!* and one of the men let go of her. She looked up to see Uncle Merlin wielding a heavy iron ladle. She kicked another in the shin while he took out the others. "Did you do it?" she asked.

"It's in place."

"Then why aren't they leaving?"

"An unexpected development." He swung the ladle again, connecting with a skull with a crack. "Without the Case, it seems the Key will still disable the protection spell—even if its other effects are contained." A last body fell to the ground. "We still have to fight."

She didn't have time to process her despair. Five-to-one odds. Uncle Merlin had taken off through the dining room, back toward the great hall, and she scrambled to her feet to follow.

It didn't look good. Mrs. Winslow had retreated halfway up the stairs, holding a coat rack aloft. Quentin was hardly discernable in the midst of a crowd of Mordred's men, while Ms. Tynsdale and Nimue were locked in a terrifying flurry of blades.

Mordred stood in the middle of it all, watching coolly. He turned as Uncle Merlin burst into the room, Brinnie two steps behind. "Merlin Ludovic," he said with a slight smirk.

"Stop this, Mordred." He held the ladle like a sword. "I'm the one you want."

"And I suppose you will give yourself over peacefully?"

Uncle Merlin looked around. Brinnie followed his gaze. Nimue had Ms. Tynsdale pinned in a corner. Mr. Winslow fell to the ground with a thud, several men surrounding him. Miss Burtle struggled as two men held her by the arms, and Mrs. Winslow was backing farther and farther up the stairs.

"Yes," Uncle Merlin ground out. "I'll give myself over peacefully. But you and all your men must leave, and they must let them go."

Mordred offered a sinister smile. "A fair deal." He waved a hand in the air. "Cease!"

The struggle came to a halt.

No. Don't do it. Brinnie's stomach squeezed as Uncle Merlin strode toward the center of the room.

He stopped in front of Mordred. He met Mordred's gaze, eyes fiery. "But I want you to know that revenge changes nothing."

Mordred drew his blade. "True. But your death changes something." He raised the blade. "It means that Wraithwood and the Key are mine."

"No!" Out of nowhere, a figure leapt on Mordred, knocking him to the ground. The two rolled, and the man ended up on top. Mordred thrust upward with his blade, burying it in the man's chest. The figure went limp. Mordred cast aside the body and stood, his blade dripping with blood.

From the left came a terrible shriek. Marcie ran across the hall and fell to her knees beside the limp form. "Jerry! Jerry, no..."

For a brief moment, Brinnie saw a semblance of fear pass over Mordred's countenance, but he quickly composed himself. He addressed his men. "What are you waiting for? Kill them!"

The struggle commenced once more. "Merlin!" Ms. Tynsdale yelled. Brinnie looked over to see her in her red-haired form once more. "Magic is returning!"

He nodded as he blocked a swing from an opponent, but he wasn't the only one who heard. Soon, the hall filled with flying fire, water, and mist. Everything from lizards to plant life erupted from the cracks. Unsure what to do, Brinnie ran toward Uncle Merlin, ducking magic and swinging blades. "Now what?" she shouted.

"Stay out of the way and help me."

"How...?" Brinnie began to ask, but before she could, Uncle Merlin had snatched up a blade from a fallen foe and raised it to parry a blow from Mordred. The two dueled with blades, but Mordred had the advantage of magic. He thrust his arm forward, and Uncle Merlin went flying as if from a mighty blast. His body slammed into the wall. In horror, Brinnie realized that Uncle Merlin's magic, the longest exposed to the Key, had yet to return.

Stay out of the way and help me. Finally, it clicked. Brinnie skirted the fighting, backing out of the thick of it. She held her breath, closed her eyes, and reached for that strange feeling, the imbalance she had felt at the battle on the road.

Something snapped into place, and Brinnie directed her energies toward Uncle Merlin. As Mordred closed in for the kill, Uncle Merlin threw out his hand and blinded Mordred with a beam of fiercely bright light. Brinnie's lips twisted up in satisfaction.

She sensed something behind her and whirled and ducked. She was barely in time to avoid capture by one of the men. Nevertheless, he closed in with a grin, certain of his victory over a weaponless girl.

Brinnie reached out toward all corners of the room. She could feel the shadows, like clay waiting to be molded and animated, to become the creatures she had seen in her delirious state before Uncle Merlin and Ms. Tynsdale found her. They hadn't been hallucinations. They had been shadows. Her shadows.

She drew them to her.

A howl ripped through her, rattling her bones. She couldn't tell whether the sound came from within or without, but from all the dark corners, her call was answered. Black eyes glowed, obsidian teeth snapped, and wolves emerged from the nebulous darkness.

Around her, combatants yelled in surprise. Brinnie felt the connection singing beneath her skin. These were her shadows, the power of hidden things. The might that lurked beyond the spotlights.

Her wolves looked at her expectantly.

She nodded.

At once, the wolves sprang forward, snarling at the enemy. The men sliced at her creatures, but the blades only passed straight through. She strode to the front door and threw it open. On the other side was a pine forest. *Chase them out.* Snarling and nipping, the wolves began driving the enemy toward the door.

Mordred and Uncle Merlin remained locked in combat. Magic

flew so quickly that Brinnie wasn't sure whose was whose. Across the room, Ms. Tynsdale knocked the blade from Nimue's hand. The Wraithwooders beat the attackers toward the door with such varied weapons as brooms and a coat rack. Brinnie's creatures didn't fight alone.

The wolves bit at the enemy, who yelled in surprise when their teeth drew blood. Brinnie's fingers twitched, directing the beasts. Fearlessly, the shadow wolves drove the attackers through the doorway, herding armed men like sheep into the pine forest.

Once most of them were through, Brinnie slammed the door.

She gulped deep breaths, pressing her back against the wall. Magic vibrated under her skin. Her tether to the shadows snapped, and the wolves ripped free, shadows whipping back into the corners and crannies.

She looked around. A few of Mordred's men lay on the floor, while Ms. Tynsdale held a knife to Nimue's throat. Uncle Merlin and Mordred battled on in the same whirlwind of magic. Brinnie wasn't sure what to do when Ms. Tynsdale yelled, "Mordred! Stop, if you want her to live!"

The storm died down as Mordred turned to see the blade at Nimue's neck. He sneered. "You wouldn't kill your own sister."

"Says the man who killed his mother." Ms. Tynsdale yanked Nimue's head back farther. "Get out or she dies."

Nimue's eyes were wide and her face burned red with anger, but any movement and she would have slit her own throat.

"What makes you think I care?" Mordred asked.

"Fine. Then watch me kill her." Ms. Tynsdale pushed the blade into Nimue's skin until a trickle of blood ran down her neck.

Brinnie momentarily glimpsed a flash of agony, or terror, in Mordred's eyes.

So Mordred did have a weakness. And her name was Nimue.

His hand slipped to his side, where a scroll was attached to his belt. "Let her go. I'll leave."

"Leave first. Then I'll let her go."

"Why would I trust you?" he spat.

"I'm more trustworthy than you are. I keep my deals."

He glared at her. "Very well." He strode to the door, opened it, and stepped through into a grassy meadow.

Slowly, Ms. Tynsdale directed Nimue forward, her blade never leaving her sister's neck. Finally, she reached the doorway. In one swift motion, she shoved Nimue out and slammed the door shut.

"Wait!" Brinnie and Ms. Tynsdale turned to see Miss Burtle limping toward them. "He had *The Case of the Master Key*."

Ms. Tynsdale slumped, leaning against the door. "But he doesn't have the Key. Or Wraithwood." Her gaze passed over the scorch marks, blood, and unconscious enemies on the floor. "This place is a mess."

"Please, help."

Brinnie turned to see Marcie on the ground, cradling Jerry's head. Tears streamed down her face. "Please. He's dying." Her eyes implored Uncle Merlin. "Can't you do something?"

Uncle Merlin hesitated. His mouth opened, then closed as he took in Jerry's pale face. "I can't. But I can find someone who can." He disappeared.

Marcie brushed the hair from Jerry's forehead. "Come on. Stay with me."

Ms. Tynsdale moved away from the door. Seconds later, it flew open and Uncle Merlin stepped in with Anika.

The healer hurried to Jerry's side. She knelt to look at the wound, then turned to Uncle Merlin questioningly. "He's human."

"I know. Can you help him?"

She shook her head slowly. "This would be difficult enough if he were a wizard, but as a human—there's little I can do."

"I'll help you." Brinnie pushed herself into motion, coming forward and placing a hand on Anika's shoulder. "Save him."

She nodded and took a deep breath. Brinnie closed her eyes to concentrate on supplying Anika with energy. Her limbs trembled, the buzz so different than what resonated through her bones when she controlled the shadows.

What seemed like an eternity later, Anika said, "It's done."

Brinnie opened her eyes in time to see Jerry's eyelids flutter open.

"Jerry!" Marcie exclaimed. "Oh, thank you, thank you!"

He blinked. "Are we all dead?"

"None of us are, thanks to you." Uncle Merlin knelt, took his right hand, and shook it. "I owe you my life."

"Well." He looked up at Merlin. "Can't say we're friends. But you were probably the only one who could keep Marcie safe."

Confusion, then tenderness, then confusion swept over Marcie's expression. She offered him a tentative smile and wiped a tear from her eye.

The Wraithwooders stood in a circle around Jerry, seeming unable to think of what to say.

Mr. Winslow broke the silence. "Reckon we did it."

"And the Key is safe, which means all the estates are secure again," Uncle Merlin added.

Smiles broke out. The Winslows hugged one another. Ms. Tynsdale laughed and slugged Uncle Merlin in the shoulder.

As the laughing and hugging spread, Brinnie's world began to spin. From far away, she heard Mrs. Winslow's voice. "Brinnie? Are you all right?"

She looked down and all she saw was red. She heard Mrs. Winslow gasp. "Merlin, she's wounded."

With that, everything went black. The last thing she felt were strong arms catching her as went limp.

Chapter Thirty-Seven

BRINNIE'S EYES OPENED SLOWLY. HER GAZE wandered around the cheerful blue room with white curtains stirring in the breeze from the open window.

"Good morning, dear."

Mrs. Winslow sat by her bedside with some knitting in her lap. "How are you feeling?"

She rubbed her eyes. "I'm not sure." She sat up gingerly and felt a twinge in her side. "What happened?"

"You passed out, dear. Anika fixed you up as best she could."

With a slight creak, the door opened, and Anika herself peeked in. "Ah! I see you're awake." She entered and closed the door behind her. "You weren't the worst case I've ever seen, but you gave it a pretty good shot. You lost more than a third of your blood with all your saving-the-world stunts."

She felt like her brain had been replaced with cotton. "Um, shouldn't I be dead, then?"

Mrs. Winslow and Anika both laughed. Mrs. Winslow squeezed her hand. "That's why it's called magic, dear."

"Oh. Then everyone's okay? Everything's good?"

"Better than good." Anika beamed. "The protection spells are up, the Key is safe, the dark wizards are in full retreat, and the man who started this whole mess is behind bars."

Brinnie searched her memory for the strange explanation. "The scientist?"

"Or at least that's what he was pretending to be." Anika crossed her arms. "He used to be the Keeper of the Key, decades ago. Looks like he faked his death so he could escape and destroy the Key. They're not sure, but they think he wanted to get rid of the protection spells so we would all destroy each other."

"Not only that," Mrs. Winslow chimed in. "I thought you might like to know. Marcie didn't tell Mordred about you. He still has no idea who you are or where to find you."

Brinnie smiled. "Good old Marcie."

Mrs. Winslow stood. "I'm glad you're feeling all right, but I have to get going. Castelon sent out the DI to investigate Merlin, and they'll be here soon."

Brinnie's smile gave way to a furrowed brow. "Wait—so after all this, they're still accusing him of treason?"

"Technically, what he did *was* treason." Anika shrugged. "But I doubt they'll want to slate him as a traitor when his estate is the only one that can keep the Master Key safe."

"Now remember, dear, as far as they're concerned, you don't exist," Mrs. Winslow said. "So keep quiet."

"But won't Quentin tell them?"

"He's had a bit of a change of heart. It seems our victory has convinced him that some rules are worth breaking." Mrs. Winslow smiled. "Rest up. Hopefully this will all be cleared up soon."

As the door closed behind her, Brinnie swung her legs over the edge of the bed.

"Where do you think you're going?" Anika demanded.

"Downstairs. I want to see what happens."

"You heard Mrs. Winslow. You can't let them see you."

"Don't worry, I won't." She raised an eyebrow. "Shadow walking has its perks."

Downstairs, the remnants of last night's battle scattered the house—overturned furniture, scorch marks, bloodstains, water damage. As Brinnie invisibly entered the great hall, Anika at her side, she saw Uncle Merlin dismiss the last remnants of Mordred's now-conscious men out the front door into what looked like a bog while the other Wraithwooders hovered nearby. The men's injuries appeared to be mostly healed, or at least bandaged, presumably due to Anika's ministrations.

I bet Mrs. Winslow insisted. The motherly woman wouldn't want even enemies to be dumped in the middle of nowhere with mortal injuries.

Miss Burtle scowled. "It pains me to let them go."

Uncle Merlin closed the door. "Unfortunately, we can't have prisoners spilling our secrets to the DI." He turned and smiled in the direction of the stairs. "Brynna! I'm glad to see you're up and around."

Brinnie turned visible. "Looks like Wraithwood has its old Master back."

"Brinnie!" Mrs. Winslow scolded.

"Anika let me come down."

"Anika!"

Anika put her hands up and laughed. "I did my best."

"I'll stay invisible."

"Not an option," Ms. Tynsdale said, back in her usual red-haired form. "They'll have magic-sensing wands everywhere. Now shoo!"

Brinnie laughed as Ms. Tynsdale and Anika both herded her back into her room. "Now, you stay here, young lady, and do not come out," Ms. Tynsdale ordered. "You can play with your shadow dogs or something."

"Excuse me, but they were wolves."

"Cheeky!"

Brinnie relaxed into bed, peace settling over her.

They had done it.

Brinnie stepped over a pile of planks on the floor and hopped from floorboard to floorboard. "Be careful," Jerry called from where he was installing a new post in the banister of the grand staircase.

"I will." She ducked a bucket of wood stain zipping over her head. "Hey!"

"Oops, sorry!" Quentin grinned as Mr. Winslow grabbed the bucket out of the air. "Next time I'll do that without magic."

"Hey, gofer." Jerry gestured at Quentin. "Could you pass me a flathead screwdriver?"

"On it." He dug through a toolbox and brought it over. "I'm still not sure about this, though. Is 'gofer' a real job?"

Brinnie laughed to herself as she pushed open the dining room doors and scurried through to the kitchen. There, Mrs. Winslow stirred something on the stove while Marcie put a dish in the oven. "Have you seen Uncle Merlin?" Brinnie asked.

"I'd try the garage." Marcie gestured toward the back door.

As Brinnie stepped out into the warm sunshine, the events of two weeks ago seemed almost as if they had never happened. But on the other hand, everything had changed.

For one, Wraithwood had gained two new members. A lot of damage had been done to the house, and Jerry was just the one for the job. Apparently, when he wasn't drunk, he was quite the handyman, and with Marcie's consent, Uncle Merlin had temporarily hired him for repairs. Despite the convenience of a repairman who wouldn't question the bloodstains, scorch marks, or sword gouges, Brinnie suspected Uncle Merlin had other motives. Even with Jerry's vows that he had sworn off booze forever, his promise would be much easier to keep in a magical mansion free of liquor. Marcie remained hesitantly optimistic, though not yet willing to consider anything beyond a friendly relationship, and Brinnie hoped Jerry could permanently change under the influence of the men and women of Wraithwood. Mordred seemed to have scared him straight for now, and he held a grudging respect for Uncle Merlin.

Then, of course, there was Quentin. Somehow in their retelling of the battle, the Wraithwooders had made the DI believe Quentin rather than Brinnie had turned the tide. As a result, he had earned the title of Protector of the Key and was commissioned to stay at Wraithwood. The DI decided not to press charges against Uncle Merlin or anyone else, considering it better to have a friend guarding the Key rather than a foe.

Brinnie stopped on the path, turned her face toward the sun, and closed her eyes. She soaked in its warmth, wishing it could seep into her soul. Finally, magic was everywhere at Wraithwood—Quentin's wild levitation, Brinnie's shadow friends, and all the small magical things that made life at Wraithwood easier, like Uncle Merlin's glowing orbs of light.

She only wished that could even begin to make up for what she had done.

When Brinnie stepped into the garage, she found Uncle Merlin gazing critically at a slab of stone propped on a workbench in front of him. Ms. Tynsdale stood next to him, her head cocked to the side.

"Brinnie," Uncle Merlin greeted her. "What do you think?"

She came around to look at the carvings. In bold letters, the stone read, *Morgana le Fey.*

"It's a little plain."

"It isn't finished," Ms. Tynsdale explained, "but we don't know what else to put. We don't even know her birthday."

"Hmmm." Brinnie picked up a pencil and paper from the worktable and began to sketch. "There. How's that?"

On the piece of paper was a simple headstone. At the top, it read, *Morgana le Fey.* Underneath, she had written, *The Lady of the Forest, Home at Last.*

Ms. Tynsdale nodded. "I like it."

"I think you've hit upon it," Uncle Merlin agreed. "Thank you, Brinnie."

"Have you found Bruno yet?" she asked.

He shook his head. "I'm sorry. I was out in the Maze and at the cottage early this morning calling for him, but still nothing."

"Oh." Her heart sank. "I'm so sorry. I shouldn't have left him."

Uncle Merlin put a hand on her shoulder. "You did what you had to do. He's a smart dog. He's probably off chasing squirrels at this very moment."

Brinnie pressed her lips together and nodded.

"You all right, kid?" Ms. Tynsdale asked. "You've seemed a little off lately."

She looked down at the unfinished headstone, debating whether to speak. "Morgana is dead, Bruno's missing, Jerry almost died—we all almost died—and...it's my fault." She closed her eyes. *It's always my fault.*

"Your fault?" Uncle Merlin exclaimed. "How?"

Isn't it obvious? "If I had never gone into the Maze, Mordred would never have gotten the parchment, there never would have been a battle, he wouldn't have killed Morgana..." She trailed off, unable to force any more words past the lump in her throat.

"Come here." Ms. Tynsdale wrapped her in a comforting and very un-Ms. Tynsdale-like embrace. "That's part of life. You don't know what's going to happen. You just do what's in front of you."

315

Uncle Merlin nodded, running his fingers over the headstone. "You can't see the future. You do what you think is right at the time. Sometimes it turns out well. And sometimes..." He paused, and Brinnie saw the sorrow in his eyes, a sorrow she finally understood. "Sometimes not."

Ms. Tynsdale released her from the hug but left an arm around her shoulders. "Besides, whether you were there in the Maze or not, Mordred would have killed Morgana if he found her. He was out for revenge."

"True. And chances are," Uncle Merlin mused, "when we came back with the Key, the Maze would have lost its maze-like qualities and Mordred would have made it through anyway."

Ms. Tynsdale's lips twitched up in a mischievous grin. "And almost dying was probably the best thing that could have happened to Jerry."

Uncle Merlin's eyes twinkled. "It certainly improved his vocabulary."

Ms. Tynsdale laughed. "Listen, kid. We're pretty used to the whole almost-dying thing." She clapped a hand to Brinnie's shoulder. "Welcome to being a wizard. You're not going to do it perfectly. But you'll still make some pretty cool shadow wolves and kick an ancient evil's butt while you're at it. That's got to count for something."

She allowed herself a smile. "I guess."

Uncle Merlin cleared his throat. "Speaking of evil and all that, we should get this finished if we want to do this tonight. You're not the only one heading out soon. Ms. Tynsdale is leaving tomorrow morning, as well."

"Tomorrow?" Brinnie looked over at her. "Why?"

"We can't keep the Key like this forever. Someone needs to find out where they're keeping the Case and get it back." She smirked. "And now that Castelon and I are quite ironically on somewhat better terms after this whole treason fiasco, that job falls to me."

Brinnie's heart squeezed. Uncle Merlin, Ms. Tynsdale, the people of Wraithwood...it seemed to never end. When would they have finally given up enough?

Nothing happened perfectly. Some people weren't saved. Some

towns burned. Sometimes dark wizards got away. But here, Wraithwood still stood, a testament to sacrifice, to the hope that was greater than all of them.

Wraithwood was more than a place to her, she realized. It stood as a reminder that there were things in this world worth fighting for, worth saving, no matter how imperfect the effort.

Brinnie saw that same determination gleaming in Ms. Tynsdale's eyes, and she had no more protests. "Be careful."

"Don't worry about me." She flashed a grin. "I'm almost looking forward to it. Two weeks without someone trying to kill me? Gets a little dull."

Brinnie laughed. "I think I could go a whole lifetime without that getting old."

"Someday, that's the goal."

That evening, they made a solemn procession through the Maze. As Brinnie stood in the cemetery where her grandparents were buried, a tear rolled down her cheek. A brand-new headstone sat underneath the tree where she had found Quentin what felt like a lifetime ago.

"It's a beautiful resting place for her," Mrs. Winslow said quietly.

Brinnie nodded. "She would have liked it."

Glowing orbs floated over them, and Marcie laid a bouquet of flowers on the grave. Jerry glanced around. "It's been a long time since I've been to a funeral, but aren't there supposed to be some words said?"

"I don't know what there is to say," Uncle Merlin said slowly. "She lived a long, good life. She was happy to move on."

"Then I guess you just said it." Ms. Tynsdale nodded. "She wouldn't want us to be too mournful. She's probably up in heaven partying like it's 1492 again."

There was a general rumble of laughter. They began to turn away when a sound stopped Brinnie in her tracks. "Wait! Did you hear that?"

She ran off through the rows of headstones and stood stock still, listening.

"Brinnie, what..."

"Bruno!" She took off through the trees, leaping over fallen logs, grinning fit to split her cheeks. "Bruno! Bruno, here boy!"

As she ran, the barking grew louder. Soon a great brown form barreled toward her. In seconds, Bruno jumped all over her and she fell to the ground giggling while he licked the tears from her face. "Good boy! Oh, good boy. I'm sorry I left you, I'm so sorry." She ruffled his ears and hugged him. His tongue wagged as fast as his tail. She patted his bony sides. "Look at you! You're getting a big giant dinner as soon as we get back."

"*Merow*!"

A cat sat out of reach, tail twitching. "Who's this?" Bruno bounded over and licked the cat's ear, in response to which it batted at his snout. Recognition dawned. Morgana's cat. "Ami?"

Ami stood and sashayed forward, head high. The cat rubbed against Brinnie's legs and flicked her tail under Brinnie's nose. She laughed. "Come here, you."

With Ami in her arms and Bruno bounding around her in circles, Brinnie started back. Within moments, she saw Ms. Tynsdale. "Oh, thank goodness. She's over here!" Ms. Tynsdale called. As everyone came from different directions and gathered around, she demanded, "What were you doing?"

Brinnie grinned. "Look who I found!"

"So this is where you've been hiding, you old rascal." Uncle Merlin dropped to his knees, smiling wide, and Bruno jumped up, putting his paws on his shoulders. Uncle Merlin ruffled his ears and laughed as the dog almost knocked him over. "I should have known. Plenty of squirrels around here."

Mrs. Winslow clasped her hands together, eyes shining. "We'd better be heading home. These two could use some fattening up. And we have two goodbye parties to celebrate."

They stayed up long into the night. Marcie baked a cake, and everyone sang happy birthday to Brinnie a week early. Uncle Merlin brought out a set of chess pieces for a game of wizard's chess, which erupted into a mock battle that ended with Quentin running into the wall on a flying chair while Brinnie chased after him with the Dread Spaghetti Noodle of Destiny.

As Brinnie stumbled up the stairs and into bed, her wide grin began to fade. She gazed at her neatly packed suitcase. It was her last night at Wraithwood.

Sometime in the night, Brinnie heard footsteps. She peeked out to see Ms. Tynsdale creeping down the hall, a pack slung over her shoulder. "Are you leaving?" Brinnie whispered.

Ms. Tynsdale whirled around. "Heaven's sake, Brinnie." She sighed. "I figured I'd leave while everyone was still asleep."

"Does Uncle Merlin know?"

"No." She gave a smile Brinnie couldn't quite decipher. "But he won't be surprised."

"Then how are you going to leave?"

"I'll just keep opening the door until I find someplace I want to end up."

Brinnie cocked her head. "But why? Don't you want to say goodbye?"

"Not really." She adjusted the strap of her pack. "I like to think that if I don't say goodbye, I'm not really leaving—I'm just going out for a while."

"Will I see you again?"

"Of course." She clasped Brinnie's right hand as if in pledge. "If not in this life, in the next."

Brinnie nodded. For some reason, that was enough. "Until then."

"Until then." A moment later, she had gone.

The next morning, Brinnie stood in front of the door, saying her goodbyes. She hugged everyone from the stiff Miss Burtle to the awkward Quentin.

Mrs. Winslow smelled like fresh-baked bread, Mr. Winslow like the grass and trees. Marcie's affectionate squeeze was coupled with a few sniffles. Brinnie could hardly tear herself away. "Are you sure you all can't come too?"

"I wish we could, dear," Mrs. Winslow said, "but humans can't travel by magic, especially by door. We'd go all to pieces."

Brinnie gave her one last hug, trying to imprint in her memory what it felt like. "Thank you. For everything." She picked up her suitcase, took a deep breath, and nodded to Uncle Merlin. "I'm ready."

He offered her his arm and she took it. Then he opened the door. Brinnie held her breath as they stepped through.

There was a gust of wind and a flash of light, then they were standing on the road outside of Lyle.

"That was so cool!" Brinnie steadied herself. "Could we go anywhere like that?"

"Anywhere we had both already been before. Otherwise we would end up someplace completely random."

She was glad she'd gotten to experience the door at least once this summer. "Amazing."

"Brinnie." He turned to face her, his expression solemn. "You realize that you're going back to the ordinary world now."

She sobered. *I realize that a whole lot more than you know.* "Yes."

"You're a powerful wizard. You'll have to be very careful to keep anyone from finding out about your powers. Not only would that be a threat to all the humans around you, but also to yourself. With your scar linked to Mordred's blade, he may come looking for you."

She shook her head and tried to smile. "He doesn't know who I am, though. He won't be looking too hard."

Her attempt to lighten the mood didn't work. "I wish that were the case. But besides being the first shadowmaster in nearly a century, you're also a helper. You can increase a wizard's power tenfold. Think what he could do with that."

She grimaced. "I'll be careful."

"There's more." He hesitated. "Any contact with wizards puts you in danger from the dark wizards' spies."

She peered at him, not comprehending. Not wanting to comprehend. "What are you saying?"

His eyes begged her to understand. "I'm saying that I may not see you again."

He couldn't be serious. She struggled to form words for a moment. "You mean, like, ever? You can still come and visit, right? And I can come here? Maybe next summer?"

He shook his head slowly. "That's what I'm trying to tell you. There are spies everywhere. If they see you with me, and especially if they see you coming to Wraithwood...now that Mordred is awakened, there's more danger than ever. I'm sorry." He couldn't meet her gaze. "You can't have any contact with us anymore. No magic. Not even your own."

Tears formed in Brinnie's eyes, and her chest burned like she'd been stabbed with another knife. "What about everyone? The Winslows, and Marcie, and Miss Burtle, and Quentin? You're saying I'll never see them again?"

"Brynna, I—"

"Then I won't go!" She clenched her jaw, determined to stand firm. "I'll stay at Wraithwood. I...I belong there way more than I do at home."

He sighed. "No, Brynna. You're young. You have a family. All we have to offer you are more battles, more war. Go home. You'll be safe, and happy."

"No! Please, no." Tears streamed down her cheeks.

His expression was pained, as if telling her was even harder than for her to hear it. "You're different now. It won't be the same when you go back. If nothing else, I think—I think you understand a bit more."

She looked down and scrubbed her toe against the asphalt. She didn't know what it was like to have friends in the real world. To feel belonging. To be herself without anyone comparing her, sighing at her.

But now, she had experienced those things. And maybe she could bring them with her.

"There is one thing, though. If you're ever in trouble—if they find you—smash this open." He handed her a small glass orb, much like a marble, except that the inside swirled with a strange mist. "It will guide you."

She took it and threw her arms around him. "I love you."

"I love you, too," he said softly. After a moment, he pulled away and held her at arm's length. "Now let's go find your parents."

Brinnie wiped the tears from her face as they walked down the road and into town. It would look strange that they came without a vehicle, but it was far better than Mom and Dad having to navigate a giant maze to find her.

Mom and Dad. She took a deep breath. Things were going to be different now. Maybe not between her and Dad. But Mom...

It wasn't right, what Mom did, squashing her, hiding her, resenting her for something she had no control over. It still hurt, knowing Mom knew she was special but never told her. It hurt being critiqued and compared. But she understood, at least a little bit. *I know now what it's like to be a wizard. And maybe, instead of hiding secrets from each other, we can share them.*

As they walked down the main street, she saw a man with dark hair standing in front of a car parked at the gas station, waving. She ran forward, dropped her suitcase, and leaped into a giant bear hug. "Dad!"

"There's my girl!"

She laughed as his hug swept her off her feet. He set her down again and turned to face Uncle Merlin. "And you must be Merlin."

"A pleasure to meet you," he said as they shook hands.

"I hope she wasn't too much trouble." Dad nudged Brinnie teasingly.

Uncle Merlin's expression softened. "None at all. Your daughter is a very special young lady."

She had missed Dad's perpetual smile, his stupid polos that never fit right, the way his eyes lit up when he saw her. She hugged him again. "Where's Mom?"

"We had some trouble with the airlines. She got booked on a different flight. She'll meet us at the airport."

"Oh." She glanced at Uncle Merlin. She wasn't sure if his expression showed more disappointment or relief. And she was pretty sure she felt the same way.

Dad snagged her suitcase. "You ready, Brin?"

"Yep."

"I'll throw your bag in the trunk. Then we better get back before your mom's flight comes in."

As he went around to the back of the car, Brinnie hugged Uncle Merlin one last time. "I *will* see you again."

"Of course. In this life, or the next."

She cocked her head. "That sounds like something Ms. Tynsdale said."

He smiled. "Where do you think she learned it from?"

Too soon, she found herself in the passenger seat, buckling her seatbelt. As Dad started the car, Brinnie clutched the orb.

"Did you have a good summer?" Dad asked.

She waved at Uncle Merlin as the car pulled out of the gas station. "The best." She tugged on the shirt sleeve hiding her scar, and for the first time, she was glad it was there. Even if she never saw Wraithwood again, and she couldn't use magic, it would be there as a reminder of one summer when magic was real and anything was possible.

"Glad to hear it." He smiled at Brinnie, then raised his hand to join her in waving.

Just for a moment, Brinnie could have sworn she saw flames dancing on her father's fingertips.

ACKNOWLEDGEMENTS

Wraithwood has been a journey. It was my first novel I finished, at the age of seventeen. By the time this book comes out, I will be almost twenty-three—six years of waiting to share *Wraithwood* with the world.

As my first, it will always have a special place in my heart. It isn't my first to be published (I've had two books out already), but it was definitely my rockiest road. Dozens of edits. Three years getting a degree in professional writing to edit some more. A few missteps along the way in the publishing process until I found my home at Mountain Brook Fire, searching for a publisher who understood my vision, who really bonded with my shy, brave Brinnie and her journey.

As you might imagine, such a process has a *lot* of important people behind it.

Thank you to my parents, who humored four-year-old me by writing down my stories as I dictated them. Thank you, Mama, for asking me, "But do you love science?" Only a crazy mother would encourage her daughter to abandon plans of med school to pursue a career in writing—or a brilliant one.

Thank you, Mama and Daddy, Nana and Papa, for helping me pursue my dreams, even when they led to a college halfway across the country for a degree in professional writing, of all things. I'd say it turned out pretty well.

Thanks, Steph, for a riotously good time as your sister. I will still love you even if you don't read all my books. (I'll do my best to get that movie adaptation for you.)

I have way too many wonderful family members to list here, but you all know who you are. I love you guys and thank you for your constant support.

Thank you to Julianna, who has been hearing me babble on about writing since fourth grade. And of course to Katie, Amanda, and Sonya, who got to deal with my existential crises. Hope Bolinger, you beautiful unicorn and wonderful agent, I couldn't have done this without you. Thank you for believing in *Wraithwood*. Thank you to Katie Heigel, my first beta reader. Thank you to Cyle Young—I have no idea where I would be without your guidance into the publishing industry. Professor Linda Taylor, "prowrite mom," and all the crazy TU prowrites—you rock.

Miralee Ferrell and the rest of the staff and authors of MBI and MBF, thank you so much for taking me into your family. I came to Mountain Brook almost by accident as an intern at a tumultuous time in my life, and I know God led me here. It was all worth it to end up here. Jenny Mertes, thank you for being the editor this manuscript needed, even though I had to go eat some chocolate and stare at a wall sometimes after getting edits back to gather my courage to dive in. This book would not be what it is without you.

But most importantly, thank you, Jesus. In the end, none of this matters without you. I know I've been a handful (and I doubt that will stop anytime soon), but you've been with me the whole way. Let it all be to your glory.

Now, A Sneak Peek at Book Two

MORDIZAN

Releasing April 2022

Chapter One

BRINNIE GLANCED UP FROM HER MATH homework and then fixed her eyes back on the page. Yes, that girl was still watching her.

She shifted on the hard metal bench, trying to focus on her equations. The late afternoon sun beating on her back did nothing to make her more comfortable. Her few minutes of productivity before the after-school programming buses showed up were turning out to be anything but.

She darted another glance. The girl had plopped down at a nearby table fifteen minutes ago, and her eyes had been glued on Brinnie in an intense stare ever since. *Am I supposed to recognize you?*

From quickly stolen glances, she knew she'd never met the girl. What with her short, light-brown hair that looked as if it had been hacked off with one swipe of an axe and her binder plastered with stickers, Brinnie was fairly certain she would have remembered if she had.

She took a deep breath. *Focus. It's just a teenager acting weird.* She fixed her attention on her math and began making calculations with furious scribbles.

"Are you a vampire?"

Brinnie jumped. Her foot caught under the table and she nearly fell over backwards in her haste to leap to her feet.

The girl suddenly stood in front of her.

Sit. Breathe. Brinnie forced a smile and a slight laugh. "Funny."

The girl blinked at her, oversized circular glasses enlarging her brown eyes to owlish proportions. "Well? Are you?"

She forced the smile to remain pasted on her face. "If I had a dollar for every time someone made a vampire joke..."

"I promise I won't tell anyone." The girl slid onto the bench across from Brinnie at the table. She set down her binder and propped her elbows on it. "I've always wanted to meet a real one."

Brinnie glanced down at the binder and saw that the stickers were all from various vampire shows and movies. *Oh, great.* She bared her teeth. "See? No fangs. I also happen to like garlic." Her gaze wandered to the gate at the front of the school. Any minute now, the buses would arrive.

"Oh. That's too bad." The girl sat back and pushed her glasses up her nose. "I thought I might have found a school that's actually interesting."

New and strange. She would probably need friends and might have trouble making them. Which meant, according to Brinnie's heart already swelling with sympathy, that was her job. *The weird ones always find me.* "When did you transfer?"

"Just got here two days ago from Colorado." She fanned her red face. "It's pretty hot."

"Welcome to Arizona." She chuckled. "And today is a cool day."

Sensation pricked Brinnie's upper arm, something she hadn't felt in a long time—a strange coolness. Her heart skipped a beat. *No. Not here.* Maybe she was imagining it.

The chill crept deeper into her skin.

She shot to her feet and gathered her belongings, stuffing them into her backpack. "Well, I have to go. Nice to meet you."

The girl stood up as well. "Where you off to?"

"Just thought of something. I'll see you later." She slung her backpack over her shoulder while scanning the courtyard. She saw the usual stragglers hanging around from the after-school programs that had been let out early, some aides, and the occasional teacher. No one who looked particularly suspicious.

What do I do? Should she stand in plain sight, making her an impossible target, or hide, before she was seen? It all depended on whether she'd already been spotted or not.

She glanced down at her arm. No light pulsing through the sleeve yet. They couldn't be too close. She had time to hide.

She strode across the courtyard and ducked around one of the buildings, pressing against the rough wall in a secluded corner barricaded on two sides by a fence and another by the building itself. Reaching down, she pulled out the pocketknife concealed in the lining of her shoe and clicked it open. With the knife in one hand, she pulled her clunky old phone from her back pocket with the other.

As she looked down to dial the number, she heard a noise beside her. She whirled and slammed the person into the wall. The figure shrieked as Brinnie's knife pointed at their throat.

"Oh, my gosh, don't kill me!"

Brinnie quickly stepped back and clicked the knife shut. She cursed under her breath. She was so done for. As soon as word got out that she had a weapon at school... "What were you doing?" she demanded.

The vampire-loving girl readjusted her glasses. "You left so fast. I was making sure you were okay." She craned her neck. "Why do you have a knife?"

Brinnie stuffed the knife in her pocket. *Deflect. Redirect.* "I didn't even hear you come up. You've got some serious stealth skills."

No luck in distraction. "Knives aren't allowed on campus."

Mom would kill her. "I know. I'm sorry." Her voice trembled with desperation. "Just please don't tell, okay?"

The girl scowled. "You almost killed me."

"I'm really sorry. I totally overreacted." She offered a sheepish smile. "I'll leave it at home tomorrow. Can we act like this never happened?"

The girl looked at her skeptically. "I don't think—"

Brinnie heard the familiar roar of the buses. "Thanks. I've got to go." She slipped past and darted for her bus. She had no other plan than *flee*. The coolness in her arm...

Mom might have to get in line to kill her.

She rushed up the steps and plopped into the cracked faux leather of a seat at the back of the mostly empty bus. Her heart didn't stop pounding until the driver pulled out of the parking lot.

Okay. Time to think logically. The girl didn't know Brinnie's name. Didn't know her grade, her classes. Even if she reported Brinnie, how would she do it? Who could prove it, if tomorrow she came to school without the knife? What would they do, round up all the black-haired blue-eyed girls in school like a police line-up?

She cringed. That couldn't be a very long list.

Gradually, the coolness in her arm faded. Brinnie got off at one of the stops farther from her house so she could clear her head on the walk home. It would be okay, she told herself. She would deny everything. And as far as she could tell, the person responsible for her tingling arm hadn't seen her. That was the more important issue anyway, even if it didn't feel like it.

She smiled ruefully to herself. Mom's wrath was scarier than any stalker.

She turned up her street and squinted at her sister's beige Buick in the driveway outside their house. What was Anna doing here? *Right. Dang it.* Anna and her husband David were bringing David's sister over to meet them. Apparently, the younger sister had gotten to be too much for the grandparents to handle, so she had come to live with her brother.

Brinnie wasn't in the mood to be polite and make friends. *But she's kind of like I was last summer, getting sent off to a relative's house to live. Of course, for me it wasn't permanent. And my parents are still alive.* Brinnie's need for space to think needed to take second place at the moment. She would have to be extra nice to the poor girl.

She took a deep breath, let go of the stress of her latest escapade, and pushed open the front door with a smile on her face. But her expression froze when her eyes landed on the stranger inside.

There, shaking hands with her parents, was the girl she had almost stabbed.

Made in United States
North Haven, CT
13 January 2023

31012205R00186